SÀBJA DE FEK and OTHER TALES
SÀBJA DE FEK e AUTRES CONTIES

by ADRIANA COMASCHI

Transation from Italian by Annarita Guarnieri

Published by
Inknbeans Press (U.S.A.)
©2015

"De ròba vèyes
E de prumes temps
A yö aldì
E vo kunté bayèdes"

Of old things
And ancient times
I have heard
And want to tell you.
(from "Entrada" Anonim. – Fabio Chiocchetti)

Table of Contents

INTRODUCTION

Opening this book, a reader might wonder, *Why a book about the Dolomites legends?*

Because...

To answer this question is at the same time easy and very, very difficult, but perhaps the explanation can be condensed into just one word. Nostalgia.

Nostalgia for that lost universe I always felt had existed long ago among those mountains, and which still exists now just in a few verses and stories—often confused and fragmentary, but no less fascinating because of this—and nostalgia for the bespectacled, insistent young girl I used to be in summers now long past when, armed with a pen and notebook, I pestered all the—more or less patient—Fassans who were unlucky enough to meet me, in order to get to 'know more' from them.

I wanted to "know more" about those stories I could feel still hovering on the peaks, in the valleys, in the local traditions and, at times, even in the geographical names; those same stories I later found in books by Wolff and a few other authors, such as Valentini, Garobbio and Lunelli, whose works, however, far from extinguishing my curiosity only fanned it all the more.

Alas, more years than I care to count have gone by since those days, and in the meanwhile I have found other interesting books and learned studies about Ladinia; I have also discovered wonderful songs linked to the old traditions, but while my head was dutifully registering and classifying all those new data, down in my soul I kept harboring the heartbreaking feeling that something had been irretrievably lost, and that more keeps vanishing, washed away by the maelstrom of time.

These are, perhaps, feelings and emotions fit only for a child, and as a matter of fact, I behaved just like I used to do as a child, when I would get to the end of a book I really loved with the feeling that there was more in it that I had not been able to capture and decipher: I told myself some of these stories—again, and my own way. Almost independently from my conscious will, as I went about this *re-telling*, the legendary elements in the stories intermingled with "learned" details coming from studies, readings and research, in tune with the long established habits of that curious young girl, now grown up and aged.

The end result is the book you are holding in your hands, in which the old Ladin legends are told again with a different, more modern, sensitivity; this is not an unheard of thing where centuries old, orally passed on stories are concerned, if it is true—as it is—what Kindl says: "Orally passed on stories are never defined in a precise form. They are fluid, and their shape varies as the person telling it and the circumstances of the telling change around them" (*U. Kindl 'Le Dolomiti nella leggenda' page 15*).

My attempt to set each story, whenever it was possible, inside a—maybe a little vague—historical frame is perhaps more unusual. I tried, in fact, to pinpoint (identify) the period in which the story I was re-writing could have taken place, starting from already existing elements within its traditional version and from my own knowledge of Italian history. I hope my experiment won't cause any outrage, since on my behalf I can call upon the undisputed authority of the Grimm brothers, who said: "*A fairy tale is more akin to poetry, while a legend tends to have more historical roots*".

While carrying on my attempt, I soon realized that in the way they were passed on to us, those legends do not form a single, coherent story—any coherence may eventually come from the ability of the single storyteller—but are... I hope you'll forgive the rather homely comparison... like onions: just like the center of an onion is wrapped into multiple, thin layers, in the same way, as time went by, other elements—alien to, or even contradictory with, the original tale—have grown around the legend's original core, elements in which similar characters, originating from the same archetype, have been confused and blended into a single character, and in which historical events clearly belonging to different periods have been molded into a single story.

Therefore, it was far from easy to identify within each legend any elements that could suggest the "real" period in which to set it, to the exclusion of others, so that I could then try to set my tale in a precise historical context, so much so that in order to manage it I had at times to "stretch" the original tale a little or, in one case, to totally deviate from it. To learn more about this, however, I invite the reader to check the 'notes' at the end of each tale.

Maybe somebody will accuse me of thus depriving, at least partially, my narration of its poetical flavor, and perhaps this is true: *Sàbja de Fek , Tanna, Dina of Lagorai, Ciadina, The Variöl, The Screaming Castle, Man de Fier, The Hike* are, with just one exception, more similar to a fantasy short story than to the product of Wolff or Zangrandi's poetical imagination, but on the other hand legends are the end result of a continuously reworking an ancient tale, where myths, fantasy and long past real events are all tangled together, and the dividing line between truth and fairy tale is lost: in rewriting them, I just added my own contribution to that 'tangle'.

I certainly do not claim that my version is the 'best' or the "most authentic" one: it is just the end result of two loves: the love of a curious young girl for those beautiful mountains, and he love an old girl has for History.

I don't even know if the readers will like my work: I had fun writing it, and reliving the tales and the landscapes of my beloved Dolomites, and I hope the reader will have fun as well in reading it, but in any case I want to appeal to the words of a real Writer, the great Carlo Goldoni, who ended one of his plays, "Il Campielo", with these words:

"No dirò che ti si bruto, né belo.
Se bruto ti sé sta, mi me despiase:
no sé bel quel ch'è bel, ma quel che piase."
I won't say if you are ugly or beautiful.
If you're ugly, I feel sorry for you:
Beauty, after all, is in the eye of the beholder

4

FOREWORD

A BRIEF OUTLINE ON LADIN GEOGRAPHY, HISTORY, LANGUAGE, CULTURE AND TRADITIONS

1- GEOGRAPHY

The Ladin region is usually divided into three different areas, where three different versions of the same language are spoken. They are:

- in Switzerland: the Canton of Grisons (language: Rumantsch),
- in Italy: Friuli (language: Furlan)
- in Italy: the area comprised between Trentino-Alto Adige and Veneto, formed by the four valleys that branch out from the Sella massif, and by the Ampezzo basin (language: Ladin), which is the area we'll call LADINIA throughout this preface.

The Dolomites Ladins, whose legends form the core of the present book, are still a community living in the valleys around the Sella massif, and specifically:

- Val Badia (Marebbe/Badia Valley)
- Gherdeina (Gardena Valley)
- Fascia (Fassa Valley)
- Fodom con Col (Livinallongo and Colle Santa Lucia)
- Anpezo (Ampezzano)

Sabja de Fek

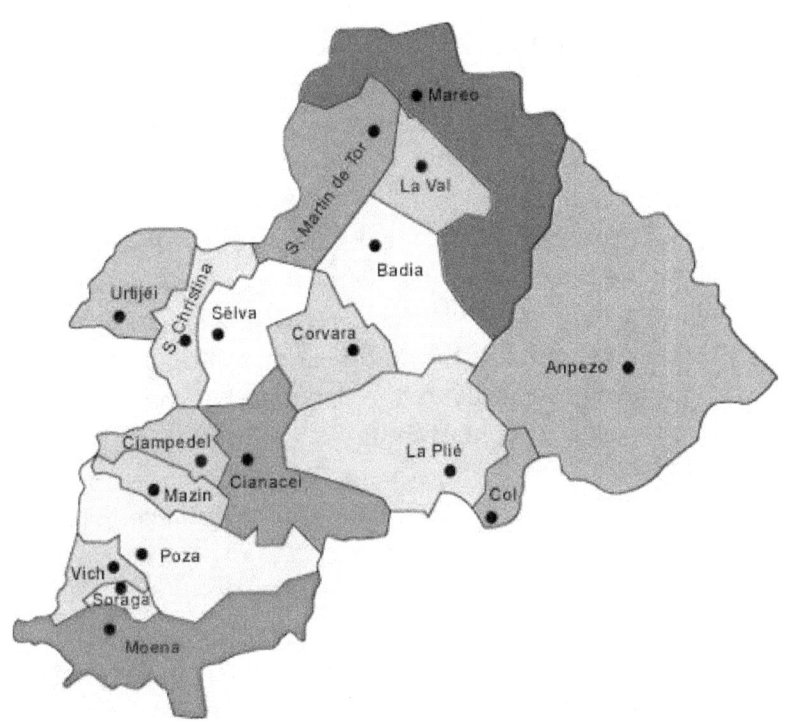

Local settlements, history and culture have always been strongly influenced by the morphological structure typical of this land, made of very high mountains (between 6,500 and 10,000 feet above the sea level) and narrow, steep valleys, and twisting, steep communication routes.

Contacts among the Ladin valleys are maintained through mountain passes (among which the most important are Gardena, Sella, Pordoi, Campolongo, Falzarego and Giau), while the nearby lands, be them Italian or German, can be reached by the roads running along the valleys themselves.

The five valleys are quite different from each other. Badia and Fassa are about 40 km (25 miles) long, and the first is narrower while the second is a little wider; Livinallongo and Gardena are shorter, with the first narrow and steep, and the second wider. Ampezzo on the other hand, lies enclosed within a wide basin, surrounded by mountain peaks.

The most important rivers are the Avisio River (Fassa Valley), the Derjon River (Gardena Valley),the Gadera River (Badia Valley), the Cordevole River (Livinallongo) and the Bite River (Ampezzo); they all have many tributaries that form smaller side valleys, either inhabited or characterized only by malgas (shepherds huts).

2- Historical outline: from the bronze age to 1500 A. D.

During the Bronze Age, the mountain area that extends from the Canton of Grisons (Switzerland) to Friuli (Italy) was inhabited by a population that the Romans (See Plinius) called Rhaeti. Defining their origins is quite difficult; their alphabet was similar to the Etruscan one, but some archaeological finds seem to imply that they had Celtic roots instead.

On the basis of some studies, it has been hypothesized that a wave of invasions by Rugians, Avars and Slavs pushed toward the Eastern Alps the populations inhabiting the Grisons area, and that those refugees ended up merging with the Celtic ethnic group already living in that area, the Breons, thus originating the people later called Raeti.

In fact, those alpine valleys had been settled long before the Romans conquered them, as shown by numerous archaeological finds proving the existence of human settlements in the Fassa Valley as early as 8,000/5,000 B.C. In 1971, the remains of a hunters' camp from the Mesolithic Age have been found at the Rolle Pass; in 1987, the skeleton of a chief has been found on Mondeval de Sora, together with a rich assortment of grave goods, all of which can be dated back to about 8,000 years ago, while stone tombs have been found in Appiano, dating back to 2,000 B.C. In order to find traces of organized human settlements where both agriculture and farming were practiced, however, we have to wait till 1,800/900 B.C. It is to that period, in fact, that can be dated back to the remains of stone built defensive walls, pottery goods, jewelry and weapons found in the vicinity of Mazzin and Campitello, in the Fassa Valley, and to 1,700 B.C. the remains of permanent settlements discovered at Sotciastel, in the Badia Valley, at Plan de Crepei, in the Fassa Valley again, and at Ciastalet (Selva), while at Scilar a place of worship has been found where sacrifices were offered to nature-related gods.

On the basis of all these findings, therefore, we can rightfully assume that the peoples fleeing from the Grisons area settled on a territory already inhabited by a pre-existing—probably Celtic—population, slowly merging with it and developing a remarkable culture from the fifth century B.C. onward.

In 15 B.C., Augustus' legions conquered the Ladin valleys, colonizing them, as proved by the various archaeological finds in the area and the Roman coins and tombs discovered at Siusi and at Tires.

The initial resistance opposed by the local population decreased as time went by, and the Raeti began to learn their conquerors' ways, most of all agricultural techniques, which is proved by the apportionment of the land, that shows clear traces of the work of Roman surveyors.

The Roman domination lasted five centuries, and in that span of time the Latin language began to spread through the area, merging with the Raetic language and evolving into the Ladin language, which is therefore a Rhaeto-Romance language.

It was during the Roman domination as well that the process of conversion to Christianity began, mostly carried on by the Patriarchy of Aquileia; some old beliefs and uses were abolished, but more often they underwent a metamorphosis in order to adapt them to Christian ways, so much so that many primitive churches were built on the ancient sites of pre-Christian cults.

During the decline first, and the downfall later, of the Roman Empire, the Ladin lands were invaded by Goths, Vandals and Huns, who all passed through those valleys, but never stopped there long enough to influence their language, uses and culture, at least until the coming of the Langobards (558-559). They came from Friuli, Cadore and Ampezzo, and extended their dominion to all the valleys of the Dolomites; unlike all the Barbarians who had come before them, they not only remained in the area, but also tried to reorganize the land and give it new laws, regulating property rights and establishing, among other things, that woods and pastures were property of the family in its whole (a law only recently abolished and still partially enforced in the Ampezzano).

The Langobards who settled in Ladinia were scarce in numbers, however, and they ended up being assimilated by their subjects' world, accepting their culture and language as their own.

In the year 560 A.D. the Baiovarii invaded Ladinia and—in spite of the strenuous defense of the inhabitants, led by Ingenuino, bishop of Sabiona—conquered the land, together with what is nowadays the city of Bolzano (600 A.D.). With their advent, the Germanization process began.

While hard on the local Ladin populations, the Baiovarian domination kept the Longobard laws unchanged and gave a boost to their agriculture; after the Baiovarii, however, there came the Franks led by Charlemagne (774 A.D.), who divided Ladinia into counties, each divided into hundreds; they also established the practice of having the heads of the households meet periodically to discuss and solve common issues (*placiti generalis*).

In the year 952, under the rule of Otto I of Saxony, emperor of the Holy Roman Empire, the Ladins finally fell into the German sphere of influence, while the church's power got stronger, also because it was supported by the Emperor, who was thus depriving the unruly and dangerous local nobles of riches and power, and at the same time was making provisions for the Alpine passes leading toward Italy to remain under the control of faithful—and, most of all, lacking any dynastic interests—vassals.

Emperor Conrad II (1027-1039), in fact, included the counties of Bolzano and Venosta into the Bishopry of Trent, while the counties of the Eisack Valley and of the Puster Valley were annexed to the Bishophry of Brixen. Those princes-bishops remained in power—at least formally—till the Napoleonic invasion, in 1803.

Among the most powerful bishops we can remember the bishop of Trent and of Brixen (the former bishopric of Sabiona), but as time went by the earls, while theoretically remaining the bishop's vassals, grew in power (with the exception of the Fassa Valley), so much so that at the end of the eighteenth century the earls of Tyrol laid claim to the Vinshgau Valley, Bolzano and Eppan, thus creating an independent realm. It was in that period that the first castles were built, usually along the border between properties, with the intent of defending them (for example, the castles of Tor and of Andrai).

During this period, the lands along the valley bottom were extensively exploited, while the areas higher up on the mountain slopes were used as pasture. The land farmed by the Ladins belonged to their Lords, but the grant of the land was hereditary and continual (with a few exceptions) in exchange for the fulfillment of some obligations. The masoes (alpine huts), on the other hand, belonged to the Ladins and could be inherited only by the firstborn, if a male, because women remained under the lifelong guardianship of the head of the household.

From the administrative point of view, the land was divided into JUDGMENTS, an evolution of the meetings of the household heads established by the Langobards and similar to them in authority; twice a year, the local Lord would take part to these Judgments to administer justice.

As time went by, however, things changed: in the year 1314 the Patti Encriciani (Encrician Pacts) were signed, and through them the community of Fiemme obtained a greater freedom in the exploitation of the land; more or less twenty years later, when the last Count of Cadore died heirless, an assembly of twelve representatives drew up the Statute of Cadore, reclaiming their independence, even if under the tutelage of the Patriarchy of Aquileia.

It was in this period that the first Communities (Regole) sprang up, the original core from which the Municipalities would later develop.

In 1420, the Ampezzo Valley became part of Venetian territory, but in the year 1511 it was conquered by the Emperor Maximilian I, who annexed it to Tyrol, to which it afterwards belonged for centuries.

The Protestant Reformation and the peasant revolts extended to the Ladin territory and in particular to Tyrol, where Michael Gaismair (1490-1532) proposed the establishment of a 'peasant republic', which failed after violent uprisings.

In the period between 1803 and 1805 the Napoleonic invasion officially put an end to the existence of the episcopal principalities of Brixen and Trent, and the County of Tyrol was assigned to Bavaria.

Four years later, following the beginning of the war between Austria and France, the Tyrolese, led by Andreas Hofer, rebelled against the Franco-Bavarians, but Austria abandoned them to their fate and they were defeated. With the peace of Schönbrunn, the Tyrol was then spilt in two: Bavaria kept northern Tyrol, as far as Meran, and central Tyrol, as far as Klausen, while the Napoleonic Kingdom of Italy got the South Tyrolean Unterlans, with Bolzano and most of the territory of the Dolomites.

At the end of World War One, the new Italian border followed the Alps divide, including the Innichen basin, and Tyrol was therefore split in two once more.

The requests for autonomy by the Ladin populations living on Italian territory were met by the rising Fascist nationalism with violent repression ('Bloody Sunday', 1921), and the prohibition of teaching German at school, while the migration of Italians toward South Tyrol was incentivized. Ladins were never considered a different ethnic group, but just Italians who spoke a 'barbarized' Italian dialect.

After World War II, an agreement between De Gasperi and Gruber called for a great level of autonomy for South Tyrol, then extended to Trentino as well, but only much later. After a succession of—not always peaceful—protests and demands for secession finally Trentino-South Tyrol became an autonomous region with considerable political autonomy.

Later, the Region officially recognized Ladins as an ethnic group with its own language, defended by the Italian Constitution, and in spite of all the administrative divisions, the awareness of the ethnic and linguistic unity of all the Ladin groups has now taken roots into the population and is supported by a thick network of associations, institutions and research centers that have developed in the Badia Valley (Micurà de Ru), in the Fassa Valley (Majon de Fuscan), at Colle Santa Lucia (Cesa de Jan), at Bocca di Cadore (Cultural Institute de la Dolomites), etc.

3- The Ladin Language

Ladin can be considered a Rhaeto-Romance language because it was born from the merging of the Raetian and Latin languages; it is, therefore, a Romance language with Raetian characteristics.

13

Sabja de Fek

According to many scholars, among which the linguist Graziadio Isaia Ascoli, this language was once spoken—even if with considerable differences—in a wide area that extended from the Grisons to Friuli. To this day, in fact, we still define as 'Rhaeto-Romance linguistic group' the group of strictly related Romance languages spoken by some 700,000 individuals living in the Central Eastern Alps. Besides Ladin, these languages include three other variations:

- **Romansh**, spoken in the Swiss Canton of Grisons;
- **Friulian**, spoken in the so-called historical Friuli, comprised of the provinces of Gorizia, Pordenone and Udine, as well as in the district of Portogruaro and Sappada.
- **Sella Ladin**, spoken in the Agordo area, Zoldo Valley, Fassa Valley, Gardena Valley, Badia Valley, in the Livinallongo area as well as in the Ampezzo and Cadore areas, for a total of about 30,000 individuals.

This language was only marginally influenced by the barbaric invasions following the downfall of the Roman Empire since very few among those barbarians chose to settle in the areas where it was spoken, at least until the coming of the Baiovarii, who settled in a wide part of South Tyrol (Puster and Eisack Valley), imposing their language, that is, the German language.

When Otto I of Saxony was crowned Emperor, in the year 962 A.D., and extended his dominion to Italy, German was first spoken together with Ladin and then supplanted it throughout most of South Tyrol as well, becoming in the thirteenth century the dominant language in two thirds of what is now the Province of Bolzano. Ladin survived however, still spoken in hidden and isolated villages, as well as in the side valleys of Tyrol, in the Vinshgau Valley, and in all the Ladin valleys of the Dolomites.

In the second half of the fifteenth century, Tyrol was under the control of the House of Hapsburg and Cadore belonged to Venice; then, at the beginning of the sixteenth century, the Ampezzo Valley became part of Austria as well, while Venice kept Cadore. In the Ampezzo Valley, however, the influence of the German language, extremely strong in Tyrol, was less felt that it might be expected. As a matter of fact, either because of the nearness of the territories belonging to Venice, or because the people of the Ampezzo Valley used to look for seasonal jobs in Venice, the Venetian language influenced their Ladin language much more than German did.

We can therefore draw a few conclusions, which are:

- The original Ladin language, born of the merging of Raetic and Latin, was mostly influenced by two languages, German and Italian, the latter under the form of the Venetian dialect.
- The German influence can mostly be felt in the areas that were under German dominion, which is Tyrol—with the already mentioned exception of the Ampezzo Valley—while all over the rest of the territory we can find more or less relevant traces of Venetian dialect.

In the five valleys Ladinia is currently made of it is possible to identify five dialects:

Fascian in the Fassa Valley, strongly influenced by the Italian language;

Ghërdeina in the Gardena Valley, very close to German;

Badiot in the Badia Valley, less close to German and, according to some scholars, the purest of them all;

Fodom in the Livinallongo Valley;

Ampezan in Ampezzo, strongly influenced by the Venetian dialect.

Besides the existence of these five different dialects and the differences often found within the same valley, the really distinctive feature of this language is that many of its structures still originate from the ancient Raetic language predating the Roman invasion; for example, we can find words like *crepa, trai, zandra,* that mean, respectively, mountain, path and brush.

All five dialects have some common distinctive features, like the palatalization of c and g when preceding a vowel, the –s suffix that can often be found in the plural (maybe deriving from the Latin –es?), the absence of the conditional tense, substituted by the imperfect subjunctive just like Latin did, etc.

Fassa, Gardena, Badia, Livinallongo and Ampezzo do not only have a language sharing a series of common characteristics, but they also share a historical heritage and a distinctive cultural tradition that stress, once more, their belonging to a single ethnic group.

3- Outline on Ladin myths, culture, art and traditions

The Ladin valleys are rich in traditions that have their origins in ancient times, but have often been adapted and transformed in the light of new beliefs or later historical events. Their origins, however, almost always have their roots in nature and farming, because the Ladins' primitive religion was bound to the worship of nature; as a matter of fact, many are the legends in which we can find references to the worshipping of the sun, the waters, the woods, which the natives' imagination populated with all sorts of fantastic creatures.

Another element that can be often found in the old Ladin fairy tales is the ability some humans have to transform themselves into an animal and vice versa, which is a surviving trace of a totemic religion and a memory of a time when matriarchy was the rule, a time seen as a sort of 'Golden Age', when Earth was not yet torn apart by war and strife.

Most of these beliefs did not disappear with the advent of Christianity, but often underwent a change, merging with elements of the new faith, in the same way the first, ancient churches were built on pre-existing, older places of worship.

Likewise, the remote, mythical years in which these legends were set often acquired anachronistic historical features, mixing up legendary events and figures with historical ones.

In a way, therefore, the Christian religion penetrated peacefully enough into Ladin culture and traditions, ending up with blending in with them to the point of often becoming a prominent element of the tale.

As a matter of fact, the value of the faith, as passed down from generation to generation, is strongly felt in all the Dolomites and highlighted by a series of traditional celebrations, such as the procession to the shrine of

Pietralba, held on the last Sunday of September, or the procession to the shrine of Sabbiona, held every three years and typically, only for male participants, or the recurring celebrations that take place on the main religious feast days (Easter, Christmas, New Year, etc), or those linked to everyday life, such as a wedding. Quite often, however, it is easy to see the original, pagan roots underneath all these Christian celebrations.

Religion and worship have had a great influence on figurative art—mostly on architecture—as well. Unfortunately, we do not have any example of churches built before the year 1000 A.D.; it seems that a church was built at Pieve di Narebbe in the year 1030 A.D., but no traces were ever found of that structure; likewise, we don't have any precise information about what is considered to be the first Christian place of worship in the Fassa valley, entitled to Saint Giuliana and—presumably— built around 798 A.D.

Most churches built in the Romanesque period were soon substituted by Gothic churches, still recognizable thanks to the distinctive shape of their bell towers, but they were all expanded and renovated in the following centuries to adapt them to the fashion of the times. Clear examples of this process are the churches of Badia, Cortina and Ortisei, all built between the thirteenth and the fourteenth century, but renovated in the Baroque period, to the point that the original structure was buried under decorations, stucco works and trumpery.

Besides the churches we can also find abbeys and monasteries, built as well around the twelfth century and renovated in later times, like the Benedictine abbey of Saint Lawrence, erected between 1166 and 1183 on the remains of another church, built in the Early Medieval Period, and next to an extremely ancient place of worship consecrated to Larentia.

Among laic buildings, the most notable and worth mentioning are the castles, initially built in order to defend the territory, that later often become the official residence of the local noblemen. There is plenty of them—so many that I cannot possibly list them all—some now reduced to evocative ruins, others still in use. Most of them were erected between the eleventh and the twelfth century, like the castles of Andrai and Tor, even if there are some dating to later centuries (the castle of Saint Cristina was built in the seventeenth century). Almost all of them, however, underwent many renovations, either to strengthen their defenses, or to make them more comfortable, or even to 'embellish' them.

Besides the castles, we can also find an assortment of typical buildings, both dwellings and workshops. All these buildings show the Ladins traditional respect toward nature, since they are all planned in order to blend with the surrounding environment.

The most ancient and typical kind of human settlement in the highest part of the Badia Valley are the *viles,* that developed from the Raetic *tambra,* the most ancient mountain hut we know of. They were made of several houses and haylofts, with a central courtyard, almost a small square, with a common fountain, oven and water through. With their lower part built in stone and the upper part made of wood, the mushroom-shaped houses— dating back to the Gothic period—are very interesting from the architectural point of view, as are the stone houses dating back to the Romanesque period.

Another typical characteristic of the area are the frescoes that could be found decorating the facades not only of the most important buildings, but often also of simple dwellings, a custom that has not been totally forgotten in modern times, as shown by the 'ciasa de i Pupe', the chemist's shop in Cortina d'Ampezzo, frescoed with allegoric images representing craftsmanship, art, technology and music.

Ladin literature is late in developing, even in comparison with the birth of other minority languages, but to correctly evaluate it, it is necessary to consider not only written documents but also and above all else, in this case, the fantastic imagination that can be found in its orally passed down legendary world.

In fact, the roots of Ladin literature can be found in the oral tradition: stories, legends and tales were handed down orally from generation to generation.

Knowing this, it is then easy to understand why it is so difficult, and at times even impossible, to separate a legend's central core from the elements that have later been added to it, century after century, in accordance with the tastes and imagination of each storyteller, or in imitation of other stories; likewise, it is often impossible not only to date these tales, but also, sometimes, to reconstruct the history of the events mentioned in them, because the same name often refers to different events and characters.

The fact that all these legends were written down very late is probably the reason why we find ourselves dealing with a lore that, while extremely rich, is at times contradictory and difficult to interpret. There are countless legends, at times very much alike, connected to history, prehistoric memories and nature, populated with mysterious beings endowed with arcane powers and yet often in tune with the agricultural/artisan world of Ladinia, that create a rich mythology in which we can find traces, or faded memories, of both Greek-Roman and German mythology.

The first documents written in the Ladin language date back to the eighteenth century: an edict, written in Fascian in 1631 and one written in Fondom in 1632. It is only in 1703, however that we find a longer document, a proclamation written by Bishop Kaspar Ignaz König to call his soldiers to arms, in which there are about three hundred words in Badiot.

It is only in the early nineteenth century—when romanticism was at its height—that we find the first translations and the attempts at writing Ladin poetry. The first poems written in the various Ladin dialects date back to 1807, and in the same year Matic Ploner wrote six short stories inspired to popular tradition, in which he used the Ghërdeina dialect.

In the same period Micurà de Rü, a priest of Badia, wrote a Ladin grammar book, sustaining the unity of the Ladin language in spite of all its different dialects, and years later the linguist Graziadio Isaia Ascoli hypothesized that all the Ladin dialects belonged to the same, Rhaeto-Romance linguistic group.

The first, real Ladin poet was Angelo Trebo (1862-1888), from Marebbe, who wrote poems and plays in Ladin, while a few years earlier, in Anpezo, Joani Gregoro Domenego Kaiser wrote his 'Satire' in Anpezan.

In the nineteenth century, under the influence of Romanticism, that reevaluated national popular imagination, Ladin legends, poems and plays, entrusted up to then to the people's willingness to commit them to memory, began to attract the attention of various scholars, who collected and studied them.

Among them, we can mention:

Nepomuceno Bolognini (1820-1900), ethnographer, researcher and journalist, who transcribed myths and legends of the Brenta Dolomites.

Don Lorenzo Felicetti (1864-1937) parish priest in the Fiemme Valley, who was interested in the myths of that area and wrote in Ladin, 'El capitèl de l'Òm Selvadech';

Tita Alton (1845-1900?), linguist, who was interested in the proverbs, curiosities and folkloristic elements of the Badia Valley, studying their mythological figures. Among other things, he wrote 'Proverbs' in Ladin, with the Italian translation to the side.

Felice Valentini, who collected and transcribed various short stories in his 'Fassan and Trentino Legends' (1908).

More recently, relatively speaking, Hugo de Rossi (1875-1940) collected and transcribed most of the Ladin legends, without any attempt to interpret or reinvent them, in 'Fairy Tales and Legends of the Fassa Valley – Part 1'. Unfortunately, Part 2 was never written.

Karl Felix Wolff (1829-1966), journalist, writer and anthropologist, personally collected from the lips of those who still remembered them not only the old legends—or parts of them—but also stanzas from ancient, lost poems written in non-rhymed verses, all elements that he then blended and transcribed, at times with a personal interpretation, in his books (*The Soul of the Dolomites, The Pale Mountains, The White Rhododendrons of the Dolomites, The Kingdom of the Fanes*).

In earlier years, a priest from Bruneck, Karl Staudacher, had developed an interest in the same legends, and in 1828 had written in German the epic poem ''.

Des Fanneslied

In recent years there has been a growing interest for the Ladin language, its history and its legends, and many scholars and writers, fascinated by those ancient tales, have studied and re-written them.

Among them are worth mentioning:

Angel Morlang (1918-2005), who wrote in 1951 an epic poem that should have become the script for a folk drama to be performed outdoors;

Biancamaria Dal Lago, writer and essayist from Bolzano, who gave us a very personal interpretation of the Fanes' story;

Helmut Brikham, eminent scholar, who tried to give a historical interpretation to the legends tied to the Fanes, and finally concluded that their core is ancient and true.

Giuliano Palmieri (1940-2007), who wrote, together with his son Marco, many essays and tales that take inspiration from the legends of the Dolomites; among them, is worth mentioning 'The Lost Kingdoms of the Pale Mountains';

Adriano Vanin (1947-liv.), speleologist and scholar, who wrote an essay and held many lectures.

Rut Bernardi (1962-liv.), native of the Gardena Valley and Professor of Romance Languages at the University of Ortisei, who has written essays on the Ladin legends;

Ulrike Kindl, (1951-liv.), from Meran, Professor at the Ca'Foscari University in Venice, since 1980 has been researching folk narrative and the fairy tales and legends of the Alpine area. Nowadays she is probably the greatest expert on these legends.

SÀBJA DE FEK

Father and King I was, and now a beggar.
Only my song I have left, and my grief.

AURONA.

Sommavida had never seen the sun, nor a tree, or a river, or a mountain; she had never felt the rain or the wind caressing her face, nor had her hair been silvered by the moon rays.

She didn't really miss the light of the sun, in the vast cavern where she lived together with her people, because thousands of iridescent crystal spheres lighted the underground halls of Aurona, their brightness shining on the gold, the precious stones and the other incredible treasures they contained, on which darkness never fell. As endless was also the noise of hammers and shovels continuously digging under the cavern floor, looking for more veins of precious metals, more gems, more treasures.

This—as the elders said—was the covenant that Sommavida's grandfather, their king at that time, had made with the underground infernal deities, who had taken it amiss at being supplanted by Sun worship: all the incommensurable riches of Aurona would belong to him, provided that he—and his descendants—would never see any sunlight, nor bend to following the new faith.

He had accepted the covenant, spending all his life inside the vast cavern, satisfied with the glint of gold and gems surrounding him and finally dying nestled among them. His grandchild and heir, on the contrary, would have gladly given all those treasures in exchange for just one hour spent freely under the real light of the sun, but it was not in her power to break the covenant with the infernal powers. She had spent her childhood and adolescence devoured by that unsated hunger, and later, as a very young woman, she had avidly listened to the words of one of her subjects, an old man who had been able to glimpse— through a long walled-up crevice—what he called, 'the outside world'. She never tired of having the man describe to her, over and over again, the colors he had glimpsed, the shapes, the smells, and the faint noises he had heard, so much so that when the storyteller died, she took to spending most of her days by the huge golden doors that inescapably sealed up the cavern.

Leaning her pale face against the doors, she could still—or at least she deluded herself into thinking she could—hear some tenuous whispers, some quivering from the outside, and her violet eyes would fill with tears as she sang her misery.

Oh, the breath of the wind,
Never felt caress on my hair!
Light of an unknown sun
On Sommavida's wan face!
Who from these fatal gems
will take me away,
and from the hated gold,
Of my dark cell,
And the heritage of men
Will give me back, the shining
Light, and from the golden chains
Finally free, my steps
Will guide among green meadows and woods?

If the Princess could only catch a few, indistinct sounds of the unknown world surrounding her, however, her clear voice, dimmed to a crystal thread, reached the ears of the shepherds pasturing their herds in the area, oblivious of the riches under their feet. One of them understood one or two words of her sad song, others caught more and repeated them to the sound of their flutes, singing them to the hunters and the wayfarers, who told about them once back at their villages; wandering bards heard and repeated them, until Sommavida's song flew from mouth to mouth, free as the Princess had never been.

At that time, Odòlghes was the king of Contrìn, in the valley that climbs up from Penia to the peaks of Ombretta; he was a young man who, while known for his bravery, loved music and poetry far more than the sword, and used to offer hospitality and rich rewards to all the musicians who would bring him new melodies and new songs.

For this reason Saldéel, a minstrel from Mazzìn, having heard the shepherds and hunters' tales, reworked their stories and headed for Contrìn, with the certainty that the king would like his new verses. It was a long march, often hindered by the bad weather, but his perseverance was rewarded, at last, and in the middle of a snow storm he finally saw the walls of the powerful city veiled by the light snowflakes falling from the sky and whirling around the shining towers and the golden merlons in a way that made them look like a vision. Cheered up by that sight, Saldéel sped up his pace and as he reached the massive doors, and gave the guards his name and the reason for his visit, he was taken to the presence of the king.

On a high platform in the wide central hall of his castle, Odòlghes was sitting on a carved seat; at his back, a large fireplace gave light and warmth to the room, and on his knees he held his great sword, while at his side a page held a golden harp. All along the walls, on which tapestries told of the glories of Contrìn and of his lord, the king's men sat at long tables while many women came and went, carrying wide trays heaped with meat and vegetables, and other pages ran from one table to the other with pitchers full of wine. The smell of food mingled with the scent of the juniper wood burning in the fireplace and of the torches slowly burning down, while calls, songs, laughter and toasts filled the air with cheerfulness and smoke rose to veil the painted rafters of the ceiling.

Saldéel stopped on the threshold and shook his shoes and cloak to free them from the snow, as he took a moment to recover, half-dazed as he was from the sudden warmth; then, as the guard escorting him prodded him, he advanced toward the king's throne and bowed to him.

"My captain has already informed me that you are a wandering minstrel, and that you're bringing me a new song," Odòlghes said, bending forward a little. The minstrel was pleasantly surprised when his trained ear registered the king's deep, melodious, and velvety voice.

Straightening from his bow, he smiled and suddenly felt quite at ease.

"It is so, Sire," he answered frankly, as if talking to an equal and not to a king; then he added: "What makes my song new and different, however, is that I did not create it, I just collected and ordered what all those who ventured on the slopes of Padon heard."

His interest piqued, the young king nodded invitingly toward the great harp to his right; with another bow, Saldéel nimbly climbed on the platform, tried the instrument strings, tuned them and started to sing softly.

Mournful and heart breaking, Sommavida's song echoed in the great hall, silencing laughter and merriment as everybody stopped eating and even the servants and the pages stopped to listen to it. When the music ended with a last note, long and sad, a moment of silence followed, then applauses and praises erupted all over the room. The king, however, sat still on his seat, staring at the minstrel with a troubled expression on his proud face. Finally he stood and raised his arm.

Immediately, silence fell once more, and all eyes turned to him.

"Yours is a beautiful song, minstrel, and you'll get well rewarded for it," Odòlghes began, signaling to a courtesan to come forward. "Here is my chamberlain, who will look after your needs and reward your talent." Then, while an extremely satisfied Saldéel was walking away together with the chamberlain, weighing the bag he had discreetly handed to him, Odòlghes raised his sword and turned to his men. "Yes, the song we heard was beautiful, but greater still is the feat it prompts us to accomplish. Men! How many among you will follow your king to Padon, to free the beautiful Sommavida and seize the riches of Aurona?"

A veritable roar followed his words: everywhere hands and arms were raised, all the faces were turned toward the throne and the king, still motionless with the sword held high in his strong hand. None of the men had a moment's hesitation, none drew back; they all clamored for their weapons and their horses, ready to follow their lord anywhere.

Six days later, the necessary preparations all made, a large force of armed men marched west, toward the bleak Padon. At their head was Odòlghes, his long, dark hair waving in the wind; as he rode, he was humming under his breath Sommavida's song, adding new verses that burned with love and hope as he left his city behind.

Love I never met
In my dreams only I saw your face,
But I want to give you back those sunrays
That shine in your beautiful hair.
The sight I want to return to you
Of the Alps, the woods, the streams
My heart I want to give you
Getting your love in return.

Right behind him, between the standard bearer and the captain, rode Saldéel, a little frightened by the turn of the events.

"My Lord," he finally burst forth, getting closer to the king, "I must warn you that the doors of Aurona aren't visible..."

"You spoke of the Padon!" immediately countered Odòlghes, as he reined his horse a little and turned a suddenly scowling face toward the minstrel. "If you lied..."

"No, no! Every single word I uttered was true, but there is an enchantment... a very powerful enchantment... hiding the access to the cavern. The underground deities wove it and nobody ever succeeded in..."

The king cut him off with a hearty laugh.

"I will, minstrel, and you'll have more material for your songs!"

In saying so he spurred his horse, his white teeth still shining in the tanned face, his dark hair blowing in the wind, and the minstrel bent over on his horse's mane, falling back in his place.

The Padon is a low range of dark rocks framing the wonderful bulk of the Marmolada and dividing the Livinallongo from the valley of the Pettorina Creek. For three days the Contrìnesi searched and dug along those black, rough slopes without managing to even glimpse the fabulous golden doors of Aurona, always prodded by their king, who could hear, faint and muffled, Sommavida's singing.

His men, however, were beginning to lose heart, and the glances they threw Saldéel were far from friendly, but none of them dared to complain with Odòlghes, who seemed obsessed, as they kept searching and digging among those dismal rocks with less and less certainty and enthusiasm. Just when they were on the verge of expressing their doubts to the king, a shovel clanged against something metal. That sound dispelled all doubts and discontent as they all took to digging with renewed energy, removing earth and rocks until the golden gates of Aurona shone under their eyes.

Joyful shouts and acclamations greeted that sight as the men raised shovels and hammers to the sky and embraced each other, shaking hands and congratulating one another in a paroxysm of triumphant joy.

Alerted by his captain, the king immediately came over and the exultant Contrìnesi drew aside to let him pass, urging him to open wide the doors to the fabulous reign. He silenced them with a wave of his hand, however, and instead of trying to immediately open a breach in the doors, he asked for his harp to accompany with its sweet notes the Lay of Sommavida, together with the verses he had added to it.

A sweet, crystal clear voice, less faint now but still muffled, answered him, singing along the same notes. Grabbing a mace, Odòlghes then hit the locked doors once, twice; those were powerful blows, but the mace broke in his hands and the doors stayed closed and unmarred in their cold glory. The Contrìnesi assailed them for days, in vain: all their tools kept breaking, and the shining doors did not show even a scratch for all their efforts.

"It is told that Aurona is under the protection of the nether regions deities," Saldéel reminded the others that evening, as he sat by the campfire together with his tired companions.

"What do you mean?" the captain immediately asked him, setting down his glass of wine on a nearby rock.

The minstrel shook his head, staring at the dancing flames, then he finally replied, "Those doors are imbued with magic... how else could they have withstood your blows?"

His words were met with a general murmur of approval, as the men gathered around him holding their plates and glasses. Encouraged by their assent, Saldéel went on, "The Vivane, magical beings whose eyes can see in the mists of the future and into fathomless depths, live not far from here. Let's seek them out and ask them if and how it is possible to open these damned doors!"

His proposal was immediately embraced with enthusiasm, and after discussing and evaluating it, the men finally submitted it to the king's approval. Even if he still had doubts about it, Odòlghes allowed a good number of his men to leave and head for the Ru de ras Virgines, where at times it was possible to find a Vivana.

A short time later, more men asked to be allowed to get back to Contrìn, because the time for harvest was getting near and they were needed in the fields. Again, the king let them go, just as he let another group of soldiers go hunting, because they were beginning to run short on provisions and the rugged, arid Padon offered no sustenance whatsoever.

Soon, by the king side remained only his squire, his captain together with two men, and Saldéel; they were all disheartened and demotivated, so much so that they did not try again to open those fatal doors, and just watched over the camp to protect their king while they waited for their companions to come back.

33

"My Lord," the captain respectfully answered to Odòlghes, who was urging them to get back to work, "four hungry men, tired from endless hours of labor, won't certainly succeed where twenty failed! Let's wait for the others to come back with news and some food, then we'll be able to get back to work at a better pace."

Grouped around him, the others nodded. Odòlghes grit his teeth. He couldn't deny the wisdom of his captain's words, but he kept hearing Sommavida's sweet voice singing about her pain, parted from him only by that damned metal barrier, and he could not bear it.

He shrugged his shoulders, motioning for his men to stay by the fire, but then he turned his back to them and went back to stand in front of the doors, alone. For seven days, always alone and in a growing frenzy, he kept hitting the golden door with his sword, prying at the hinges with its sharp point. Both under the sun and in the moonlight, for seven days he tirelessly attacked those golden doors, trying to force them open with such strength that a rain of golden dust fell on his blade, forever covering it. From that moment onward, it started shedding such a brightness that men called it sàbja de fek, sword of fire.

During the seventh night a blow, more powerful or perhaps just luckier than the others, ripped off a hinge covering. The young king then concentrated his renewed efforts on that hinge until it also surrendered to his fury, opening a wide crack that shed a reddish light into the night's gloom, and allowed a joyful cry to escape... Sommavida!

Multiplying his blows, Odòlghes hammered, and hit, and smashed until the other hinges gave way too, together with the bolts. The king had to jump aside and bend one knee to the ground to avoid being flattened by the massive doors crashing to the ground amid a small rain of dirt and pebbles, and clouds of dust. Then, as he got back up, his incredulous eyes were finally able to see Aurona's full splendor.

He saw a huge underground hall, lit by countless lamps, globes of glass and crystal hanging from the ceiling on golden chains; while so numerous, those lamps shed only a dim, reddish light, but it was enough to make the incredible treasures heaped in the cavern shine and sparkle. From the walls hung panels made entirely of gold and precious stones, silver and gems encrusted all the furniture, while more precious metals and jewels were heaped inside vases and baskets.

Odòlghes, however, had no eyes either for the gold or the silver feebly shining in the light of the hundreds of lamps hanging from the ceiling, or the rare gems shining inside the baskets, or the exquisite furniture of the hall. Likewise, he did not even see the lavish clothing of the courtesans huddling around Sommavida. The Princess alone captured his gaze, and he could not take his eyes off her.

The dawning sun lent a faint shade of pink to the girl's pale cheeks and made her violet eyes shine brighter than the amethysts and the gold gracing her long, white neck, her slims wrists, her beautiful golden hair. Bathed as she was in the suffused lighting, she appeared to the king more similar to a vision or a dream, than to a real woman. On impulse, he crossed the threshold and reached for her with his right hand.

"Sommavida, my Princess, banish all fears! I am Odòlghes, King of Contrìn, and it was hearing of your beauty and of your sadness that brought me here. Your mournful song stole my soul, and even if I had never seen you, I came to love you... will you... can you... return my feelings? Will you leave Aurona and its treasures behind to follow me to Contrìn as my bride and my queen?"

Many emotions... hesitation, relief, joy... chased each other on the young woman's troubled face. Shyly, she raised her eyes on the king, who kept staring at her: he was handsome, young, tall and strong, with black hair and very light eyes shining in his face tanned by that sun she had never seen, and had always yearned for. She smiled, and with a gesture full of grace and majesty, she put her small, white hands on the king's strong, dark, sword calloused one.

They looked at each other and smiled, by now totally oblivious of Sommavida's courtesans, who were beginning to move and to get out of the cavern, looking around with incredulous eyes. Finally, the two embraced, Odòlghes proud, fierce face pressed against the girl's soft hair. They moved away from the cavern still holding each other, carelessly leaving behind Aurona and all its treasures.

While the king helped her on his horse, the princess watches absentmindedly her people leave the cavern, slowly—almost hesitantly—at first, then running anxiously. Few of them stopped to retrieve some of the treasures among which they had lived, and those few ended up with letting them fall to the ground in order to pick up, instead, those colored flowers they had never seen before, or to incredulously plunge their hands into the clear water of the creek, or to chase colorful butterflies fluttering around.

While Odòlghes spurred his horse toward his kingdom, his Princess in his arms, and the people of Aurona began to disperse, a sudden rumble shook the mountain: boulders and earth fell from the low surrounding peaks as dense, dark clouds of dust rose to hide the sky, where the sun by now shone bright. When the dust blew away and the avalanches subsided, no trace was left of the doors of Aurona: in their anger, the deities had pulled it down into the bowels of the earth.

THE TRUSANI

There were seven municipalities in the Fassa Valley: Ciampdel, at the feet of the Sassolungo massif; Moena, built in the embrace of a small valley between the Catinaccio, the Sassolungo and the Latemar massifs; Vigo, at the feet of the Catinaccio; Ciananei, enclosed between the Marmolada Mountain and the Sella Group; Pozza, in the shadow of Marmolada's high peaks; Mazzin, near the Antermoia Mountain; and Soraga, on the banks of the Avisio River. Even if they all belonged to the Ladin ethnic group and their lands bordered with each other, there had often been bad blood among those municipalities, because that very same nearness tended to give birth to fights over pastures ownership or the establishing of borders, fights that at times degenerated in out-and-out battles. And those battles left in their wake a trail of blood, hate and vengeance.

That day, however, all seven Fassan *regolànes* met in the wide Conca de Gardecia; grim and brooding, all the same they shook hands and embraced each other like brothers, because a great and common danger loomed over them all.

Coming from the lands beyond the Marmolada, the Trusani were crossing the steep Ombretta passes and advancing toward the Fassa Valley, and there was no doubt whatsoever that their aim was to conquer the whole valley and its thriving villages.

It was a clear summer day and the sun, by now riding high in the sky, shone on the last, little dew drops bejeweling the bed of long, lush grass, painted in gold the thick foliage of the trees offering their cool shadow to the gathered men, and drew new, shining colors from the multitude of wild flowers dotting the pasture. Swallows were chasing and calling each other against the background of the blue sky while, down below, the constant, droning concert of the insects blended as a counter melody with the crescendo of whispers rising from the Fassans who were gathering behind the barriers erected for this occasion, to listen to the decisions made by their leaders, and maybe influence them with their approvals or vetoes.

The seven *regolànes,* who had already settled under the great elm tree growing almost in the very center of the field, were waiting for the crowd to quiet down before getting started with the meeting, and their faces were looking more and more earnest and somber.

At last, when the sun had almost reached its zenith and all the Fassans were pressing against the barriers, Moena's *regolàn,* who was also the oldest of the seven, stood up and explained the nature of the danger looming over all the Fassa Valley before leaving the floor to those who had witnessed the invasion first hand.

Hunters—who had adventured almost as far as the Agordino province while stalking their prey—told about the armed troops they had seen marching toward the Fassa Valley, and the same tale was confirmed by the shepherds who had run away from the mountain plateaus where they kept their cattle to pasture when they had seen the Trusani's polished armors shine under the sun.

The *regolànes* questioned those witnesses for a long time, all together and separately, compared their tales, and finally stood silent, pondering on what they had heard, as sheer dismay transpired from their expression; all around, everybody else was silent too. Finally, the Captain from Vigo took the floor.

"My friends, what we just heard confirms our worst fears: the Trusani will soon swoop down on us. We know they are strong, well-armed with powerful weapons and armors made of a metal our blades cannot pierce, and merciless. Will we wait helplessly for them to come to slit our throats and grab our lands and our women, or will we draw our weapons to defend ourselves?"

Immediately, Gordo from Soraga and Ghedìn from Pozza stood up applauding to his words, but old Gardis from Mazzin, the only female leader present, shook her head.

"Youngsters," she huffed. "Always ready to come to blows! You have no idea whom we are facing..."

"Men, just like us," Fedèr from Ciananei interrupted her.

"Men who have already been defeated by King Odòlghes!" Londo from Ciampedel cut in; his words drew cheers from the citizens pressed against the barriers.

Gardis fell thoughtfully silent while all eyes turned to the Ombretta, whose narrow valley guarded Contrìn, the royal city, defended by strong crenellated walls, covered with a layer of gold that shone under the sun. It was the seat of Odòlghes, who had thrown down the golden doors of Aurona, disregarding all its reaches and carrying away only Princess Sommavida; Odòlghes, whose glory was sung by bards and poets, who told about his valor as a Warrior King and his talent as a musician, and about his great harp he always carried with him everywhere, even at war. And he had fought many wars, always coming back victorious to his city and his wife's arms, even when confronting the feared

Trusani, which he had defeated in a bloody battle at Plan de Norèjes.

The king and his people, however, had grown in pride because of all their victories, so much so that they had been the only Fassans to refuse to be part of the local militia, the Arimanni. As he thought about that, the old *regolàn* from Moena sadly shook his head.

"If Odòlghes were to join forces with us, we would stand a chance of victory," Gardis admitted, however.

"He won't!" the Captain immediately interrupted her, then he bitterly added, "The Contrìnesi have grown in hubris, and now they disown our ancient blood bonds. No, it is just the seven of us who will have to face the enemy."

His words were followed by a disgruntled, but approving, murmur; Londo, however, persisted in asking that they would at least try to persuade the King to side with them, sending a delegation to him. The discussion went on for a long time, with the support of the cries and shouts from their people, until they finally reached a compromise. A delegation would leave immediately for Contrìn, but at the same time, the Arimanni would convene under the leadership of their commander. Three days later, while the Arimanni were already gathering in Vigo, two ambassadors left Soraga, heading for Contrìn.

Twenty-five years had gone by since Sàbja de Fek had broken down the golden doors of Aurona, and in that time, before her death, Sommavida had given him three sons, Verrénes, Verloj and Vidòr, now fully grown up, and a daughter, Elionda, who had been born many years after her brothers and was still a child.

Odòlghes loved his children with all his heart, just as he had loved their mother, and after her death his love for his children had grown even more. Among them, however, he loved best the last two, perhaps because in the gold of their hair and in the traits of their faces he could see something of his lost Sommavida, while his first two sons had inherited his dark hair and blue eyes.

He was proud of them all, proud of his older sons' prowess at Plan de Norèjes, proud of his third son's talent at singing and playing the harp, proud of the beauty little Elionda's delicate features already showed, and his love and pride prevented him from judging them correctly, so much so that he kept trusting them with the most delicate and important responsibilities, without ever wondering if they were really up to the task.

Therefore, when the Fassan ambassadors came to express their fears and present their proposals, the King received them together with his sons, and his sons' opinion was the only one he asked for, afterwards. Immediately Verrénes, the oldest, shook his head.

"My father and my King," he exclaimed. "We are Contrìnesi! Our city is well fortified, with high, strong walls, and after the defeat they suffered at our hands, certainly the Trusani will never dare to get near it. If we now join forces with the Fassans, however, we might run the risk of exposing our people to their retaliation. It is harvest time, and they will be out in the fields, exposed to the danger."

While Odòlghes nodded, pleased that his son was so cautious and attentive to the safety of those who would one day be his subjects, his second-born—Verloj—cut in, "Are we expected to join forces with the Arimanni and accept as our commander Tarlùi, a shepherd who has just exchanged his

42

staff for a sword... we, who are the sons of a King?" he asked, his voice full of scorn. "If the Fassans really need us, they must first recognize your authority and pay homage to you. Only then we'll discuss of alliances and help!"

Odòlghes nodded again, recognizing in his son's haughty words the very same pride he harbored in his heart, then he turned to Vidòr, who sat on the steps leading up to the throne, his fingers idly plucking at the strings of the great royal harp.

"My Lord and my father," he began, with his sweet, clear voice that always reminded Odòlghes of his lost bride, "we must also remember that, across the years, by your will and our mother's, all the art, the knowledge and the beauty created by our people have been gathered here in Contrìn. Look at the frescoes that adorn our houses, think of all the manuscripts painstakingly written year after year, to preserve our history and customs, remember the melodies composed, transcribed and stored only here, in our city! Would you run the risk of having this priceless heritage scattered and destroyed? All of Fassa's soul is here, and Contrìn's first duty is to preserve it!"

For the third time, Odòlghes nodded and smiled, for it pleased him to hear his sons give voice to the ideas and thoughts he had voiced himself in past situations; he did not stop and think that past circumstances had been different, he just turned to the ambassadors, who were waiting with a resigned expression.

"You have heard what has been said, and my heirs' words are my own. Go, then, and pass them on to your cities."

Dejectedly, the ambassadors headed back home.

Surrounded as it was by a six feet deep moat and defended by an earthwork with a palisade on top of it, the well laid out 600 tents square encampment looked bigger and stronger than most of the villages its occupants were getting ready to strike.

Two long streets, one vertical and the other horizontal, crossed the quadrilateral encampment, and along each of them soldiers wearing short tunics and shiny armors marched back and forth. Armed with wide swords and daggers, their heads covered with heavy helmets sporting colored crests, those soldiers carried themselves with strength and pride, like men dedicated to war and proud of it.

A bigger, higher tent, surmounted by the host's insignia, rose at the center of the encampment, where the two streets crossed each other. Its sides were partly rolled back, thus exposing some of the interior to a casual observer: rectangular in shape, the tent held a table strewn with papers and a seat, presently occupied by a young man whose tough, stern face betrayed years of heavy responsibilities and hard choices. His helmet, shield and sword lay at his feet; standing in front of him were three armed men, all older than he was, but all showing deference through their expression and behavior.

"It is so, Legatus. Those barbarians have taken up arms and their militia—a citizen's militia—is getting ready to face us. They have primitive weapons, and they lack in discipline, but we must consider that we'll be facing real soldiers and not ploughmen who are holding a sword for the first time in their lives," said the oldest among the three, a huge, bald man.

The young commander nodded thoughtfully, then he threw a fleeting glance at the second man, silently asking for his opinion.

"We will defeat them, of course," the man immediately spoke up; he was leaner than the first one, but still strong and brawny. "It would not even be worth discussing the matter, if our march were to end here, among these mountain valleys, but..."

"But it is not so," his commander concluded in his place, instinctively lowering his gaze on the map covering the table. "No," he went on, rising to his feet, "we cannot afford to lose time fighting against these people, if we want to cross the Northern passes before winter sets in."

"And so...?" asked the third man, who had been waiting one step behind the others, triumph vibrating in his voice.

"And so, I find myself forced to follow your plan, Caio Valerio. I don't like it, but I find it expedient. Are you sure..."

"Without any doubt, Claudio Druso! My contacts are more than trustworthy, and my own woman answers for them. Not all the Contrìnesi are faithful to their King, and even less to his heir apparent. Contrìn will fall in our hands, thus offering us a different way to reach the high passes from the one where we would find the Arimanni blocking our way."

"Moreover, this will allow you to avenge the death of your comrades who have been killed on that damned plateau... what was it called?" the commander insinuated.

"Rhododendrons Meadow, Legatus, or Plan de Norèjes, as they call it in their barbaric language," the centurion hastened to answer, a wide sneer on his face.

He would never forget the slaughter in which almost all his companions had met their death, nor the tall, dark haired man who had mercilessly chased them down, spurring his own warriors with his words and his example, a flaming sword in his hand. Just as he was never going to forget the scorn with which that crowned Barbarian had had the bodies of the defeated soldiers thrown in the Pettorina Creek. The centurion had barely escaped with his life, lying down in a depression of the ground, hidden by the moonless night, but he could still see the slaughter in his mind's eye, his commander's head flying through the air, sheared off his neck by that flaming blade, his comrades falling to the ground bleeding on that hostile soil, the smell of their blood and the screams of the wounded as they were mercilessly put to death.

"It is true, Legatus," he admitted, gritting his teeth. "I have sworn to avenge them, and I will. This is why I chose to live on these mountains, why I took a barbaric woman as my companion, spying on my old enemies to the advantage of the Empire, and now I finally know where to hit. Trust me and my hate: it will lead you to victory."

Whilst refusing to join the Fassan league, Odòlghes thought it better to strengthen Contrìn defenses, and he charged his sons with the task of keeping watch over the borders and patrol them.

"You all proved yourselves to be wise counselors, my sons, but you must now prove your readiness to sacrifice yourselves to the safety of your people," he admonished them, as he shared among them the control of the garrisons and of the gates.

Full of self-confidence, the three young men accepted the responsibility, finding it worthy of them and gratifying, but they soon discovered that it entailed more toil than honors when the endless inspections, training sessions and watch shifts prevented them from carrying on with their usual, easy and pleasant everyday life, while their way of handling things kindled complaints and unrest among their underlings.

The first to give up was the youngest, whose character was ill-suited to weapons and discipline, most of all at harvest time, when singing and poetry competitions took place in every farmyard—contests he always used to win. He held out for some ten days, then he took to delegating his underling to carry out his duties, often forgetting to supervise them, absorbed as he was in his art. As it was to be expected, surveillance soon wavered in the areas under his responsibility, becoming discontinuous at best.

He told his brothers that he might have to go away 'for a few days', but instead of adding his load of work to their own, they initially got angry with him and then, since his defection did not seem to be causing any trouble, they ended up following his example.

Verloj got a message from fair, young Mèina, a married woman he was having an affair with, who was asking him to come and see her since her husband was going to be away for a few days. Deeming it absurd to miss such an opportunity just 'to keep watch over the mountains', as he told Verrénes, he ignored his elder brother's grumblings and left his post, secretly getting back to Contrìn.

Verrénes was deeply annoyed by his defection. Of course, he was not even thinking of taking over his brothers' duties, but he felt very stupid at staying there with the soldiers, deprived of all the comforts and amusements he was used to and that—as he kept thinking with growing anger—his brothers were still enjoying. After some inner debate, however, he chose not to say anything to their father because, in spite of everything, there was still a strong bond of solidarity among the three brothers; at the same time, though, he also decided to take advantage of any pleasant occasion that chance might offer him.

He did not have long to wait: barely two days had gone by since Verloj had left when a small group of merchants presented themselves at his post. The merchants carried wine and exquisite food with them, and had in their train jugglers and wandering minstrels. Their arrival boosted the bored young man's morale and he went out of his way to organize a pleasant evening. So, that night not only Verrénes, but his officers as well indulged in revelry and, made thirsty by the heavily spiced food, they drank excessively, made more than a pass at the artists—all young and quite compliant women—and finally ended up drinking themselves into a stupor at what should have been their guard post.

At that point Caio Valerio who, through his wife's relatives, had been spying upon the King's sons, rejoicing in their deserting their post one after the other, shed his disguise as a merchant and used torches and fires to signal the Trusan army to advance, while he and his men slaughtered Verrénes and his guards.

The Trusani swooped on Contrìn almost without any fighting, since Vidòr hadn't scheduled the patrolling that should have guarded all the ways into the city, and found the city gates open and undefended because their protection had been entrusted to Verloj, who was then enjoying Mèina's charms. Left to themselves, without a leader, only a handful of his men had kept to their duty, and they had been easily overcome by Caio Valerio's brothers in law.

In his castle, built on a small plateau from which it overlooked the whole city, Odòlghes slept in his bed, unaware of what was happening and yet restless in his sleep, because twice already he had dreamed of his dead wife, Sommavida, seeing her surrounded by flames, her beautiful face distorted with terror, her hands extended imploringly. When that vision came back to haunt him a third time, the King managed to rouse himself from his slumber and sat up on his bed; immediately, his eyes were drawn to a glimmer of light filtering through the heavy, dark drapes even if morning was still far away, and he heard a growing commotion outside. Spurred by a sudden foreboding, he left his bed and ran outside on the balcony, pulling back the curtains and immediately drawing back with a horrified cry: Contrìn had been set to the torch.

The high, shining towers were on fire, and so the golden merlons and—within the protective embrace of the walls—the haughty abodes of the Contrìnesi, with their graceful frescoes and carved wood decorations; everywhere, on the ravaged streets, in the torched fields and in the devastated squares, he could see the bodies of his subjects caught and killed in their sleep, the wounded breathing their last, bodies still contorting as the fire consumed them. And looming over it all, the Trusan eagles advanced, bringing death and ruin, taking possession of his land.

With a scream in which despair merged with pain and disbelief, Odòlghes dashed to the door as he was, only grabbing on the way out his great sword, sàbja de fek, and ran down the stairs, then in the courtyard and out, in the streets, to fight and die with his Contrìn. While running, he shouted with his powerful voice, waking up the whole castle so that everybody–men, soldiers, women, even children– would join him in what he himself recognized as a desperate fight, to save at least Contrìnese honor.

His squires heard him and followed him, helping him don his golden leather cuirass and his helmet before he went out on the streets; a groom, who had heard him even before the squires did, met him at the doors with his great stallion, the golden harp hanging from the saddle, and a second groom handed him his shield. Thus armed, the King of Contrìn spurred his horse toward the invaders, his war-cry ringing in the air.

Scantily dressed and even worse armed, the people of the castle followed him, aghast and fearful for their lives and those of relatives and friends who lived in the city and in the surrounding countryside, and that group of desperate men first threw themselves against the wall of flames that by now surrounded the castle, and then against the invaders, fighting with weapons, bare hands and teeth.

Only little Elionda–totally forgotten in the ensuing chaos–remained at the castle with her nurse and a couple of serving maids; too terrified even to try to run away, they locked themselves up in a small room in the castle dungeons, praying and hoping that the King would send somebody to take them to safety.

The battle raged savagely among the ravaged streets and the gutted buildings of the burning city, because in the Contrìnesi fury and despair made up for their lack of numbers and weapons. Self-assured and disciplined, however, the Trusani kept advancing, conquering the city street by street, house by house.

The naked bodies of the two lovers were thrown down from Mèina's balcony, almost at the King's feet, while on the bell tower–whose bells nobody had rung to give the alarm–was being hoisted Vìdor's lifeless body, after the young man, coming back the victor from a song competition, had been caught while he was trying to get back to his post.

The high towers collapsed in a cloud of dirt and ashes, the powerful walls were crumbling, and yet in the center of the devastated city, on the narrow path leading to the castle, Odòlghes was still fighting furiously, together with the last Contrìnesi who were rallying around him. Then, under his eyes, Verrénes body was hung up beside Vidòr's.

Caio Valerio, who was at the head of the Trusani besieging the King, was quick to take advantage of Odòlghes momentarily lowering his guard and, with a tremendous blow of his sword, he cut through the King's wrist. The Trusan gladius cut through flesh and nerves, broke the bones and, while blood spurted copiously from the wound, the King's hand fell to the ground, sheared off, the dead fingers still grasping the sword hilt. While his men gave out a horrified scream, Sàbja de Fek swayed on the saddle, folding on himself and letting the shield fall as well. Before anybody could come to his rescue, the Trusani surrounded him, hitting him with gladii and maces until the

King crumpled to the ground, his helmet broken and his face covered with blood.

Having heard their fellow citizens' screams, more men rushed over, and the battle raged on, fiercer than ever over the King's body, so much so that when the Trusani finally managed to push back the last assault, forcing the Contrìnesi to surrender, Odòlghes body was by then buried under those of his subjects and, in the elation of victory, nobody thought of looking for it.

"Ave, Nerone Claudio Druso! Victory is yours!"

The Legatus, who was slowly riding through the bloodied streets, full of bodies and rubble, nodded, a piece of cloth still pressed against his nose to defend it from the acrid smell of the fires still burning in the ruined city.

"I did not wish for such a slaughter, centurion! You spoke of disgruntled citizens who were going to help us, of a surprise attack!"

Caio Valerio shook his shoulders.

"So it was, Legatus, otherwise the count of the dead would have been much higher. They are a brave people, these Contrìnesi!"

"Which is why I hope it will be possible to find a way to live in peace with them."

"They will end up with accepting our Pax Romana as well, Druso, just like many other defeated populations have done," cut in a grey haired man carrying a Prefect's insignia, who had come up to them; smiling to the Legatus, he went on, "What really counts is for this victory to be a first step toward opening a safe communication route to Southern Germany."

Brightening up, Druso eagerly reassured him. "It will, Prefect! We have already found some guides who will show us the way to the mountain passes, and once across the Alps, my brother Tiberio will help me to catch the German tribes in a vise and inexorably crush them." He paused, his smile growing warmer as he watched a small group of crying women, among which could be seen a beautiful blond girl of five or six years of age. "And as far as the defeated are concerned..." He dismounted and approached the small group; resolutely pushing aside the women, he picked up the girl, who stared at him with bewildered violet eyes, too frightened to keep crying. "This little girl, Elionda, Sàbja de Fek's last living offspring, will become a bond of peaceful cohabitation between us and them."

In so saying, he got back on his horse still carrying the child, motioned for Elionda's serving maids to follow them and together with the Prefect left that scene of death.

The fight had raged through all the night and the following day, the sun finally setting while fires still burned here and there and the echoes of the battle still rang in the air; now, however, the moon's rays were shedding their light on a scene of death and destruction, where everything was still and quiet.

Many Trusani had gone back to their encampment, taking their wounded with them, others were patrolling the crumbled walls and the streets choked with rubble, and others yet were busy heaping the bodies outside the walls, for the funeral pyre.

Inside the city—now a ghost of its former self—squads of legionaries patrolled at regular intervals the streets and the houses, the sound of their marching in time the only noise breaking that sinister silence of death... at least until in the starry night a song rose, high and powerful, from the ruins of the destroyed city.

Odòlghes had slowly come back to life, a defeated and maimed man, a King without a people or a homeland. He wanted to run away, to save himself, but he could not: all the dead lying around him, and the memory of his dead sons had held him there, on the scene of his utter defeat, as if their wounds were open mouths still asking something to their King. As he painfully dragged himself to his feet he saw it nearby, half hidden by a burned out curtain but miraculously undamaged: his harp. And he understood.

Dragging himself forward, falling down and painfully getting up again, he covered those few yards and finally let himself fall down by the instrument, gripping it between his knees, and as his left hand gently touched them, the harp strings answered to his touch with a soft keen. Then the King lifted his bloodied face toward the starry sky and intoned a song of death and glory that would accompany his sons, his soldiers and all those who had died in and for Contrìn in their last journey. That was all he could do for them now, celebrate their death singing of their deeds, their bravery, so that they would never be forgotten.

Once more his warm, powerful voice rose under Contrìn's sky, singing of valor and tragedy, of heroism and defeat.

Crags white as snow, icy brooks,
Golden dawns, fiery sunsets,
Of the land that was mine, hark:
Let this be the King's last song.

Sabja de Fek

Where are the brave youths, the pride
of Contrìn, where the golden walls
And the sleek towers and the royal keep?
Betrayal opens the never breached
Doors to our foes' offense
And impetuous, a river of enemies
Pours into the dreaming city.
Dirt and smoke, and fire and blood,
Torn down walls, ashes and ruins,
Clashing swords and assaults and flights
And shining blades, horror and death
Wails and screams, mothers' cries,
And a shout, just one: for Contrìn we fight!
Then, silence, and the hissing of flames.

O my Fallen, o Children! May
The strong valley wind spread
Your ashes on the beloved cliffs
Of the breached passes, and
In our mountains' bosom.
Not in the Heroes' fair abodes
May grieving souls find their rest.

Father and King, I was, now I'm a beggar.
All I have left is my song, and my grief.

The Trusan patrols heard him and ran to inform their centurion; Caio Valerio hurriedly followed them, already suspecting who the unknown singer could be, but when he found himself before the defeated King he came to a sudden standstill, choking on the scornful, threatening words already rising to his lips.

Surrounded by corpses, Odòlghes was sitting with his back against a collapsed column, his eyes on the faraway stars, the golden harp on his knees. His cuirass had been broken in many places and his ripped, bloodied tunic showed through the gaps; his maimed arm hung motionless from the shoulder and his long, dark hair was matted with gore, but he had been singing an ode so powerful, heartbreaking and intense that the centurion stepped back, speechless; his men stepped back as well, without reaching for their weapons, and they all silently listened to that song, finding in those words, in those notes something that belonged to them as well: pain, bravery, honor.

When the last note died, the singer slowly got to his feet, stared at his enemies for a long moment, then turned away from them and moved a few, uncertain steps toward the fallen walls and the freedom offered by the woods.

One of the soldiers—not Valerio, who had already walked silently away—reached toward the singer, asking:

"Who are you? And that song... why?"

The defeated froze. Then, without turning back, he answered in a soft voice.

"I'm nothing. A beggar, an exile, just that, and for the last time I have said good bye to my land and my people, singing the death hymn of the free Contrìnesi."

Then he walked away, and nobody dared to stop him.

REVENGE

Almost twenty years had gone by since that fateful day when Contrìn had fallen under the swords of the Trusani, and many things had changed. Most of the houses had been rebuilt or restored, and the Trusani themselves, after taking possession of the city, had had its walls rebuilt as well; under their supervision, those walls had lost their golden gleam, but were now stronger and enduring, in accordance with their engineers' rational criteria. Within that reborn Contrìn, the population had slowly got used to live side by side with the maniple of Trusani that Nerone Claudio Druso had left there as he marched on toward Germany; slowly, some of them were even beginning to appreciate the Trusan rule, which gave them reliable laws and protection against the Arimanni's incursions.

Great honors had been bestowed on Centurion Caio Valerio and his Contrìnese family. His brother in law, who had been at the head of the dissident Contrìnesi and had opened the doors to the invaders, was now the city's *regòlan,* and Valerio himself was its military governor. Both had done their utmost to erase even the memory of that terrible night, forgiving those who had accepted their authority, helping in the rebuilding of houses and streets, and distributing food supplies during those first, hard months. They had also done their best to make the cohabitation of the two, different ethnic groups easier, to the point of providing the bride with a dowry in a mixed marriage, and of helping the new families thus created.

By the Legatus own decision, Little Elionda—who the new *regòlan* had raised like his own daughter—had been promised at an early age to Publio, Caio Valerio's son, as a living symbol of that pacific cohabitation strongly pursued by Claudio Druso before his departure, and that his men had tried to consolidate.

"Twenty years of hard work, Caio, but we can be well satisfied with the results," the *regolàn* said, as he poured a drink for his guest, and the Trusan nodded, smiling. "Augustus himself, in Rome, was well pleased with them, as the Quaestor he sent here told me, and Elionda's wedding with Publio will seal the peace we won back for our people."

This was the actual reason of the meeting—to talk about the wedding of the two youngsters, by now both in their twenties. They had decided it was going to be a major, unforgettable event, to which representatives of the other Fassan cities—that had always prudently kept their distance from Contrìn—had been invited in the hope that the sight of the newfound peace and prosperity of Contrìn might bring them to look more favorably at the presence of the Trusani on their lands.

"Have you already told Publio?" the *regolàn* asked, well knowing his son-in-law to be was on watch duty on the Ombretta passes.

"Of course! He's hurrying back home" assured Caio Valerio; then he raised his half-full glass and added, "You know, I have the distinct feeling that my son has developed a new interest toward fair Elionda, of late..."

The two men exchanged a knowing look, then both laughed, as they toasted with their glasses.

"Speaking of your daughter, what is Elionda doing and saying about her wedding?"

The *regolàn* laughed again as he poured himself more wine.

58

"What would you have a girl to do when her wedding is drawing near? She is giggling with her friends, supervising the preparations for the ceremony, and most of all working on her wedding dress!"

They laughed and toasted again, well satisfied.

As a matter of fact, right in that moment Elionda was sitting on the balcony, in her room, together with her best friends, but she was looking at nothing in particular, her gaze lost beyond the gracefully carved wood railing as she listened absentmindedly to her friends cheerful chatter.

The previous day, as she was looking around the house where she had grown up, searching everywhere for nice trinkets for her wedding, she had seen something that had been preying on her mind since then. It was a long, strong sword, whose oddly gleaming point looked like it had been coated with melted gold, and it was hanging on the back wall in the wide room on the first floor where her foster father used to receive delegations of citizens or ambassadors from the other Fassan communities. She seldom went into that room, and usually only hurriedly, so that had been the first time she had really seen that weapon, which she had never noticed before.

That day, however, as she studied it in detail, she had felt something frightening waking up in her heart and fighting to surface, something she was attracted to, but at the same time feared and tried to ward off. She ended up running away from the room, her white tunic flowing behind her, and seeking refuge in the wide kitchen, where she knew she could find the old maidservant who had looked after her ever since she was a baby, and was perhaps

59

the only one who could—and would—tell her something about that weapon that so intrigued her.

Elionda found her there, just as she expected she would, sitting by the fireplace where she was peeling vegetables, and went to sit on a stool at her feet as she used to do as a child, resting her beautiful face on her knees; as they old familiarity resurfaced, Elionda overwhelmed the old woman with a barrage of questions.

The maidservant had a moment's hesitation that did not escape the girl's notice, but after a while she quietly replied.

"I don't know why you were so impressed by that weapon, my child! It is a fine sword, which the *regòlan* picked up after the battle of... when..."

Stammering, the old woman turned bright red and broke off.

All the children had always been told very little about the Trusan invasion and the terrible battle following it, both for unspoken agreement and as an answer to open appeals from the *regòlan* and the governor. Because of her birth, Elionda knew even less, since she had been told only that many years ago some misunderstandings between Contrìnesi and Trusani—fueled by a group of deceitful citizens—had degenerated into riots immediately suppressed by the Trusani. The perpetrators had then been banned from the city and her real father, *regolàn* of Contrìn at that time, had joined them of his own accord, almost as a penance for his inability to prevent those events.

She had not been told about the destruction of the city and her killed brothers, much less about her royal ancestry, and in that tale Odòlghes had been represented as just a *regolàn*.

To this they had always added that, in leaving, he had left Elionda in the care of his good friend, the present *regolàn*, to be raised as his daughter.

And as such she had been raised, so much so that up to now Elionda had never had any suspicion about that tale; after seeing that sword, however, she had been having doubts that the slave's sudden silence were now corroborating.

"Go on, please!" she urged her. "What else did you want to say?"

The old woman pushed her back and got up, straightening her apron.

"Nothing, you silly child! What else would you have me to add? You father kept that sword in the hope that her owner would come forward and claim it, because it really is a fine weapon, worthy of a king..." On those words her voice cracked for a moment, but she recovered with an effort, and hurriedly finished her sentence... "But nobody ever claimed it, so the sword ended up where you saw it, hanging on a wall. And this is the end of my tale, child, because I have to go into the pantry."

Stroking Elionda's check, the old woman hastened away, but by now a doubt had taken roots into the girl's soul.

During the day she appeared to be the same as ever: she would joke with her friends and with the handmaidens while embroidering her trousseau and taking an interest in the preparations her father was making for her wedding day, or she would express her anxiety and eagerness to see the wedding crown Publio was going to give her. At night, however, while lying alone in her bed, she would be assaulted by new, different images populating the surrounding darkness.

In them she would see a tall, dark haired man, with very light colored eyes shining in a sun tanned, proud face, who would hold her in his arms. And there were three boys as well, who played with her and let her ride piggyback, or taught her to run on the meadows. She also saw a city she knew to be Contrìn, but at the same time did not look like it, with golden walls and high towers shining under the sun. And more gold—a royal crown— shone on the head of the man holding her in his arms, while at his side he carried the sword she had seen hanging on the wall in the *regolàn* meeting room, and a golden harp glittered at his feet.

Every time she would wake up crying and with a heavy heart, without knowing why. She would then tell herself she was being silly and would hasten through her daily chores with a quiet, happy countenance. Nobody ever suspected something was undermining her peace of mind, and if at times she looked absentminded or a little nervous, everybody ascribed that to the natural anxiety of a young girl on the verge of leaving her home and family for a new life at her husband's side.

The preparations were therefore carried on without problems, and as he arrived at the head of his maniple of Trusani, Publio found the city all decked out and his betrothed more beautiful than ever. He joyously presented Elionda with the wedding crown, beautifully crafted in silver filigree and colored enamels, and in placing it on her golden, curly hair, he dared to kiss for the first time her rosy cheek, then laughing at Elionda's visible self-consciousness. "I see you went the whole hog here," he then said to his father.

"And you haven't seen anything yet! Before the ceremony proper we'll have a contest of bards and a weapons tournament, followed by dancing, parades and choruses. I want this wedding and this feast to seal the triumph of Pax Romana, putting an end to hate and rivalry once for all!"

"I'd say you already reached your goal, if these acclamations are any indication."

And among those acclamations, Caio threw his arm around his son's shoulders as together they headed for home, escorted by their stolid legionaries.

The beginning of the celebrations was only a few days away, and already the city was packed with guests, peddlers, musicians and jugglers.

All squares, crossroads and courtyards were crowded with people in their best finery, who would mill around the merchants' stalls and get in and out of the various taverns, eating, drinking, and enthusiastically applauding the first musicians to arrive at Contrìn.

An harpist in particular—an older man with long, silver hair and very light eyes on his tanned, lined face—drew the attention and the ovations of the crowd both with his merry drinking song and his recitation of ancient poems telling of past glories, because the soul of Fassa itself seemed to quiver in his powerful, deep voice, and the notes of his harp were as deep and harmonious.

All over the city people were soon saying a bards' competition was going to be superfluous, because none of the other bards could compete with that harpist; as his fame grew throughout the city, it reached also Elionda's ears: her curiosity awakened, she persuaded a recently married friend to go with her to listen to him.

Sunset was near when the two girls reached the small square where the bard was performing; the last, red rays of the setting sun wreathed his silver hair like a crown and lit his eyes, gleaming on the big harp the man played only with his left hand. The performance had already begun when the girls reached the square, and at first they had some difficulty in following the song. Then, as sudden and painful as a stabbing dagger, the feeling that she knew that music, those words, and—most of all—that voice hit Elionda forcefully.

She could feel the blood drain away from her face, but the cloak she had wrapped herself into to avoid being recognized hid her pallor and her emotions from her friend as after twenty years she listened again, shivering with disbelief and rapture, to the tale of beautiful Sommavida and of Aurona.

And she remembered everything: the royal palace and her brothers, the golden walls of *her* Contrìn—the same city she lived in... and yet not the same anymore—her mother's sweet face, and her father. Her father, king and musician, tall and strong, the royal crown wreathing his dark hair, the golden harp lying at his feet, and at his side... her hands contracted into fists under her cloak, as tears of disillusionment and anger filed her violet eyes... at his side sàbja de fek, the great shining sword now adorning the *regolàn's* wall.

They had all lied to her, always: her foster father, the Trusan governor, her betrothed, her friends... even her maidservants!

She felt dizzy with the surge of anger now suffocating her: they had taken everything away from her, her name, her status, even the right to cry for her family! With a few muttered words to her friend, she threaded her way through the crowd and, shaking with fury, went back home, where she immediately retired to her room and her bed, pleading a strong headache.

During her sleepless night, however, spent crying and chasing after her childhood memories, she thought back to those odd dreams she had been having, and she realized that she had been reliving in her sleep her life of old, seeing her true family and her city as it used to be in the past.

Dawn found her out of bed already. Again, she wrapped herself up in her wide cloak and covertly left the house on shaking legs, with her heart hammering in her chest, bent on finding the harpist again. Intuitively, she knew who he was, just as she knew that from his lips she was going to learn the truth about herself and her family. That certainty frightened and yet fascinated her, so much so that she broke into a run as soon as she learned from a passerby where she could find the man, and still running entered the small courtyard where the harpist had settled for the night.

While running, she had kept wondering at what she was going to ask him, and how, but in the end there was no need for words: as he saw her, still breathless from running and from her strong emotions, with her cheeks flushed, her violet eyes shining and a smile quivering on her lips, the harpist opened his arms to her.

They embraced, tears and smiles mingling as they stared at each other, recognizing their own features in the other's. Finally, still holding each other, they sat on the poor bed the former king had made for himself with his cloak and his traveling bag.

They talked... only broken, meaningless sentences at first, but after a while Elionda managed to ask her father about her story, and that of her family.

Odòlghes could tell her only little, at first, because he feared that the girl's absence might raise suspicions at home, but they met again in the following days, aided by the festive atmosphere, and soon Elionda knew everything. She learned of Contrìn's past glory and of its kings, of her brothers' wretched end and of the destruction of the city, and she cried both out of grief for her losses and out of bitterness for having ignored them up to then.

Finally drying off her tears, she looked at Odòlghes with loving eyes as she stroked his maimed arm.

"At least you are safe, father! But how, and where, did you live all these years?" she asked.

"I earned my exile's bread like a beggar, playing and singing. I knew the misery of the street life, and the splendor of many a court, I have been called with many names, but I have never forgotten my Contrìn, not that I was its king."

The girl huddled against him, savoring the pain and the pride of those words, then she shyly reached to stroke his face. "Why didn't you look for me? I would have been happy to follow you anywhere!"

Odòlghes rejoiced inwardly, because he had come back driven by vague rumors according to which his daughter was still alive, as well as by a secret thought. He refrained from saying anything about that, however, and merely held her more tightly in his arms, whispering gently,

"I believed you to be dead as well, my love, and I had resigned myself to a wandering life, alone, without a country or a family of my own. Now that I have found you again, however..." He broke off, looking at her. She looked so much like his beloved Sommavida! And yet, in spite of those violet eyes and blond hair, he could still see something of himself in her sweet face.

"Now that you have found me again?" Elionda pressed him, because she wanted him to keep speaking. Instead of answering her question, however, her father replied with a question of his own.

"Are you in love with Publio, that young man you're going to marry?" he asked.

The girl fell silent, uncertain, nervously playing with her long, blond braid. Was she in love with her betrothed? They had grown up together and she had known him all her life, just as she had always known they would get married one day. She had agreed to that without any problem and she liked him well enough, but... did she love him?

She thought of how her friends in love would blush, and feel jealous, and giggle or cry, and she shook her head. No, she did not anxiously wait for news of Publio or for his visits, even if she was happy to see him. She did not cry when he was absent, nor feared he could fall in love with another woman, nor did she blush, quiver or hope in reaction to his nearness.

"No," she answered, with utmost certainty, and a wolfish smile lit Odòlghes face.

"What about the *regolàn* who raised you? What feelings do you have for him?"

This time, Elionda's hesitation lasted for a longer time, because her foster family had always been good to her. Seeing it, Odòlghes pressed on, "He never told you anything, did he? Just that you were a poor orphaned child he had adopted and raised out of sheer goodness of heart."

The rage Elionda had already felt at the thought of having been deceived all those years long kindled once more in her heart, and she raised her head with a prideful gesture so much alike his father's.

"They lied to me, all of them!" she exclaimed. "I was grateful to him, very grateful, but my gratitude had been built on his lies!"

"It is so, my daughter," Odòlghes gravely nodded. "They lied even about your name, your descent! But you must pretend still, just a little longer. I have to leave you, my dear... but only for a short while, very short! Then we'll be together, forever. Wait for my return with faith, and remember: nobody must harbor any suspicion that I'm still alive, or that you now know who your father is."

He kissed her, then he picked up his harp and his scant belongings as he hurried toward the city gates.

Tarlùi shook his head, his lips compressed into a stubborn grimace.

"No," he repeated in a hard voice, turning his eyes from the man standing in front of him, the left hand extended in a pleading gesture, the right one hidden under the simple dark cloak. "When you were powerful and we were still weak, you scorned and derided us, rejecting our offers for an alliance. Why should we help you, now that your pride cost you the loss of Contrìn?"

The other stiffened in reaction to those harsh words, anger and outrage surfacing in his clear blue eyes, but he managed to control his emotions and answered in a low, quiet voice, his head bowing in a cascade of silver hair.

"Because the Trusani are your enemies, just as they were mine. Because it won't be long before they turn their weapons against you, and holding the new Contrìn could give you the victory. Because now I can let you get into the city, armed, without any problems."

As he spoke, he raised his eyes on the Arimanni captain, and saw doubt fight on his face against his old diffidence. He stared at the Arimannus for a long, silent minute; then, since the other was still shaking his head, he pleaded again, desperately and passionately.

"I admit I wronged you, that in my pride, in my folly, I rejected all friendship proposals, but I exhort you not to make my same mistakes now that fate offers us the possibility of winning together!"

"You're begging now, Odòlghes, because you don't have a throne anymore, nor any power. Your words sounded quite different, years ago."

"I'm begging, yes! I'm pleading you, but on my Contrìn's behalf, not my own... and if my pleading is not enough, look... Sàbja de Fek is kneeling at your feet."

And he bent both knees to the ground in front of all the Fassan Arimanni, while his proud face, lined by time and suffering, turned a deep red. His movement unfolded his dark cloak, showing his humble wandering musician's tunic, his harp and his maimed right arm, where the hand was missing.

The soldiers looked at each other, uncertain and self-conscious at the sight of that pleading man, kneeling before them, who had been a legend of their land, and Tarlùi angrily motioned for him to get back to his feet.

"Stand, king of Contrìn! Enough. You said you can let us into the city with our weapons... how?"

Odòlghes struggled to his feet and turned his eyes on those who had witnessed his humiliation, before bringing them back on their captain.

"The wedding they are going to celebrate is my daughter's, and if she'll ask for the Arimanni to parade in her honor, they will allow it."

"Are you sure?"

"Yes."

"But will the girl agree to it?" another Arimannus cut in. "She's been raised by the Trusani and their allies, after all, she's betrothed to a Trusano and..."

"She's of my blood!" Odòlghes raised his face in a proud gesture and wrapped himself in his cloak again. "Be ready to fight, once inside the city. As soon as you hear my war cry, you'll pounce on the Trusani and on those Contrìnesi fighting at their side. Spare the city, however, and the defenseless, because they are my people."

Tarlùi nodded, taking the king's left hand in both his hands, while the Arimanni gathered around them, their swords held aloft to seal the agreement.

Persuading Elionda to go along with her father's wishes was not very easy, but Odòlghes found the right words and managed to overcome her doubts, appealing to the resentment and outrage he had seen on her face when she had realized how people she considered relatives and friends had deceived her for so many years. To fully persuade her, he did not hesitate to mention his own situation as a refugee, always in danger, and how different her life—their life—would be if he could win back that place that was rightfully his.

"More than anything else, father, I wish to see you back on your throne!" Elionda then exclaimed, pacing nervously around the clearing where they were secretly meeting. "However, I wouldn't want innocent people—maybe even friends of mine—to die because of me..."

Her father silenced her with a gesture, then the former king got closer to her and took her hand as he gently reassured her.

"Nobody will get hurt, my child, if they won't try to hurt us first! The Trusani just have to throw down their weapons and leave this land that belongs to me! Let them get back to their homes, and nobody will touch them!"

"But they are a warlike people, and I don't know if..."

"This is why you must let the Arimanni in the city! Upon seeing that their opponents are soldiers, as trained and skilled as they are, and not simple rebellious citizens, they will surrender without a fight and will leave Contrìn. We won't pursue them, you have my word on that, and will let them get back to their own country."

Only half persuaded, Elionda nodded hesitantly. Seeing her troubled face, Odòlghes went on: "Unless you lied to me, my child, and you are in love with that Publio..."

"No, father, no! I care for him, but I don't love him!"

A smile appeared on the king's lined face.

"This is for the best! You deserve much more! A prince of royal blood, maybe, or a great warrior, such as Ey de Net, who won Princess Dolasilla's love."

He paused for a moment, thinking, then his smile widened as he concluded: "They say that the last prince of the Fanes still lives, and he would be worthy of you and your

71

lineage! If it is true, I'll find him, and if you want him, he will be your husband, because you will be a great queen, Elionda!"

Beguiled by his words, the young woman nodded again, with more persuasion this time.

"If it can help you win back your throne and make that winning back less bloody, I'll ask the *regolàn* to let me attend the Arimanni's demonstration of their weapon prowess."

"That's my good little girl! Your dead brothers bless you, and you have your father's gratitude, savior of our land! Just remember my sword..."

"It's already hidden inside my trousseau chest, which will be on the dais, beside me."

"Throw it to me when I start singing. That will be the signal for our reconquest!"

The new Contrìn had never seen so much luxury and merriment since it had fallen under the Trusani's power. The whole city was celebrating, but most of the population and the guests had gathered around the dais where the wedding between the *regolàn*'s daughter and the Trusan governor's son was going to take place. The young couple was already there, together with their families, and everybody could see Publio's cheerful smile and Elionda's understandable confusion, her sweet, troubled face hidden behind the folds of her saffron colored veil. Behind them, upright in their shiny cuirasses, were lined the legionaries of Publio's maniple, and at the feet of the dais was Tarlùi, who had unexpectedly accepted the invite to take part to the games the *regolàn* had sent him on his daughter's request, proudly wore the winner's laurel crown, because the Arimanni—now crowding around him— had once more been victorious in the games.

It was now time for the musicians to entertain the crowds, and many of them had already offered their performance, telling ancient tales of the *vivane*, who still lived in the woods and by the quiet lakes of the Dolomites, of the ambiguous *anguane*, who were sometimes friendly toward men and other times hostile to them, of the icy *Croderos*, insensitive to human emotions and pain, and of their blond queen, who had instead experienced those emotions and pain.

Those songs had been met with applause and appreciation, but an absolute silence fell on the audience when the old harpist came forward, his cloak thrown on the right shoulder and his harp in his left hand: nobody wanted to miss either one single note or one word of the song that would certainly win the contest.

Feeling his daughter's intense stare, Odòlghes slightly bowed his head before sitting on a rock and starting to play.

His music was sad and solemn, and yet full of memories, of ancient glory and battles long past, of a lost, forever mourned greatness. Enthralled, the audience had eyes only for the musician's silver hair and his great, deft hand skillfully plucking the harp strings. Then the man raised his face and slowly, almost imperceptibly, started singing. It was just a long keening sound, at first, a moan that shook the audience to the core, then the words came, strong and echoing... words that awakened old memories in the governor. Before he could react, however, Elionda disengaged her hand from her betrothed's and swiftly bent on her trousseau chest, pulling out a long, wrapped up object she threw toward the harpist. The object flew through the air and on the ground, freeing itself from the cloth wrapping it and thus revealing itself for a long and strong sword, its blade shining with a golden glow.

"Sàbja de Fek!" the musician thundered then, as he sprang to his feet and grabbed the sword; his cloak fell off his shoulders, and his harp overturned on the ground, forgotten.

Everybody could the see that his right arm, always hidden under the cloak up to then, was maimed and the hand was missing, and in a moment the news spread that Odòlghes was alive and had come back, that revenge was going to be exacted for the wrongs of the past.

"Sallòi!" Before either the regolàn or the governor, both caught by surprise, could get up, impart any command or simply take cover, the Arimanni's war cry sounded high and frightening, swords and daggers blazed in their hands, and the first arrows cut through the air.

And the massacre began.

Finally— when it was too late—Elionda understood what she had set into motion, and her desperate scream went lost in the clamor of clashing weapons.

After the first few moments of bewildered disbelief, the governor drew his sword and called his legionaries to him, while the terrified regolàn tried to run away instead, jumping off the dais; Publio, on the other hand, having immediately realized what had happened, grabbed his betrothed, insulting and threatening her. The girl managed to escape him, however, and jumped off the dais as well, leaving behind in his hands her bridal veil. The young man then grabbed his bow and nocked an arrow, taking aim with a steady hand while Elionda ran toward her father.

Odòlghes did not even notice her, however, because at that moment he had just pounced on the *regòlan* —the Contrìnese who had betrayed his king and his city—like a hawk on its prey, the shining sword raised high over his head. Vain was the defense put up by the *regòlan* and his brothers, who had come to his aid, because the former king slaughtered them all like a wolf would a flock of lambs.

Meanwhile, the battle raged around them without quarter nor mercy; while still sowing death around them, the Arimanni had not yet managed to reach the dais, where Caio Valerio was valiantly defending himself, but they were taking control of the square and of the nearby streets; some of the Contrìnesi were fighting them while others, mindful of their past, were siding with them, and brotherly blood was spilt.

At the same time Odòlghes felled his last few enemies and raised his sword, now covered with blood that dulled its golden glow, as he insulted and challenged the governor. Valerio sneered at him, however, and scornfully shouted back, "Run away, old man, and give thanks to your gods that I won't stoop to fight against a one-handed old man!"

Blinded with anger, the king increased his efforts tenfold, so much so that, alone, he managed to cut through the legionaries and to jump on the dais, facing the centurion of old. His sword was now covered with blood to the hilt, fury shone in his light blue eyes and a fierce grimace contracted his face.

The Trusano was not a coward, and he also thought that killing his enemy could turn the tide of the battle in their favor; therefore, he threw himself at him, his gladius held high.

As they faced each other in a fight to the death, in a frenzied succession of slashes and lunges, the blades screeching as they shone under the hot sun, Tarlùi finally managed to reach the dais together with a handful of his men, and the fight raged even more savagely around the two foes.

By now Caio Valerio was in a bad shape, perhaps because he hadn't been wielding a sword for too long, or perhaps because his foe was fighting like a berserk, possessed as he was by thirst for revenge, because in his mind the memory of the past had smothered any perception of the present and he was still the king of Contrìn, fighting to save his city.

A sequence of feints, followed by a lunge and a downward slash of sàbja de fek, sent the centurion's head to the ground, where it rolled until it rested by the lifeless body of the *regolàn* who had betrayed his king.

A little short of breath, Odòlghes drew back, and as he wiped his sword on his cloak, he finally looked around... and what he saw appalled him.

On the bedecked dais and the cobbled square, amid the flowers adorning the balconies, everywhere lay the slaughtered bodies of Trusani, Contrìnesi and Arimanni, whose blood had reddened the decorations, the plants and flowers adorning the square. Even his daughter, Elionda, lay dead on the ground, an arrow sticking into her back and her eyes still full of the desperate denial she had shouted upon realizing what she had unleashed. A few feet away her betrothed, Publio, still held in death the bow he had used to kill his traitorous fiancée, an Arimannus spear holding him upright and nailed to the dais on which the two youths should have exchanged their vows of eternal love and fidelity.

From the nearby streets and the invaded houses, the clangor of weapons mixed with war cries and the moans of the wounded, with women screaming and children crying; and above all that roared the flames of the fires the Trusani had set as they drew back, to better hinder their attackers.

The king of old closed his light blue eyes as he fought to keep at bay his awful feeling of reliving something he had already experienced.

"I had been attacked, then, and betrayed," he tried to tell himself. "Now I'm exacting vengeance."

How bitter was that revenge, however, since it was not giving anything back to him while taking everything away from his people. He could not fight with the same strength and conviction, nor was he able to concentrate all his will, all his attention on the foes surrounding him. Too late he realized that a small group of legionaries had surrounded him from behind while he was facing two Trusani. He was now facing many foes, too many, so he shouted his war cry to call for help. Before his men could reach him, however, a blade held by an unknown hand slipped under his guard and his left arm, raised to deliver a blow, and pierced his heart, stilling it forever.

The former king of Contrìn still stood for a moment, while his proud face paled and astonishment filled his light blue eyes, then he crashed to the ground, his dead hand still gripping his sword, while the fight went on over his dead body, more savage and merciless than before, and the flames—finding an easy prey and abundant fuel in the wooden houses—roared all around them, devouring the dead and the dying alike.

All day long Trusani, Arimanni and Contrìnesi from each faction fought with the utmost fierceness, wounding and killing each other in the city where the flames were still devouring buildings and streets, and the bodies of both the dead and the wounded. Then the night came, and the moon rose over still smoldering ruins, where nothing moved anymore, and over hundreds of horribly wounded and maimed bodies, whose dead eyes stared at a light they would never see again.

The years went by, and the grass grew back among the ruins, ivy vines covered whatever was left of the houses and the walls, and brushes thrived among abandoned weapons and unburied bodies. Slowly, the vegetation grew thick and lush, covering the burned ruins, the rusted metal, the whitening bones, until trees and brushes and flowers obliterated any trace of the ruins and the dead, and of their battles.

Nothing is left nowadays to remind a wayfarer of the passion and glory of Contrìn, twice destroyed to never raise again in the shadow of the huge Marmolada, under the peaks of Ombretta. But at night, when the moon is shining at its brightest, it is possible to see a cloud crossing the starry sky, and it looks like a cloak flowing on the wide shoulders of a strong warrior, while the whistle of the wind becomes a mournful song, and the chirping of the night birds turns into the melody of a great harp, singing of past glories and of the follies of men.

Historical Notes to "Sàbia de Fek".

There are at least two sources for this legend: the first–the one about Aurona–is very ancient and linked, under many respects, to the myths concerning the mines because it is similar to the legend of the Delibana, the young woman who had to live underground for at least seven years in order to guarantee that the mines would be productive. The second, instead, belongs to a later era, and conceals under its veil a time of trouble and invasions of the Dolomites valleys by a foreign people. These two stories, belonging to different times and having different origins, are linked by the names of Odòlghes and of Contrìn. This doesn't mean anything to an historian or a researcher, because we already know similar archetypes (the warrior king, a powerful city) existed in the Ladin culture, even if there is a time span of many centuries between the two characters, but I decided to ignore any pseudo-historical plausibility in favor of blending the two fragments (because they are just that… fragments) into a single tale. Let's call it a poetic license, and I hope the readers will forgive me! History, with a capital H, has certainly already forgiven me, because it is long used to this kind of misuse!

The so-called "Trusani" deserve that I spend a few words about them. Many scholars identified them with the Langobards, but in the different legends portraying them we find enough discrepancies in their behavior to make it legitimate to suppose that the term "Trusani" may not refer to a specific people, or a single invasion, but to any foreign "enemy", to any invader. And invasions were a common occurrence in many western cultures. We still have to explain the origins of that name, though. The Ladini have always seen it as a distortion of the word "Trevisani", but *Tarvisium* was still a small hamlet at the time of the Roman conquest, which is the same era in which most of the legends about the Trusani, and in particular the one about Sàbja de Fek, take place. We could speculate about an allegiance between the Duke of Treviso and the Langobard arimannia of Roccapietore, but it took place in a later time.

Giuliano Palmeri, and others after him, speculated that the term "Trusano" could originate from "drusiano", instead, and refer to Tiberio Claudio Druso's legionaries who, in the year 15 b. C., subjugated that part of the Dolomites area in the attempt to open what would later be known as Via Claudia Augusta.

Far be it from me to put forward my opinion in a debate I'm not qualified to take part whatsoever into. I just opted for this theory not only because I found it plausible, but most of all because it fueled my storytelling inspiration more than the others.

Let me spend just another word about the *Regolànes* and the Arimanni. Again, I must plead guilty of bending history to my needs, but to my defense I must say that these figures appear in the traditional version of the legend, together with Odòlghes.

The truth is that the *Regolànes*, a sort of "majors" or chiefs of a tribe or a village, but most of all the Arimanni, members of a military caste, are historical figures of the Ladin valleys who existed in a much later time, and their presence in Sàbja de Fek's myth serves most of all to the purpose of stressing again how this legend existed in two very different times.

A curious reader will be able to find more about both the *Regolànes* and the Arimanni in the notes to *Ciadina* and *L'Varjol*. On my part, I can only beg forgiveness again for wronging History thus: it fascinates me, and feeds my curiosity, but when I write I'm first and foremost a storyteller.

Dina from Lagorai

El mal d'amor l'è na gran maladìa
El mal d'amor nia no pol più I sanar
El bruja e l'art còme legna de tia
Nince la nef no la I pol destuar.
Heartache is an illness of the heart
Heartache can never be healed
Like resinous wood it burns and sears
Nor even snow can put it out
(anonymous, Ladin version by L. Canori)

She belonged to an ancient family, so ancient its origins were lost in time, as ancient as the place where she lived, which the handful of peasants and shepherds living in the area used to call, "the castle"—just as they called her, "Dame"—even if in all probability it had originally been just a *castellier*, a fortress that had been enlarged over the centuries to become a mansion for the owners of the surrounding meadows and woods.

There were still rumors about one of her ancestors, wife to the founder of her House, who was not human but belonged to the mysterious people who had inhabited those lands well before humans settled on them; according to those far-fetched stories, she had been a *ganna*, a creature endowed with strange powers and bound to the woods, the rocks, and the water courses.

Those tales had always amused Dina, but now in her soul amusement had given way to melancholy, and she wished with all her heart for those fairy tales to be true and to have inherited some of those powers.

The only thing she had in common with her legendary ancestor, however, was the bond she had with water and the attraction she felt toward the small lake by which her castle stood, a clear pond that reflected the gloomy crags of Lagorai enclosing it, and was surrounded by the thick pine woods covering the mountain slopes.

Her betrothed, Ubaldo, had not come back home.

Almost one year had gone by since Emperor Henry II had come from his remote country to help Uldarico—prince-bishop of Trento, and the lord Dina owed fealty to—to repel Arduin of Ivrea's invasion of their valleys. A terrible battle had been fought at the Locks of Valsugana, and in the end Arduin had been defeated, but the blood price for that victory had been very high. The surviving soldiers told of hundreds of bodies still lying unburied on the battlefield.

Ubaldo had to be one of them. She wasn't going to see him again, or to hear his voice, and she would not even have a grave on which to grieve for him.

She had no idea why those powerful lords had waged their war, nor she cared to know; all she knew was that if they hadn't fought that war, she would now be happy as Ubaldo's wife, and maybe their marriage would already have been blessed by a son, to carry on her dynasty.

Now, Dina knew, she was going to be the last of her family, and after her death nobody was going to live in her castle, that would fall in disrepair, forgotten on the shore of that small lake.

As she dwelled on those sad thoughts, her elbows propped on the windowsill and her chin resting on her interlaced fingers, Dina felt the overpowering desire to visit the lake shore again and dip her hands in the water, almost seeking some kind of comfort in it.

Dina raised her head, pushing back her sleek auburn hair, and glanced out of the window. Outside, the sky was darkening and the massive Lagorai range loomed in the incipient twilight, but she did not change her mind. She called Lizeta, her old servant who was both maidservant and duenna, and ordered her to help her get ready to go out.

"At this time of the day?" the woman asked, disapprovingly, but she proceeded to braid Dina's hair all the same.

"It's not dark yet, and it's not very cold. Spring is here already!"

Her voice caught in her throat because that had been the time when, the previous year, Ubaldo had last said goodbye to her. She fought back her tears, however, as she wrapped herself in her cloak and left.

There wasn't a trace of wind in the cool air, and the lake was a silver mirror on which the reflection of the dark peaks of Lagorai drew a dark crown. All around, the surrounding woods were a vague dark mass, but the surface of the lake was shining softly and, as usual, Dina was attracted by it like she would by a friend.

Sitting on the humid shore, she pushed back both her hood and her cloak to soak her hands in the water, and even if it was very cold, she felt refreshed by it. Away from her poor people, in front of whom she had put up a show of strength, Dina allowed her thoughts to wander: her beloved's death, her solitude, her melancholy that was now her only company...

Dina pulled out of the water her hands, by now numb with cold, and she bent forward to gaze in bitterness at her own reflection: she had lost too much weight, had a pinched face and her eyes were swollen from crying. She sighed, then she gave a sudden start as she looked more closely at the reflected image. Those eyes were as green as hers, but shinier and framed with blond eyelashes; and blond was also the hair framing a face that looked very much like hers, but was more beautiful, and seemed to stare at her from the bottom of the lake. Those lips, redder and fuller than her own, curved into a smile, showing small, white teeth. Frightened out of her wits, Dina stood up and backed away with a terrified scream, covering her face with her hands. When she finally found the courage to lower them, she saw with incredulous trepidation that the image was now floating over the lake shore. It was a woman, wrapped in flowing blue-green veils and with long, blond curly hair, but her body looked like it was not made of mortal flesh, but rather of interwoven water and air. And yet she spoke, with a thin, delicate voice that sounded like a whispering breeze or murmuring waves.

"Don't be afraid of me, Dina of Lagorai!"

"Who... what are you?" the girl managed to stammer, and the Apparition smiled again.

"Who I was, who I am and who I will be... what does that matter? I am water, and wind, and memories. Your tears called me back to these shores and here I am. You grieve for the man you lost..."

"Oh, yes! Can you give him back to me?" Dina passionately interrupted her, and when the Figure shook her head, she pressed on: "Or, at least, can you allow me to see him one more time, to hear his voice again, to know where he fell so that I can bury him properly?"

She reached pleadingly with her hands, and the Ghost seemed to ponder on her words for a moment. Her voice was already fading, and her body was losing its shape to become just a blue-green blot, a misty cloud in the surrounding darkness, when she whispered, "Valfloriana, Dina! It's where the crows carry the souls of those who have fallen in battle and lie unburied. The blue flowers... you'll have to water them, one by one, for seven days, and the dead will appear and talk to you. Beware, however, it is dangerous..."

By now the Apparition wasn't visible anymore, it was just a lighter shade in the darkness, a pale reflection in the lake, but in a last whisper that faint, and yet urgent, voice went on, "The water, only the water... remember! Remem..."

Then it vanished, and the young woman was alone again in the darkness, broken only by the faint light coming from the castle, behind her. Dina hesitated for a long moment, then she headed back to the castle, her mind in turmoil, swearing to herself, *Valfloriana! Yes, I'll see you again, Ubaldo.*

The hot summer sun shone on the wide expanse of blue flowers covering the meadows like a huge, silky blanket. Under its burning rays the little blue corollas bent forward a little, dried up by the heat and almost begging for water, that same water that flowed, fresh and swift, through the dark, green woods, softly singing on its bed of white pebbles before splitting in a thousand white sprays down a small, silvery waterfall.

Her face flushed from the heat and her auburn hair gathered in two braids wrapped around her head, a woman went back and forth between the woods and the meadow carrying a bucket full of water, her tunic sleeves rolled up above her elbows as she carefully watered all those small flowers.

Dina had kept her promise and left her castle and lands in the hands of her old tutor, heading for the Vallefloriana by herself, on horse. She had been there for two months now, which she spent tirelessly watering the flowers and calling back from death, for a few moments, dozens of warriors. Up to now, however, the only one she was desperately seeking had not come to her.

She was not ready to give up, tough, and once more she patiently and carefully sprayed with the water from her jug a small area of that meadow where green and blue blended; once more from the flowers rose the faint, shimmering images of dead warriors, and once more she listened to their dead voices telling, asking, praying for a few short minutes, until the earth soaked up all the water and, with it, those pale ghosts.

Once she had poured down the last drop, and the last ghost had disappeared after whispering his name, his story and where his body lay unburied, Dina trudged toward the creek, tired and disappointed, but upon reaching it she staggered and fell with her face on the pebbles and her hands in the water. For a moment all went dark around her, and she felt extremely weak, but then the coolness of the creek revived her, even if she still felt somewhat dazed and confused.

This was not the first time she was seized by an inexplicable discomfort since she had embarked on her quest, but she had never fainted up to now. As she raised herself with difficulty to a kneeling position, she brought her hands to her face, stinging from the impact against the pebbles, and leaned over a small pond in the creek to check if there were any damages. At first the water reflected her pale and tired face, now sporting a cut on a cheekbone and a bruise on the forehead, but then the image slowly shimmered and mingled with the white foam, and when it reformed, it had changed.

Two green eyes were now staring at her from a pale, oval face with long, golden hair floating in the water, now framing the face, now covering it, while the Apparition slowly gained substance until the young woman saw again the face of the mysterious being who had already shown itself to her once in the past.

"Dina from Lagorai" warned the soft voice she remembered so well, "beware! You have brought back to life too many warriors, and now they want you to join them on the Cece, the highest peak of the Lagorai. Get back to your castle, or you will soon be just one more shadow among theirs."

Shaken, Dina shivered as she thought back to the discomfort, the fainting fits, the weakness that for days had been overcoming her, and yet she shook her head.

"Ubaldo! I want... I must... see him again, talk to him, and I haven't yet..."

"Young maid, are you sure that your love, your fidelity aren't for nothing? Is your man really lying unburied?" The Image's words were so faint they mingled with the murmur of the running water. "Give up this useless quest, get back to your valley, to your life!"

As Dina shook her head again, the slow, whispering voice went on: "Remember the water, then! The water of this river can still..." Then it vanished, and in the creek the beautiful face lost substance, becoming a whirlpool and disappearing under the eyes of the frightened, shaking young woman.

If Dina had ever doubted of the Apparition's words, her persistent illness, her feeling faint and weak would have persuaded her it was telling the truth, but she didn't give up and, day after day, she carried on her search, even if she had to slow down her pace. More and more often, in fact, she had to stop and soak her hands in the water, which seemed to be the only way to cure her collapses, and after that she had to rest for hours in the shade of the pine trees that grew thick and luxuriant around the range, or inside the little hut where she had now been living for months.

It was while taking one of those breaks that she heard a child crying deep in the woods, a sound that gave her the strength to rise from her pallet and run in the direction of the sound; there, curled up among the pine needles, she found a child of about six or seven years of age, his small face dirty and stained with tears.

Picking him up in her arms, she spoke to him gently as she rocked him soothingly. At the same time, she noticed that his clothes, while dirty and a little torn here and there, were not those of a peasant, but of a nobleman's son. It took her quite a while to get the child to stop crying, and in the meanwhile it grew dark, so that it was impossible to take the child back home, even if she had managed to learn that he lived in a castle nearby, whose towers rose high and grim above the trees.

He must be the lord's son, at least judging from his clothing. Tomorrow I'll take him there, she said to herself, as she took the child to her hut, the boy's hand trustingly holding her own.

As they walked, the boy—who by now was much calmer—told her in his childish way that his mother had scolded him, and that he had then run away, getting lost. The memory of the fear he had experienced brought a new spate of tears, but Dina hugged him and comforted him with gentle, loving words; as soon as they reached the hut, then, she made him sit down on her pallet and got busy cooking him some supper.

While going back and forth between the cupboard and the fireplace, she realized she was humming to herself, as she had not done since a long time. The child was watching her from the bed, clapping his little hands happily, so she raised her voice and for his sake found again the music and the words of those old legends that, so many years ago, her own nanny used to sing to lull her to sleep.

"Mami, conteme na storia/ dla bolp, del corf, de la regina/dla strìa, del soreie, de la luna/del picol pop che dorm te cuna..." ("Mommy, tell me a story/about the fox, the crow, the queen/about the witch, the sun, the moon,/ the little people so that I can sleep..."

(from *"Fior e foa, reisc e magda"*verses by Rosi Mussner).

She felt happy as she hadn't been for a long time: she was not alone anymore, had somebody to take care of, somebody who needed her.

The next morning, as promised, she took the boy to the wide clearing where the castle rose dark and massive with its four towers, and she looked after him as he ran away and disappeared through the great gates, smiling as he blew her a kiss.

Dina clung to that kiss and that smile to fight back tears, because her heart had sunk at letting the child go, and repeatedly told herself she had to be glad the child had gone back to his mother. She had no sons, nor a husband, only a sad memory and a bitter hope. And she went back to watering the blue flowers.

One month had gone by since that meeting had broken her solitude, and she was sitting by the creek, her naked feet in the water, trying to find her strength back after one of her fainting spells, when she heard a small voice calling her.

"Dina! Dina!"

With a start, she put on her clogs and ran toward the woods, seeing *her* child run out of the trees.

91

"I found you at last!" the boy exclaimed, grasping her hand. Then he added, happily: "I've come to live with you!"

"What?" Dina was dumbfounded. "But... what about your mother?"

"She's bad! She's always angry because my father never spends time with her, and so she scolds me. But I did nothing... nothing!"

Dina sighed to herself, realizing that family had unresolved issues, but then she had to concentrate her attention on the little runaway, who was on the verge of dissolving once more into tears.

"Come on, dry your eyes, I'm sure we'll find a solution! In the meanwhile, come with me, I'll show you the blue flowers growing on the range and then we'll have our midday meal at my home. Do you like... one moment, I don't even know your name!" she exclaimed.

"Alarico, but everybody calls me Rico."

"Rico, then! And now, come with me."

The morning went by swiftly, and, calmly reasoning with him, Dina finally persuaded the boy to get back home.

"You can always come and see me: I cannot move from here," she promised, with a sad smile. "We'll spend more nice days together, and in the meanwhile your father will get back and your mother will be happy. Nobody will scold you anymore, you'll see, because you are a good boy."

Comforted and reassured, Rico threw his little arms around her neck. "You are so good, Dina, and I love you, so very, very much!"

Since that day, the young woman's habits changed drastically; when she was alone, she would tirelessly carry on her search, with her illness worsening as the number of the warriors she awakened grew; but when Alarico came to see her, she would devote all herself to him, which gave her a bittersweet feeling of satisfaction, because the child she was hugging was not her own: the children she had dreamed of had died with her beloved Ubaldo, nor she was ever going to have any.

One day, however, the child unexpectedly came at an unusual time, while Dina was still evoking the dead with the water, and she did not see him until she was done and straightened up, turning around.

Rico stood still, frozen with fear, on the edge of the woods, with fright in his eyes and a hand pressed against his mouth. She ran to him, then, but before she could say anything the child broke free from his paralysis and hid his face against her skirt, crying, "What are those things? Are they ghosts? I'm afraid! Send them away!"

"Don't be afraid, honey. They are... yes, they are poor souls, warriors who fought and died, and now lie unburied. The crows took their spirts here, and now they live inside those blue flowers, and they can appear and speak if somebody waters them. You must not be afraid of them! They cannot... and don't want to... harm you."

Somewhat reassured by her words, Rico raised his head and, while still grasping his friend's apron in his little hand, he dared to look once more at the meadow, now free of any presence, where the small blue flowers slowly swung back and forth under the caress of a light breeze.

"It's so weird, Dina! And they will stay here forever?"

"No, they won't. They'll stay here as long as they retain some memory of their earthly life, and some hope that somebody will come looking for them, then they'll go up there, on the highest peak of the Lagorai."

As she spoke, she had walked away from the meadow and toward the creek, because she could feel she was on the verge of fainting away, but she could not reach it and fell on her knees, while all around her the whole world lost substance, as if enveloped by a sudden, thick veil of fog. She felt like a whirlwind had taken hold of her; she could hear Rico calling her with fear in his voice, but she could not answer to him. Then she felt like a strong wind was suddenly blowing, and in between its whistling gusts she heard a woman's voice, faint and weak.

"All my warnings have been in vain! Dina from Lagorai, you will soon join us on the peak of the Cece."

It seemed to her that two green eyes were staring at her, framed by flowing golden hair and long veils, then she found herself back on the stony creek bank, with Rico bathing her face and hands.

"You saved me, little one!" she gasped, as she felt life flowing through her once more. "Please, oh, please, remember: if you see me feeling ill, pour some water on me, because this is the only way I will be able to stay with you, at least a little longer."

"A little longer? Why? I want to stay with you forever!"

"It won't be possible, because I will soon join the dead I awakened, up there, on the peak of the Cece. Don't cry, my child, I..."

Alarico, however, had already dried his eyes and had raised his head to stare firmly at her.

"I'll come with you, then, on that mountain. With you."

Dina hugged him, shaking her head and smiling in spite of herself; still holding him tight, she headed toward the hut.

Many more days went by, and the fallen leaves were already heralding the oncoming of autumn, but on the meadow the blue flowers still shone changeless, and the young woman was still watering them in the hope of seeing her Ubaldo again, but also because of the compassion she felt for those forgotten dead. Having overcome his initial fear, Rico was often at her side, his little face grave and solemn as he carried a bucket of water, with which he often managed to wake her up from her fainting spells.

Fall was there, at last, when one evening a cheerful fanfare echoed through the valley, and many knights, preceded by flags fluttering in the wind, headed for the castle. The next morning Alarico did not come. In the afternoon Dina, worried and anxious, was already thinking of going to the keep to ask about him, when the child ran out of the woods.

"My father is back," he announced, kissing her.

"From now on everything will be fine at home, then! Your mother will be happy and your father will look after you," Dina replied, trying to pretend the news gladdened her, while she could feel melancholy already growing inside her. She had to be happy for the child's sake, and she *was* happy, but she could not help but think that now he would come more seldom to see her, if ever.

However, Rico gravely shook his head.

"I don't think so. Yes, we were together, this morning, and he showed us the presents he brought us, but right after the midday meal he retired in the library with my mother and I heard them shout at each other. They were fighting and bickering, so I ran away and came here, to you, because I love you more than I love them!"

Dina scolded him gently, then she questioned him some more, worried for him, and while his answers were often confused, she finally understood that the lady of the castle was reproaching her husband over his frequently being away from home, his indifference toward his own family and the little care he had of the estate she had brought him as her dowry.

"And it is true, you know... he always leaves us alone! I saw him when I was very little, and then now. It's been..."Rico counted on his fingers, a little awkwardly, then concluded: "It's been four years. It is not right, is it?"

Then, without waiting for a very ill at ease Dina to reply, he forcefully went on: "My mother was angry with me, too, and with you, because I always come to see you and I'm happy here. She kept saying you are a witch, but I know it isn't true, that you are good and love me! I don't want to get back home, I want to stay with you forever! Do you want me to?"

The young woman was still trying to find an answer that would not hurt her little friend feelings when another voice, scornful and ironic, broke the quiet of the woods.

"Let's see, then this enchantress who bewitched my son!" A tall, strong man, with a hard, handsome face lit by dark eyes and framed by thick black hair, pushed aside the lowest branches and came out of the woods, immediately and possessively placing his hands on Alarico's shoulders.

At the sound of that voice, Dina's heart skipped a beat as she slowly turned to look at the newcomer. All traces of color left her face, while her knees gave way: in front of her, dressed with the luxurious clothing of a nobleman, was the man over whose death she had been grieving for years, the man she had awakened so many warriors for, in the hope of seeing him again.

And now she was seeing him, handsome and proud as she remembered him, but married to another woman.

While she crumpled to the ground, she realized he had never loved her. Already married, and a father, he had deceived and betrayed her, and at last, tired of her love, he had used war as an easy pretext to leave her behind.

The pain, the disillusionment, the bitterness choked her, and her heart throbbed painfully in her breast, doubling its pulses, while her head seemed ready to burst, a roar rose in her ears and her eyes grew sightless. Merciful, darkness enveloped her then, and she lay still among the blue flowers.

Ubaldo had recognized her as well, and he immediately thought of his already jealous and suspicious wife, from whom he derived most of his present prosperity. This fear mingled with shame, and he instinctively turned his back to Dina, to run back to his castle. His son's desperate crying and fighting against his hold, as he kept staring at the unconscious woman, finally stirred him.

"Let me go!" the child cried, confusedly, kicking and squirming to get free. "The water! She must have the water, or she will go away and I'll never see her again!"

If there was something the castellan was certain of, however, it was that he was not going to allow his son to have any more contacts with the girl he had deceived and betrayed, so he held him tighter and called for his squire, who was waiting nearby, ordering him to find the creek and get some water from it.

"I can't see the use for it, but maybe this little fiend will calm down then," he concluded, and the servant left him.

Ubaldo waited for a long time, his gaze that kept lingering on Dina's still body only to stare away from it, while Alarico went on sobbing and fighting, shaking so violently he almost seemed prey to convulsions. It took almost an hour before the servant, who did not know the area and had lost his way more than a few times, finally came back with a jar full of water. At a gesture from his master, he knelt down to bathe the young woman's face and hands. Many minutes went by, the silence broken only by the child's labored breath, then the man got up and shook his head.

"It's no use, Sir Ubaldo. She's dead."

Incredulous, the castellan stared at him; overcome by remorse and shame, he raised one hand to cover his face, but in so doing he loosened his grip on his son, who wriggled free from his grasp an threw himself on Dina's body, hugging her as he cried and sobbed desperately.

For a few minutes, his father stood still, them he shook himself and called Alarico, gently at first, then more sternly; shaking with a nervous tremor, the boy did not even glance at him, so Ubaldo tried to draw him away from the body by force, but in the end he needed his squire's help to manage to detach him from it.

Glancing at the child, who was wide eyed and cyanotic, Ubaldo hefted him on his horse and, holding him in front of him on the saddle, spurred the horse toward the castle, thinking all the while how on earth was he going to explain to his wife what had happened.

I'm afraid it won't be easy to get out of this mess, he pondered. *Even if I were to keep the lid on it and have my squire do the same, nobody will ever make Alarico keep his mouth shut! If only he were to keep silent, I might...*

As Ubaldo indulged in those thoughts, he glanced again at his son, who had finally calmed down and lay still in his arms, his face hidden against his chest, and a horrified, incredulous cry escaped his lips: the child was not going to talk, not ever again. Alarico was dead, his face stiffened in a grimace of pain and still wet with his tears.

All Ubaldo could do was to take back the little body to his wife, stunned with grief.

"I found him like this on that meadow covered with blue flowers," he lied; his voice was hoarse, however, and his eyes wet with tears, because his grief and his remorse were genuine. "Don't ask me anything, I beg you! Not now... I cannot... and then there is nothing to say. Nothing!" And with a parting glance to the squire, whom he had already warned, he locked himself in his room.

Silent, the lady of the castle readied her only son for burial, and once the boy lay arranged on the high bier she had had built in the courtyard, she stood staring at him for a long while, unable even to cry, not a single wail escaping from her pressed lips. Then, while the shadows of the oncoming night already veiled the high peaks surrounding the castle, she called to her two trusted servants and sent them in the woods and on the meadow, to search for the causes of that tragedy.

She waited for them in the courtyard, sitting by her son's coffin, gently caressing his hair with eyes staring at nothing, while her face grew harder and harder.

99

"Lady..." A couple of hours later the uncertain voice of the older of the two servants roused her from her reveries. She turned toward them, noticing in so doing that it was now late and quite dark, and motioned them to speak.

"We found nothing in the woods, mistress, just the tracks left by Sir Ubaldo and his squire, but on the meadow, amid those strange flowers, there was a young, beautiful woman, and she was dead."

"A woman..." the lady of the castle repeated mechanically, then she suddenly flared up with anger. "A witch, you mean!" she screamed. "The witch who charmed my child and then killed him!"

The two men exchanged a glance, far from persuaded that it was really so, but they had long learned not to contradict their mistress, most of all when she looked like that and had that tone of voice, now made shrilly by anger and grief, so they bowed their head.

"Get back there," the lady ordered them. "Behead her and then burn that foul being to ashes!"

"It's too dark to find the way and put together the wood for the pyre, my lady," objected one servant, and the other added: "We'd better wait till tomorrow morning. Dawn is not that far away, anyhow."

The lady hesitated. On the one hand, she wanted to have her orders immediately carried out, but on the other hand she had to admit her servants were right, so in the end she relented and sent them away.

She remained there in the dimly lit courtyard, alone with her dead child, thinking about the past with a still face and staring eyes. She could hear the rhythmic thread of the guards on the battlements, and the banners rustling in the

100

light wind that made the light flames of the candles dance erratically. She felt her face burning and her head was aching, while her eyes—which had not been able to shed a single tear—felt swollen and aching. She closed them for a moment, leaning back against the marble backrest of the bench she was sitting on, and she finally realized she was exhausted, with no strength left. Perhaps she slept.

Yes, she must have fallen asleep—she told herself—because what she was seeing could only be a dream.

The high peak of the Cece seemed to burn with a blue flame, and inside that flame some shining figures appeared slowly. They were all warriors, armed as if heading for battle, but they carried on their bodies and their faces the wounds that had killed them, and their helms were adorned with blue flowers. Form that peak, the highest of the Lagorai, they descended toward the meadow were Dina lay dead, while the light surrounding them grew to become blinding; slowly, that shining army of ghosts flew back toward the peak, carrying with it the young woman's body, covered with blue flowers.

A moment later, the blue light suddenly appeared above the castle, in the courtyard, where it surrounded Alarico's small coffin with a glare stronger than a flame, making it almost invisible, before rising again toward the mountain peaks.

I dreamed, the lady told herself again, rousing herself and staring at the blue cloud, now just a little lighter than the night sky as it dispersed around the rocky heights of the Cece, but a moment later a horrified scream escaped her lips.

Her son's coffin was empty: the dead warriors had come to take him away, to reunite him with Dina on the highest peak of the Lagorai.

Historican notes to Dina from Lagorai

Unlike the previous one, this legend has a clear Medieval setting, and its only relationship with myths from the bronze or iron age can be found in the recurring reference to the water and its power, a reference that I took the liberty of expanding and deepening, adding to the story the ghost of Dina's ancestress, a *gana*, a water spirit.

I also identified (rather arbitrarily) the war parting Dina from her betrothed with the one opposing Arduin of Ivrea to Emperor Henry II and ending with the bloody battle fought at the Locks of Valsugana, which gives a precise timeline to my story, that consequently takes place more or less between the year 1004 and 1007 A.D.

TANNA

Their heart is made of ice and stone,
Love is unknown to the Crodares;
But only when love broke it to pieces
My heart of stone once more became.

In the good season, the Ampezzo Valley shepherds and farmers used to harvest the hay and graze their cattle on that wonderful natural terrace they appropriately called "The Oxen Plain", or else the "Mountain of Sovergna", a mountain pasture that, while almost 6000 feet above the sea level, still looked far from high, almost overwhelmed by the high peaks of the Marmarole surrounding it.

The villages—just a handful of houses huddling together—were strewn across the bottom of the valley, among luxuriant woods through which a rushing creek wended its winding way; the houses set nearest to the mountain pasture where those that climbed the slopes of

Colle Tamber, and the people of the area used to call that small village Luzius, after the name of its legendary founder, a warrior from a faraway country.

Whether they lived there, or in Adrunco, built almost in the shadow of the Ajarnola peak, or in Laurentius, a slightly bigger and more important village because it controlled the Muria Pass, through which it was possible to reach the great road heading south, all those people agreed on one single thing, which they kept repeating to each other, sadly shaking their heads: that place would have been a real Heaven, and their houses much safer, without the Crodares, the magic lords of the Marmarole.

As the elders used to whisper, they were a merciless people, enemy to all human beings, which they loved to torment in a thousand ways: they lived in beautiful mansions carved inside the living rock of the mountains, and brimming with all the things that could make a man's heart happy, and yet they took no pity of the wretched humans deprived even of a roof on their head by the avalanches they unleashed. Their life was so long they could be rightfully called 'immortal', but they would not lift a finger to save the short life of a man fallen into a chasm; they were extremely rich, because all the treasures of the Marmarole belonged to them, and they were the detainers of a millenary knowledge, interwoven with magic, but they had never shared those gifts with men, or had used them to make the human life less hard.

The inhabitants of the villages all agreed on that, and they would offer a great profusion of examples to sustain their opinion: the avalanches, the ice, the abundant snowfalls, the droughts... and yet, they were all wrong.

The Crodares were neither good nor evil, they simply had no feelings. Their hearts were made of stone, and their life—devoted to the safeguard of the mountain—was ruled only by the laws of reason and necessity; insensitive as they were to pain and love, they could not... did not know how to... be moved to pity by human suffering.

It had always been so, and things would have remained the same if one day the crown of the Marmarole, made of ice as shining and beautiful as a diamond, gleaming of a bluish light, had not been placed on Tanna's head.

All prophecies and oracles had pointed to the young woman as to the predestined *Rejna* of the Crodares, but her disconcerted subjects soon realized they had put all their powers, their mountains, their very existence, in the hands of a creature in whose breast pulsed a human heart.

As if she were a real human being, Tanna would often leave her ice palace and the highest crags of the Cimon del Fropa to seek the company of those beings she felt more similar to her, and she could then be found among the shepherds who came to the Oxen Plain in the summertime, or among the farmers harvesting their hay, while she joked and laughed with them, or danced with their women, her face rosy and bright, her blond hair flowing in the wind.

For the Crodares, however, the worst was yet to come: when two snow slides wiped away the houses of the valley village nearer to the slopes, killing most of their occupants, Tanna—her beautiful eyes brimming with tears from the stories she had heard from her friends—forbade the avalanches to fall, and after that the thankful words, the celebration, the gratitude shown to her by humans made her order boulders never to fall down from the mountain peaks, and the creeks to hold their rushing currents in check, so that they would not endanger whoever went fishing on their banks, or the women washing their laundry there—all this without caring about the damages her orders were causing to the mountains.

Deaf to the stern reproaches from her subjects, by now Tanna had taken to living like a human being, happy to talk with shepherds and farmers, and to listen to the things her human friends told her in confidence about their families, children and lovers.

Love. That was something Tanna had never experienced, and she often wondered what her friends felt when they blushed in reaction to a smile from a young man, or cried because of his indifference toward them. Many a man had looked at her with desire in his eyes, because no other woman was as beautiful and desirable as she was, but her heart had never quickened its pulses until Guido, a young stranger, came to Luzius. He was a handsome young man, strong and a head taller than anybody else, with long, dark hair that curled up against his neck and shoulders, and blue eyes so cocky and confident that they did not fear meeting and holding her gaze. He walked with a nonchalant self-assuredness, like a king among his subjects, and he would tell her about things the others ignored, tales of faraway lands and unknown customs, of a body of water so vast you could not see where it ended, which he called 'sea'.

His hard, almost commanding voice, would grow mellow and warm when he was speaking to her, and he was not afraid to meet the challenge of the steepest crags and the most treacherous crevices to bring her a flower or a rock that had caught her fancy.

Soon Tanna got to know firsthand the blushing and the quivering pangs of love, as joy and doubt fought for predominance inside her until one summer evening, when Guido drew her aside, away from the chorus of singing shepherds, and showed her the stars filling the sky, pointing at each of them and calling it with the name it had in his country; then, laughter curving his mouth under his dark mustache, he asked her the names of the surrounding mountains.

While the young woman was pointing at the different peaks, he leaned forward and kissed her lightly on the cheek, where a dimple appeared every time she smiled; feeling her human heart rise all the way up to her throat, Tanna stared at him with her blue eyes, made shinier and wider by the feelings pervading her, and Guido kissed her again, finding her lips with his own.

The Crodares could not believe their ears as they listened to their Queen. Of course, they could not feel either anger nor indignation, so they were only trying to assess what consequences Tanna's decision to wed a human and go to live with him would have for the Marmarole, and for their race.

"For the moment, we'll settle on the Oxen's Plain, where there is a cottage already," Tanna explained to them, her eyes shining with her joyous elation. "Guido will be often away, to take care of his business in that faraway country of his, where one day I might go with him..."

"Will you thus forsake the Marmarole and your people?" one of her Councilors cut in, a Crodar so old his blue eyes were now almost white and blurry.

The young woman knew a moment's hesitation, because her human heart was rebelling as well at the thought of never seeing her mountains again, and of leaving her people behind. She lowered her gaze, thoughtful, but the image of Guido's handsome and brave face immediately came to her mind, together with the memory of his contagious laughter, of his strong arms holding her tight. She raised her head and met the old councilor's eyes.

"Yes, if my man will ask that of me. Isn't it every woman's lot?"

The Crodares met her words with silence, then the old councilor exchanged a glance with the others and spoke again.

"Every woman's, maybe, but not the Crodares' Queen's lot. Tanna, when you donned the blue crown and took upon you the powers belonging to our *Rejna*, you also took upon you the duties this entailed. Are you reneging on them now?"

The young woman stood quiet for a long while, her small hands toying nervously with her long, blond curls. Not only could she feel her heart sink at the thought of leaving her world, but her mind as well—the mind of a true Crodar—rejected the idea of forsaking it, because it tasted to her like a betrayal. On the other hand, however, she wanted to live like men did, not like the Crodares, and she wanted to listen to her heart, not only to her mind.

And then, she would have never been able to give up Guido and their living together, loving each other. What was the dominion of the Marmarole, what the blue crown, compared to that overwhelming feeling filling her heart? Suddenly, she realized she had made her choice, and that it had been quite easy to make. Slowly, she raised her arms and removed the crown from her brow, gently placing it on a shiny block of ice. She lingered a while longer, letting her fingers brush gently against that gleaming circlet, but it was in a resolute tone that she spoke to her subjects.

"Here, I'm not the Crodares' Queen any longer. Together with the blue crown, I renounce to all my prerogatives, all my powers. Choose among yourselves somebody who can carry it in a manner more in tune with your wishes. From now on, I'll live among men, like a mortal woman.

In spite of her assuredness, she felt a sort of inner quiver, a painful yearning; but once her small speech was over, she felt only relief at having made her decision, one she was certain she would never regret. Now she could live among people who acted and thought with their hearts, not only with their minds, she was free to live with Guido and to give him children they would rise teaching them love and compassion.

Laughing, she stood. Her face, usually of the same diaphanous paleness as the snow, was now rosy and lively, her blue eyes shone like the fleurs-de-lis that, in the summertime, dotted the meadows, and not with the pale, bluish glare of the glaciers.

"Good-bye. I won't wish you happiness, because you cannot know what happiness is!" she said to her former subjects who, still and silent, were mentally evaluating her impulsive gesture. "May you at least live peacefully, in the serenity of the mountain."

Then she turned and ran away, out of that icy palace, away from those bare crags, down the narrow path known only to the Crodares that led to the high plain covered with lush green grass, down among the shepherds and their cattle, and in Guido's arms, who was waiting for her there.

"It's all over, my love! I left everything and everybody behind, and now I'm yours, forever," she cried happily, and she did not see that even if her lover was holding her tight in his arms, a shadow had crossed his handsome face.

Inside the great palace of ice, the Crodares were still sitting around the vacant throne. The blue crown shone feebly, but no one had spoken up to claim it, because ambition and thirst for power were emotions, and therefore unknown to them.

Finally, one of them voiced what everybody was thinking.

"No one can take Tanna's place, because she was the chosen one. What will we do, then?"

"We'll wait." The voice of the old Crodar sounded calm and assured.

"It was you who prophesized she was going to be a great queen," another cut in, but with no resentment... he was just remembering, and asking.

"It is true... and she will."

"But her human heart..."

The old man had a slight, frosty smile, devoid of any trace of joy.

"We'll wait for it to get broken. Men are real masters at this. She will get back to us, then, and she will be the greatest queen the Marmarole ever had."

It was almost noon of a late summer day. By now very near to the high peaks of the Marmarole, the lowering sun beat down on them and made the whole valley look like a wide golden lake of light.

Three men were riding along, very slowly because the way had got very steep and any trace of the path they were following had vanished since they had left the Oxen Plain behind them.

"In a short while we'll be forced to continue on foot," muttered the oldest of the three, a stocky man with receding gray hair bound at the nape of his neck.

"My thought as well," agreed the strong young man—actually, almost a boy—riding beside him. "The thing is... what does *he* think?"

And he gestured at the rider ahead of them; his companion rolled his eyes with a grimace.

"Are you really sure, Mastro Gutmondo?" the boy whispered suggestively, laughter his eyes.

"I know what he told me and what I saw with my own eye, Romildo. Our lord lost his head after a local peasant woman!"

"A peasant woman! And him being the Lord of Montanara!"

"Or a shepherdess, if you prefer. In fact, I'd say she's a shepherdess for sure, since they always meet on the high pasture where the local people take their cattle to graze," Gutmondo replied, his lips pressed unhappily together. Of Langobardic descent, he had always been in the service of the Montanara, as Guitcillo's squire at first and then as his son's master at arms, that same Guido who was now the head of that noble family.

"Is she beautiful, at least?" Romildo wanted to know, a leering little smile curving his lips, but before the other could answer him the third rider stopped his horse and at the same time jumped from the saddle with an unusual agility for a man his size. He was very tall and, while slender, he was wide in the shoulders and chest, with powerful muscles that fully lived up to the nickname of 'Guidone' his followers had given him.

"You two will wait for me here," he ordered sharply, as he threw his reins to Romildo who had dismounted as well in answer to his commanding gesture; before Gutmondo could voice his protests against such a rash behavior, he disappeared behind the rocks in two long strides.

Guido was burning with his desire to hold Tanna in his arms again, that mysterious young woman who had charmed him. He knew nothing about her, just her strange unusual name. Peasant woman, shepherdess... what did it matter? He wanted her with all his heart, won over by the mysterious, alluring aura surrounding her and by her strange beauty, so different not only from that of the other local women, but also of the ladies of his court. They had been living together for almost two years now, and from time to time he would leave his castle with one pretext or the other, to spend a few days with her in their small house clinging to the slopes of the Ciareido, above the Oxen Plain. He knew, however, that it all had to end, because every time he journeyed there he jeopardized his life and his future, that very same future that was opening ahead of him so full of promises and glory.

While formulating those thoughts, he had reached the house, and he stood for a moment by the threshold, panting a little from the exertion and peering through the open doorway.

Tanna was sitting by the fireplace, her back to him, her long golden braids reaching to her waist and exposing her white neck, bent over the wool-winder. She was singing softly to herself, her song matching the movement of her shoulders and foot, and...

Guido blinked his eyes, perplexed. Once again, for a fleeting moment, he had thought a bluish glow crowned his lover's pale brow and her golden hair, and once again the same obscure mixture of awe and fear had cast such a chill on him that he could not bring himself to touch that weird glow.

In the meanwhile, Tanna stood up, graceful and lithe as usual, and she got closer to the fireplace to stoke the fire, lifting the lid of the big copper pot of hot water hanging on a chain over the flames, and as he watched her act so comfortably normally, Guido forgot his disturbing feeling. All he could feel now was the enchantment wrought in his heart by the harmony in the young woman's movements, the delicate beauty of her lean body, and of a face that could be sweet and proud at the same time. As Guido observed the way she moved around the room, his regret at having to leave her was more bitter than ever, but he had spent far too much time in that poor cottage, allowing that beautiful woman to seduce him! He had to find his old self again, and become once more Guido da Montanara, Lord of Fregona, the man who had saved Conrad I of Franconia's life, thus earning his rich castle and the Emperor's protection. He had to get back to what he knew was his real life, made of wars and conquests, of ambition and honors.

In a short while the first snow would fall, and getting back to his lands was going to be difficult then; he had to leave before the season changed and forsake Tanna.

He felt his throat constricting painfully at that thought, and on impulse he crossed the threshold with his arms extended, calling his woman. "Tanna!"

But as he held her in his arms, hiding his face in the pale gold of her hair, kissing those sweet lips, reveling in the nearness of that perfect, yielding body, he knew that was— had to be—their last time together, that in the morning he was going to leave her never to see her again, to get back to his life as a *condottiero* and a lord, in order to carry on his ambitious plans. He owed that to his house and his noble forefathers, and to himself as well: he had loved Tanna— and forgotten everything else for her sake—for two long and wonderful seasons. Now, it had to come to an end!

"My love," he said, propping himself up on an elbow, "tomorrow morning I have to go to the village. Winter is coming, and I have to buy many things and conduct some business as well."

The young woman nodded as she lovingly straightened the blankets, and offered a smile devoid of any suspicion. It was not the first time Guido left her to go and buy some supplies, or to take care of his mysterious business that would keep him away from her for long periods, but he had always come back with a present for her, glad to see her again and starving for her caresses and her smiles.

"My absence might be longer than usual, this time," he added nonchalantly, as he played with her long, curly golden hair. "There are some important matters I have to take care of..."

"I will wait for you," Tanna smiled trustingly, her head on his chest. "I'll always wait for you."

And she did.

She waited for him as fall became winter, and as winter receded with the oncoming of spring, and while summer replaced spring; she waited for him, and the wait was less painful than she had feared because she was not alone anymore: with the oncoming of spring, together with the flowers, a new life had blossomed and issued from her, and she was now waiting for her man holding their child in her arms. The marvel of that new life helper her live through the months and years in which her patient wait slowly burned down to tired resignation, which became disillusion and pain, even if for the sake of her son she kept pretending she was certain his father would come back.

"No, you cannot climb up to the peak of the Croda Bianca," she would warn him, her crystal clear voice now a little veiled. "Not by yourself, at least. I'm sure however that your father will take you there, once he gets back."

And for him she brought back to life the tales her lost lover used to tell her, stories of turreted castles, courtesans wearing luxurious garments, banquets and tournaments... and, finally, the sea, that huge expanse of water she had never seen, but that was near the place where Guido lived.

Mother and son would spend their evenings like that, sitting in front of the big fireplace that gave light and warmth to their small cottage and staring into its flames. Wide eyed and fascinated, the child tried to imagine all the wonderful things her mother told him about, but all Tanna could see in those flames was always and only the face of the man who had forsaken her, and then she would feel the painful throbbing of her human heart that had caused her to renege her people and renounce her throne. And yet, she did not regret it, not yet, because she thought that to feel pain was still better than having no feelings at all, and also because she had her son—whom she had called Salvanel—with her.

Actually, she would have liked to name him after his father, or one of his forefathers, but she had then realized how little she knew about her man: little more than his name, even if she had guessed that he was an rich and noble warrior among his people, and that his country was very far from those mountains among which she had met him and fallen in love with him.

"Your father is an important man," she told the boy, who—as he grew up—was growing more and more impatient at the simple, humble life they led. "And he lives beyond the mountains. It's not easy for him to get back here, but sooner or later..."

She was trying to lull him, and herself as well, with those false hopes, but Salvanel was determined as he was impatient, and kept pressing her with his questions, day after day, dreaming of finding in that unknown father a way to change his life, to leave the plateau where he had grown up and see other lands, other peoples.

To appease him, Tanna tried to remember every word, every gesture of her lover, she even showed him the presents Guido had given her and which she jealously treasured... even if, of late, she had felt tempted to sell some of them because she had used up almost all the things she had taken with her in leaving the Crodares, and also the money Guido had left her.

"They are beautiful!" Salvanel exclaimed with wonder, gently picking up a silver necklace set with garnets, while he stared at the other jewels, the small sculptures, the combs encrusted with precious rock crystals. He then turned toward his mother, looking at her with a new look of respect in his eyes.

"You were right, mother. My father is a rich and powerful man, and he must have loved you very much..."

He fell silent, thinking. More than ever he wished to be with that unknown father, sharing glory and dangers with him, and he lowered his eyes again on the small, carved chest containing those little treasures, rummaging inside it. He wasn't admiring the exquisite workmanship of the jewels, nor the mixed glow of gold and precious stones; no, he was looking for a hint, a sign telling him who his father was and where he could find him. He searched in vain, though, and in the end he closed the chest, disappointed.

"Nothing," he murmured, his young face clouding over, then he ran his fingers on the lid and he suddenly started, looking down at it.

"Mother, this chest belonged to him as well?" he asked, a new tension in his voice.

Tanna nodded, perplexed.

"It belonged to him, yes. He forgot it here when he left, and I kept it, thinking that I was going to give it back to him when... when..."

Her voice broke, and she lowered her beautiful blue eyes, but Salvanel did not even notice her inner turmoil.

"Then I know who he is, and how to find him! Look, mother, look here! This is his coat of arms, and it will tell me my father's name! I'll find him at last, and I will be able to talk to him, to tell..." Choked with emotion, he broke off and hugged his mother, laughing.

Tanna hugged him back and forced herself to smile as well, even if she could feel a fist of ice squeezing her heart. That lively voce, that laughter, those shining, eager eyes... never the two men of her life had been more alike! And she knew that her son was soon going to leave her as well.

He left a month later, as summer ended and the first autumn fog rose to veil the rugged rocks of the Cimon del Fropa. He had sold a few jewels to buy the necessary supplies for his journey, for he knew he had a very long road ahead of him; he was certain of his success, however, because he had showed the coat of arms around, made questions, and he finally had his answers.

Now his unknown father had a name and a clear social standing: Guidone da Montanara, Lord of Fregona, feudatory of the patriarch of Aquileja, connected with the Emperor of Franconia.

He cheerfully set off, whistling. Behind him, unnoticed, Tanna waved once more a long scarf in farewell and waited for his son to disappear along the road to the valley bottom, then she retreated inside her small cottage and sat beside the cold fireplace.

She was really alone now... alone with her memories, where the bitterness blended with the sweetness, suffocating it. Distractedly, she moved the cold ashes around with a poker and she marveled at feeling only tired bitterness in her human heart, a dull, resigned disillusionment.

Salvanel's journey was long, much longer than he had anticipated. He left behind the mountains among which he had been born, the great plateau where he had lived up to then and the villages dotting the valley bottom, following at first the rushing waters of the Boite, and then other rivers and unknown roads, trusting the directions he was getting along the way.

He saw the ruins of Miljera, the city founded by Zan de Rame and Donna Dindia, but he stopped only at the castle of Botestagno, where he got more information about the da Montanaras.

"He's grown in arrogance, that Guidone, since the fief of Camino has been promised to him!"

"He's set his eyes on this castle a well."

"He goes by the name of Count of Camino, now, but his Collalto cousins will soon drag him down from his high horse!"

This was how Salvanel learned that there was a blood feud going on between his father and the powerful Lords da Collalto, to whom he was related, and that his father lived in the castle of Fregona, on the foothills of a low mountain, the Cansiglio.

He had no idea what use he could make of the information he had got, but he committed it to memory, just as he did with the directions to get to Fregona. He spent the night at Botestagno, bought a horse and set off again, now bitterly conscious that his journey was going to be far longer than he had imagined, and that his mother would be up there alone, to face the oncoming winter by herself.

Not even the thought of his mother could take his mind off his obsession, to find his father, to be acknowledged by him, and to learn why he had abandoned him. While holding in his hands the garnet necklace and the small chest with the da Montanara coat of arms, which he had brought with him to prove his identity, he suddenly realized that his eager hope was slowly becoming something else: doubt, suspicion, maybe even resentment.

He rejected those thoughts and spurred his horse.

Winter was well underway when he finally got to Fregona, and he made it there only because he managed to join a caravan of Venetian merchants who were taking back to their city a load of pelts and were trading and bartering here and there along the road. He went with them till Cansiglio, then he reached the castle of the da Montanara following the directions the merchants had given him.

By now, nothing was left in him of the naïve and inexperienced boy who had left the Marmarole with the certainty he was going to find his father in just a few days. He had traveled for months, seen villages, hamlets, and castles, things he had never even imagined could exist, and yet the sight of the castle of Fregona impressed him deeply, perhaps not so much because of the majestic grandeur of the building , as because he knew his father to be its Lord.

Upon seeing the high walls, the wide moat and the armed sentries manning the gates, Salvanel realized that with such strong defenses getting inside the castle was not going to be easy. For a while he wandered about the walls, with the only result of making the guards suspicious;

disappointed, he finally headed for a nearby cluster of houses.

Even before he dismounted, he noticed an unusual activity. Many men and a few women, all dressed up in clothes they certainly didn't wear for work, were gathering in the open space amid the houses. Many carried baskets or bundles, while other held a parchment in their hands and had a doubtful expression on their face; all of them, however, were staring at the road he had just come from, the one which led to the castle, and a small group was already heading that way.

Mingling with the others, Salvanel listened to them, even if with some difficulty because the language they spoke was a little different from his own, and after a while he dared asking a few questions.

"But... where are you from?" wondered a fat woman, who had a basket full of vegetables in one hand and held a child with the other. "Today our lord, the Count, will see those who want to appeal to his justice, and his tenant farmers as well, who will have to bring him their produces," she huffed, as she pointed with her chin to her basket while twisting her mouth in a meaningful grimace before she hurried toward the road.

"I can tell from your clothing and the way you speak that you are a stranger," another villager cut in, a lanky man who had come closer, his curiosity aroused. "Are you going to ask the Count to take you in his service? If so, you'd better talk to the head servant and..."

Salvanel shook his head. "No, I'm not, but thank you all the same for telling me," he answered; then, as a sudden afterthought, he added, "But I have to appeal to the Count's justice, so I'll come with you, if you don't mind."

Nobody raised any objections; ten minutes later ten men-at-arms carrying the da Montanara coat of arms on their tabards chest came to escort the small group to the castle.

Already impressed by the majesty of the castle seen from the outside, the young man was struck speechless by the sight of the courtyards, the broad staircase, and the wide halls. Used as he was to his humble cabin and the poor houses surrounding it, he stared unbelievingly at the thick walls, the wide rooms, the rugs covering the stone floors, the richly inlaid furniture. And then there were the people! Courtesans, servants, vassals, men-at-arms! He had never seen so many men and women all in the same place, and all dressed much more richly than the people in his village, even on the holy days. There were people coming and going everywhere, greeting each other with short nods or deep bows, shouting orders and exchanging pleasantries. Some instruments could be heard playing softy somewhere, and a couple of times a high voice sung with the music, while the scent and warmth of the lit torches could be felt everywhere.

Staring around, dazed by all those lights, those noises, that hustle and bustle, for a moment Salvanel felt very proud at the thought that his father was all that people's Lord, the owner of that wonderful place; in the wake of that feeling, however, as he stared at the simple tunic of undyed wool his mother had woven and sewn for him, at his large, shapeless trousers and rough shoes, he blushed, ill at ease.

In the meanwhile, the men-at-arms escorting them had reached a huge double door of thick oak wood, strengthened with shining copper studs; it opened before them and the peasants were herded into a great hall where a heavy tapestry with the great black and silver shield of the da Montanara hung from the back wall; in front of it, two high seats of carved wood were placed on a high platform, with two other seats set at a lower level. All around there were men-at-arms and a great number of richly dressed men and women.

Before the young man even had the time to ask to the nearest peasant what was going on, there was a loud blare of trumpets, and while the men removed their hats and the women curtsied, a couple came into the room, preceded by heralds, some men-at-arms and four pages, and followed by two young men and, a step away, by more courtesans. The couple came forward slowly, majestically, nodding now and then to this or that courtesan; upon reaching the high seats, the two took place on them, while the young men sat on the lower seats and the rest of their train stood around them.

Judging from the few gray hairs spread through his long dark hair, the man had to be in his early forties; he was tall and strong, but a little ticker in the body than he used to be; his heart hammering in his heart, Salvanel recognized his own features in the Count's light-colored eyes, the strong line of his jaw, his high cheekbones, even if his face looked harder, more determined and lined with age. Ignoring the man-at-arms who was motioning for him to stop, he stepped forward, but then he looked at the lady and the two young men and he stopped, as a suspicion grew and took roots inside him.

A few years younger than the Count, that lady had the da Montanara coat-of-arms embroidered on her bodice and cloak, and that same coat-of-arms was reproduced on the small tiara shining on her dark hair, gathered in two thick braids circling her head. Her proud behavior matched quite well her rich clothing and her pretty but stern face, whose stronger trait was her Roman nose, and inexorably implied that she was not a vassal to the lord of the castle, but his peer.

His sister, she could be his sister, Salvanel frantically said to himself; but as he looked at the two young men sitting at each side of the couple, at the way the features of the Lady and those of the Count blended on their faces, he could not believe that himself.

In the meanwhile, a courtesan whose garments were even richer than the others' stepped forward and as his Lord gave him permission with a nod, he announced that His Grace the Count da Montanara would be granting an audience.

While petitions alternated with homages and the Lord of the castle handed out boons and punishments, Salvanel kept staring at the couple, until he could not hold himself in check anymore and, ignoring both the protests from the other petitioners and the guards' orders, he shouldered the others aside and got at the feet of the two thrones.

Immediately two men-at- arms grabbed him by the shoulders and dragged him back so fiercely that the small chest he was carrying flew from his hands and fell on the floor. It opened on the impact and the silver necklace fell out of it, shining faintly in the torchlight.

Murmurs of surprise and choked exclamations sounded throughout the room, and even the Lady lost her solemn stillness and leaned forward to better look at those two objects, while the Count frowned as he looked questioningly at the guards holding Salvanel.

"He doesn't carry any weapons, my Lord," one of them assured him. Guido then signaled that they could release Salvanel, before nodding to a page, who picked up both the chest and the necklace and handed them to him with a deep bow.

For a long while the nobleman stared at those two objects, schooling his face so that it showed no emotions, even if he had recognized them both and was feeling unusually ill-at-ease, then he finally made a decision. "If it was a present you wanted to bring me, young man, you definitely chose quite a strange way to do it," he began, irony heavy in his voice. "The more so since the coat-of-arms on this chest shows it belongs to me."

He broke off, aware he was blushing, and looked at Salvanel. That hair, those eyes! He swallowed, and as he did so Salvanel moved a step forward and hesitantly bent one knee on the floor. The natural elegance, the nimbleness of his movements, and those long, tapered hands! Guidone nervously swallowed again, regretting he had given the boy the opportunity to talk to him.

"And they used to belong to you, my Lord," that cheeky youngster was saying, holding his gaze as if to challenge him, "but almost twenty years ago you gave them as a gift to my mother, together with many other beautiful and precious things. You remember it, don't you? And do you now understand who I am and why I am here?"

Guidone didn't look at him, but glanced again at the chest as he lifted the fragile necklace with two fingers. He could feel all the courtesans staring at him; even worse, he could perceive the bewilderment and the doubts on his sons' faces, and his wife, whose family he relied upon to fight the Collalto, was staring at him with suspicion and outrage in her eyes.

He opened his fingers, letting the jewel to fall back inside the chest, and a small wry smile surfaced on his previously inscrutable face.

"Nice trinkets!" he exclaimed loudly, as if he had not heard the young man last words, then he leaned informally toward Salvanel, who was looking at him with uncertainty, and added, "Tell me the truth, where did you steal them?"

The young man drew back with a start as if he had been slapped, and while chuckles and murmurs rose all around the room, Guidone stole a glance at his wife and sons, and went on: "Yes, because I don't know how else a beggar like you could have got hold of them! You'd better stop pretending and tell the truth. Tell it for your own sake!"

The he leaned back on his seat, satisfied that his sons were smiling and his wife had reverted to her previous proud and detached behavior.

Once over his initial bewilderment, however, Salvanel was overwhelmed by rage, in which disbelief and disillusionment mingled with outrage, and furiously threw himself at the Count, his fists raised to strike. He never even managed to touch him because the squires standing at the feet of the throne promptly grabbed him and pulled him back, throwing him on the ground and holding him there at sword point.

"My Lord?" the oldest among them asked Guidone.

The Count had a moment's hesitation. One gesture, one word, and that brainless young man would stop being a problem, forever. And yet, he could not bring himself to say that word; instead, he merely shook his strong shoulders.

"He must be mad. In any case, throw him out of my castle and teach him a lesson, so that he won't dare getting back here."

He them motioned for a page to bring him some wine, clearly showing he considered the matter closed, while his wife and sons openly smiled and all the courtesans exchanged comments as they looked at Salvanel with pity or mockery in their eyes.

Those looks, those chuckles, and his father's disdainful refusal to acknowledge him hurt the young man more than the rough handling and the blows the men-at-arms rained on him as they dragged him out of the hall, through the wide rooms and the long corridors he had gone through just a short while before with his heart full of hope, finally pushing him across the drawbridge to throw him in the mud by the moat.

"There!" sneered the group leader, kicking him a couple more times. "That's the place you belong to, in the mud! Never dare setting foot in Fregona again, beggar, or bother my lord with your filthy lies!"

He pushed Salvanel's face in the mud with his foot, as if to hammer down his warning, then he growled an order to his men and led them back inside the castle. The drawbridge was immediately raised behind them, and the great gates locked.

Salvanel remained on the ground, aching all over from the blows, with his clothing dirty and torn, and his heart weighing like a stone in his chest, a lump in his throat from his pain, bitterness and shame. He pushed himself up on his elbows, then he slowly got up on his feet, and as he tried to clean himself from the mud and the blood, he suddenly realized that he did not have the chest or the necklace anymore; more important still, he had left his horse in the courtyard, so it was lost too, together with the bag tied to the saddle and containing all his things.

His hopes and dreams were gone, and with them also part of his credulous naivety; the memory of the humiliation he had suffered, of the rough way his father had rejected him brought tears to his eyes, tears of anger and helplessness. The only thing he wanted now was to take his revenge on that man who had disowned and humiliated him, but he also realized there was nothing he could do against him. Nothing at all!

As he indulged in those thoughts, a name came to his mind, as sudden as lightning: Collalto. Leaning with his back against a tree, he made an effort to remember. He had heard that name more than once, while seeking information about the da Montanara. The Collalto were a noble and powerful family, with strong blood ties with his father, but also at war with him. He straightened up and stared at the castle. He did not care why the Collalto had come to hate him, or how it had happened, just as he did not care who had wronged whom. All he wanted was revenge for what had been done to him.

"Collalto," he whispered, nodding to himself.

Their castle wasn't far away, or at least it was not that far for somebody who had already traveled from the Marmarole to the Pian del Cansiglio. For a moment, the memory of his mountains, of the simple life he had led there, and of his sweet mother, Tanna, overwhelmed him, but he pushed it away, determined to get his revenge. He was going to join the Collalto, it did not matter if as a servant, a man-at-arm or even a groom; all that mattered was that the moment would come in which he was going to face again—weapon in hand—the man who had thrown him out.

I will succeed, he wowed to himself, raising his fist against those battlements upon which the da Montanara banner fluttered in the wind, *should it take all my life, I'll succeed*! Limping, he set out for Collalto.

On the still frozen ridges of the Marlarole, in the shadow of the Cimon del Fropa, which hid in its bowels the great ice palace where she had once lived, Tanna was still waiting, resigned and tired, knowing by now how much a heart could hurt that wasn't made of stone, a human heart wounded and forgotten by other human beings.

Two years later, the contention between the da Montanara and the Collalto became open war, and the two families faced each other on the battlefield.

Guidone himself was at the head of his men, with his sons Alberto and Guecello by his side, both anxious of proving their prowess, but with the Collalto rode also Guidone's firstborn son, Salvanel, who—through months of humiliations, wiles, pleading and efforts—had managed to enroll in the army of his father's enemies and to prove himself to the point of becoming their standard bearer.

Proudly carrying the Collalto banner, he was now anxiously waiting for the bugle call that would give the signal to attack. He had already located Guidone, tall and strong on his roan stallion, and was ready to throw himself at him, to defeat him and drag him down into the mud as had had his guards do with him.

The thought of the vengeance he had desired and anticipated for so long was not the only reason his heart was hammering so wildly in his chest, however. While living at the Collaltos' castle, he had met Marcora, his lord's youngest daughter, and their eyes had spoken to each other even before the young man plucked up courage enough to really speak to her; simple words were followed by sighs and then by a kiss, just one, but enough to set fire to Salvanel's heart. Were he to really defeat Guidone and maybe kill or capture him, then perhaps the gulf between him and the maiden he loved would become less wide and he would be allowed some hope. Perhaps... the drum roll, the trumpet calls and orders shouted on both sides of the battlefield shook him out of his daydreaming, and he spurred his horse, together with his comrades.

And the battle was engaged.

The sun was just rising to the east when the two armies met on the battlefield, and a red summer moon was already high in the sky when two squads carrying respectively the da Montanara and the Collalto banner started combing the battlefield to collect the wounded and the dead.

The fight had been savage, but it had not lasted long and had pretty much ended in a draw, so much so that now the two counts were meeting in a huge tent erected near the battlefield, to discuss the terms for a truce, if not peace.

Rambaldo of Collalto was unscathed, while Guidone da Montanara had his head bandaged and a broken arm. During the fight, the Collalto standard bearer had fought his way through the men of his guard and engaged him, wrenching his sword away from him and turning it against him. Guidone barely managed to deflect the blow, so that the blade just nicked his forehead before hitting his arm with such strength that it broke the chainmail and the arm under it. Before giving in to the pain, Guidone managed to spur his horse forward and against his attacker's, throwing him to the ground where he got trampled by the knights rushing to their lord's aid, and in so doing he recognized his opponent as the son he had reneged.

As he sat face to face with his cousin and enemy, trying to enforce his point of view and fighting the pain from his wounds, Guidone also had to fight against an odd feeling of weariness and chagrin totally new to him.

He did not even know if Tanna' son was still alive, and he certainly could not ask after him. He was the Count da Montanara, and he could not forget himself to the point of inquiring after the boy, with the risk of confirming, in so doing, his claim of kinship, the more so since the surreptitious glances and the whispers the Collalto men were exchanging behind his back seemed to imply that they already knew about it,

Rambaldo, however, did not know, and things had to stay that way.

With a huge effort, Guidone squared his strong shoulders and forced himself to carry on the negotiation.

"A marriage, you say. I would not be averse to it, my cousin and lord, since it would cement our newfound alliance, but I'll have to discuss the matter with my lady wife..."

"Of course." Rambaldo's knowing smile was barely hidden by his long mustache, and Guidone silently gritted his teeth.

The terms they were agreeing upon were more than acceptable, and the proposed marriage between Marcora and either Guecello or Alberto was a honorable solution, that somehow recognized his being equal to Rambaldo, who still saw himself as the head of the family.

Pleased with how things were shaping up, the two men went on with the negotiation.

Barely alive, Salvanel had been taken to the castle and in the great hall by the armory, where all the wounded were being gathered. Two barber surgeons and a few men acting as their assistants were working among the makeshift pallets, taking it easy because the fight had been brief and only a few among the wounded were in critical condition or required particular attention. In fact, within a few hours the hall almost emptied and only four soldiers were left on the makeshift beds of straw and rags. The torches shed an eerie, reddish glow on the wounded's bodies, their grimaces of pain, the bloodied bandages and the silhouettes of the assistant and of Master Graziadeo, the only surgeon still there after most of the wounded had been taken care of and had left the room.

"This one won't last the night," the surgeon commented to the groom who was helping him, nodding toward a middle-aged man with his head and torso al bandaged up and a death rattle already escaping his mouth. Eying the wounded with pity, the groom crossed himself while the surgeon examined the next man's leg, and went on: "And this leg will have to come off, if it doesn't get better by tomorrow."

His assistant crossed himself again—he did not have that much confidence in the barber surgeon's science—

then he glanced at the third man, who was already trying to sit up, to the extent allowed to him by his broken ribs.

"You will be able to get back home in a couple of days," Master Graziadeo told him, "provided that you keep your chest tightly bandaged as long as I tell you to. As for this one..." He shook his head, uncertain, as he looked at the last wounded man. "His broken arm and assortment of bruises aren't anything to worry about, but since he was trampled by horses I'm afraid there might be some internal damage. He should be looked after assiduously..."

"And he will," a low and musical female voice cut in. A dark veil hiding her luxurious dress and her thick chestnut brown hair, Marcora stepped into the hall, holding her dress train on her arm to keep it away from the blood and mud dirtying the floor. "Have this man taken to the tower rooms. Now!"

"Damsel!" Both the surgeon and the groom stared dumbfoundedly at their lord's daughter, who was bending on the wounded. "Certainly the Count your father..."

"My father and my brothers have left to accompany Count Guidone da Montanara to Fregona, where the peace treaty will be signed. Right now. I'm giving orders in this castle, and the first one is to take immediately this wounded man to the tower rooms usually reserved for guests."

The two men exchanged another uncertain glance, while Marcora's small foot impatiently tapped on the floor, then the groom shook his shoulders and with an effort picked up Salvanel and headed for the door, calling to his fellow assistants for help; pressed by the young lady of the manor, the surgeon hurried after them.

Put up in the sunny and comfortable rooms in the tower, carefully looked after by the surgeon and served by a pair of handmaids, Salvanel quickly got better.

"It was your luck that I had with me my *Potio Mirabilis!*" the surgeon explained, as he placed on the table at the wounded man's side a glass full of a thick, smelly liquid. "It works wonders with internal damages. Real wonders!"

As he turned his nose up at the horrid taste of that 'wonderful' cure, Salvanel smiled to himself, thinking that the real miracle was due to his strong mountaineer's constitution, the good treatment he had got, and most of all to Marcora's loving presence by his side.

During those days, in which they had been able to see each other and to talk freely, the feelings already budding between them had grown into a passionate love. Salvanel told her about the faraway place where he was born, the ice and the snow that in winter made it almost impossible to reach his house, unless one knew the secret paths through the high, forbidding mountains enclosing the plateau like a king's crown, and finally of his mother, sweet Tanna, who was patiently waiting for her son to come back, just as she had waited for her lover to come back. And he told her the name of his father, the man who had reneged him, allowing her to see the depths of his pain and bitterness.

As Marcora avidly listened to his words, the compassion they aroused in her heart fueled her love for Salvanel, and that overwhelming feeling made her decide that she would never marry anybody but that young man who had been the first to make her feel like a woman... a loved woman.

She told him that much, simply, a light blush on her round cheeks, as she looked at him with shining eyes from under her long, chestnut brown eyelashes, shy and tempting at the same time. Together, they swore undying love and faithfulness to each other, while the moonlight flowing through the open window threw a pale light on Salvanel's blond curls and Marcora's long, dark braids, and on their joined hands.

The next morning, at the crack of dawn, a courier brought a message in which Count Rambaldo announced his daughter's engagement with Alberto, Guidone's second-born son, and ordered his daughter to get ready to welcome her husband, who was going to come back to the castle with him in a few days. Silent, Marcora and Salvanel were now sitting one in front of the other in the room where their love had grown and they had exchanged their pledge, the message that was going to part them forever lying there between them.

The young man was wringing his hands as he fought back tears of anger and pain, but there weren't any tears in his beloved Marcora's eyes, nor there was any tremor in her voice as she suggested in a low but determined tone, "Let's run away." As she spoke, she pointed at a bundle she had taken with her, containing the few valuables she had been able to put together. "Let's go to your mother's, on the mountains. We will be safe there."

At first Salvanel merely stared at her, bewildered, then he nodded. Where else could they go? He did not have any help, any friend in the area, and the people Marcora knew were certainly going to side with her father and with Guidone. For a moment, he could feel again in his throat a bitter taste of bile at the thought of the man who had fathered him only to throw him away like a discarded toy, but then he forced himself to forget him: his mother, his beloved Marmarole and Marcora by his side, forever. He did not want to think of anything else. He did not need anything else.

He nodded again, more firmly this time.

"You're right. Let's run away before your father gets back."

The snow fell thickly, heaping up on the already whitened peaks of the Marmarole, among which the Cimon del Fropa shone with the thick layer of ice shrouding its jagged peaks and sparkling treacherously on the bottom of its deep gorges. Curled up and wrapped in the cloak made with the pelt of the first wolf killed by Salvanel, Tanna was looking at the white, thick snowflakes whirling around the high peak and on the plateau, and down at the valley floor, as she pondered dubiously on the orders she had given more than twenty years previously, when the blue crown was still shining on her head. Shepherds and farmers had certainly benefited from them, since they did not have to fear avalanches any more, but the paths that used to connect the valley to the plateau, and the plateau to the mountain itself were now buried under many years' worth of frozen snow and were difficult to find and follow, most of all during the winter, and especially during a storm like the one raging outside.

And besides that... she closed her eyes and sighed. Besides that, the mountain itself was suffering. She was not the Crodares' queen anymore, her heart was human, and yet she could still hear the voice, the pain of her Marmarole, crushed under that incredibly huge mass of ice.

She sighed again, and in that moment she thought she could hear a human voice amid the whistling and howling of the wind. She listened more carefully... nothing. She had been mistaken: the wind howling and the ice creaking from its years long forced immobility must have mislead her.

She got up, pulling her cloak tighter around her shoulders, and reached to stoke the fire, but she froze with a log in her hands, her heart jumping to her throat. No, she had not been mistaken! She ran to the door, threw it wide open, oblivious to the snow whirling around her, and ran outside, her cloak blowing in the wind that also blew her pale hair on and around her face.

"Mother! Mother!" a voice was crying from the gorge. A voice she knew quite well and had wished to hear again for many a month: Salvanel's!

Sinking in the snow at every step, sliding on the ice underneath it and fighting to regain her balance, Tanna finally reached the gorge edge and searched its depths with her eyes, in vain, because the dark night was made darker still by the layer of clouds hiding the sky, and by the thick curtains of snow still whirling around; in the meanwhile, her son's voice kept calling her urgently, filled with fear.

"Please, mother, help us! They are right at our heels, and will reach and kill us! The path, show me the path to get to you, or all will be lost!"

By now, Tanna's heart was hammering so strongly it seemed it would erupt from her breast, while she tried to discern through the darkness and the ice that road she used to travel so often in the past, but on which she had not set foot for more than one year, the path that would save her son, but to no avail: all she could see was snow and ice blanketed rock, where all traces had been hidden by that white layer. That very same darkness that prevented her from seeing the path would also hide her son to his enemies' eyes, however. She had a little time left, and she knew how to use it.

"Wait, Salvanel, my son! I cannot find the path, but I can still help you. All I need are a few minutes, I think... hope."

That last word died on her lips, turning into a whisper full of uncertainty, then Tanna turned away from the gorge and started to run desperately in the thick snow, fighting against the gale, toward the Cimon del Fropa, in whose icy bowels the Crodares had their dwellings. She did not ask who the men were who wanted to kill Salvanel, nor why; she did not even ask who the other fugitive was she had seen by his side. She did not ask anything because there was just one thing that mattered to her: her son was in danger, and she had to save him.

I'm their queen, or at least I was! she told herself as she trudged on, sinking in the snow and sliding on the ice, fighting to hold her cloak closed around her with her numb fingers. *They will listen to me, they have to!*

When she got to the secret gates of the Marmarole people, however, she knocked, shouted and cried in vain. She warned about the dangerous conditions of the mountains, overloaded with ice, and then begged, shouting her love and her pain, but to no avail: there was no answer and the gates remained locked and hidden under the shining layer of ice covering the whole ledge.

Heartbroken, Tanna went back the way she had come—with her heart in a turmoil of hope and fear—just a short while ago, feeling a painful vise constricting her chest, full of tears she was not able to shed anymore. When she reached the gorge edge again, she called her son and—her voice broken with unshed tears—explained to him she had not found the hoped for help.

"But you mustn't worry, my son! With the first light of the day I'll be able to get my bearings, I'll find the path and I'll come to get you. I'm sure the barest light will be enough, because I know the place so well. Your enemies are foreigners to these lands, aren't they? So they will need a stronger light to see by."

Tired, Salvanel's voice answered her, confirming that the people chasing him came from far away. Then, as the night hours swiftly went by, he told her mother all that had happened to him, his voice getting hoarse while he told her about his father, and then filling with emotion when he spoke of Marcora, who had left everything behind for his sake and was now there by his side, shivering and worn out, but not voicing a single word of regret.

Appalled, Tanna cried silent tears while she tried to find some words of comfort and hope, and in the meanwhile the darkness turned to gray, the snow stopped and a pale sun slowly rose above the mountain peaks.

That faint glimmer of light allowed Tanna to look around in search for any trace, any sign showing the only safe path that could bring her son to her... a path no stranger could easily find and that could be blocked without difficulty. The coat of ice and the recent snowfalls had altered the whole appearance of the area, but she kept scanning it with her eyes while heartening the two fugitives with words full of hope, even if she could feel that very same hope slowly die in her heart. The daylight was already much stronger when she finally recognized a huge boulder that Guido had placed at the beginning of the path, which allowed her to locate the whole path.

"Here it is!" she called joyously, as she started walking along the path. "You should find a cluster of three firs by your position. The path begins to their left. I'm coming toward you, but in the meanwhile you'd better start moving, following my directions."

Looking anxiously around, she saw two figures, so bent forward they almost seemed to be crouching, who were climbing up the steep path, helping each other, and she smiled tenderly while she climbed down as swiftly as she could.

They were very near, only two bends of the path between them, when Tanna saw a group of armed men standing by the beginning of the path.

"They are here!" she cried, as she felt her blood run cold. "Hurry! They won't find the way, and in any case we can block it. "Come on, make haste! It's beginning to snow again... they won't get you!"

In fact, the leader of the group stopped, swearing as he stared at the big flakes falling down, then he raised a hand to make his men stop as well.

Tanna's shout of joy turned into a horrified cry when she saw the longbows the soldiers were carrying, that could hit a target even at a great distance, and realized they were nocking arrows.

"Hurry!" she cried again, leaning toward the fugitives. "They are aiming at you... oh, hurry, hurry! Salvanel, my son!"

Right then Marcora lost her footing, and the young man stopped to help her, then he pushed her toward his mother, whose face he could now glimpse in between gusts of snow-laden wind.

"Help her, mother, help her! Ah, mother!"

As Tanna caught hold of the young chatelaine and dragged her up to safety, pushing her behind a rock that would shield them both, a cloud of arrows sliced through the air from below.

Salvanel, who was still climbing to safety, barely had the time to see the two women he loved get behind shelter when two arrows pierced his arm and leg. He fought for balance, trying to take hold of a branch or a rock with his good hand, but he found only slippery ice and snow already melting under his feet while turning red with his blood.

He plummeted down under the eyes of Tanna, who was running toward him, and of Marcora, who had fallen down to her knees.

The gorge, so deep it seemed to have no bottom, swallowed up his body.

Long months went by, in which the two heartbroken women lived together in that same cabin that had seen Tanna as a woman in love and then as a mother. There she looked after Marcora, who was all she had left of her son: Salvanel had loved her, and had been loved in return, and for the sake of that feeling they had shared, Tanna loved the ill-fated young woman like a daughter.

For her she kept the fire going in the fireplace, and for her—when the weather allowed it—she bartered with the shepherds the few things she still owned, to get food and blankets; for her she weaved and spun, and found the strength to tell her own story, the story of Salvanel; for her, she recalled all the old legends and songs. And more. Tanna, who did not have anybody to wait for and anything to hope anymore, knew only too well in the depths of her wounded heart that it was necessary to have something to cling to if you wanted to live on, and she found that something for the young woman her son had loved so much.

"You know, my child," she told her one day, barely rising her pale face from the distaff, "the glacier always gives back what it swallowed. One day, maybe tomorrow, maybe in a year's time, or who knows when, it will give Salvanel's body back to us. We will be able to see him again, to hold him in our arms, to properly bury him by our house, where he will be near us forever."

She then fell silent and raised her head a little more, careful not to let the young woman see the tears veiling her eyes. Unexpectedly, Marcora was smiling, the first smile since her arrival.

"To see him again!" she exclaimed. "Oh, yes, mother! To see him once more, even if for the last time! When... when do you think..."

"I don't know, my dear," Tanna replied, a smile mirroring Marcora's one still shining on her face. "I don't know. But whenever it happens, we will be there to greet him."

And so they did. From that day onward, every morning the two women would go to the gorge that had swallowed the man both had loved and still loved, and would stare into its depths in the hope of glimpsing its body, while the layers of ice kept getting thicker.

It wasn't always easy to carry on that pilgrimage because the shepherds, who used to graze their herds on the plateau in the good season, started muttering against the two women. Tanna and Marcora had very little to barter with them now, and that little was seldom of any interest, so the shepherds started blaming them for the fact that the pastures, once lush and green, were now covered with ice most of the time, so much so that the sheep could hardly graze there and the paths were almost impassable.

A sudden and unexpected hail storm finally unleashed all that simmering hate. With the furious shepherds throwing stones at them, the two women ran away and found shelter in one of the many caves opening in the rocky face of the mountain, from where they stared, bewildered and terrified, to the smoke and flames rising from their house.

Making do with the few things they managed to save from the fire, they endeavored to turn the cave into a livable shelter and settled there, nearer still to the gorge that had swallowed Salvanel.

By now, their sorrowful morning pilgrimage had become their only reason to go on living, and even if the shepherds and the inhabitants of the surrounding villages were still harassing them, every morning they went to kneel on the gorge edge, praying for the body to be given back to them.

'Stries', witches, the people were calling them by now, 'stries de la djassa', the ice witches, and since all their attempts to chase them away had come to naught, a delegation of peasants and shepherds went to see Zan de Pizagul, the regolàn of Luzius, asking him to intervene and to bring armed men to chase those two evil creatures from their pastures.

The regolàn was a good, old man, so old he remembered the anomalous thickening of the ice dated back to a long time before the apparition of those two alleged witches, but he thought it better to go and see by himself what was happening. Therefore, he solemnly agreed to come, and a couple of days later he went to the pasture with a group of armed men that, to tell the truth, was quite small: only four men.

It was a very clear day, even if unseasonably cold; a few clouds lingering around the high peaks were soon driven away by a chilly wind, but the sun shining now in the blue sky barely shed a little warmth on the men and herds crowding around the *regolàn*, as they all waited for the two *stries* to appear, as they did every morning.

Zan felt perplexed and uncertain: he had come to prevent the worst from happening, but now he did not know what to do and, to tell the truth, he was also a little afraid.

After all, those two creatures might really be two witches, or beings bounded to the Unmentionable One! he thought, crossing himself and regretting he had not thought of bringing along a *preve*, a priest, instead of those four soldiers that now appeared to him an inadequate protection.

He was still debating what could be done, when one of the soldiers let out an astonished cry.

"Look, there! Just below the ice rim... a man!"

Crying in wonder and fear, crossing themselves and whispering words of protection, the men crowded around the gorge, where Salvanel's body could now be seen clearly, but they did not have the time to exchange a single word, or opinion, that they were pushed aside. Her long disheveled hair framing her tear-stained face, her arms open as if to hold that frozen body to her heart, Marcora furiously pushed her way through them and threw herself on that ice coffin, lying on her lover's chest while shouting incoherently words of love and pain that ended in one last, desperate, choked sob.

Behind her, pale and dignified, her face turned to stone, stood Tanna.

Almost unwillingly, the gathered men stepped back to allow her to reach those two still bodies, and the woman knelt down to gaze at her son's face for the last time. Gently, she put her hands on Marcora's shoulders to pull her up against her, and the young woman's body limply seconded her movement. Tanna then bent to look at her face, and slowly closed her eyes.

Dead.

Marcora was dead, she had died on Salvanel's body. She had gone on living all those long months only to be able to see and hold in her arms again the man she had forsaken everything for: home, family, riches, power.

Tanna had made a similar choice herself, and she also had lost the man for whom she had made that choice, but she had at least got a child to live for, while Marcora had nothing left, just her memories and her sorrow.

As she thought so, kneeling by those two dead who were all she had left of her dreams, it surprised her that she was not feeling either grief or anger, or even resignation. She had no feelings at all, not even regret for what hadn't been, or anger for what had happened. Her heart—her human heart—was silent, mute like...

She slowly got to her feet. She could feel the movements of the mountain like never before, but she did not turn to look at it; instead, she turned toward the men who had caused Salvanel and Marcora's death. She stared at them and, again, she felt nothing. She simply saw them for what they were: stupid, narrow-minded, short-lived beings, blinded by their passions. And as she stared at them, while pitchforks and hoes fell to the ground, the *regolàn* pointed at her with a shaking finger, shouting:

"*Férmete, compagnes, l'è l' Reìna de Crodares!...* Don't move, friends, she is the Crodares' Queen!"

It was only then that Tanna, still standing by the edge of the chasm, realized that an azure light was shimmering all around her. Rising a hand, she brushed her fingers against her forehead, not at all surprised to find it wreathed again with the azure crown, just as it did not surprise her to see her ragged clothes change into the snow-white tunic of the Queen of the Crodares. And at her back she heard the hidden doors open—those giving access to the abodes of her people—and her subjects come out to honor her, kneeling before her.

Yes, she was the Queen of the Crodares, as icy and unreachable as the mountains she reigned and watched over, the Queen of a people so long-lived that it was called 'immortal' by those wretched human beings, a Queen who felt neither love nor hate, whose only laws were those of reason and necessity. And she knew it was now necessary to free the Marmolada from the ice that had enshrouded it during the years of her folly, a time when—out of love for a wretched people—she had ordered the avalanches not to fall, the storms to quiet down, the snow to fall only on the highest peaks, sparing houses and fields alike.

She raised her arms in a gesture of command, barely conscious of the wide, shining bracelets now encircling her wrists, and she looked at her subjects as they picked up Salvanel and Marcora's bodies to carry them inside the mountain, then she turned her gaze to her persecutors again, now huddling in a quivering, small group, reverently holding their hats in their hands, their weapons forgotten on the ground. Many fell on their knees under the impact of her icy stare, begging forgiveness, blaming each other, wailing.

Behind them, in the valleys below, stood their poor homes.

For a moment, a single instant–shortest than the blink of an eye–Tanna once more understood their terror, their misery, and pitied them.

"Run!" she shouted, but her voice was once more the voice of the Queen of the Crodares, the voice of the Marmarole. "I unleash what I bounded: all my bans are hereby rescinded and the mountain takes back what's rightfully hers! Run, or you will be swept away!"

As the mountain dwellers ran away, in the hope of reaching their homes and families in time to save themselves and their loved ones, a deep rumble shook the mountains all around them.

Deep quivers ran through the shiny surface of the glaciers–of all the glaciers enveloping the Marmarole–and deep cracks appeared all over it until it broke apart with a sinister creaking sound, and huge ice slabs crashed down from each peak, dragging down in their descent all the fresh snow accumulated over them and sweeping away everything in their way, while a suddenly stormy sky released a thick snow storm that soon enveloped the Cimon del Fropa, hiding forever Tanna, Queen of the Crodares, from the sight of men.

However, since she had given in to the feelings of her human heart one last time, every year, for just one day,

Tanna still feels it beating inside her breast, feels love and grief, anguish and disillusionment. In that day everything is silent on the Marmarole, there are no avalanches, no scree landslides, and the mountains are open to whoever wants to learn their secrets, as the *Scholars of the Black School* well know. Tanna spends those hours sitting on her obsidian throne, in the deepest, most hidden room of her ice palace, a black veil covering her head below the azure crown and falling over her shiny, snow-white robe. At her sides, two gold-inlaid coffins made of eternal ice hold the bodies of Salvanel and Marcora, and in that day the Queen finds her human heart again and cries once more for her betrayed trust and love, her lost hopes, her grief.

Historical Notes to "Tanna".

In "Tanna" we find again a story which is in some ways related to medieval legends and yet presents figures that remind us of much older myths, those linked to nature and its hard laws. Such are, in fact, the Crodares, the sons of the rocks, apparently similar to humans, but unable to have any feelings. Related to them, and to their queen, Tanna, are other characters of the Ladin mythology—among the most primitive and unsettling ones—who almost seem to underline the blind power of the mountains: Samblana, queen of Marmolada's perennial glaciers, whose azure cloak reminds us of Tanna's azure crown; Cè de Lu, the Merciless, the *Om de la jacia* (Man of ice), all figures tied to the high picks and the ice.

However, this is the only 'primitive' element I found in this story, which is otherwise similar to the traditional medieval tales.

Therefore, in my retelling it, I fully respected the figures of the Crodares, portraying them with their peculiarities and their powers, but I also tried to place the story in an historical moment as precise as possible.

After rejecting, as historically unacceptable, the reference I found in a version of the legend to a "Count of Aquileia", city that was never ruled by a count, but was instead the seat of a powerful patriarchy, I tried to imagine who could have been the noble and important man who seduced Tanna, and after some searching I chose Count Guidone da Montanara who, with his sons Alberto and Guecello, founded the Da Camino dynasty. Of course, there isn't any proof of a relationship between him and the Crodares and Tanna—a relationship born exclusively out of my imagination—but all the other details about him are real, or at least historians deem them plausible.

The da Montanara family was probably of Langobard origins, descended from a side branch of the Collalto, and Guido (or Guidone) got his castle, set on the slopes on the Cansiglio Mountain, and the title of count as a gift from the salic Emperor Conrad of Franconia for—it seems—having saved his life (around the year 1015). The disputes between the Da Montanara and their cousins, the Collalto, are borne out by historical data as well, while Marcora and his love story are a product of my imagination.

CIADINA

Tose e fenc, tose e fenc, chi l'è più fort
Che che è bon de tor via sta colana!
Maids and young men, who's the strongest
Who can take this necklace off me?
Cursed, devilish necklace,
'cause of you he wants me not!

From Ciadina, words and music by Luigi Canori.

The good wives of the village all agreed that if Ciadina's mother, God rest her soul, had lived, she would have prevented her daughter from indulging in every whim crossing her pretty head. However, that sainted woman had died when her daughter was still a baby, and being raised by her maidservants, her father and two older brothers,

Ciadina had grown into a fickle and vain girl. Their husbands and sons, however, would laugh up their sleeve whenever they heard that because they felt sure those were words born out of sheer envy.

In fact, Ciadina was undoubtedly the most beautiful girl in the village and in the two nearby valleys, Pellegrino Valley and Saiùc Valley, where her father had most of his properties, fields and pastures where his flocks could graze. Piere was a rich man, and Ciadina was not only his youngest child, born to him when he was already getting on in years, but also his only daughter; it went without saying, therefore, that she had been pampered somewhat, and that she felt proud of her beauty and her social standing, also because her father had never tried to dampen what he saw as her legitimate pride.

He was ambitious too, so much so that the previous year he had tried to be elected as the *regolàn*, and had been defeated only because of the opposition of a couple of *fade*. Far from being disheartened by his failure, he was going to try again and he felt certain he would succeed.

In the meanwhile, he was doing his best to get in the good graces of the Arimanni Captain Nikolo Pilat, who held sway over the Capifuoco's assembly, which was the reason why he had invited him for dinner together with his wife.

"Sadly, I'm a widower," he complained, and immediately added: "But my daughter, Ciadina, will do the honors." He then paused, thinking. Spending the evening in the company of two older men who only talked about the local situation and the dangers deriving from the Trusani's demands, as well as of a stern matron who only spoke to support her husband, certainly was not going to please his daughter! Therefore, he had to find a solution to prevent

153

the girl from exploding with one of her renowned tantrums. "If you want, you could bring a couple of your men with you. Young people love the company of their peers," he suggested with a smile.

Nikolo smiled too and nodded. "I'll tell Tone, whom you already know, and I'm sure he'll feel glad and honored," he answered. He had a moment's hesitation, then he cleared his throat and went on, choosing his words carefully, "He's almost thirty, but he never married, even if he could certainly afford to! He is an Arimanno, but he also owns the *tabiàs* and the land he inherited from his mother, on the mountain pastures."

The two men exchanged a look of mutual understanding, then the Captain added: "I'll tell him to bring a friend, and I'm sure he will come with his comrade at arms".

That was how Ciadina met Verrènes for the first time.

She knew her father would have welcomed her marriage with Tone, and she tried to do her best to please him, but even while speaking and smiling to him, her eyes kept straying toward the other man, taking in with clear appreciation the blond curl of hair that kept falling forward on his forehead, his odd lead-gray eyes, and his slim, agile body; compared to him, the dark haired, stout Tone appeared as rough as a big bear.

Soon Verrènes started glancing back at her, then those glances gave way to smiles, shy at first, then conspiratorial, as if the two youngsters shared a secret, even if they had exchanged but a few words. By the end of the evening it was clear to everybody that a very strong attraction had developed between them, so Piere was not surprised when the young Arimanno—as he thanked him in taking his leave—asked him if he could come and visit with them again. He agreed, laughing, and threw a meaningful glance at Ciadina, who was blushing with happiness. Of course, Piere would have liked better the elder and richer Tone, but he did not want to go against his daughter wishes, the more so since she already had a dowry that would suffice by itself to give her a comfortable life. Moreover, he thought, Verrènes was as good a catch as Tone: being an Arimanno, he not only received a handsome salary, but he also had rights on the lands traditionally allotted to those warriors.

Moreover, Nikolo guaranteed for the boy, saying that he was respected by all his mates for his bravery and loyalty, and even Tone, bearing no resentment for the choice made by the girl, put in a good word for his brother-at-arms' sake.

"He's brave and he will go far. I wouldn't be surprised if he would become our captain a few years from now, once Nikolo retires.

Captain of the Arimanni... those words tickled Piere's ambition and totally reconciled him with the idea of having that young soldier as his son-in-law, so he encouraged his visits that grew longer and more frequent.

Winter came, and covered with its white mantle of snow the meadows and the rocks around Costabella: the days grew darker and an icy wind could often be heard moaning outside, but inside Piere's comfortable house the fire burned merrily in the fireplace, chasing away both the cold and the darkness, and every time Verrènes knocked at the door he would find a goblet of hot mulled wine to warm him, Piere's hearty welcome and beautiful Ciadina's shy and tempting smile.

Then, after the usual courtesies had been exchanged, Piere would usually take his leave, pleading some urgent business to take care of, and an old servant would slip discreetly into the room and keep herself busy with some chore in the shadows. Ciadina would then sit on the bench set in front of the fireplace and hem a sheet or an apron while Verrènes sat beside her and told her in a low voice of his life as a soldier, the battles he had fought and the faraway places he had seen. While still young, in fact, he had traveled a lot and been part of other Arimannie before enrolling in the one he now belonged to.

"I was in Fassa, a valley surrounded by the most beautiful mountains in the world," he told her, "and there I climbed to greet the rising sun on many of those white peaks, such as the Marmoleda, as the Fassans call it. They are a hard-working people, and speak a language similar to ours, even if a bit harsher. They have a large Arimannia, whose main task is to protect the passes; I spent two years there, and the captain did not want to let me go, but after that bad business of the Latemar..." Verrènes broke off, as if he already regretted mentioning that; Piere, who was still in the room, intent on carving some ladles wood handle, raised his eyes and stared at him with sudden interest. "Have you been on the Latemar? They say there are veins of precious metals up there."

Verrènes shuffled his feet, ill at ease, but Ciadina insisted that he finish his story, so in the end the young man gave in.

"I went there, yes, through the Pas de Costalongia, together with a group of the companions I had then. And, yes, there are still gold, copper and precious stones to be found in the bowels of that mountain. It is inhabited by small men, strange creatures—dwarves or Silvanes—who dig into its bowels and extract precious metals and stones they then patiently and skillfully work into jewels. It is rumored that they have great treasures amassed inside their mountain. Their greed awakened by those stories, my companions captured a few of those men and threatened to burn them alive if they did not lead them to where their riches were hidden. Together with some of my companions, I was against it. We ended up having a row, and while we were fighting among ourselves our prisoners escaped and disappeared inside their mysterious underground tunnels. Nobody got wounded or killed, but since then I felt ill at ease and I left as soon as my period of service ended."

His mind filled with the image of all those treasures, Piere pressed him with his questions, but Verrènes did not feel like talking about it any longer and soon changed the subject, nor he ever spoke about that again during his by now almost daily visits, that were getting longer and longer.

Outside, the wind blew strongly or the snow fell slow and soft, but in the room the flames burned warmly and shone on the polished boughs decorating the walls, on the young warrior's blond hair and gray eyes, and on Ciadina's long braids, that were neither fair nor dark, but in the firelight glimmered with one thousand nuances, from bronze to gold and copper, while a delicate shade of pink lingered on her face. From time to time, the words would die on Verrènes lips, and the needle would slip from Ciadina's fingers: they would then stare at each other, exchanging a smile that would end in a sigh.

Spring chased winter away, and the snow slowly melted from the dark soil, which was soon covered with green grass, dotted with the delicate colors of the first, shy flowers; the chilly winter gale turned into a gentle breeze, whose warm breath seemed to stroke the meadows, the bushes, the budding trees. The sun drew shards of light from the snow and the glaciers covering the mountain peaks surrounding the Pellegrino Valley, and its rays were now bringing new warmth. In the village, people seemed to emerge from a sort of hibernation and started to leave their houses to work the fields or to repair whatever damages the winter cold and wind had caused, or simply to have a little talk with neighbors and friends.

At first, Verrènes and Ciadina managed to meet as if by chance in the little village square, by the washhouse, whenever the Arimanno had a day free form the service, but later on they could always be seen together. They would walk side by side, the girl with her eyes demurely lowered but shooting quick, passionate glances to the tall young man who, a little awkwardly, stared at her with adoring eyes, smiling. As usual, either the old maidservant or Piere himself would discretely chaperon the couple, while Ciadina's friends and Verrènes comrades-at-arms smirked as they watched them go by, because by now everybody thought of them as of a couple.

Therefore, it was not a surprise for anybody when, on a warm spring morning, Verrènes knocked once more at Ciadina's door, a box in his hands and a determined—albeit a little fearful—expression on his face. Tone, who had been his confidant all those long months through, saw him to the door, and after patting him encouragingly on the shoulder stood there whistling, a wide smile on his face, looking after

Verrènes as he disappeared down the hall. During the winter, Tone had been courting a young widow, and he was already looking forward to a double wedding, with their comrades-at-arms applauding, joking and singing merry songs.

In the meanwhile, Verrènes had been ushered in, not in the usual room with the fireplace, but in the long hall reserved for special celebrations, which was actually seldom used and looked like it had been hurriedly and recently cleaned up. There, stammering a little, Verrènes asked Piere for Ciadina's hand in marriage.

As soon as they shook hands in agreement, a side door opened and Stina, the old maidservant who had been a silent witness of that love, came into the room, carrying a heavy, well-polished copper plate with a mound of cookies still warm from the oven, a jug of wine and three pewter goblets artfully placed on white embroidered doilies. A moment later, answering to her father's call, Ciadina came in through the central door, wearing her best dress and an embroidered apron, her face flushed and her thick braid a little disheveled because she had been eavesdropping.

With her arrival and her predictable assent, the engagement was made official and Verrènes, as he kissed for the first time her round cheek, silently offered her the box he was carrying. Ciadina hastened to open it, and immediately her blue eyes went very wide.

Inside, lying on a soft piece of cloth, shone some translucent gems encased in thin, gleaming threads of gold and copper. Dark gray, those gems had unique blue and silver highlights.

The jewel was proof of a craftsmanship and an elegance never seen before in the whole Pellegrino Valley.

"Do you remember what I told you about the Latemar and the bad experience I lived up there?" the young man asked, as he fastened the necklace around his betrothed's neck. "Some time later, on the Grand Mugon, I met one of those strange creatures again. It said it knew me and offered this necklace to me as a 'token of its gratitude'." He finished fastening the necklace and, as he brushed her neck one last time, he pleaded: "Promise me, my Ciadina, that you will never take it off, at least until we get married. The one who gave it to me weaved into it..." He broke off, then he simply finished: "Promise me, I beg you!"

Even if an eerie shiver had run through Ciadina's body when the necklace had circled her throat, and Verrènes odd, cut off sentence had upset her somewhat, she promised, and the evening ended in good cheer.

Only one thing marred the young Arimanno's happiness: he would have liked to marry Ciadina as soon as possible, but Piere had been adamant about it.

"You will get married only by the end of autumn, when my sons will get back from the mountain pastures with the herd. This way, we will have the time to organize an unforgettable wedding, and Ciadina will be able to put together her trousseau," he said, then he added, comfortingly, "Cheer up! Five months will fly by, and in the meanwhile you two will be able to enjoy your engagement, one of the best moments in life!"

Those were indeed days full of happiness and joyful hopes, but they soon ended, and brusquely: ancient enemies moved from the faraway Ròća, heading for the passes above the Pellegrino Valley, from which they wanted to invade the Fassa Valley. Ladins called them 'Trusani', like those first invaders of long ago, but they were Langobards from Roccapietore, possibly allied with Belum or Tarvisium. Ciadina's village was on their path, and the order had already been given to the Arimanni to get ready to move to stop them.

"We will chase them away, my love, and will be back in time for us to get married when and how we decided. Don't be afraid, I'll come back to you. Keep carrying the necklace I gave you as a token of my love: it will bring me luck, I can feel it," Verrènes said, in an attempt to comfort his betrothed, who had been crying for days. The girl clung to his neck, sobbing, but the young man kindly disentangled himself from the frantic grasp of those small hands, kissed her on the forehead, took his leave from his soon to be father-in-law, and left to join Tone, who was waiting for him in the courtyard.

The Arimanni left the next day, among the good wishes and the handkerchief waving of the farmers, and the crying of the women left behind to wait for their return.

Ciadina waited as well, burdened not only with her worrying over Verrènes safety but also with boredom, because her being engaged prevented her from taking part to the simple celebrations and the dancing that celebrated the end of the harvest and the shepherds' return from the mountain pastures, and also to the long night vigils, when stories were told, old songs sung, and gossip exchanged.

Three long months went by, then two breathless messengers reached the village, bringing the news that the Trusani had been driven back and that the brave Arimanni were coming home.

All the people turned out on the streets, rejoicing, talking, singing, toasting, and this time Ciadina, escorted by her father and brothers, joined the celebration, applauding the soldiers as they reached the small square.

Once they had all come back, and were surrounded by the joyful villagers, however, Ciadina was still standing there on the road to the village, together with a group of other women whose smile had died. Some of them had a child in their arms or beside them, others still had in their hair the flowers and ribbons they had worn to greet their men, who had not come back. Slowly, the small group dispersed as all those women sadly went back home without a word, without even looking at each other, while the air still echoed with the songs and laughter of the others, who had been able to hug their loved ones again, and of the returned warriors.

Ciadina still stood there by herself, incredulous, the useless scarf she had embroidered for her betrothed dangling from her hands, while her eyes filled with tears as she slowly realized Verrènes wasn't going to come back, that she would never see him again. With that thought, tears started running copiously down her cheeks, and the lump in her throat grew into desperate sobbing.

Right then, a voice called her. "Ciadina!"

She turned, drying her face, and in the growing darkness she saw Tone's stout figure as he left his betrothed side to hesitantly approach her.

"Forgive me for intruding upon you on such a moment, but your grief is mine as well. We fought side by side, defending each other as usual, Verrènes and I, but in that last engagement a group of Trusani managed to cut us off from our forces. Verrènes fell to the ground, hit by an arrow, and I narrowly escaped with a wounded arm, and that only because our captain came to our rescue and dragged me away."

"He's dead!" sobbed Ciadina, but Tone shook his head, looking at her with uncertainty in his eyes.

"No, I don't think so," he finally said. "His wound was on a leg, and then they clubbed him, knocking him out, but in my experience neither wound was lethal." He broke off, coughing nervously, then he lowered his gaze and went on: "If I hadn't been wounded as well... if my captain hadn't dragged me away... enough! I left him there on the ground, I deserted him, and I fear he has been taken prisoner." He then clasped the girl's hands in his own, murmuring, "Forgive me! I'll never forgive myself."

The girl nodded as she returned his clasp, but as she did so she realized with wonder that she wasn't as happy as it would have been logical to expect at the prospect that Verrènes might still be alive.

Such prisoners were seldom seen again—she reasoned, as she headed for home, silently escorted by a sorrowful Tone and his betrothed—and even if and when they did, it was after months, or even years, a time that she would have to spend in seclusion, waiting for somebody who might never come back.

Two months went by, and autumn gave way to a long, cold, and dreary winter, which Ciadina spent at home, almost always shut up in her room, there to brood over the terrible loss that had befallen her; then the cold relented, there were no more snowfalls, and with that improvement of the weather a delegation from the Fiemme Valley came to the village, to debate about some pastures rights. Having managed to get elected as the new *regolàn*, Piere was the one who received the delegates, and for once he asked Ciadina to forsake her seclusion to join them as the lady of the house, since his two sons and their families lived elsewhere.

"I know I'm asking a lot of you, my dear, but this is the first important situation I'm facing as a *regolàn*, and I certainly don't want to make a bad impression," he told her, and the young woman nodded, lowering her eyes to conceal her sudden joy at the thought of mingling with other people again after so many months of loneliness, basking again in other people's admiration, talking and laughing.

She chose her clothing with care—something unusual for her of late—and gathered her hair into two big braids, leaving the lower part unbraided to make her hair softness and luster better stand out. Once ready, she looked at herself in a polished copper tray and smiled to her mirrored image, pinching her cheeks a little to give them a nice pink color. She then hesitated for a moment, her hand on Verrènes necklace clasp, then she decided to keep wearing it.

"I promised," she told herself, with a steadiness she wasn't feeling. Moreover, the gems' color perfectly matched her blue corselet and the embroidery on her wide skirt. She fastened a brocade apron around her waist, grabbed a soft wool shawl and almost ran to the long hall, where the guests had already been admitted, careful to allow her embroidered slippers to be half-seen, together with her slim ankles, sheathed into white stockings.

While doing the honors, she cast sidelong, curiosity filled glances to their guests, and she immediately felt attracted to Ghebardo, the head of the delegation, who in turn was looking at her with a smile on his lips, while he lithely wandered around the room, giving orders and pouring wine.

He was a fine young man, not very tall but well proportioned, with lively dark eyes and shiny black hair, carefully cut as the latest fashion demanded, and his clothing was so elegant and rich that it made Ciadina's eyes widen with appreciation. He was self-assured in the way he spoke and moved, like one used to be in command... as a matter of fact, Piere soon whispered to his daughter that the young man was the head of the delegation and belonged to a rich and noble family, which made him one of the most important members of the Magnificent Fiemme Community.

All evening long, while the negotiation was carried on among the general satisfaction, Ciadina and Ghebardo kept fleetingly glancing at each other, with the young man's smile getting wider and filled with growing admiration, while Ciadina's eyes shone and she kept blushing.

It seemed to Piere that the negotiation kept dragging on even after they had reached a general agreement, and he understood why it was so when, in taking his leave, the young man asked if he could come back to 'reformulate some minor provision', as he put it, his eyes never leaving Ciadina.

And he came back the next evening, and the one after that, while his companions resignedly waited to get back home. After the first few visits, Ghebardo set aside the pretext of the negotiation, by now fully settled, and started openly courting the young woman, who on her part did not draw back nor returned to her previous seclusion, but always greeted him with a smile.

"I realize I'm barely acquainted with your enchanting daughter," Ghebardo told Piere, after a couple of weeks, "but I will soon have to leave and I don't want to do that before first taking my chance and asking for your daughter's hand."

The *regolàn* hesitated. That request wasn't coming as a surprise to him because he had been present during the young man's recent visits, and he held no doubts about what Ciadina's answer was going to be, since she was clearly flattered by Ghebardo's admiration, but the promise made to Verrènes—as well as the young man's uncertain fate—troubled him. He mentioned the problem to Ghebardo, carefully choosing his words and paid close attention to his reaction because, in spite of his misgivings, he kept thinking that such a marriage would not only secure her daughter's social standing, but would also be very useful to his aim to expand his influence to the nearby villages.

The young man immediately cut him off, laughing. "I've already been told the whole story, but it doesn't look like an unsurmountable impediment to me, if Ciadina agrees to marry me and you give us your blessing! They were just engaged, after all, and not already married!"

"Yes, this is true," Piere muttered, already feeling somewhat relieved, then he promised he was going to talk to his daughter the next morning, and that Ghebardo was going to get his answer by the next evening.

"See to it that the answer is yes, *regolàn!*" insisted Ghebardo.

"It is, as far as I'm concerned, but Ciadina might..."

"... might want to waste her youth away waiting in vain, ending up a spinster?" the young man cut him off. "I don't think so; in fact, I'm sure it's not so."

As he spoke, he laughed again, and Piere realized that there was already some sort of understanding between the two young people; therefore, he felt totally untroubled the next morning, when he knocked at his daughter's door.

The girl brightened up as soon as her father started speaking, but she hid her smile and listlessly raised a couple of objections, mentioning Verrènes and her solemn promise to him.

"Much to my regret, my daughter, I must point out to you that there aren't many chances for that poor man to ever get back home. The Trusani are anything but soft in dealing with their prisoners, most of all if they are Arimanni. Even if he were still alive, which I strongly doubt to be the case, and were able to come back—many months from now, maybe, or even years—who knows in what state he would be? He could be maimed, or an invalid... and by now Tone has become the new Captain of the Arimanni," reasoned the *regolàn*, then he remembered Ghebardo's words, and he added: "Moreover, Verrènes was not your husband yet, you two were bound only by a promise he cannot fulfill any more, even if through no fault of his, the poor man!"

"I surrender to your wisdom, father. Do tell my noble suitor I feel honored and glad to accept his proposal, and that this evening, with your blessing, I'll welcome him as my betrothed."

At dusk, a great celebration was held in the *regolàn*'s house, and the new suitor offered his betrothed the gifts he had sent for from his village: two silver combs, a thick bracelet of the same metal, and lengths of white brocade and velvet, so beautiful and valuable that the girl was left speechless as she brushed them with her fingertips. "You will use them for your wedding gown, my dear, for I want you to be the most elegant bride ever seen in this valley," Ghebardo said, then he added, jokingly shaking a finger at her: "And you must have it ready in a hurry, too. In a few days I'll get back home to get everything ready, but I'll be back in a month, at most, to marry you."

Starting the next day, Ciadina took again to strolling around the village at her betrothed's arm, introducing him as her fiancé in every yard and house, flaunting his presents and drawing on herself her friends' envy and admiration once more. Of course, there were a few who frowned upon her behavior, thinking she had been too quick in forgetting poor Verrènes, among them Tone and the young widow who by now was his wife. The Arimanno got to the point of resolutely turning down Piere's invitations and avoiding to ever meet the engaged couple.

Nevertheless, Ciadina was happy: the compliments she received, her friends' good wishes, her betrothed's elegance and refinement made her dream of a new world, one in which she was going to be a respected and admired lady. So she walked along the humble, narrow streets of her village with her head held high and a smile on her lips, pride and joy shining through her eyes, as she kept telling herself the had made the right choice. And yet, something was troubling her.

At night, once Ghebardo had taken his leave, when she was lying in her bed, alone in her wood paneled room, she had trouble falling asleep, and when she finally managed, hers was a troubled sleep. She could never remember her disturbing dreams, but she often woke up feeling like something was choking her, as if the necklace of polished gray gems she kept wearing—partly out of sheer superstition and partly because she liked it very much—was strangling her. She would then sit up on the bed, panting, and would suddenly remember Verrènes blond, curly hair, his cheerful smile, his sweetness toward her, and the love he had always had for her, and she would then feel a sense of unhappiness, an uneasiness she was reluctant to label as remorse, but for which she could find no other name.

When the sun rose, however, it's light chased all those shadows away, everything was forgotten and Ciadina would feel happy and excited again as she devoted herself to working at her trousseau, visiting with friends, and most of all sewing her gorgeous bridal gown, as her betrothed had advised her to do before getting back to his village.

Some days had already gone by since he had left, and Ciadina—still awake in her room— was counting the days separating her from the big day, when the door opened slowly and old Stina came into the room, uncertainty and emotion etched on her worn face.

"He's back, Ciadina!" she announced breathlessly. "And he wants to see you right away!"

"So soon!" the girl exclaimed, thinking it was her betrothed calling on her; then she added, uncertain: "And my father has gone to take care of some business in the nearby village. I don't know if it is proper that..."

"No!" the old woman interrupted her. "It is Verrènes. Verrènes has come back! After long months of imprisonment, he escaped risking his life and traveled the whole way on foot... the poor boy! He still has a limp and he's awfully skinny, and... he's asking for you."

The old woman barely whispered those last words, because her mistress had first blanched and was now turning bright red.

"Send him away, Stina! Tell him I'm ill, or whatever you want, but send him away! I cannot... don't' want to... see him!" the girl cried through trembling lips, avoiding to meet her maidservant's eyes, then she lay in bed and pulled the covers over her head.

The old woman stared at her for a moment longer, then she slowly left the room, dragging her feet and shaking her head.

Ciadina remained in bed, tossing and turning with her mind in turmoil; as the hours went by, however, the memories and her remorse were replaced by a different feeling, almost of anger, because the Arimanno's return was endangering her future, that very future full of riches and honors she had been daydreaming of up to that moment.

She did not want to see him, or to speak to him, ever: she wished him all the best, but far from her, her home, her betrothed. After such a long time he could not— must not—put forward any claim on her, now that she was engaged to another man. Even if a small voice in her heart insistently reminded her of the days of their shared love, of the promises exchanged, she firmly silenced it, telling herself that by now Verrènes, in the state he was in, could not aspire to the hand of the *regolàn*'s daughter anymore.

With those thoughts well rooted in her mind, the next morning she took Stina to one side and ordered her not to mention the young man's return and short visit to anybody, and to send him away, should he ever come back.

Sure enough, the Arimanno came back many times, always asking for his betrothed, but the maidservant always sent him away, even if she felt sorry for him. By now, all the village knew about Verrènes return, but Ciadina avoided both the prying eyes and malicious questions shutting herself up in her home, hiding behind the excuse of her father and brothers being away, and of her being busy getting her trousseau ready.

One night, however, she was already in bed when she heard something tap against her window shutters; that noise sounded again and again, preventing her from falling asleep, and she finally got up to open the window, thinking some of her friends were playing a joke on her.

It was Verrènes, instead, his worn, thin face raised up toward her, hope shining in his eyes.

"Ciadina..." he began, pleadingly, but an angry cry from the girl immediately cut him off. "No! I already had Stina tell you, and now I'll say it myself: go away! It's all over between us, I'm engaged with another man and I'll soon get married!"

"Our promises, Ciadina! Your promise... you pledged yourself to me, you assured me you were going to wait for me, faithfully..."

"And I did, for many, long months, but you weren't coming back..."

"I was wounded, and a prisoner, but I escaped as soon as I could stand, and crossed rivers, roads and mountains to get back to you! I still love you..."

"It is too late! But if it is true you still care for me, then go away! Your presence here is an obstacle to my happiness."

"At the side of another man, whose luck was better than mine."

Verrènes voice was betraying all his bitterness, his disillusionment and a deep, almost resigned, exhaustion. For a fleeting moment, the girl could feel that bothering sense of remorse knocking at her heart, but then her eyes fell on her splendid bridal gown and its sight was enough to chase away any guilt she might be feeling.

"With another man, yes," she countered. "I did not want it, nor did I look for it, but it happened. You'd better accept it and leave me alone."

In so saying, she tried to remove the necklace he had given her so that she could give it back to him, but the clasp got stuck, or perhaps it was broken, and she wasn't able to unclasp it. She drew back from the window then, and in the moonlight she could see the Arimanno slowly turn around, his head bowed forlornly as he waked away with a slight limp, his shoulders bent.

She sighed with relief and pity, but as she watched him disappear behind a house, looking through a crack in the shutters, she told herself that it was unthinkable for the *regolàn*'s daughter, the beautiful and rich Ciadina, whom everybody admired and envied, to leave her noble betrothed for that man. And she returned to her bed.

Verrènes was never seen again, not at her door nor anywhere else in the village, and a few days later there was a rumor going about that he had left his Arimannia to enroll elsewhere, in the Fassa Valley, where they feared the Trusani would soon attack them.

Again, Ciadina sighed with relief and tried to dispel her remorse burying herself in the preparations for the by now imminent wedding. The presents were already being delivered, her gown was ready and her rich trousseau filled three wood chests decorated with cheerful paintings of alpine flowers. In the meanwhile, Piere came back home, and he immediately looked inquiringly at his daughter, for he had already been told that Verrènes had come back, even if for just a few days; the girl's rosy face showed only peace of mind and joyful anticipation, and Stina kept her mouth shut.

She clearly doesn't know anything... just as well, thought the *regolàn*, reassured, and he forbade everybody to say anything about the Arimanno.

So the preparations for the wedding went on without trouble, but the marriage ceremony was just a few days away when one night Tone knocked at the *regolàn*'s door; he was followed by a very young, slim, dark haired boy who carried a heavy, round object covered with a rough black cloth.

"Tone!" Ciadina exclaimed, surprised because she had not seen nor heard from the Arimanni Captain and his wife for many months. "You're looking for my father, I suppose, but unfortunately he's not here. He's on the mountain pastures, with my brothers."

"No, girl, it is you that I was... or, rather, we were... looking for.

In so saying, he gestured for the young man to come forward, then he added, in a dry voice: "Verrènes is dead."

The girl paled and instinctively raised a hand to the necklace, while with the other one she leaned on the back of a chair.

"He died fighting heroically at the Fedaja, thus preventing the Trusani to cross the pass, and with his sacrifice he gave the Fassans time to reorganize their army and to push the invaders back." Tone fell silent, lowering his eyes to conceal his inner turmoil, and again he motioned for his companion to speak.

"I was with him, my lady," the boy awkwardly began, stepping forward. "Of the whole squad at Verrènes orders, only three of us managed to survive, but Fassa is safe! He was a hero, a great hero, and without him we'd never have made it! He fell by my side, covered with wounds and blood, and with his last breath he asked me to bring you this."

And he removed the back cloth covering the object he was carrying. With mixed horror and shame, Ciadina recognized her betrayed fiancé's shield, on which could now be seen a red circle.

"He drew it with his blood," the boy explained, "and a moment later he collapsed with his face against the rocks, never to move again."

"No, no! I don't want it!" the girl screamed, drawing back, but Tone was leaving already, dragging the boy with him.

"I don't care what you want or do not want, girl," he countered from the threshold, his voice hard. "Verrènes didn't want for it to end this way either! But this is how it was, and now enjoy your new betrothed and your wedding, if you can."

Those last words almost seemed to convey a sort of threat. Trembling, the girl hurried closed the door after the two messengers, then she stared at the shield through a veil of tears. Her heart was in turmoil, but she could not even tell if it was her shame and remorse upsetting her so, or the fear that object aroused in her, or even the fear that what had happened would soon become common knowledge and the jealous Ghebardo would hear about it.

In the end, that last fear prevailed and she wrapped up the shield again, hiding it under her bed before anybody came back home, determined not to say a word about what had happened; as soon as Stina came back, then, Ciadina pleaded a terrible headache and took to her bed.

She slept poorly and was up before dawn, determined to put everything behind her and to think only about her imminent wedding, and while she was hurriedly dressing for the day, mentally going through all the little things she had to do, a smile came back to her lips. Once ready to go out, however, in glancing at the big, polished copper plate placed on her ottoman, she froze as she looked with horror at her mirrored image. The necklace Verrènes had given her, and that she still carried at her neck, had changed color and now in its gems shone a sinister, changing red light, now pale like the blood running through the veins, then the darker red of arterial blood or almost brownish like clotted blood.

Ciadina immediately remembered the Fassan boy's words, and frantically tried to get rid of that cursed necklace once for all, but to no avail. For all that she tried, she could not open it, and her attempt to use a small knife only gave her a small scratch at the nape of her neck, while the gems kept pulsing with lighter and darker nuances of red.

In the meanwhile, all the household had woken up. Ciadina heard Stina calling her, then her father as well, so she choked back her tears, together with her fear and shame, and she hid the necklace under the scarf covering her neckline before she went downstairs, where she forced herself to appear as smiling and calm as usual.

During the following nights, she secretly tried again and again to get rid of the necklace, which resisted all her efforts, and in the meantime the day of the wedding arrived.

The *regolàn* had outdone himself, not minding how much he was spending: the streets the wedding procession would walk through had been bedecked with flower garlands, and the small square was already filling with people, all in their finery because they all knew that after the ceremony the wedded couple was going to treat everybody with roasted meat, bread and sweets; by the water trough, a raised platform had been built, on which some musicians were already gathered, ready to liven up the ceremony with their music. That was where the marriage vows were going to be exchanged in front of the parish priest, who was already on his way, and then the dancing would begin.

Ciadina was still getting dressed when she heard a horse galloping outside: she looked outside and her heart started hammering in her chest when she saw her betrothed, richly dressed and mounted on a bay horse, who was approaching under the garlands, followed by a small retinue that threw flowers and small trinkets at the applauding crowd.

Beyond herself with happiness, Ciadina twirled around, so that her white velvet gown billowed around her. "Hurry up, hurry up," she spurred her maidservants, "he's at the door already! Stina, give me that shawl, and the apron... and you, hurry up with doing my hair! He's here and I'm not ready..." oh!"

A little cry escaped her lips when the door opened and Ghebardo came into the room, followed by a valet carrying a small chest.

"You shouldn't be here!" Ciadina scolded him. "As you can see, my hair hasn't been done yet, and..."

"On the contrary, my love, I had to get here before you finished dressing, so that you could wear this."

Ghebardo then motioned to the servant, who bowed and opened the chest, containing a wonderful white and gold lace headdress, adorned with small god and silver filigree flowers and shining with little pink pearls.

"Your wedding crown," the young man simply said. "Allow me to put it on your head with my hands, and leave your beautiful hair down."

So surprised she was at a loss for words, Ciadina merely nodded, her red lips opened in a smile; Smiling back, Ghebardo picked up the headdress and stepped forward, but then he stopped while perplexity and fear wiped off his smile.

"What's that thing you're wearing around your neck?" He asked, his voice suddenly hard.

Ciadina flushed. She had tried to hide that cursed necklace under the laces of her blouse, but its red glow shone through them. Under Ghebardo's inquisitive stare, she had to pull them aside and show the necklace.

"It... it is a present," she explained. "I thought it became me... don't you like it?"

"No." Ghebardo's voice sounded dry and determined. "I don't know how you got it, but I know that sort of jewels: they are made by the mysterious Latemar people, and they are enchanted. Take it off your neck right away, those things bring ill luck."

177

"As you wish." With trembling hands and a heavy heart, Ciadina tried again to get rid of the necklace, already knowing she wouldn't succeed. "Something broke, I cannot open it," she complained.

Without a word, her betrothed stepped forward and tried to open the clasp, but all his efforts were vain. And in vain first Ghebardo's servant, then Stina and her daughter, and finally even Ciadina's father and her brothers joined his efforts. The necklace kept pulsing with its bloody red light around Ciadina's neck.

Finally, Ghebardo stepped away, a disgusted expression on his face. "You lied to me, Ciadina! I don't know who the poor wretch was you drove to his death, but his blood is on your hands, and guilt burdens your heart."

With an angry, final gesture, he threw the wedding crown to the ground and crushed it under his foot, then he turned away from the girl and the small group of relatives and servants surrounding her and still vainly trying to get her rid of the cursed necklace.

On the door, Ghebardo looked back for a moment. "The engagement is broken," he announced, dryly, then he turned to his retinue, crowding the stairs, and added: "We're getting home, right away."

Ciadina cried, wept and begged; Piere tried to intervene, even if by then he had guessed what had happened, and Ciadina's brothers threatened Ghebardo, but he adamantly ignored them and left on his horse, his head held high, followed by his retinue, leaving the wretched *regolàn* facing the difficult task of finding some explanation to give the guests, the parish priest, the musicians and the crowd, who were all still waiting for the wedding ceremony to begin.

Sabja de Fek

While Piere and his sons did their best to explain why the wedding would not take place, saying and not saying, Ciadina chased out both servants and relatives, and locked herself in her room, knowing she could never face the malevolent, disgusted stares of the villagers, nor endure their malicious and mocking innuendos.

Collapsing into a chair, the useless, ruffled wedding gown widening around her, her beautiful hair flowing down her back and shoulders, she cried her heart out while her fingers kept worrying at that cursed necklace that had robbed her of everything, forever. She knew now that nobody would ever want her, that everybody would forever mock and despise her. As she sobbed, she thought back to poor Verrènes, who had died defending a foreign land, and finally realized she had been the one who had driven him to seek his own death. Suddenly, remorse—that remorse she had been keeping at bay, thinking only of her future happiness by the side of the man who had now forsaken her the same way she had forsaken her first love—hit her with heartrending strength.

Her tears then stopped with a last sob, and Ciadina stood up. She donned a dark shawl over her white dress, pulling it up to cover her head, and ran away.

She ran away from the village, where everybody talked about her disgrace and her guilt, ran away from the meadows, where the shepherds sang of her sad story, ran through dark woods and up black, jagged rocks—where nobody ever set foot—until she almost reached the Costabella peak.

There was a little, abandoned mountain hut up there, and that was where she sought shelter. Her father came to beg her to come back home, and then her brothers

179

did the same, but Ciadina stubbornly refused. Then, as time went by, nobody came to seek her anymore, and Ciadina was left alone on that rugged mountain, with her remorse as her only companion, her eyes always staring at the Fassa Valley.

It is said that she's still there, and that at times it is possible to see her, slim and white in her wedding gown, as she stands on a high rock and looks toward the Fedaja, where ill-fated Verrènes met a hero's death, thus finding at last that peace her rejection had robbed him of.

Historical notes to Ciadina

Here we find again the arch-enemy, the Trusani. Of course, this name cannot refer to the Romans, since the original story doesn't seem to date back to their remote age, but rather to a more recent time, probably around the Eleventh Century.

Therefore in my story, while using the classic term of 'Trusani' to refer to the invaders, I stressed the fact that 'Trusani' was actually a term used to indicate any enemy force, also suggesting that this time the attackers were the men of Roccapietore, trying to extend their control to the nearby valleys.

In the legend of Ciadina, the warriors facing them are the Arimanni, a term of Langobard origin indicating free men who had the right/duty to bear arms and had a particular bond with the lands entrusted to them, both a right of usufruct and a duty of defense.

The term, however, survived the fall of the Langobard kingdom and was later used to indicate groups of men who had freely chosen to be warriors, in exchange for a salary and the collective ownership of the lands assigned to them. Therefore these warriors were bound to a territory, often the same one they originated from, and weren't just mercenary troops.

There was then another problem to solve, which was the identity of the 'prince'—or, according to another version of the story, the *gran scior*, the 'great lord'—who usurped Verrènes place in Ciadina's fickle heart. The term 'prince' had to be ruled out because at that time it was not known in those valley, or at most used to refer to the prince-bishop of Bressanone, which is why I chose to identify him with one of the rulers of the Magnificent Fiemme Community, implying that he came from the village of Carrano, and thus implicitly setting my story around the year 1200.

The only element in this legend that harks back to the ancient Ladin myths is its mentioning the 'Latemar dwarves' as the makers of the magic necklace which, in fact, is the only 'dark' element in the whole story. As it happens in all the other Ladin fairy tales and legends mentioning them, here these dwarves are seen as expert miners and casters who worked in the mountain bowels.

Finally, let's spend a few words to explain the term *regolàn*: a 'regolàn' was something like a modern major, elected by the assembly of the *capifuochi* —which literally means heart-heads and indicated the household heads— and charged with the task of enforcing the laws (*regole*) and administrating the territory.

L' VARJOL

"Gio è vedù I louf co la bolp e I lieber
Gio medema è encantesimè
Gio è vedù I louf co la bolp sautè."
I saw the wolf, with the fox and the hare
I bespelled them myself
I saw the wolf, the fox and the hare sing together
From 'I bal de la stries' (the witches' dance), Ladin version
by F. Chiocchetti.

At the feet of Mount Faloria, among the hills through which the Bigontina Creek flowed, on the green meadows dotted here and there with white and dark gray by the small houses, three times already had been heard tolling the bell calling to an special *Faula*—a special assembly—all the members of the local Regola, the heads of the most powerful families who owned most of the surrounding land.

On the wide Plan de Ranpoiei, where in the past the primitive tribes used to meet to worship their gods, all the Regolieri of the 'family hearths' had convened already, grim and worried, and they were only waiting for the Master Ainardo, the Marigo, to arrive before getting the meeting underway. Almost all the inhabitants of the village, both men and women, were crowding around them, massing against the wooden fence that, together with some big boulders, kept them away from the actual meeting ground, anguish and despair transpiring from their faces as well. More astonishing than that massive participation, made even more noticeable by the late hour, was the elevated number of children present, all firmly held by their hand or carried in their arms by their parents. There were so many that it really seemed none of them had been left at home, and the steadfast refusal on their parents' part to let them go and play on the meadow, which was causing whining and tantrums, only made even more clear that the fear etched on every face was about the safety of those children, who embodied the future of the whole community.

And that fear had to be really strong, if all that people, in spite of their being bone tired after a day's work on the fields and in the house, had not only convened there to listen to what their leaders were going to say, but were also totally silent. In fact, only a few infants' cry could be heard from time to time on the great meadow, immediately silenced by the whispering voices of the parents, and barely a murmur rose from the crowd when the Marigo arrived, accompanied by two *laudatores* and escorted by a small group of *saltari*.

Master Ainardo was a middle aged man with gray hair and sporting a still dark beard; his keen blue eyes stood out on his deeply tanned face, and he was so tall and stout that the two *laudatores* appeared short and thin by comparison; even the *saltari* leader, Zane, the strong village blacksmith was dwarfed by his nearness.

The Marigo took his place, waited for everybody to settle down, silenced with a stern look the murmur now raising from the crowd, and finally, after clearing his throat, he began calling upon God and all the Saints, praying that they would assist him and his people in this difficult moment. Then he explained the reason for that special meeting.

"The reason why I summoned you all here is serious, very serious. Few among the village family-hearts ignore it because—alas—very few of them have been spared, but I'll briefly sum up the facts that have brought us here, before questioning both the victims and the witnesses to these crimes."

All eyes turned for a moment to a small group of villagers who kept a little aside from the others, their eyes lowered and grief deeply etched on their faces, and in the meanwhile Ainardo went on, "Since last spring, many children have disappeared in Fraìna. At first, we thought that those children, left momentarily unprotected, might have wandered away and got lost, or that they might have been attacked by a wolf, or fallen into some ravine, but since these disappearances kept happening, and always in similar circumstances, I soon asked Master Zane to look into it with his *saltari*."

The Marigo nodded to the blacksmith, who flushed and awkwardly stood up.

185

"I'm not very good with words," he immediately apologized. "I'm much better at handling my hammer and anvil! In any case… however…" He coughed nervously, dragged his feet on the ground and finally he laconically blurted out, "The thing is, those children didn't get lost in the Faloria woods, nor fell into some ravine or were attacked by some animal, because in those cases my men would have found traces of their passage. We combed the area inch by inch for months, but to no avail! They have disappeared into thin air. I'm sorry." Spreading his huge hands in a helpless gesture he sat down again with a sigh of relief.

His words didn't generate comments of any sort because everybody already knew the search had not given any result, and also because many of those present had actively taken part to it. Everybody was silent while, at a nod from the Marigo, one of the *laudatores* slowly read through the list of the disappeared children.

At this point, the assembly began to lose its initial composure, because the mothers' weeping, the fathers' angry cries, and relatives and friends' bitter comments punctuated that sad roll call, so much so that a couple of times Ainardo had to intervene and threaten to break off the meeting. After a while, however, as the list of names grew longer and longer, a deathly silence fell on the wide meadow, where all those present, who up to then had not fully grasped the import of what was happening, looked at each other, aghast, reading on their neighbor face, in his or her eyes, their own grief.

The sun was already painting the mountains with a veil of pink, forerunner of the imminent darkness, and the air had gotten quite cold, when finally that terrible roll call ended and the *laudatory* stepped back to his place, an almost apologetic expression on his lean, honest face for the pain he had aroused.

The Marigo waited for sobs, shouts and threats to die down to a grieving murmur, then he stood up again and called, "Let Verloj of Fernamusino, the first one to lose his son, step forward."

Immediately, a young man came forward, detaching himself from the small group of witnesses. He was tall and strong, with a charming face enlivened by vivid green eyes and framed by a short and curly beard, of the same chestnut brown of the hair covering his forehead and neck.

Murmurs of sympathy and encouragement followed his steps, for they all knew his story only too well. His very nickname, 'of Fernamusino', said that he came from a ruined family, whose properties had been in that village, wiped away some years previously, when the Boite River overflowed.

Verloj had grown up between the memory of a rich and powerful past on one side, and his present poverty on the other, and this exerted a bad influence on his character. Until he got married, in fact, he used to be one of the most regular customers of Master Massaio, the local innkeeper, and his hands were better used to handling dice and playing cards than a plow or a sickle, so much so that after his parents' death he squandered whatever little money he had left and started getting into debt. At this point, another man would probably have been ostracized by that hard-working, earnest community, but Verloj had always been very good at exploiting his innate congeniality, his sad story and his handsomeness to win young women over; therefore, it came to nobody's surprise when on a Lent

Sunday of six years ago, the parish priest announced from his pulpit the imminent wedding between Verloj and Biaquina, a few years older than he was, but only heir to her rich family's assets.

Of course, there had been many malicious comments, because Verloj had already played many other girls along only to disappoint them, and it was also whispered that he had broken a solemn engagement—with whom, however, nobody knew—in order to marry his heiress. Once he had married Biaquina and gone to live in her house, under her relatives' keen eyes, Verloj seemed to have sorted himself out, however, and the birth of a son, which all the family had been looking forward to, had apparently strengthened his marriage. Not even the child's disappearance had strained the relationship between the two, at least judging from the anxious tenderness with which Biaquina kept looking at her husband as he easily jumped over the fence and stepped into the circle of the Regolanes, stopping right in front of the Marigo.

"Tell us then, Verloj, how your son disappeared, and also put forward your suspicions, without any fear," Ainardo encouraged him. The young man seemed to have suddenly lost his usual glibness, however, and he merely shook his head; only after a few minutes of silence filled with anxiousness and anticipation, he finally started to speak, his voice low and uncertain.

"I have very little to say, Master Ainardo, and everybody already knows every single word of it. Anyhow, for what it may be worth, here is my story." He paused again, looking at his wife, then he went on: "Gordo had just turned five and he was a very lively child, tall and strong for his age, who would never stand still even for a minute. That morning his mother wasn't feeling well, so I decided to take him with me; together, we reached our *britte*, on the pastures by the Bigontina. I had some matters to discuss with Marieta, the *brittèra,* and while we were talking Gordo sneaked away unseen by either of us, absorbed as we were in our discussion. Suddenly, the sunlight filtering through the windows of the room darkened for a few moments, as if veiled by a great cloak, and immediately after that I heard my child scream in the courtyard. Just one cry, short and choked! That was the last time I heard my son's... my only son's voice." He broke off, bowing his head, while among the attentive, moved crowd Biaquina hid her face in her shawl. "I ran outside to look for him, and called him repeatedly, while the *brittèra* searched the house before running outside on the meadow... but to no avail! My Gordo had vanished, and there was no trace on the ground that could help us understand what had happened. We never saw him again, his mother and I..." As he got to the end of his tale, Verloj raised his hands to cover his face, and Ainardo had to clear his throat repeatedly before being able to go on with the questioning.

"So, on the day he vanished there was no forewarning, no strange occurrence that..."

Lowering his hands to expose his troubled face, the young man emphatically shook his head; the Merigo glanced at the scroll he held and went on, "Anything in the previous days? Nothing strange happened? No suspicion, run-in, quarrel of any kind?" Then, as Verloj kept shaking his head, Ainardo burst out, "Come on, Verloj! Here we come to blows over a boundary stone moved a few inches from where it should have been, or the disappearance of some old axe! It is not possible that you and your wife do not have some enemy who…"

"We have no enemies, *messere*! Of course, we had our fair share of disagreements and quarrels, but there is nobody who can hate us to the point of taking it out on our innocent child!" Biaquina cut in, since her husband kept shaking his head wordlessly; the woman had elbowed her way through the crowd to reach the palisade, her face already lined by age still wet with tears. Glancing at her with eyes full of gratitude, Verloj addressed the Marigo again, fighting to keep his voice steady. "It is as my wife says. We don't know of any enemies that could be so ruthless; moreover, the way our poor child disappeared doesn't suggest any human agency, but rather…" He broke off suddenly with a warding gesture against evil, while all around the villagers whispered in hushed tones the names of ancient terrors that not even their faith in the Holy Virgin and the Saints had been able to erase from their mind: the *Samblana*, *Ce de Lù*, the *Om de la Giazza*.

All the Merigo could do was to thank and dismiss Verloj, before calling forward Marieta, who confirmed what Verloj ha said, stopping every two words to reaffirm her innocence, of which nobody had ever doubted.

By then, the sun had already disappeared behind the peaks, the sky had darkened and the crispy air was turning chilly. After letting his eyes rest on each *regolàn*, to be sure they all agreed with his decision, Ainardo called the meeting to an end, adjourning it to the following day; the wide plateau slowly emptied of most of the crowd, as the people hurried toward the warmth of their houses, holding their children tightly by their hands or in their arms. A few people lingered on in small groups, to talk about the recent mysterious events and Verloj's account of his son's disappearance. Two people stood out among them, the lanky sexton, Giacomo Saonèr, who was always ready to regale everybody with pearls of his wisdom, whether they wanted to hear them or not, and the old, stooped herbalist, Martina, known as Betònega. Those two kept glaring at and contradicting each other, throwing their respective beliefs and superstitions in each other's face, as the onlookers incited them, while a young man who had arrived almost at the end of the meeting wandered from group to group, asking questions in an attempt to understand what had happened. Of middle height, but well-proportioned and agile, he had thick, reddish hair, amber colored eyes, and a handful of freckles on his chiseled, smart face. While the last lingerers finally dispersed, driven away by the chill of the night, the sexton's self-important exhortations, and Betònega's colorful curses, somebody finally recognized the young man.

"Look if that's not Ghedìn! He's back, after all these years!"

That exclamation was followed by others, and after briefly discussing the matter, all the lingerers agreed on the young man's identity, sharing comments, memories and conjectures while they got back to the village.

"He left six or seven years ago, I think, without saying a word to anybody," someone observed.

"Right. But then he did not have anybody to say goodbye to, since even the aunt who had raised him was dead, by then," Tita immediately cut in; he was the son of the local publican, and was prone to be late every time he could, because he was anything but eager to get back to work by his father's side.

"I seem to remember he was engaged, though!" panted the Betònega, as she caught up with them. Immediately, the sexton contradicted her, "Engaged, my foot! When one is penniless...."

"You are wrong," Bertol dal Pian, one of the wealthiest *regolànes* in Fraìna, intervened. "There was a girl... don't you remember? And she was as pretty as they come, too. She was that female painter who spent a couple of seasons here. She painted a few portraits and even started frescoing..."

By then, they had reached the village center, and as Bertol spoke all the eyes turned toward the Ciasa de ra Regole, on whose front wall it was possible to see even in the faint starlight the masterful sketch for a clearly unfinished painting.

They all stopped to gaze at it for a moment.

"She was to paint Zan de Rame and Donna Dindia's story" huffed Bertol, and the Betònega finished the sentence in his place, her lips tight with disapproval, "But she barely sketched the foundation of Miljera before packing up and disappearing!"

"Without saying a word to anybody, just like Ghedìn. Six years ago..." The regolan's voice trailed off as he got struck by a sudden thought. "Almost one year after Ghedìm left. What if those two facts are connected somehow?"

A chorus of objections silenced him. Standing there under the great, unfinished fresco, gesticulating excitedly, his friends pointed out to him that such girls were born wanderers, and also that the beautiful stranger had been courted by loads of young men much better off than poor Ghedìn, a penniless hunter with neither a family nor a plot of land to his name!"

"Verloj courted her too, before he got engaged with Biaquina!" Giacomo Saòner suddenly remembered. With that remark, the conversation shifted back to the couple's predicament and the danger looming over Fraìna, and Ghedìn and the beautiful painter were forgotten.

The Faula met again on the morrow, again surrounded by the local people, come to listen to the statements of other fathers whose children had disappeared; the fathers only were called as witnesses because all the children had always disappeared while entrusted to them, and not to their mothers. Master Ainardo almost immediately put the accent on that detail and tried to dig deeper in the matter as he questioned Menico dal Pian, wealthy Bertol's youngest son, who had lost his one-year old son while going to the mountain pastures.

"We were on our way to the pasture when suddenly..." The witness—a lanky young man with a long nose and thick, unkempt corn colored hair—stammered, then he felt his father's exasperated stare on himself and bluntly finished, "Puff... my son wasn't there anymore."

He fell silent, wiping sweat from his forehead as he looked first at his wife and Bertol, then at the Marigo, who looked rather perplexed at the sudden end of his statement. Before Ainardo could think of something to say, however, a strong voice shouted, "How were you carrying the child? At that age, he certainly could not be following you on his own!" Pushing his way through the crowd, Ghedìn came forward until he could lean against the palisade, his smart face red and alert.

Menico turned toward that new tormentor, then he swallowed a couple of times while his Adam's apple shifted up and down, and finally mumbled, wringing his hands, "Eeeeh, no. No. I was carrying him on my back..." He then turned back to the Marigo and with an urgent note in his voice asked, "May I go now?"

Ainardo had a moment's hesitation, because something didn't sound right to him in those awkward answers, and yet at the same time he did not want to make an enemy of powerful Bertol, but he was saved from that embarrassing situation by unruly Ghedìn, whose voice broke the silence again.

"On your back? How? He could certainly not hold on to your neck by himself!"

After vainly casting a beseeching glance to the Marigo, who motioned him to answer, the young man hung his head and answered, "In the basket. He was in the wicker basket."

"Weren't you afraid he might fall off it?" the hunter pressed him.

"He was fasten..." Dismayed, Menico suddenly broke off pressing a hand against his mouth, but that word had already escaped his lips and had been heard and understood; a murmur spread through the crowd while his wife, Stina, came forward, with arms akimbo and anger painted all over her face.

"Young man, it is already difficult to believe a child can vanish without a trace in the few minutes he's out of his parents' sight, but it is quite impossible that somebody, or something, can steal a child from his father's very shoulders, and from within a basket he's been fastened to!" Master Ainardo sternly reproached him, half standing from the rock he was sitting on, and at the same time he stole a grateful glance to Ghedìn, who was still leaning with his elbows on the palisade, his eyes on Menico.

Stina, whose face was already stained red as it always happened to her when she got angry, was joined by her frowning father-in-law, who kept lashing the air with the thick willow cane he used to prod his cattle, his eyes still boring into his son's.

From beet red, Menico turned green in the face.

"You won't have us believe that the child simply untied himself, or that somebody untied him without you realizing it!" the hunter kept pressing him, taking advantage of the Marigo's silence.

The unfortunate witness swallowed a couple more times, opened and closed his mouth, cast his eyes all around in search for a source of inspiration, and finally, not finding any, he ended up confessing it all, further lowering his already faint, hesitant voice.

"Eeehhh, no. No. I... I freed him because..." It was almost impossible to understand the rest of his sentence. "A... a girl. Yes... I freed the child... to help her find her bracelet... One moment, one single moment! I lowered myself into a crevasse to look for it, and... a shadow, a great black shadow covered the sun... and they weren't there anymore! The girl, my son, they were gone! Only the basket was still there..."

The crowd's murmur grew into an uproar, which wasn't loud enough to cover Stina's growl of rage and Bertol's roar, as he kicked down the fence and strode toward his son brandishing his stick, followed by his daughter-in-law who now held a thorny branch she had just torn off a bramble bush.

195

Menico did not wait for them. Ignoring both the Marigo calling after him because he wanted to question him further, and the *laudatores* shouting in an attempt to restore the peace, he darted for the woods, chased by his enraged relatives, while comments, shouts, exclamations, protests and jeers noisily mixed all over the wide meadow in the crisp air already heralding the oncoming dusk.

It was almost dark, and the mountains surrounding the Plan dei Rampoiei were now only gloomy, looming shadows, when the assembly finally found a semblance of calm and decorum again, but by then the hour was so late that Ainardo adjourned the meeting to the next day once more, and everybody headed back for the village, more upset and full of suspicions than before.

During the night, however, other men who had lost their children knocked at the Marigo's door and all of them secretly confessed that they had been distracted from looking after their child by a girl asking their help for several, different reasons: she had lost something precious, or she had fallen and hurt herself, or she had gotten lost. All the men added that they'd rather tell him all that in private, to avoid creating the same bad impression as poor Menico.

The description each of them gave of the stranger was similar enough to the others to persuade Master Ainardo that the woman was always the same one, and as he finally dismissed the last of his nighttime visitors, he scratched his head out of sheer bafflement.

While he settled down again in his warm bed above the *stube*, careful not to wake up his wife, the patient Namaria, for the umpteenth time, he tried to sum up all he knew about those mysterious disappearances, but soon enough facts, confessions and evil spirits got all mixed up in his mind and he fell asleep. Somebody loudly knocking at his door woke him up again: he choked back a curse as he opened his eyes, because it felt as if he had closed them barely a few minutes before, but then the faint light filtering through the shutters made him realize it had to be dawn already.

Shivering, he left the warmth of his bed, randomly grabbed something to wear and as he put his clothes on he went to open the door, barefooted and puffy faced from lack of sleep.

Ghedìn was there on the threshold, fresh and rested and all tidied up as if the sun had already been high in the sky, and was not just a barely seen gleam above the mountain peaks. And the young man was smiling placidly, as if it was normal to bother the village Marigo at such an ungodly hour.

"Good morning, Master Ainardo," the cheeky youngster greeted him, still smiling, as he pushed him a little too the side to get into the room; then, without waiting to be asked to, he sat down on a bench. "Certainly there was an interesting parade of people here tonight," Ghedìn affably went on, and before his unwilling guest could reply he added, "All men, all young, and all have lost a child... really, Menico's confession started a flood!"

"But... but... but..." The poor Marigo could not decide if to throw the young man out or to have him stay for the breakfast his wife was already putting together in the other room, at least judging from the clatter of plates coming from there.

"How do I know it, you mean?" Ghedìn easily guessed then he spread his arms wide, laughing, as he added, "It was an easy guess, and besides, after telling you

197

everything, many of them felt the need to pour their story into my ears as well, so here I am."

"Yes, here you are." Baffled, Ainardo scratched his head again, then he smoothed his mustache down as he repeated, "Here you are. To do... what, if I may ask?"

"To help you, of course! You see, I know all of Ampezo quite well..."

"We do as well! We live here."

"Yes, but you work on its pastures, gather your firewood in its pines and larches woods, at times you hunt on its bluffs, up on its mountains, but then you always get back to the valley, to your village and your homes. On the other hand, I lived on those crags and in those woods, I slept in caves, drank the Bigontina's icy water and roasted my prey in the open air, in a clearing by the mountain pasture."

"But you've been away for quite a few years!" Ainardo countered, cutting him off. A shadow crossed the young man's amber eyes, and he fell silent for a long minute, as if thinking back to the past; when he spoke again, his voice still sounded firm, but had lost most of its cheerfulness.

"That's true. I went away when..." He broke off, shaking his shoulders, before concluding, in a dryer tone "...when I realized there was nothing left for me to do here." He then shook his shoulders again, thus silencing any foreseeable question on Ainardo's part, and continued, "In any case, now I'm back, and I want to help you because..." He stopped again, and his expressive face betrayed some awkwardness and uncertainty, but he quickly found his composure again almost before the Marigo could realize something was wrong, and it was with his usual self-confidence that he finished, "I was in Gherdeina when I first heard about all these disappearances, and I hurried back here immediately. Even before arriving in Freìna, I collected rumors, suspicions and fears along the way, and I developed my own theory about it all." Refusing to explain his theory to his guest, he went on, "It's too early to speak about it, but... I bet it's been a long time since you last went to the Faloria woods, and to the Aga de Montedeserto spring, isn't it?"

More confused than ever by that sudden chance of subject, Ainardo merely nodded.

"I've been there right before I came here, instead, and I discovered the *sarella* had been removed... and quite a long time ago, judging from the state it's in!"

As he spoke, he took from his pouch a small object, corroded and damaged by the mold covering it, and showed it to Ainardo.

It was a *sarella*, the wooden tap applied to a spring to draw water.

While the two men were staring at it in silence, they were shaken out of their thoughts by a faint cry. Namarìa was on the threshold and was staring at them with fear in her eyes, a hand pressed against her mouth. The milk she had been going to offer the two men lay in a puddle around her feet, together with the broken pieces of the jug containing it.

"But then... the Evil Spirits of Faloria!" the woman exclaimed. "That's how they are evoked, how they come among us! It may be that the Sva..."

"Hush, wife! Do not even mention her, she could hear you!"

The woman immediately shut up; suppressing a shiver, she bent to pick up the broken jug and clean the floor, while the two men stared at her in silence.

It was only after Namarìa left the room that the hunter spoke gain, in hushed tones.

"Yes, this is witchcraft. I realized it even before I found the *sarella*, because there were too many clues pointing to that conclusion. Just think..." he went on, getting more excited as he spoke. "The dark shadow appearing every time a child disappears, the kidnappings always happening while the children were entrusted to their fathers..."

"And the mysterious girl who always appears to divert their attention from the child and then vanishes into thin air!" the Marigo vehemently interrupted him, but his words made Ghedìn shut up quite abruptly. When he spoke again his voice was quieter, almost devoid of any emotion.

"Yes, it may be. Or perhaps it was only a coincidence, and..."

"Come on! This so called 'coincidence' happened so many times it really looks more than a little suspicious!"

"Provided that it was always the same girl!"

"According to the description we got..."

"In any case, this is not important right now." The young man sprang to his feet and looked toward the door, suddenly anxious to cut that conversation short, but he held himself in check and hurriedly finished, "Allow me to keep investigating on the matter and you won't regret it."

"As far as I'm concerned, feel free to do whatever you deem necessary. I'll let it be known that nobody should be a hindrance to you, and that people should give you all the help you might need. However, could you tell me why are you so interested in all this, since you have no children?"

Ghedìn hesitated, one hand on the door already. Lowering his eyes to avoid the Marigo's gaze, he finally stammered, "I... I mean, I live here, or at least used to, and... in short, it is logical for me to feel involved, or even..." His words overlapped, his voice faltered, and a faint blush was coloring his face.

"Alright, alright," the Marigo cut him short, putting an end to those barely intelligible words with a curt gesture of his hand. "Let's just say you do this out of love for your birthplace."

"Well, yes, that's fine! So, with your permission I'm leaving now, to carry on my investigation."

"Good luck!"

After the hunter left, Master Ainardo stood in the middle of the room, thoughtfully shaking his head.

"There's something that doesn't add up there, *tos!*" he finally said. "You're way too clever and smart for me to put a spoke in your wheel, but I'll keep an eye on you!"

The sun was already riding high in the clear sky, shining mercilessly from that blue expanse where not even a hint of a cloud could be seen. Even the wild crags of Soràpis and those high walls of rock the valley inhabitants called *Macài de Marcòra* shone under its golden rays, that drew a shining symphony of colors from the thick forests of larches, red firs and pines covering their foothills, blending all the different nuances of green and brown of leaves and boughs.

Even if used to that glorious sight since he was a child, Ghedìn lingered for a moment to gaze at it, and the sight soothed his anxiety and sharpened his mind as it always did. Sitting on a rock, he wiped sweat from his forehead and took a sip of water from his canteen, and in doing so he realized it was almost empty.

"So, to sum things up..." he told himself. He refused to allow his mind to dwell on the awful suspicion that had made him leave the Gardena Valley to get back to Fraìna as soon as the rumors about those mysterious disappearances had spread far and wide, and concentrated instead on the present situation. Actually, he had been back at the village for quite a few days already; after collecting stories, rumors and suspicions from the shepherds, he had spent all that time wandering about on the *Macài*, because there was one single thing all accounts agreed upon: that dark shadow several people had seen when the children had disappeared always headed for those crags. *That's where I'll find you! Everybody can well deny it, but a trace was right there, for those who knew how to find it!*

Thus thinking, he removed his backpack from his shoulders and rummaged inside, carefully pulling out a small silver filigree cage of beautiful making. He stared admiringly at it for a few moments, because at that time and in that area nobody had ever seen any such thing. *It certainly isn't a flower that bloomed on the Soràpis! And I never saw anything like it, neither here nor in Gherdeina, where skillful artisans abound, nor in any other place I have been across the years. And yet, I found it abandoned under one of the Macài great rock walls, half buried in the foliage of a larch as if fallen from the grasp of somebody—or something—flying well above it.*" He took a moment to ponder on that last thought, then he stood and picked up his backpack, the cage and his canteen as he glanced toward the sun. It was very hot and his canteen was emptying quickly; almost without any conscious thought, instead of heading uphill he turned right, following the faint murmur of water coming from beyond a tangle of brambles and low bushes.

He was already anticipating the pleasant coolness of the creek running under their shade, and in fact the sunrays seemed to have lost much of their heat and power inside that green alcove, wet and shadowy. The clear water of the creek gushed out of a fissure in a white rock and swiftly flowed downstream on a narrow but deep bed of small round pebbles, so light in color that they almost shone. All around, the ground was soft and covered here and there with dark green beds of musk mixed with short plants and small, colored flowers.

As it spurted out of the rock, the water would split in thousands of small, invisible droplets forming a silver mist that fell back on the meadow, the flowers and the plants, as well as on Ghedìn himself as he bent over the spring and drank avidly from it, afterwards refreshing his face and hands with its cool water.

So absorbed he was in his thoughts that he did not notice the figure that was slowly appearing behind him, almost taking shape from the water droplets. It was a diaphanous, slim young woman, whose long, fair hair blended with the veils covering her, and she was staring in fascination at the small silver cage. It was only when the apparition touched its bars, making them tingle, that Ghedìn became aware of her presence.

He spun around, his hand already on his big hunting knife, then he froze as a smile chased away the aggressive grimace on his face.

"An *anguana*! You are an *anguana*, aren't you?"

"Yes, I am." The young woman stared at him through silver, shy eyes, uncertain. "And you are Ghedìn, son of Tònele. Your father was always kind to us, he never chased us away, and as a child you would at times leave a piece of bread or a fruit on a rock, saying, 'for the *anguane*'. We remember those who hurt us, but also those who are good to us! We aren't evil…"

"I never thought you were!" the young man exclaimed, then he gestured toward the little cage. "Do you like it?"

The *anguana*—who had grown more solid in the meanwhile, without losing any of her strange, non-human beauty—stared at it with a shine in her eyes. "Yes, I like it a lot, but…"

"Do you perceive anything evil in it? Is it a work of witchcraft?"

The creature ran her long fingers on the delicately wrought bars, the silver lace of the door, the small, elegant dome. "No. Whoever made it belongs to your race, hunter, but it is also made of tears, regrets and remorse. It is odd that such a beautiful object should be so full of grief! And yet it is."

Ghedìn, who had paid the utmost attention to her words, found in that simple statement a proof that his painful suspicions were well founded, and averted his gaze. Then, almost to create a diversion, he sat on the bed of musk, pulled out of his backpack a piece of cheese, some bread and a fruit, divided everything in two, and pushed one half toward the *anguana*.

"Share my meal, and don't leave yet, if you can! Many children have disappeared from Fraìna, my village…"

The *anguana* stared at him without showing in any way that she understood what he was speaking about, and probably it was just so, because for many years now men had been walking on a different road from the original inhabitants of the woods and the waters of the Anpezo. Conscious of this, Ghedìn rephrased his question.

"There is a great, black shadow that often crosses the sky, maybe heading for the *Macài,* and its flying past always means grief for my people..."

"The *Varjol!*" immediately exclaimed the *anguana,* happily capping her slim hands, glad she could be of help to somebody who had befriended her.

"A vulture?"

"Or an eagle, maybe, I don't know. Or it may be neither, but a Creature who can take their shape, but is much bigger and faster than either of them. It flies above us like a black cloud driven by the wind, and vengeance, remorse and shame whirl around its wings. Is this damned Being what you are looking for?"

Ghedìn bowed his head and nodded sadly. "Yes," he whispered, after a long moment, crushing in his fist the handful of musk he had pulled from the ground.

The *anguana* stared at him with big, compassionate eyes in which thousands of droplets of spring water seemed to shine.

"Then you have to climb the *Macài,* up high, until you reach those reddish rocks up there. I can show you the way, if you wish, but beware... there is danger, and cruelty, there."

"Show me."

A determined look on his face, the young man stood up and put his few belongings back into his backpack.

The way to the red rocks—which rose among stony terraces and scree beds, nestled on a bare cliff whipped by icy winds—was long and hard, but Ghedìn kept climbing without taking any break, without hesitation, up the sheer scree slopes and rock shelves, taking advantage of any fissure, any handhold, to get higher and higher. The sun was almost setting, and his hands were bleeding, when he finally managed to pull himself up on a ridge, right behind those red rocks, and he had barely caught his breath when he heard, loud and sweet, a chirping sound, as if many little birds nestled among those crags.

It's not possible, they could never survive up here among the rocks, it's far too cold for them! he told himself, as he headed for the rocks, and felt a vague fear grow inside. A moment later, however, he froze with amazement. Scores of small silver cages like the one he had found hung from the rocks, many of them holding inside small birds that twittered sadly. He wanted to get nearer to them, but right then the already faint sunlight darkened even more when a great, black shadow drew near, and Ghedìn barely had the time to hide behind a rock spur before a big black bird that looked like a huge vulture and held in his claws an unconscious child, swooped down among the rocks, lying down his little, motionless prey on the ground.

The huge bird stared at it for a few moments, its great wings spread wide as it turned its head about, then something in it began to change: a veil of darkness hid its figure, and within that dark halo the wings fluttered like hair in a breeze, whirling around the figure as it grew thinner, straightened and changed. Now a young woman stood among the boulders of the Macài, delicate and slim, wrapped in a black cloak that hid her whole body, her pale face framed by very long, black hair frozen in an expression of horror and shame. Stiffly, with some difficulty, she bent over the child who had woken up and was now crying, and her light, melodious voice rose in a slow, bewitching lullaby. Soothed by that sound, the child calmed down and closed his eyes again, but as the young woman's song got stronger and louder, another dark vortex enveloped both of them. When it dissipated, the horrible bird of prey stood again where the girl had been, a small bird trapped in its claws. It placed the little bird inside one of the small cages, closed its door with a flap of its wings, and then took flight again, a dark, nightmarish shadow ready to mete more terror and grief.

Hidden behind the rocks, Ghedìn had witnessed the whole scene, falling on his knees and hiding his face in his hands, as if to deny the truth of what he had just seen. He struggled to his feet, as tears rose to sting his eyes and his heart hammered in his chest, while pain, anger and denial fought for predominance inside him: his worst suspicions had just been proved true. Neither the seven years that had gone by nor the appalling way that beautiful face had changed had been enough to prevent him from recognizing in that fiendish being the female painter he had silently and passionately loved, even if with no hope of being loved in return, because she had given her love to another man. His devotion, his love had been for nothing, just like his newfound talent as a painter that should have brought them closer, since her art meant everything to her. Verloj was her love, Verloj who had charmed her with his sweet words, his handsomeness, his careless cheerfulness... the same Verloj who had then betrayed her to marry the wealthy Biaquina, the same Verloj whose son had been the first to be kidnapped.

A vague suspicion, a sort of awful foreboding, had been growing in him since he had first heard the news, taking away his peace of mind to the point he had decided to come back in the hope of being able to prove himself to be wrong.

But he now knew that the woman he had adored and still loved with all his heart was... what? Or rather, what had she changed into?

As he stood still by the rocks, his fists clenched, his heart full of pain and anger, Ghedìn tried to reason things through, but only a single thought managed to emerge from the maelstrom of despair raging in his brain: he would save her, a resolution he clung to in order to regain his usual clarity of thought. He could not lose heart, not now, not while *his* painter needed his help; no, he had instead to find a way to give her that so much needed help!

He slowly pushed fear, horror and dismay back, locking them in a corner of his mind, then he drew a deep breath, sat on a rock—ignoring the biting cold that intensified as the night fell—and finally managed to sum up what he knew and what he had figured so far.

She wanted to get back at Verloj, this is clear, he pondered. *Since she could not do it by herself, she removed the sarella from the spring to evoke the evil Spirits and get their help, and they answered her plea, giving her feathers and claws to kidnap her unfaithful lover's son. But what then?* His lips pressed in a tight line, he shook his head, unsure, perhaps rejecting the idea that the girl could have grown so cruel as to exact vengeance even on people who had never hurt her. *I don't' know what happened then,* he finally concluded, *but I'll have her tell me.*

He stood up and scanned the surrounding area— carefully avoiding to look at the silver cages, where now a score of little birds was sound asleep, the little head hidden under one wing—until he found a large crevasse, almost a cave, which opened a few yards below the stone ledge. Carefully, he climbed down and surveyed it in the faint starlight before curling up inside, wrapping himself in the few spare clothes he had in his backpack.

There he spent a dreadful night, made even worse by the freezing cold and his tormented thoughts. He slept little and poorly, but his stubborn determination to learn what had happened to the woman he loved, to save her and take her away from that place, to make amends for the wrong she had done, won over his instincts, which were telling him to run away from that freezing cold and the ordeal he was going to face the next day, when the grim bird of prey would come back.

The terrible night was finally over, and with the first light the hunter crawled out of his shelter, stretching and rubbing his hands, numb with cold, his red hair disheveled and his freckles standing out more than ever on his pale face. Stubbornly, he climbed back on the ledge, hid behind the same rock again, and waited.

He did not have to wait long; the sun had just dawned over the Fedaia, chasing away both the clouds and the freezing cold with its rays, when the great, black bird of prey showed up on the horizon, flying around the *Macài* to finally land there. Horrified, Ghedìn saw it lower gently another child to the ground, but he forced himself to stay hidden and quiet till the end of the grim rite.

As soon as the bird took its human form again and locked its prey—fast asleep through the effects of the magic song—into one of the cages, the young man came out of his hiding place.

"Don't go!" he cried. At the sound of his voice, the dark smoke already enveloping the girl's body thinned until it disappeared altogether. "I know you, even if you never told me your name... don't you remember me?"

"Ghedìn," she whispered wearily, as she flopped down on a boulder. "Yes, I remember you! It was long ago, in another world." All of a sudden, a hint of a smile curved her pale lips on the wake of those memories. "I taught you to paint, and you were good, very good, but then..."

"But then... what? What happened to you? You were good-hearted, generous, totally committed to your work, and we all loved you! What have you done?"

"I loved, Ghedìn. I loved and was deceived and betrayed." She suddenly jumped on her feet, quivering with anger, her dark eyes full of fire. "Do you know what it means to love somebody with all your heart, passionately, and to be let down? What..."

"Yes, I do, because I've always loved you, without any hope of being loved back," the hunter quietly replied. Speechless, the painter lowered her burning gaze. When she looked up again, a new light—almost of hope—shone in her eyes. In the meanwhile, Ghedìn went on: "I love you so much that I ran away when you got engaged with Verloj, and now I'm back because some instinct told me that you were somehow involved in these children's disappearance, that you were in danger. I still love you, I love you so much that I'm ready to do anything I can to save you, to turn you back into the woman you once were. I ask nothing in return,

I do not expect you to return my feelings, I just want to give you back your life and happiness."

At those words, two tears ran down the girl's pale cheeks, but she drew back all the same, avoiding Ghedìn's extended hand and wrapping her dark cloak more tightly around herself. "You love me... a slave of the *Svalazza*!"

Upon hearing that much feared name, a shudder ran through the young man. However, he pressed on: "Whatever may be the curse holding you prisoner, I'll defeat it, because my love is greater than any sorcery, even greater than the queen of the *stries*' power."

The girl stared at him for a long time, while her pale face slowly found its rosiness again, her eyes lost their wild, desperate look, and her long, raven-black, disheveled hair framed her face in a sea of soft, dark waves.

"I believe you," she finally sighed. "Oh, why didn't I listen to you, instead of..." She did not pronounce that name, but shook her head and hesitantly went on: "You are right! I appealed to the *Svalazza* to obtain my revenge, but in so doing I fell in her power and how I have to obey her cruel orders, kidnapping those children and changing them into birds, just like I did with the son of the one who betrayed me. I was free to tell my story only to somebody who still loved me, in spite of what I have become, and..." She stopped, hesitating for a long while. Not even finding the nerve to look at Ghedìn, who was attentively listening to her, she finally added in a whisper: "... and to show him how to break the spell."

"I can free you, then! So, tell me: I'm here, I love you as I always did, and if I could hope that you would return my love, I'd be happy to make you my bride!"

For a moment, a long forgotten joy gleamed in the painter's eyes. "It will be hard, very hard, for you to overcome the oncoming trials," she warned, however. "You already overcame the first one right now, though, asking me to marry you. Now you should get back to Fraìna and complete the fresco I left unfinished."

"I will. What else?"

"Then you'll have to come back here and face the last, more difficult trial. If you'll make it, I'll be free, the village won't be haunted anymore by the grim vulture and the children will be returned to their human shape and to their homes, because the strength of your love will have won over the *Svalazza* and her wickedness."

"Fear not, and wait for me. I'll complete the fresco and come back to you right away."

Almost smiling, the girl nodded, but again she prevented him from getting near and turned away from him, hidden by her cloak. Burning with hope and love, Ghedìn was already hurrying down the slope when she added, in a shy, tremulous whisper: "Filadressa... this was once my name. It is all I can give you now, to support you in your endeavor."

"Filadressa! This name will be my talisman. Invoking it, I will be able to defeat the *Svalazza*'s evil spells and to free you."

For the second time in a span of just a few days, Master Ainardo was suddenly pulled out of his peaceful sleep before dawn by somebody furiously banging against his door, and for the second time the sight that offered itself to his drowsy eyes was that of a thoroughly drenched, dirty and disheveled Ghedìn, his red hair all ruffled and a fanatic light shining in his eyes.

"Marigo!" he shouted, preventing the poor man from uttering even a simple invitation to come in, since it was pouring rain outside. "I need your permission to complete the fresco at the *Ciasa de ra Regoles*, but I have to do it right away, before the weather takes a turn for the worst! And I also need the necessary tools... brushes, and..."

"*Cet, tos*! And step inside before you say anything else, because the weather has already taken a turn for the worst, at least as far as I'm concerned!" The young man came in, and while he was trying to dry himself as best as he could, the Marigo went on, fuming, "And now explain yourself! You left four days ago, vowing you would look for the missing children, and now you come back asking for brushes and paint for a fresco nobody was ever able to complete? Holy cow! Make up your mind once for all. What are you, *'n ciaciador, n' comandador o n' moler?*"

The young man suddenly laughed and shook his head, spraying raindrops everywhere.

"I'm none of those things, or maybe all three of them. Or, perhaps, I'm just a desperate man who suddenly found hope again, a man who was lost and has found himself again, a..."

"I see. You're in love. Uhm."

Sitting astride a stool, Master Ainardo took some time to think things through. Born and bred in Fraìna, four times serving as its Marigo, he boasted of knowing everything about his village. Seven years before, when that foreign painter had come to live at the village, Ghedìn—who lived in a small cabin above the Pocòl—had started to come to the village more and more often, and had even begun to take painting lessons from the girl, only to suddenly disappear once the girl's engagement with Verloj became common knowledge. That engagement had later been broken by Verloj, the painter had left, and soon after that the children had started to disappear.

Ainardo felt a shiver run down his back as all those facts clicked into place in his head, creating a clear picture there.

"Ghedìn, just tell me if… no, don't say anything." Ainardo pondered on the young man's last, passionate and rambling words, then he made up his mind. "Don't say anything," he repeated. "You have my permission, and I'll let you have all the things you need to finish the fresco. I trust you, your courage and your honesty. Just remember that, besides your personal feelings, there are dozens of families grieving the loss of their children."

"They will have them back."

A grave look on his face, the hunter offered his wide, strong hand to Ainardo, who vigorously shook it.

Summer had come and gone, so hot and dry that the harvest had been at risk until the first autumn rain had come to wash all fears away. Ghedìn had worked every single day, not allowing himself to rest even for a moment, and he managed to complete the fresco before it started raining again.

In coming back from the fields or the pastures, the villagers often stopped to admire the brilliant colors of the fresco, the masterfully drawn figures, the easily recognizable mountains sketched in the background. There was a subtle difference between the young man's hand and his teacher's, who had employed more delicate colors and paid more attention to the faces and the clothes of the portrayed figures than to the surrounding landscape. The hunter's hand was less refined and stronger, but as a whole the two styles blended with each other, and everybody concurred in saying that it would have been difficult to do a better job.

The author, however, was not there to accept compliments and thanks from the villagers: the last brush stroke had not yet dried when Ghedìn had disappeared in the Faloria woods, heading for the *Macài*.

The day was drawing to a close when he got there, welcomed by the little prisoners' chirping, and he immediately called the painter.

"Filadressa! Filadressa!" As soon as the young woman appeared from behind some rocks, her anxious face framed by the long, dark hair that, together with the cloak, totally hid her figure, Ghedìn joyously exclaimed, "I've finished it, and everybody says it is beautiful! The fresco, I mean! The people say my style reflects my teacher's." He laughed, and tried to take the girl's hand in his own, but in spite of the joy that had fleetingly appeared in her eyes, she still drew back.

"Wait! As you know, there is one more trial, the hardest."

"I'm not afraid of it. I fear nothing, now that I've found you again. Tell me. Whatever it is, I'll overcome it."

"Look, then!" With those words, the girl let the cloak fall to the ground.

The young man cried out in horror and disbelief: Filadressa's small, nimble hands had turned into monstrous birdlike claws.

"This is the *Svalazza*'s brand," she whispered in a low, trembling voice. "I... I have changed, you know I have. I'm what I once was, and I feel horrified and remorseful at what I did, but my hands... my hands..." Her voice broke and she burst into tears.

Feeling stunned and crushed, Ghedìn kept staring at her, his eyes moving from those awful claws to the beautiful, tearful face. Inside him, disgust, fear and anguish fought against compassion and love. The he took a step toward the girl.

"It doesn't matter," he resolutely assured her. "A sort of illness, that's what it is. I'll always think you were ill through no fault of yours, and that it left its mark on you. You will keep those... things... covered, and your voice and face are so beautiful everybody will envy me. If... if you agree to marry me, that is."

Filadressa raised her face, where the tears had now given way to hope.

"Do you still want me, then, in spite of this?" she asked, hiding her claws under the cloak she had put on again.

"I love you," the young man answered, simply. At that, Filadressa broke into a sweet, delighted laugh.

"Look at me again, then!" she exclaimed, as she lifted her arms. The hunter could not believe to his eyes when he saw those small hands he remembered so well instead of the ugly claws that had replaced them. A moment later, Filadressa threw herself into his arms.

"I could be freed forever from the *Svalazza*'s enchantment only if a man had loved me to the point of wanting to have my by his side for life, my awful deformity notwithstanding. Your love and your generosity have saved me!" she explained, as she held to him, returning his kisses. "And now, my love, let me wear the Varjol's feathers one last time," she added a few minutes later, disentangling from his arms and turning toward the little cages with a sweet, awkward smile. "Now these little ones, that the *Svalazza* forced me to take from their families and imprison in the cages she made mi build, will get back to their loved ones, free as well, thanks to you."

Then she took once more the shape of the bird of prey and opened the cages. Two by two, three by three, she quickly flew the little ones back to their village. As soon as it was lowered to the ground, each little bird immediately turned again into a child who had no memory of what had happened to him and happily ran toward home, calling out to his mother and father.

It was with the utmost joy and delight that the whole village poured out into the narrow lanes to gather in the small square, in front of the *Ciasa de ra Regolas*; Giacomo Saòner started ringing the bells for all he was worth, and the Betònega rushed out of her home muttering something about the virtues of her potions, while *laudatores* and *saltares* vainly tried to bring back some order, and the parents, grandparents and siblings of the missing children hugged them, almost smothering them with kisses, as they cried with joy and emotion.

Verloj was there too, with Biaquina, and Menico as well, with his father and wife by his side, and all the other young fathers who had allowed Filadressa to distract them... but in the happiness of the moment, everything seemed to be forgotten, and forgiven.

So it seemed... but in fact it was neither forgotten nor forgiven.

217

When a smiling Ghedìn walked into the square with Filadressa at his side, at first their appearance just caused a few curious stares, but in a short while somebody started murmuring and pointing at the girl. Verloj was the first to recognize her; he immediately realized what had happened, and what his betrayal had unleashed, and he wisely persuaded his wife to get back home with their son in her arms. Menico, however, had nothing to fear or to reproach himself with, and he immediately pointed his finger at the painter.

"There she is! There can be no mistake... she's the one looking for her bracelet, the one who distracted me when..." He broke off and hugged his child, while his wife and father turned toward the girl, who fearfully drew closer to Ghedìn.

Half of their own will, and half pushed forward by their wives, Firmino and Maso—two of the young men Filadressa had charmed in order to kidnap their children—stepped out of the crowd and stood staring at her, uncertainly scratching their head.

Before they could say a word, however, a menacing murmur rose from the crowd, growing in volume as the people gathered around the hunter and the girl, all eyes staring at them full of animosity. A few angry shouts rose from the crowd; Firmino and Maso hesitated, looked at Menico, who kept nodding his head, and finally mumbled uncertainly, "Yes. Maybe. There's some resemblance." Immediately the hubbub turned into screams full of hate.

Right then Master Ainardo—who had been sent for by a *laudator* at his wits end—stepped forward.

"Enough! Be quiet and still, all of you!" he shouted. Immediately, everybody turned to him with explanations and accusations.

"She's the one who tried to kidnap our children!"

"The one who kidnapped them, you mean! As for the fact that..."

"She's guilty, and she must pay! Together with him, who's siding with her..."

"Monsters"

"Scum!"

"Enough, I said! And let me through, for goodness sake, so that I can have a look at those supposed monsters!"

"Menico! Menico recognized the girl, and after him Maso and Firmino also said that..." somebody shouted, among the crowd, and other malevolent, hate filled voices followed that cry.

"Witch!"

"She must burn!"

By then, however, the Marigo had threaded his way through the crowd and was now standing in front of the accused pair, staring at them. Unable to meet his eyes, Filadressa hid her face against Ghedìn's shoulder, while the young man stood tall, defiantly meeting all those accusing eyes.

On its part, the crowd quieted down a little, most of all because Zane had appeared at the Marigo's back, together with a group of saltari. Then Ainardo suddenly burst out laughing.

"You stupid dupes!" he exclaimed, turning toward the crowd. "So this girl should be the witch? She's my cousin's daughter, just arrived from Gherdeina to look for her fiancé!" And he nodded his chin toward a dumbfounded

Ghedìn, before sternly addressing to him. "And you, young rascal, you aren't thinking of leaving her, are you? Beware, should I find out that you came back here in order to avoid keeping faith to your vows…"

"No, no!" Ghedìn interrupted him, laughing, because he had understood Ainardo's ploy. "On the contrary, I'm ready to marry her even now, in front of everyone, or tomorrow in front of the parish priest, if he will consent to give us his blessing."

"Uh, don't rush things, now! First, we must see if the girl will have you."

Pale and trembling still, but with a light of hope in her eyes, Filadressa looked at her lover and silently put her small hand into his.

A thick silence fell on the square, as the villagers looked uncertainly at each other, not knowing what to think anymore.

"I told you it was just a resemblance…" Maso muttered.

"And I said I wasn't sure," Firmino added, then both backed away through the crowd, turned their back to the scene and walked away, while Menico's grim-faced wife and father pounced on the unhappy young man.

"Well, well," approved Ainardo, with a good natured smile. "Between your being both painters, and Ghedìn's job as a *saltero* you won't have any problem in supporting yourselves and any children that will come. Yes, as of now you are enlisted, *tos,* and do not try to say a single word about it!" Then he turned toward his house and shouted: "Wife! My cousin is going to get married: let's bring out a barrel of wine, so that everybody can drink to the bride and groom!"

The Marigo's words, and the barrel Namarìa hurriedly provided, together with some loaves of bread, a few cheese wheels and some fat sausages, melted the villagers' suspicions like snow under the sun, and soon peace and cheerfulness were restored, while cheers and good wishes replaced threats and curses, the children took to running all over the place and on everybody's feet, their mothers shouted themselves hoarse trying to contain them, the fathers drank wine and talked about the harvest, the weather, the flocks, and the young men gawked at the girls of marriageable age who, on their part, flirted with them while affecting false modesty.

Everything was back to normal in Fraìna.

Historical Notes to "The Varjol"

Since the valley of Cortina—where this story takes place—had no permanent settlements until the Middle Ages, this legend must be set around that time, probably not before the seventh century, when some colonies of Langobardic origin were established in Cadore and in Ampezzano.

In the figure of Filadressa, however, it is still possible to find some of the physical traits belonging to the *Bregostane* of old, now seen only as evil witches, and her ability to shapeshift can be linked to the primitive myth of the vulture.

Other elements, however, suggest that at the time of this legend the figure of the *regolàn* already existed, and that it is therefore possible to set the time of the story after 1235 A.D., when the First Statute of Cadore was approved by Count Biaquino da Camino, and the *Regola* became a commonly accepted government system.

This is why I could introduce in my tale some of its elements, such as the Marigo, the *Laudatores* and the *Saltares*.

Elected by the Cadore General Counsel—on a nomination by his outgoing predecessor—the Marigo's duties included managing the Regola estate and keeping watch on the woods, collecting revenues and taxes, paying all expenses, and administering justice, as well as applying the sentence according to the provisions of the *Laudi*. In his job he was supported and controlled by two Laudatores, and helped by foresters and by the saltares, who were then the equivalent of the local police.

The Screaming Castle

"Through perjury you had it built
Through my blood its stones you knit..."

PART ONE: WILENDA

Ruthgard von Stättenecke slowly set down on the table the parchment he was reading and lowered his head to hide his emotions from his men.

For more than twenty years he had been a mercenary captain, renowned not only because of his bravery, but also because of his strong personality and his inflexible strictness in commanding his mercenary company. Therefore, now he could not allow his lieutenants to see the sudden tear that had risen to veil his eyes as he read the formal document through which the Grand Duke Lodovico—whom he had served under for the last five years—had come to terms with the Prince-Bishop of Bressanone, obtaining from him that after more than thirty years the title, lands, riches and honor the Stätteneckes had lost to the hate of their cousins, the Lorfeils, would be returned to them.

Ruthgard would never forget the day when betrayal had put his castle in the hands of his hated cousins, the following headlong flight with his wounded father, and the wide cave on the high Mount Balest, far above the castle, where they had sought shelter together with a handful of trusted servants, and where his father had died in his arms... but not before being forced to helplessly look on the total destruction of his castle and the massacre of his people, not sheltered anymore by those high stone walls.

Now a few fire blackened ruins were all that was left of Stättenecke, but to Ruthgard that heap of rubble still was his home, the emblem of his House, and he vowed to himself that his castle would be rebuilt, finer and more beautiful than before, but most of all that it would be built in such a way that nobody was going to be able to conquer or destroy it ever again. This was the oath he had taken as a child, staring at his father's body, and this was the only revenge he could take on the hated Lorfeils, long disgraced and driven away from the country.

Six months later—after discharging part of his company and taking his leave from the Grand Duke and the Princes Wulfstaffen, his mother's relatives who had taken him in and raised him—he came back to his regained feud of Stättenecke, and he immediately sent for builders and carpenters, offering them all the men, raw materials and money they needed to make his castle impregnable and sturdier than the rocks themselves on which it was going to be rebuilt.

In spite of all the resources and the efforts freely spent on the endeavor, however, the work went on at a slow pace and the foundations—most of all those of the battlements main tower—sank twice into the ground.

"My lord Count, you will spare both time and money if you will agree to move the site for your castle a little more downslope! It is clear that the fire..." the master mason began, after the walls collapsed for the second time, but just one glance to Ruthgard's hard face was more than enough to make the good man shut up and hasten to order his men to remove the rubble.

No, the castle had to be rebuilt right there, where the Stätteneckes' mansion had always been, and the Count turned a deaf ear to the artisans' excuses, as well as to the malevolent whispers already spreading throughout the village, according to which the ruins had been cursed by the defeated Lorfeils' matriarch, the same, terrible woman who had been the driving force behind the tragic, fateful fight between the two Houses.

"Everybody was afraid of the Baroness around here, and not just because of her bad temper," helpfully told him the innkeeper of the *Brown Boar,* the inn where Ruthgard had temporarily taken his lodgings, as he set down on the table a mug of beer. Then he went on, in a confidential whisper, "They said she was a *bregostana...*"

The Count merely shook his shoulders.

"That's just an old superstition," he replied, curtly, but the innkeeper insisted, while drying his hands on his apron and warily glancing at the front door, as if he feared to see the Baroness on the threshold, even if the woman had been dead for years.

"It may well be as you say, my lord. I'm just an ignorant innkeeper, but it is common knowledge in the village that the *bregostane* could destroy a poor man's harvest through hail or drought, make women and cattle barren, split the ground under a house, cause illness..."

"Enough."

The Count sent the innkeeper away with a brusque gesture, but a feverish light was burning now in his eyes. As he went to bed, he kept pondering on the innkeeper's words. He knew about the *bregostane*, women that—according to local rumors—still practiced old, bloody rites and had magic powers; he even knew that the last *bregostana*, an old woman who had escaped the persecution that had officially put an end to those cruel rites, still hid in a cave on the peak of Mount Balest. He was not surprised that the Lorfeils' matriarch might have been one of their number, but he could not believe that merciless woman's hate and power could have survived her death. And yet, the seed of doubt had taken root in his mind, and it kept growing while the construction work resumed at Stättenecke.

A month later, the newly laid foundations sank again, and after a heated argument the master mason left, taking all his men with him.

It was pouring rain, with a cover of lead grey clouds hiding the mountain peaks and looming over the ruins—old and new—of the castle; oblivious to the rain drenching him, the Count was sitting on those boulders, looking around and remembering, when an idea slowly took form in his mind, so absurd that at first it seemed crazy and blasphemous even to his own eyes. He pondered on the matter for a long time, looking for alternative solutions and even trying to persuade himself to move his castle elsewhere, but with his mind's eye he could still see smoke and flames rising from the torn down walls, he still heard the screams of the wounded and his enemies' victorious cries, while his father was dying in his arms and he was swearing that Stättenecke would be rebuilt where it had always been.

The rain ran through his dark hair, slid down his strong neck, drenched his dark cloak, and collected at his feet to run away in a thousand small rivulets. Nearby, another foundation boulder sank into the wet ground with a slight sucking noise.

Cursing, Ruthgard sprang to his feet, looked once more at those disheartening ruins, then he turned away from them, resolutely striding toward the peak of Mount Balest and the hideout of the last *bregostana*.

He came back four days later, grim and thoughtful. He immediately charged another master mason with the rebuilding, but this new attempted failed as well, as if the ground were swallowing during the night the stones erected during the day.

Then, at the third try, the ground suddenly opened under the builders' feet and swallowed the part of the foundations they were working at, together with one of the men. The Count called a halt to the work and dismissed all the workers.

They saw him leave that very night, wrapped in his dark cloak, his face hard, his eyes haunted. Berta, an old servant who had been with him for many years, was the only one who dared to ask him where he was going all alone, at night, while the wind heaped great, dark clouds over the mountains and the smell of rain was already in the air.

For a moment, it seemed the Count wasn't going to answer, then he reined in his horse.

"I must solve this problem!" he exclaimed, angrily pointing at the surrounding ruins. "And I know somebody who..." He broke off and lowered his eyes, then he resumed, more slowly, "Yes... I know another master mason, a foreigner, who has already found a solution to such a situation. I'll bring him here." He drew a deep breath and concluded, in a more confident tone, "Tell the master mason the work will resume in a few days."

And he spurred his horse.

Obedient, the old woman spread the news through the village, where everybody took to waiting, full of curiosity, the lord's return with the foreign builder. It was however on a dark new moon night, made even darker by the ominous clouds shrouding the sky, that Ruthgard finally came back to Stättenecke, riding self-assuredly along the old path of Troi Paian, which had always connected the Isarco Valley with the mines of Fusil and ran by the ruins. An old, ragged woman hobbled behind him; her long grey hair was a tangled mass and she carried at her belt a curved knife, under her black shawl.

Nobody saw them go by, and nobody saw them the following morning either, because the castle ruins offered them both a refuge and a hiding place, but for two nights in a row the village people saw lurid greenish flames dance all around the walls perimeter.

On the third night, however, a patron of the *Brown Boar*, who was trying to sober up in the cool night air, by the road, suddenly heard a galloping horse getting near, then he saw the Count riding at break-neck speed through the village on his bay horse, wrapped in his cloak, a wild look on his face.

So upset he was by his lord's expression that he barely managed to avoid the horse's thundering hooves, rolling away from the road and into the gutter. The following morning he hastened to tell what had happened to everybody he met, but nobody truly believed him because he was a well-known drunkard.

That night, however, while the oblivious villagers slept in the safety of their houses, away from the winter cold that seemed intentioned to last forever, something happened among the burned out old ruins, among the new building stones half buried in the mud. That night, the unnatural green flame rose higher than ever toward the sky, the only, ghostly light shining on the mountains and the valley because of the moonless night and of the clouds obscuring even the faint starlight.

Hisses, moans and weeping—like a thousand lost souls crying together—rose through the darkness, followed by the old woman's voice, screaming words in an unknown tongue. A strong gust of wind answered those sounds, bringing in more black, rain-laden clouds instead of dispersing the existing cloud cover.

A faint weeping then echoed, sudden, tremulous and uncertain, to be immediately followed by a dreadful scream, filled with terror and hate. Then there was only silence, even the howling wind quieted down until it fell altogether, and the first, fat drops of rain descended like tears on the ruins of Stättenecke.

A few of the villagers might have heard something, and the greenish light of the flames might have filtered through some shutters, but the oncoming dawn washed away any disturbing memory: after many days, rain and wind were now but a memory, and the sun was shining on Stättenecke, with the birds flying around the amassed building stones... and the foundations, which were going to be the main strength of the castle, appeared to have already been laid, deep, safe and solid.

Perplexed, the villagers looked inquiringly at each other, not daring to openly voice their questions because they were now beginning to fear the Count the same way they used to fear his enemies in the past; the old servant made it her business of reminding everybody of her master's words, which generated theories and discussions... whatever the means used by Ruthgard, however, the end result was that the builders were summoned again and, among the general disbelief, the castle was soon rebuilt, big, powerful and magnificent.

The following years went by peacefully and prosperously: thanks to the Grand Duke's support and the Princes Wulstaffen's help, the Count of Stättenecke was able to form alliances that made the county a safer place, with the consequence that the village grew larger and richer, and the merchants took to visiting it again, bringing in more prosperity.

"However he managed to rebuild his castle, it is undeniable that the Count's return has been a stroke of sheer luck for the whole village!" happily commented the cook, who had just got news that her sons had finally managed to start their own workshop at the village.

"Since he came back here, the roads are safer, even if there are still a few brigands who..." approved the head groom.

"They won't last long, I swear!" cut in Halmer, the men-at-arms captain, who had been in the Count's service for many years. And the governess hastened to nod her agreement, with an enthusiasm as accented as the interest that wide shouldered, mustached soldier awakened in her.

"How true! In any case, things are already much better in comparison with the past! And this castle is really magnificent!"

"It is strange, then, that our lord hasn't brought home a bride yet..." the wine steward suggested slyly, glancing toward a sturdy peasant in her thirties, simply but well dressed, who held on her knees a child of about five years of age.

There was an awkward moment of silence.

The rumor had been going on for quite a while that the Count had rejected a few advantageous marriage proposals because of a child he had brought to the castle as an infant, when he had first come to live there.

He was a healthy, strong boy, and the Count had named him Thorvald, after his legendary ancestor. Nobody knew anything else about him, neither his exact age nor his descent. In any case, he was certainly treated more like a relative than a servant, even if it was well known no Stättenecke had a child of that age. Intrigued by his presence, servants and villagers had long come to the conclusion—not devoid of a little malice—that the boy had to be the Count's own son, born on the wrong side of the blanket, and that the lord did not want to wrong him by marrying a noblewoman who could give him legitimate heirs to his title and lands.

Of course, nobody dared mentioning it with the Count, and even among themselves servants and villagers barely hinted at the matter with half sentences and glances, just as they were doing now in the big, dark kitchen of the castle, where the only light came from the fire burning in the fireplace. That silent exchange of glances and suggestive grimaces was brusquely cut short by old Berta, who came into the room, glanced first at the small group by the fire, then at the boy, who was looking questioningly at his nanny with his blue eyes, and burst out: "You rumormongers! Get back to work, instead of wasting your time gossiping!" She was laughing as she said that, however, and her mischievous laughter silenced and intrigued them all. "Our lord, the Count," the woman went on, in a more solemn tone, "will leave in three days for the capitol, there to take Dame Wilenda of Wulstaffen—the Princes' niece—as his bride. So, do you still have something to say, you gossipers?"

A whirlwind of comments and cheers followed her words.

Just as Berta had said, Ruthgard left three days later, headed for the capitol city, where the wedding took place with great pomp and circumstance at the presence of the Great Duke himself; a month later, the Count came back home with his young wife.

Wilenda was just twenty years old, but she had willingly agreed to marry the Count of Stättenecke, who was almost thirty years her senior, even if she had some qualms at the idea of spending her life in that lonely, far away castle, so different from the lively, magnificent court life she was used to. After some hesitation, however, she had reasoned she could not hope for a better suitor, with the small dowry she had left after her father—cadet brother to Prince Wulstaffen—had gone bankrupt and died, and she had accepted the Count's proposal.

Better to be the lady of a rich castle among the mountains than a poor relative at the Wulfstaffens' court! she thought, facing first the wedding and then the journey to the mountains with a smile on her lips.

The young bride was cheerful and full of life, and at first the novelty of her wedded status, the luxurious elegance of her rooms, the rugged beauty of the surrounding mountains reassured her about the wisdom of her choice. As autumn gave way to winter, however, wind and rain put an end to her daily riding outings and at times even prevented her from going out in a coach, forcing her to stay at the castle for days in a row, and that soon spoiled her happiness.

Besides her maidservant, the governess and old Berta, her only ladies in waiting were a widow belonging to the lesser nobility, Dame Britta, and her nubile daughter, but the long, monotonous winter days, the leaden cover of clouds that seemed to cut the castle away from all the rest of the world, the fireplaces vainly fighting against the cold, inexorably dampened any cheerfulness, and the few words the women exchanged as they sat weaving or embroidering seemed to die down in the wide, gloomy halls and the long, dark corridors, smothered as they were by the pounding rain and the howling wind.

Between the two of them, the governess and Berta efficiently ran the castle, barely listening to Wilenda's uncertain suggestions, and once she had run out of conversation topics—very few to start with—with the widow and her daughter, Wilenda found herself listening more and more to her ladies in waiting's gossiping, suppressing yawns and pretending she was concentrating on her embroidery.

That was how she first realized how strange was little Thorvald's position at the castle. The child lived in her husband's rooms, apparently with the only task of pouring his wine, as if he were his page, but wore the Stättenecke livery, was looked after by a woman charged with taking care of him, and was instructed in the use of weapons by the sergeant of the Guard. Moreover, every ten days a deacon would come to the castle to teach the boy to read and write. In other word, Thorvald was getting the same education a noble born child would get.

Wilenda knew very well that the child could not in any way be related to the Wulfstaffen or Stättenecke family, however, unless the relationship was of a secret and unmentionable kind—a suspicion supported by her ladies in waiting's words and even more by their silences—and at that thought she always felt her face burn with anger.

She might have agreed to marry a man so old he could have been her father, and she could endure living a cloistered life in that gloomy castle, just as she could have accepted the existence of a bastard son of her husband, but his silence on the matter... no, she could not tolerate that! She felt deceived, mocked even, and the fact that everybody at the castle but her—the lord's bride, the lady of the castle!—knew about it and perhaps was laughing behind her back annoyed her so much that at the umpteenth time Dame Britta hinted at the topic, she brusquely put away her embroidery and asker her women to leave in a tone and with such a face that they immediately lost any wish to ask her what was amiss.

234

Quivering with anger, Wilenda stood for a moment in the now empty room, then ran upstairs and locked herself in her room, sending her maidservant away. Ruthgard was out hunting, but he would be back the next day and he would then have a lot of explaining to do.

Her angry thoughts still turning in her mind, she went to bed. Contrary to what she expected, she fell asleep right away, but her uneasy sleep was troubled by eerie, obsessive noises, like a frantic knocking at the castle doors combined with disquieting sounds that seemed to rise from the very foundations and reach up through the whole castle, to the merlons. Wilenda tossed and turned, trying to wake up, but even when she finally managed to surface from sleep, she kept hearing those furious thumps, together with a howling sound that seemed to enshroud the solid walls. When even her room's shutters started to bang rhythmically, she finally could not stand it anymore and buried herself under the covers, too frightened to get up, light a candle and call for somebody. She kept telling herself that was what she should have done, but at the same time she did not want to appear as an easily frightened child, so she remained curled up under the covers, making herself as small as she could, her eyes tightly closed, until she finally gave way to sleep once more, when the grey light of dawn was already filtering through the window.

The sun was higher in the sky when more shouts and yells woke her up, but this time she immediately recognized her servants' voices, and then her husband's as well, strong and commanding as usual.

Jumping from her bed, she ran to the window and opened it: on the wings of a gust of cold air, the

235

exclamations of the small group gathered around Ruthgard rose to her ears in a confused clamor.

"Down there in the moat, my lord Count!"

"Some rotten ropes were around the body, as if it had been secured to a boulder, but..."

"The water must have worn them out and it surfaced again during the storm, last night, but..."

"Shut up!" The nobleman's tone couldn't have been sterner or more commanding, effectively making grooms, men-at-arms and servants fall silent. Piercing them with a last threatening glance, the Count strode toward the makeshift stretcher lying by the well, motioning for somebody to lift the old blanket covering it.

Pushing the shutter open a little more, Wilenda leaned out, curious about what was going on, but she immediately drew back, pale and upset.

On the plank used to move it, lay a half-decayed shapeless thing, bloated with water and covered with filth, which still retained some human resemblance in the skull's empty sockets, in the shape of a hand, whose contracted fingers seemed to try to keep a desperate hold on life, in the slim chest, whose broken ribs revealed a tangle of small vermin that had been feeding upon the flesh and innards of that unknown dead.

Fighting against nausea, the Countess collapsed on the bed, cold sweat beading her face, her hands trembling, and she curled up there for some time, barely registering that the noises were dying off in the courtyard, while Ruthgard's voice sounded louder, more commanding and steady.

That was how her handmaid found her, when she came upstairs to bring her mistress her breakfast; oblivious to her lady's distress, the woman proceeded to tell her what had happened, while she busied herself lighting the fire in the fireplace.

"What an awful thing, my lady Countess! During the night a body surfaced in the moat... half decayed and eaten by fish! Our lord the Count thinks he was some sort of scoundrel, and ordered for his body to be thrown in the ravine, behind the castle..."

"What?" Wilenda remonstrated. "Just like this, without a prayer, or..."

The handmaid shook her shoulders.

"We found it odd as well, but nobody dared to say a single word. Our lord the Count's tone and expression were..." The woman suddenly broke off, shaking her head, and in the following minutes fully concentrated on serving breakfast to her lady.

At the mere sight of the food, however, the taste of bile rose again to Wilenda's mouth and she pushed the plate away as she got up.

"I'll talk to him," she decided, while in her mind that latest, grim discover added to the rumors about Thorvald and the frightening noises she had heard during the night, fueling her anger against her husband.

"We would all be very grateful to you, my Lady! It is already impossible to find some quiet in this castle, with those dreadful sounds that..."

Wilenda gave a start, jerking back from the maidservant, who was helping her to dress.

"Sounds? What do you mean?" she asked aggressively. Perhaps frightened by her reaction, the girl hurriedly took back her words, explaining them away with vague hints at the howling wind and the shouts of the guards on watch; in the meanwhile, heralded by a discreet knocking on the door, the governess came in to discuss the day's housework.

"I've had enough, my Lady. Your being my lady wife doesn't mean you can interfere in my decisions."

In so saying, the Count stood up, staring at Wilenda with those icy gray eyes that always had the power to silence her. But not this time... no. There were too many things she needed to understand, to accept... and a new, quite compelling reason to insist on getting some explanations. Standing tall, she faced her husband, who had walked around his large ebony desk to loom over her.

"As the Lady of Stättenecke, and a believer, I feel responsible for that poor creature that..."

"Enough, I said!"

The Countess stared at him, unable to believe her eyes. Not only Ruthgard's voice was quivering with anger, but he had also raised a hand, almost menacingly. Wilenda instinctively drew back, but then her indignation won over her fear.

"How dare you threaten me, a Wulfstaffen!" she shouted. "And this only because I'm trying to defend the good name and the honor of your family! Yes, your harsh treatment of that poor, dead..."

"He was a brigand, Wilenda."

Suddenly calm once more, the Count walked back to his desk and sat at it, drumming with his long, strong fingers on the chair armrests. "He probably got hung on the slopes of Mount Balest and was dragged down here by the storm."

"Are... are you sure?" Her husband's calmness was affecting the woman even more than his anger had done.

"We found the rope and... yes, I'm sure."

All of sudden, Wilenda felt as stupid and gullible as the lowliest among her servants, and she did not like it at all. She searched in her mind for more questions, for those other causes of worry and annoyance that had brought her there, that had prompted her to look for explanations from the man she had married but that she did not really know. Her fears now appeared very childish to her, though, and in the end all that was left was a name. She whispered it.

"What about Thorvald?"

Ruthgard stiffened, and that icy, and yet furious, look surfaced in his eyes again, but he managed to hold himself in check.

"May I ask why are you mentioning him right now, after we discussed about a brigand's body? Or do you suspect there might be some crime connected to that boy as well?"

His calm, controlled voice sounded almost amused, so much so that the young woman felt more stupid than ever. But she wanted to get to the bottom of what she had started.

"Of course not! But I cannot help but wonder who he really is, and why he is treated as..."

"Now I've really had enough of this." The Count stood up again, looming once more over her. "Find yourself something to do, instead of listening to the servants' gossiping! Keep in mind who you are, and learn to silence those lazy gossipers surrounding you."

Hurt, the woman tried to defend herself, but before she could utter a word, her husband went on, "I warn you, Wilenda! This is no business of yours, and I exhort you not to mind anything that doesn't involve you directly! Now or ever!" He then cut off the young woman's remonstrations with a curt gesture as he concluded, "Would you now please leave me? I have things to attend to." And he motioned her out, as if she had been a mere servant.

Her cheeks burning with humiliation and anger, Wilenda left the room, barely noticing the men-at-arms' captain waiting outside as she headed for the rooms she shared with her husband. Once there, she lingered for a moment with her hand on the latch, then she resolutely turned her back to the door and climbed the narrow stairs leading to her small, personal four-room apartment, locking herself inside.

As she sat on the four-poster bed, nervously tapping her foot against one of the post, she thought back at how her conversation with her husband had turned out and felt her anger grow.

She decided she was going to stay up there in her rooms, with her women, until Ruthgard would come to apologize to her. Only then she would tell him her secret, which had been growing inside her for three months now, and maybe that would make him look at her with different eyes, listen to her fears and dispel her doubts. Maybe. For the time being, however, she was going to stay up there, in her apartment, there to sleep and eat, so that she would not have to sit at the same table with him.

She was determined to carry out her plan, but during the night those dreadful sounds that seemed to rise from the castle foundations to its merlons came back to torment her, so that the next morning she cast aside her anger and pride, and ran back to her husband, thoroughly distraught.

The anger Wilenda had felt the previous day, the sleepless night and the fear haunting her made her look so fragile and fearful that the Count greeted her with concern and kindness, so much so that Wilenda forgot her intentions and sank with relief into his reassuring embrace.

"Calm down, my lady!" he told her. "You must remember this is a mountain castle and not the Wulfstaffens' palace! The wind was blowing through the merlons all night long, and you mistook its furious howling for cries and screams." He looked down at the young woman and saw she did not believe him. "Or maybe what you heard was the frightened shrieking of the birds nestling on the towers, upset by the wind storm. Those can be frightening noises, and may sound like human screams if you do not know their real source."

Wilenda stared at him and tried to force herself to believe to that explanation, because at that moment she needed her husband's protection and help, badly.

"Perhaps you're right... no, you certainly are. How silly of me! But, you see... you must bear with me and be patient, right now, because I'm... I mean, we..." she stammered, blushing.

"What are you trying to say? The Count asked, his hands on her arms. Smiling, and blushing even more, Wilenda lowered her eyes and finally told him she was pregnant.

Ruthgard hugged her without a word, but for the first time in a long while a joyous smile lit his hard face.

The Countess then moved back to the large apartment she shared with her husband, which was better shielded from the wind because it was in the main body of the castle instead of on one of the towers; at the same time, the servants were sent to destroy the nests the birds had built under the roof.

Some time went by, and as nothing untoward came to disturb the young bride's sleep—besides the castle's usual noises—Wilenda put her mind at rest and started to impute her past fears to some nervousness due to her pregnancy, a belief fully shared by old Berta.

By the sixth month of her pregnancy, however, the phenomena came back, always at night; this time, others in the castle first complained about those sounds and then began to fear them. It always started with a persistent scratching against her shutters, followed by the frantic noise of the gates being shaken and by furious blows against the main doors, as if somebody was trying to get into the castle. They would end at dawn with a long moan, leaving Wilenda terrified and drenched in cold sweat, too frightened even to scream or call for help.

In any case, neither her ladies in waiting—as terrified as she was—nor anybody else in the castle could have helped her, because every attempt to locate the source of those noises had been vain, and by now everywhere it was rumored that the castle was cursed.

The Count might have been able to assuage those fears, at least in part, but he had left almost a month before to hunt down the brigands that for some time had been making the roads unsafe on his lands, and it had not been possible to inform him of what was happening at the castle.

So, Wilenda was alone in the large bedroom on the first night of the new moon, when the last sliver of moonlight disappeared, as if swallowed by the black sky, and those long claws scratching against her shutters woke her up from her uneasy sleep. They were scratching and digging in the wood, which seemed to begin to give way, to open...

Her heart rose to her throat, choking her screams; paralyzed with fear, she could not move, while the furious blows against the main door joined the persistent scratching, and the darkness in the room became deeper, thicker.

Trembling, Wilenda curled up on herself, drenched in cold sweat, with her hands pressed against her ears under the covers. Then a ghastly scream, sudden and piercing, echoed through the castle, followed by more screams—dull and choked sounding, but just as frightening.

Terror finally lent Wilenda the strength to leave her bed, grab a shawl and run to the door, but then her strength failed her and she fell on the floor, unable to get up, to run away, while those moans filled the room and the shutters shook, threatening to give way under the violent blows *somebody* was raining on them, and the choked scream—that seemed to rise from earth's own bowels—turned into a desperate wail.

The next morning her servants found her still there, barely conscious and delirious, running a very high fever but still able to put up a fight with what little strength she had left when they tried to carry her to her bed. In the end, her women were forced to settle her in another room, while yet another messenger was sent out, with the order of finding the Count at any cost.

"What do you think might have happened, Berta?" Britta asked the old woman, panting a little as she spoke, as she used to do when she was upset.

The women were all together in the small room adjoining the main bedroom, where they used to sit to embroider, weave and exchange gossips. Even though it was broad daylight outside, the windows were shuttered and the three doors leading from the small room to the bedroom, the dressing room and the corridor were all closed.

The old woman silently shook her shoulders, but Rella, the maidservant, cut in, "It was something really bad! I was sleeping in the Lady's dressing room, but I heard something too: it felt as if somebody was crying and scratching against the wood to get in… and then, that scream!"

"It was heard all over the castle!" interjected the governess, as she came in to bring the Countess a hot herb tea. "It frightened everybody!" she went on, as she set the cup down on the table. "It's enough to say that the cook is threatening to leave, while a couple of scullery maids and a groom have already packed up and left, without even waiting for the master to come back!"

"The shameless rascals!" Britta commented, but at the same time she could not help but think that if so many people were so afraid, they had to have a valid reason for it. And she was stuck there in that castle with her daughter!

"I've never been at ease here, with all the rumors circulating about this place, it's being so isolated, those sounds at night… and then they found that body in the moat and threw it in the ravine like a dead beast!" wailed the girl… who could not really be called a girl anymore since she'd already been on the other side of thirty for quite a while. Her mother hurried to comfort her, whispering soothing words in her ear, while the governess turned to Berta.

"What's your say on the matter?" she asked.

"I say that if you don't get moving, that herb tea will be ice cold by the time the Countess gets to drink it. About all the rest, it's up to our lord the Count to do something," the old woman replied sharply, and she hurriedly limped toward the dressing room.

In a pique, the governess grabbed the cup and disappeared into Wilenda's room; since Britta and her daughter where still talking in whispers without so much as looking at her, Rella took advantage of their being absorbed into each other to leave for the stables. Her fiancé worked there as a groom, and she was certain she would be able to persuade him to leave that cursed place with her.

It took more than a week for the messenger to reach the Count and for him to get back to Stättenecke, and in the meanwhile that awful mixture of moans, screams and blows against the windows and the main door recurred every single night, even if that other, dreadful death scream was never heard again. By now, it was known all over the countryside that the castle was cursed, because the rumor had been spread by the servants running away from it.

Therefore, when Ruthgard got back home, he found there less than half the servants he used to have; his wife was still sick and beside herself with terror, and little Thorvald was jittery and tearful.

His nanny came out to meet the Count in the courtyard, and immediately apologized about the child's state, not even waiting for her lord to dismount.

"He always was a restless boy, just has he has always driven me crazy on any new moon night. He would cry and refuse to go to sleep, asking me to leave a lit candle by the bed and to stay with him. This time, however, he was so bad I could barely stand him! He screamed and fought and tried to run away from me: believe me, there's something wrong with that boy, and you should have..."

"Would you tell me you cannot help a boy you raised to fight his quite normal night terrors, you impudent good for nothing?" the Count burst out as he dismounted, angered by the woman's impertinence and anxious to run to see his wife, but the nanny stubbornly blocked his way.

"What I mean is that there is something... something wrong, and evil in this castle, and that Thorvald—the poor boy—is part of it all! I..."

"Shut up!"

The Count lifted his riding crop, as if to strike the woman, but while she fearfully stepped back, he restrained himself and added, his voice as calm as it was frosty, "Collect your wages from the governess, get your things, and leave, right now. Thorvald is now too old to be entrusted to an ignorant and superstitious peasant."

The woman tried to protest and even shed a few tears, but the Count was adamant in his resolve and strode away toward his apartment. After a few moments, the nanny shook her shoulders and went to pack her things; it saddened her to lose the comforts offered by the castle, and also to leave the boy she had raised, but she took heart in the thought that at home she would at least be able to sleep peacefully, with the chirping of the crickets and the croaking of the frogs the only sounds to break the silence of the night. After getting her money from the governess, she left the castle, but only after spreading her personal version of what had happened among the servants first, and the villagers afterwards, with the result of increasing tenfold the rumors about Stättenecke. More servants left the castle, and even a few villagers decided to move to the neighboring county.

Halmer, the captain of the guards, and the governess pointed then out to the Count that the situation at the castle was deteriorating fast, because they were running out of servants and it was not easy to find any replacements. Ruthgard barely listened to them, however, because his main source of worry was his wife, and their unborn child.

Wilenda was having trouble recovering from the fever and nausea wrecking her body, and she spent every night in a paroxysm of terror, saying she could still hear that frantic scratching against her window, the huge gate rock back and forth, as if furiously shaken by some invisible hand, and the moans and cries carried to her ears by the wind.

Her husband tried to tell her again that it was just the wind blowing, mixed with the rain pouring down and the birds' calls, but those explanations didn't ring true even to his own ears, and as the new moon night drew near, Wilenda grew frantic with terror.

"I cannot hear that scream again," she sobbed, curled up on the wide bed with her hands pressed against her ears. "And those other screams, rising from the earth itself... no, I cannot tolerate it! I beg you, I implore you, let me get back to the capitol, and to my aunt and uncle's palace! Do it for our child, if you don't want to do it for me, because here I'll go crazy, I'll die, and what will happen to the child then?"

Sitting by her side, the Count listened to her with more patience than he would usually show, and he tried to cam and hearten her in a quiet, reasonable voice belied by the dreadful look in his eyes. When his wife's protests and pleas finally died in a desperate sob, he bent forward to caress her tangled hair as he fought back a sigh.

"I'd gladly agree to let you leave, Wilenda, if only it were possible. No, my dear, listen to me: it is the dead of winter, one of the worst winters ever, and the roads are very dangerous, not only because of the weather but also because plagued by highwaymen again. How can I allow you to leave now, in your state..."

"But I have to go, or we'll both die! Oh, I beg you, I beg you! Don't tell me no! My aunt..."

"Now try to calm down. I'm here now, ready to protect you and the child. I'll find a way to..." Ruthgard broke off with a choked curse and stood up, his fists clenched, as he moved away from the bed. Wilenda's crying turned into desperate sobs, and Ruthgard approached her again.

"Take heart," he told her, his jaw clenched. "I'm not saying you cannot go, but just that I need time to think about it, to see if it is possible to have you travel in complete safety. I'll see to it, and in the meantime you just try not to worry."

Then he kissed her on the forehead and left the room, displaying a self-assurance he was far from feeling.

Winter was gone by then, but spring had brought continuous downpours of rain, turning the roads into freezing rivulets and the fields around Stättenecke into a quagmire, while the relatively warmer weather was causing avalanches and landslides. It was therefore impossible even to think of leaving for the princes' estates right then, but deep down Ruthgard knew only too well that they simply *had* to leave. He was still debating the problem when Halmer knocked at the door.

An informer had come to him with news about the brigands' hideout, offering to guide them there. The outlaws were going to gather there in six nights' time to split their loot, which would offer them the chance—maybe the only one—to set up an ambush and get rid of them once for all.

The captain's eyes were shining with satisfaction at the prospect as he finished reporting the news, but worry darkened the Count's face.

In six nights' time... that meant the first night of the new moon, the one Wilenda was so terrified of. On the other hand, he could not and would not ignore such an opportunity. After a long inner fight, he summoned Britta and Berta, entrusting his wife to them for those few days he was going to be away, then he gathered his men and left.

Ill-fated Wilenda saw him leaving from her room balcony and realized she'd been left alone. She threw herself on the bed fully dressed, her face turned toward the wall, and withdrew into herself, refusing to speak and sending even her women away.

Two days later Britta, in a huff over her lady's refusal to open up with her—and also secretly terrified at the thought of the oncoming new moon—took her leave together with her daughter, giving as a pretext some relative's sudden, unlikely illness.

That left only Berta at the Countess' bedside, with the old woman also having to look after Thorvald, who would alternate moments of cheerfulness to grim silences and long bouts of crying. Berta could not expect any help from the governess, who had to double as cook and administrator, since both of them had left soon after the Count... and the next night was going to be the first night of the new moon.

The wind had already been blowing for days around Stättenecke, amassing over the castle and the surrounding mountains layers of dull gray clouds, swollen with rain, that rolled through the darkening sky like long gray rags, painting the horizon with vague shapes that looked like ghostly figures to Wilenda's terror filled eyes. All of a sudden, the faraway rumble that had echoed in the distance throughout the afternoon turned into a deafening peal of thunder, while a bright bolt of lightning wove through the sky, dark and full of electricity. Rain followed, a heavy, steady rain that lashed at the castle walls and pounded against Wilenda's shutters like a monstrous hand trying to burst through them.

Even if half asleep from the sedative herb tea the governess had given her, Wilenda was still moaning and thrashing under the blankets. Berta was trying to soothe her with some comforting words when Thorvald's desperate crying came from the small room he had been put into for the night, which could easily be reached from Wilenda's bedroom by means of a narrow spiral staircase.

Berta hesitated. The Countess seemed asleep, even if fitfully, while the little boy was sobbing and almost choking in his own tears.

"I'll get him and bring him here," she finally decided. "He'll sleep on that bench." Berta cast another glance at her lady, who was moaning softly, her eyes closed. Another peal of thunder seemed to shake the castle's very foundations, and was followed by dull screams. Shuddering, Berta picked up the only candle holder in the room: whatever might be happening, the boy could not be left alone. She opened the small door and climbed down the narrow staircase; she had almost gotten to the bottom, however, when her foot slipped and she fell, lying down there half-dazed and unable to pick herself up, while the candle went out. Her cries for help went lost in the frightening cacophony of the thunderclaps, the wailing wind, the choked screams and the furious blows against the main doors—whose echoes now seemed to reverberate through the whole castle; then, from the bowels of the earth came the chilling scream Wilenda had already heard in the past, and for a moment it overcame all other sounds, almost drawing their power, terror and threat into itself.

Thorvald heard it, and left his bed; in the dark room he came across Berta, who was moaning on the floor, and sought refuge in her arms. Wilenda heard it too, because the other sounds had already woken her up from her uneasy sleep. Beside herself with fright, she left her bed, falling and getting up again until, shuddering and swaying, she managed to open the door and get out into the corridor; from there she climbed down the stairs holding herself to the railing, reached the hall and finally the courtyard, barefoot, in her nightgown, her loose, disheveled hair blown in her face by the wind.

Fighting the fury of the elements and the pouring rain—so heavy that it blinded the watchmen on the walls to what was happening in the courtyard—the young woman moved a few steps toward the great main doors, that were really moving, as if somebody was pushing at them from the outside; when the choked sound of human voices rose again from the earth bowels, she then cried in terror and crumpled senseless on the ground, lying there with her face in the puddles; her long white nightgown and her hair still blew in the wind for a few seconds, then the rain drenched them and the Countess lay still in the courtyard, like a heap of wet rags.

Nobody realized what had happened till the next morning, when the governess entered the apartment, finding the bed empty and the door leading to the spiral staircase open. She found old Berta, still moaning with little Thorvald asleep in her arms, and she was trying to understand what had happened and calling for help when she heard the watchmen shouting outside: the Countess had been found, still unconscious and running a very high fever... and as soon as they settled her back in her bed, the governess saw with dismay sure sings that her lady was going to give birth way before time.

A servant ran to the village to call for the midwife and two men-at-arms were sent to find the Count, but by the time he got back to Stättenecke it was all over.

Wilenda lay dead on the wide bed, her hair framing her livid face and her hands crossed on her breast; nearby, in a small cradle, on embroidered linens, was a newborn baby girl, as pale as her mother; the baby cried weakly and rubbed her eyes with her tiny fists, as if grieving her mother's death.

The Count named her Sylverna, had two wide rooms refurbished for her and looked for a wet nurse and a couple of maidservants to look after her.

Finding them was not easy in spite of the good wages promised, because by then the news about the tragic circumstances of the Countess' death had spread all over the village and, together with the already existing rumors about the castle, they made many village women refuse the

Count's offers for fear of that *something* haunting the castle and its inhabitants.

Whenever he happened to hear those rumors, the Count would merely shake his shoulders dismissively, and he went on living at Stättenecke. In spite of his show of indifference, however, it was quite clear that something was eating away at him. Dark circles marked his eyes and stood out in his pale face, his hair had turned grey and he had lost weight, so much so that he looked like the ghost of the strong, resolute man who seven years before had stubbornly managed to rebuild his ruined castle, against all odds.

Moreover, to vindicate the persisting rumors that the castle was haunted, by midsummer Ruthgard sent a messenger to the Prince Wulfstaffen, asking him to welcome Sylverna to his home for some time to come, because he feared she might suffer from the harsh winter weather and the absence of a motherly figure.

The princes were still grieving Wilenda's death, for which they felt responsible to some extent, so they immediately agreed and, well before autumn gave way to winter, Sylverna arrived at the princes' manor together with her wet-nurse and old Berta—both quite relieved at leaving the grim castle behind.

PART TWO: **SYLVERNA**

Sylverna leaned out of the coach window to look around. They were traveling along a narrow, windy mule track, surrounded by dark green firs and enclosed by bare rocks, partially covered with musk and lichens, where low bushes grew here and there; dark mountains loomed everywhere, their peaks still shrouded with snow even if it was spring already, and the great castle of Stättenecke stood out over it all. Her new home. She shivered, almost without realizing it.

Even if the journey had been long, it had cheered her to travel across the verdant lands and through the nice, pleasant villages that were part of her father's fief, but the sight of that dark keep, so imposing and grim, silhouetted against the background of an equally darkening sky, gave her a subtle feeling of foreboding. High mountains surrounded it on three sides, while on the fourth the castle rose on the edge of a deep ravine. Everything in it... the powerful, crenellated walls, the six high and strong towers, the narrow windows with their protective iron bars, the locked gates and the still raised drawbridge... seemed to reach out to her with hostility and malice.

The girl drew back, leaning against the backrest and closing her eyes. She had been traveling for two weeks and she felt tired, cold and lost. She was missing her comfortable rooms at the Wulstaffens' palace, the colors and sounds of the large city, the voices of her friends and servants, but most of all she was missing her uncle and her aunt, who had taken her in when she was an orphan only a few months old and had lovingly raised it like a daughter.

But she was not their daughter, she was the Count of Stättenecke's daughter, and after fifteen years he had decided he wanted her back by his side; the Count was now riding beside her coach, wrapped in his dark cloak, apparently as solid as his keep, and as impregnable.

During those fifteen years, her father had come to see her as often as his new responsibilities as a law officer for the prince-bishop of Bresanone—who held him in high esteem—would allow him to do. The Princes Wulfstaffen had told the girl her mother's story, but many years before they did, the young girl had already heard from her nanny those terror filled stories about how the castle had been rebuilt, spiced with many hints at the strange spells and unholy rites needed to accomplish that aim.

Perhaps it was the shadow of those old, confused childhood memories that now made her feel strangely repelled by the castle, or perhaps it was the thought that it was the place where her mother had died, only a few days after giving birth to her... her mother, that she had never known and yet had missed so much The rumors circulating among the servants, she remembered, had it that the young woman had been terrified by that very castle that would now welcome her daughter. Her growing sense of foreboding made her squirm a little on the seat, and immediately—as if he could feel her edginess—Ruthgard leaned toward the half-closed window.

"Are you asleep, Sylverna?" he called, and when she shook her head, he went on: "There are still a few hours of travel between here and the castle, but if you feel too tired we can stop at the village of Saccun, at the foot of the mountain, and spend the night there. If we hasten a little, however, we could be at home, where everything is already

ready to welcome us, before midnight. Anyhow, the choice is up to you."

"I can't wait to see the castle, Father, and I'm not tired... not much, in any case. Please, let's go on."

The careful upbringing she had received from her aunt and uncle had prompted her to say the exact words her father hoped to hear, and her reward was one of those rare smiles, which for a moment brightened his hard face before he rode away, shouting orders. And the journey continued, at a faster pace than before.

Their goal had finally got so near that the ravine isolating the castle and the wide drawbridge were now in clear view, when a new, unknown voice shook Sylverna from her drowsiness. The voice belonged to a young man who was greeting the Count with an affection barely held in check by respect, asking about his journey and giving him news about the castle and its inhabitants, and the Count's reply came in an unusually warm voice. Her curiosity piqued, Sylverna was on the verge of pulling aside the window curtain to peer at the newcomer when she heard her father call his name.

Instinctively, Sylverna drew back. *Thorvald.* Yes, that was it, she had heard it right... and that was a name known to her through the Wulfstaffens servants' gossiping, since rumors had it that the young man was the Count's illegitimate son. Still curious in spite of herself, she pulled the curtain aside again and leaned out of the window, finding herself face to face with a strong, fair haired young man, who was reining in his horse and trying to peer into the coach, prompted by the same kind of curiosity. For a moment the two young people looked at each other, then they burst out laughing and the journey ended on that merry note, with Thorvald riding by the coach as he made small talk with his lord's daughter, while the Count himself rode at the head of the small group.

The young man spoke with the utmost admiration of the Count's war deeds, but once he realized that the young woman did not seem to appreciate very much those tales of valor and blood, he told her his own story in plain words, almost to show her how generous her father could be. He was an orphan, and his father had been one of the Count's men-at-arms; when his mother had died too, killed by a plague, the Count had taken him in and raised him like a son, giving him a status and a proper upbringing, the people's malignant innuendos notwithstanding. He politely stressed that point, making Sylverna blush as she regretted her previous suspicions.

"Our lord the Count is a valiant warrior, but he is also a good and generous man," Thorvald went on. "You must not fear his abruptness and terseness! He's so lonely, you see, and he's been anxiously waiting for years for you to come back, to make you the lady of his castle."

Sylverna leaned out of the window and raised her eyes—a lighter gray than her father's—to meet the squire's ones.

"The castle frightens me a little," she confessed. "It's so huge and massive and dark, almost choked by those bare mountains!"

"Just wait and see the apartment you father has had readied for you, before you say anything! I'm sure you'll change your mind," Thorvald laughed, as they headed up the last slope leading to Stättenecke.

As a matter of fact the rooms she was immediately taken to were as plush and elegant as those she used to have at the Wulfstaffens' palace, and in addition to that the next day her father summoned her to his study an greeted her with kind, loving words, almost apologizing for having made her leave her aunt and uncle.

"Perhaps I've been selfish in bringing you here, but I'm alone, my daughter... I've been alone for years... and I wanted so much to have you here with me! I realize life was more cheerful and lively in the capitol, but you won't miss parties and guests here either... and on top of that here, at Stättenecke, you will be the lady of the castle!"

Sylverna, who had actually shed more than a few tears at having to leave the Wulfstaffens to follow her barely known father to an unknown castle, felt moved by his honest words. Flattered at the idea of becoming the lady of the castle, she finally raised her modestly lowered gaze to smile at her father, who opened his arms to her.

The following days were cheerful and happy. The girl concentrated on learning the layout of the castle and as much as she could about its management with the utmost good will, and it surprised her somewhat to notice how few the servants were around the castle, so much so that many tasks were carried out by the Count's men-at-arms, who had originally been members of his mercenary company.

"The people are afraid," the governess—an old woman who was among the few who had been living at Stättenecke for many years—admitted one day, but she immediately added, "I mean... winter is quite hard here, there have been avalanches in the past, and... and... there were rumors about brigands..." Her sentence ended up in a faltering whisper, but Sylverna wasn't listening to her anymore. She had seen Thorvald, with whom she had developed a growing friendship, standing by the stables door, and she ran toward him, looking forward to a nice ride together through the woods, that were already donning their dark red autumn cloak.

That evening, however, while she was brushing her hair and getting ready for supper, her father suddenly came up behind her.

"Look here, Sylverna, I have something for you!" he told her, his voice warm with love, as he set down on her dressing table a big bunch of keys she had occasionally seen in his hands. The girl stared at the keys with widening eyes, not daring to touch them.

"The castle keys? For... for me?"

"Yes, my dear, for you. You are the lady now, and everybody will have to obey you. I've been watching you in the past few days, and I'm very satisfied with you.

He then showed her the different keys, telling her what they were for; finally, he detached four big ones from the key ring.

"I will still keep these, because they open the armory, the men-at-arms barracks, and... and all the other rooms used by them, which certainly aren't any concern of the lady of the manor. Because this is what you now are, my daughter: the Lady of Stättenecke".

Proud and happy, Sylverna hugged her father and then, childishly enthusiastic about her new role, she wrote a thrilled letter to her uncle and aunt, telling them she was quite happy and satisfied; that letter assuaged the doubts still haunting the Wulfstaffens, and they finally decided to undertake a trip to a far estate they owned abroad, a journey they had been postponing for quite a long time.

They left ten days later, their mind at ease, after briefly writing to their niece to inform her that they were leaving. Little they knew that Stättenecke's fate was soon to be fulfilled.

Sylverna was so absorbed and pleased with her new life that she did not even miss the company of girls her own age; the Count, on his part, was always ready to humor her whenever she wanted to go for a ride or to visit some nearby village and do some shopping there. And when the Count was busy or away, Sylverna always had Thorvald to keep her company.

"Unfortunately, the roads are plagued by brigands again, my lady," the young man told her that morning, seeing she was pouting a little at her father's absence, since he had promised to take her to a fair in a nearby village and had left before dawn instead, without even informing her. "They tried to hold up a caravan during the night, and the surviving merchants too refuge at the castle. The Count immediately left to chase down those rascals... leaving me behind, at home."

Thorvald crossly whispered those last few words, which prompted Sylverna to look questioningly at him.

"He told me I'm still too young and emotional," the young man muttered reluctantly, but then he burst out, "It is not true, though! I'm more than twenty years old, and I haven't been having nightmares or..."

"Nightmares!" Sylverna immediately jumped to her feet and held his eyes for a long moment, before she asked, in a low, hesitant voice, "Tell me, Thorvald, do you sleep well here, at night?"

Then, before the young man had time to answer her, she went on, more vehemently, "Most of all in the moonless nights, when it's all so dark! I... my sleep is so uneasy."

She broke off for a moment, almost regretting her words that almost sounded like a betrayal of her generous father but a strange light now gleaming in Thorvald's eyes prompted her to go on.

"I keep waking up at all hours, I don't know why, and I'm afraid, so very afraid, even if it's all quiet and still outside. Other nights, I have bad dreams... nightmares, even... and when I wake up I hear strange noises, as if somebody were scratching at my shutters, or... In other words, I sleep badly most of the time."

She looked at him again almost expecting an explanation of some sort, or reassuring words, but the young man—who had listened to her words with more gravity and attentiveness than her short story seemed to call for—looked suddenly upset. A long, silent minute went by before he finally got closer to her and asked in a low voice, "Dreams... nightmares... do you still have some clear memory of them?"

Sylverna already regretted confiding her fears to him, and her first reaction was to refuse to answer, but the young man pressed her so urgently that in the end she had to admit, unwillingly, because putting it into words seemed to give the nightmare new substance, "I'm somewhere, I don't know where, and it is fully dark. Suddenly, a livid, greenish flame flares up, and I realize I'm at Stättenecke, but the castle is just a heap of ruins, with deep diggings where the corner tower should be. I can hear a hoarse, evil voice screaming words in an unknown language, and somehow I can understand them... 'Where it was and as it was!' it cries, and then, 'By the promised blood, what was bound is released!' Or... Thorvald! What's wrong with you?"

The squire—who had been listening to her with growing attention and excitement—had grown suddenly pale and had leaned against the wall, his eyes closed. He did not answer to her anxious cry, and he seemed to come back to himself only when Sylverna, frightened by his behavior, shook him.

"I... I... forgive me! I just remembered..." He fell silent for a moment, then he straightened away from the wall and in a stronger voice went on, "I just remembered a very important errand I have to run. The blacksmith... I have to go, right away."

And he walked away swiftly, without even taking his leave from her.

Thoughtful, Sylverna went back to her rooms. There she scheduled with the governess the tasks for the day, summoned the gardener to choose the flowers for the main hall, distributed among the maidservants both the yarn for the weaving and the clothes that needed mending, but all the while her brain kept pondering on what had happened with Thorvald, unable to find an explanation for the young man's 'flight'. She could not help but think that her story had upset him, which led her to suspect that there might be something real at the root of her fears. She was still uneasy and upset by those thoughts when she finally went to bed, which perhaps was the reason why that night her dreams turned into nightmares.

She dreamed of a vague figure, whose cadaverous face was marred by wounds and old age, and saw it standing menacingly in front of Stättenecke's gates. Feeing troubled, Sylverna tossed in her sleep and immediately found herself in her bed.

"Thank goodness, it was just a dream!" she said, or at least she thought she was speaking aloud, but right then some resounding blows against the main door made her jump, while *somebody*, outside, demanded to be let inside, screaming hideously.

Thrashing about under the covers, Sylverna finally managed to cry out. Just one cry, faint and choked, but it was enough to wake her up. Her fright turned into panic mixed with horror when she realized that something was actually banging against the castle's doors, shaking the massive outer gates as powerfully as a gale.

The taper fell from her trembling hand, and she couldn't make herself reach for it, almost fearing that *something* might grab at her; she curled up in her bed, her head under the covers, unable even to call for help, until a thin sliver of light on the floor told her the so much invoked dawn was finally there. Hesitantly, she threw the covers away and sat up on the bed, listening carefully, but all she could hear was silence... or rather, she only heard the usual morning sounds: birds chirping, a rooster crowing in the distance, her maidservant's steps in the corridor. Sylverna immediately called her, anxious to leave that room where she had lived so many hours in sheer terror, but she did not say anything about her nightmare, even if her pallor and the dark rings under her eyes aroused the woman's curiosity.

It was not the servants she wanted explanations and comfort from, however; no, she wanted them from the castle's lord, her father.

Sylverna went to see him as soon as he came back, but upon reaching the door of his study she hesitated, uncertain. She knew the Count loved those massive walls as much as—perhaps even more than—he loved her, and feared his reaction. The memory of the awful night she had just gone through finally won over her fears and she slipped into the wide, dark room decorated with gold and velvets, with a high, coffered ceiling.

Ruthgard sternly stared at her from behind his wide desk, annoyed by the urgency with which the girl had asked to see him, and under his gaze Sylverna suddenly felt quite silly and nervous. She plucked up her courage, however, and told him what had happened to her during the night, bashfully hinting also to the rumors she had heard at the castle and at the village. As she spoke, she kept looking at the Count, who sat very still with his hands on the desk surface, his grey eyes staring icily at her, his jaw clenched.

The more his face hardened, the more Sylverna's words grew hesitant and timid, until they died in a sigh, even before the Count effectively silenced her striking the desktop in anger. Cursing, he then jumped to his feet and strode toward the cringing girl.

"Hell's bells! You're just like your mother!" he angrily cried out. He then stared at his daughter's pale face, at those wide, smoke-grey eyes staring at him in fear and disbelief, and he clenched his fists, forcing himself to calm down.

He had lost his wife, but wasn't going to lose his daughter as well.

"Forgive me, Sylverna," he went on after a moment, his voice now calm. "I'm tired."

"You must then forgive me if I bothered you with my fears. But... what about my mother?"

Her aunt and uncle had told her that her mother had died giving birth, but the servants' gossips and even more the way old Berta—who had served her mother first, and the her, at the capitol, till her death—would avoid the subject had told her that there had been something strange in the way her mother had died. She had always rejected that thought, so much so that of late she had even forgotten it, but the words his father had just let slip out of his mouth had reawakened her suspicions.

The Count was now smiling, however, his hand on her shoulder in a loving gesture.

"Your mother... yes," he interrupted her, before he started walking back and forth across the wide room, his hands clasped behind his back. "During her pregnancy she suffered from insomnia and depression. Everything would make her nervous, frighten her... it is not unheard of for an expectant mother to act that way, most of all if pregnant with her first child, but the night sounds would terrify her and in spite of all my efforts to calm her, those fears poisoned her last days of life, even if actually there was nothing... nothing at all... to fear.

Sighing, the Count took Sylverna's hands in his own.

"Wind gusts, the birds crying from their nests on the walls, the flagpoles rattling in the wind... the very same sounds that frightened you last night. That's all there is to that. I still get angry at the thought that those simple noises, together with some silly rumors, frightened your mother to the point of making her sick! But it won't happen to you, no! You are my daughter, a Stättenecke, and you will react, you will be strong." Ruthgard suddenly broke off, biting his lips, then he hurriedly went on, before Sylverna—quite bewildered by those sudden revelations—could utter even one word.

"I'll have the shutters and the roof tiles of your apartment checked, my dear, but I cannot promise I'll prevent the wind from blowing!" he soothingly reassured her. "On your part, you must promise me you'll try not to think about it anymore; just try and be cheerful, and your fears will disappear. Go, now, the gardener is waiting for you. As you go, order the grooms to have our horses ready: later on, I'm looking forward to challenging you to beat me to the cemetery chapel."

And he smiled at her, full of love and care. Somewhat reassured, not wishing to displease him again, the girl sought the sunshine of the courtyard as she tried to push her fears and doubts back into a corner of her mind.

As soon as he was alone, however, the Count furiously hit the wall in front of him with his fist, then he slumped on his chair and raises his hands to cover his face, contorted with anger and fear.

"You cursed old woman! Goddamned *bregostana*, and may I be damned too, for asking your abominable help!"

He sat like that for a long while, overwhelmed by his memories and fighting against regret and remorse, then he calmed himself and stood up, striding toward a small cabinet, almost hidden between the huge bookshelves; unlocking it, he took out a vase full of grey powder, then he called the governess, who had been in his service for almost twenty years and was absolutely trustworthy.

"The young Countess has started suffering from insomnia and nightmares," he told the woman, his voice even. They exchanged a long, knowing glance, then the woman lowered her head with a sigh. "You will put one spoonful of this powder into her herb tea every evening. It is just a harmless sleeping drug that will help her sleep well. Mind you! Neither my daughter or anybody else must know about this or the rumors will start circulating again."

The woman bent her grey head even lower and sighed again, avoiding her master's eyes.

"As you wish, my lord Count. And... I'll make sure that she drinks it all."

Since that night, Sylverna slept more soundly and never woke up before down, but her dreams grew more frightening, even in her slumber. Her inability to wake up made them even worse, so much so that at times her distress would drive her to get up and leave the room while still half-asleep, with the result that the rumor started circulating among the servants that their young lady was under a spell that made her walk around in her sleep, at night.

So it was in a state of half-wakefulness that in a moonless night the girl found herself leaning out of her window, the one that overlooked the wide courtyard. She never knew how she had managed to get there, or to open the balcony's heavy shutters, but there she was, staring at a small, bent figure that trudged across the large paving stones, holding a smoking torch which gave off an odd greenish light. The figure stopped under her window and raised her face toward her, as she leaned out even more, strangely attracted by the torchlight. Sylverna tried to make out the figure's face, because she couldn't remember any servant at the castle who looked like it, but the torchlight itself prevented her from seeing anything more than a vague, white face half-hidden by a black hood and framed by tangled grey hair, and a thin body under a tattered dress.

As she stared with puzzlement at the woman, noticing that the only visible hand—the one holding the torch aloft—had long, sharp nails, the old woman's voice floated up to her, almost slithering over the walls, soft and alluring.

"Young Countess, young Countess... my poor little girl, beautiful, beautiful little queen!"

"Who are you? What do you want?" Enthralled and repelled at the same time, Sylverna could not keep silent, much less draw back from the window.

"Oh, oh... I'm just a poor, old woman, but I can help you."

"I need no help, and I didn't ask yours!"

The mysterious old woman's only answer was a hoarse laugh, then she went on, "My little queen, beautiful young Countess! You want the truth, you want to know... yes, yes, it is so. Therefore, my heart, that herb tea you must not drink anymore! It contains a sleeping drug, which makes you blind and deaf, keeps you away from the truth. If you don't believe me, just throw it away once, only once! And you will see, you will see... you will see!"

Those last words sounded different to the girl's ears, almost threatening, and she leaned out even more to try to make out whom she was speaking with, but right then the greenish light flickered and went out, plummeting the courtyard in the deepest darkness and in an absolute stillness.

After calling out for the old woman a couple of times, in vain, Sylverna felt ill at ease as she returned to her bed... or at least that was what she thought she had done when the next morning she woke up there, a little dazed as she'd been feeling of late every morning.

As she ran her usual errands, however, she kept thinking back to that night's conversation, and the more she thought about it, the more she convinced herself she had been dreaming. In the morning she had found her heavy shutters still closed and barred, and a quick check of the servants had confirmed to her that none of them looked even remotely like the old woman. Her suggestion kept haunting her, though, so much so that she decided to follow the old woman's odd suggestion and that night she distracted the governess, pouring the herb tea into a vase while she was not looking, before going to bed as usual.

At first, nothing disturbed the darkness and quiet of the night, but later on a sound dragged her out of her sleep.

She recognized it even before she was fully awake: it was the same, frantic knocking against the front doors that had terrified her so much in the past, and it was soon followed by heavy, shuffling steps trying to climb the stairs; finally, strong blows shook her window shutters, and long nails scratched at the wood.

Terrified, she hid under the covers and spent the night curled up there, trembling, with her eyes wide open in the absolute darkness and cold sweat trickling down her forehead, as she waited for dawn, praying for a sliver of light to come and put an end to that horror.

The next morning, however, she got up as usual, even if everybody could see how pale and listless she was, and she did not speak about what had happened with anybody, not even with Thorvald, firmly telling herself that it had been only a bad dream.

Everything was quiet for a few days, but on the evening of the seventh day, on the first night of the new moon, Sylverna could not resist that odd mixture of terror and curiosity that had been tempting her since the night of her weird nightmare, and again she only pretended to drink the herb tea before going to bed with a small lamp lit on her night table.

This time she heard a dreadful death scream, full of hate and threat, which rose from the castle foundations up to her window, to the merlons themselves followed by a cacophony of choked human screams that seemed to come from the very bowels of the earth.

Sylverna tried to get up, to call somebody who could listen with her to those dreadful sounds, explaining them, helping her; in her terror, however, she knocked against the lamp that went out in a cloud of greenish smoke, leaving her rooted to the spot, sitting on the bed with her hands grasping the covers, wide eyed, while meaningless words— the same she had once heard in her nightmares—escaped her lips.

"The blood... the promised blood..."

When her maid came to wake her up, the next morning, she found her trembling, delirious, and running a high fever. The maidservant called the governess, who in her turn called the Count. He immediately rode to the village to come back a short while later with Nirika, the healer, whom he took to his daughter's side before retiring in his study, ordering that he shouldn't be disturbed for any reason.

When the Count gave an order in that tone, and with that look in his eyes, nobody dared disobey him, so he was left alone with his dreadful memories and his dire forebodings until Nirika vigorously knocked at his door.

The healer immediately reassured him about Sylverna's health. She had been suffering from brain fever, but she was now out of danger and would recover in a few days, provided that—the woman added, her voice now grave and suggestive—she was spared any fright or trauma of any kind.

As she spoke, the woman stole a glance at the Count, who was nervously drumming his fingers on his desk, then she lowered her voice as she went on, "Perhaps, my lord Count, it would be better for her to leave the castle." She openly ignored the Count's sudden jerk, and she added, insinuatingly, "Her poor mother used to have these visions as well, these same nightmares, and you well know how it ended."

"Enough, woman!" Abruptly jumping to his feet, Ruthgard threateningly loomed over the healer. "If I ever find out that you're frightening my daughter with such ridiculous yarns, you ignorant woman..."

"Yarns?" immediately countered the healer, stung by his words. "Would you call it a yarn the terror that made the Countess run out into the courtyard, barefoot and in her nightgown, even if she was in labor already?" Her voice grew lower, hissing. "A yarn the way your castle's foundations kept collapsing until one night you managed to lay them, nobody knows how or with whose help? That same night, the green flames of the *bregostane* rose high into the sky!"

"Shut that mouth of yours or I..."

Livid with rage, the Count lifted his hand as if to strike the woman, but he managed to restrain himself and he merely threw some gold coins at her feet, as he added frostily, "Take your money and leave. You'll never set foot in my castle again, and you'll be careful not to spread your poisonous words around the village, or I'll ban you from it as well. And now, go!"

Suddenly realizing her own brazenness, the healer was now afraid of the consequences, so she held her tongue and left in a hurry after picking up the coins; however, rumors about that short quarrel quickly spread through the castle, and Nirika's words—with all the exaggerations and the comments they collected along the way—together with all the other rumors already circulating among the servants, generated more fear.

As soon as Sylverna felt better, she hastened to tell her father what had happened to her during that dreadful night, but to her astonishment, the Count immediately shut her up.

"I don't want to hear such nonsense!" he told her, showing a harshness she had never seen in him before. "And you will never mention it again, is that clear?"

Surprised and hurt, the girl insisted, at first trying to stay calm and then in a more urgent tone, when the Count silently turned away from her to stand by the window.

"Father, I'm afraid! I swear that... that *thing* was full of hate, of malice!"

"That's enough! You probably had too many sweets, last night. I'll tell Kursa not to give you any with your supper, and that old woman of yours won't appear again, you'll see."

Sylverna stared incredulously at her father's back, the only part of him she could see since he hadn't even turned to answer her plea. As her eyes filled with tears, she begged again, "I cannot stay here any longer, I don't want to! Let me get back to Wulfstaffen, with my aunt and uncle! I beg you, I implore you... yes, to my aunt and uncle, to my cousins, my family! I'm afraid, here!"

The Count slowly turned about, staring at her with such hard, uncompromising eyes that she was left speechless.

"*Enough*, I said!" he ordered. "I don't want to hear another single word about this ridiculous story, and I won't. I just want to remind you that the Princes Wulfstaffen are away from the capitol, and won't be back there for quite a while."

Sylverna's lips trembled, as her determination to stay calm and reasonable slid away together with her first tears. She raised her pale face toward her father in one last, silent plea, but he had an angry reaction.

"Don't be childish!" he drily replied. Any other attempt on Sylverna's part to pick up the discussion again was met by her father with a silence heralding anger.

If the Count was silent, however, the same could not be said of the servants—in spite of their having been sternly warned against 'frightening their young Countess with ridiculous, out of whole cloth stories'—or of the peasants living in the nearby villages, where the girl would often go under some pretext or the other. So, little by little, one word here, another word there, Sylverna started putting together a rather disturbing general picture.

She found confirmation of her suspicion that her mother, before her, had been plagued with nightmares, made of terrifying sounds and dreadful screams, but she also came to realize that others, at the castle, had heard those sounds and kept silent about them, maybe out of fear of the Count, or maybe out of fear of that *something* haunting the castle. In fact, by now she was at least certain of one thing: something dreadful lived in the castle.

She had not told anything to Thorvald yet, in spite of the friendship they had developed between them... or perhaps because of it. Guided by the instincts of a girl on the threshold of womanhood, she had guessed that the young man was falling in love with her, and that made her rather self-conscious, or rather unsettled her, because she felt attracted by him and at the same time she knew Thorvald could never be to her anything more than a devoted servant.

In that moment of fear and confusion, however, she cast aside her qualms and decided to take advantage of the young man's love for her to get his help and made him tell her what he knew, since by now she was certain Thorvald was part of the mystery enshrouding Stättenecke, and that he was probably keeping quiet about it out of his love and gratitude toward the Count.

She asked Ghitta, her personal maidservant—whose devotion she had already made sure of by means of a few small presents—to let Thorvald know that the next morning she was going to wait for him in the greenhouse, giving her maidservant the impression that it was a secret date.

Her heart was racing as she got ready for the 'date', checking in the mirror her clothing and hair with more care than usual while trying to persuade herself that she was doing that only to better carry out her plan. Once in the greenhouse, however, as soon as she saw Thorvald waiting for her seated on the edge of the well, one long leg bent and dangling idly, her heart jumped to her throat as she ran toward him, a smile on her lips. She stopped a few feet away and greeted him with a nod as the young man jumped on his feet to bow, removing his hat.

For a moment they both stood still, but soon their usual comradeship resurfaced, dissolving their initial self-consciousness, and they strolled around the greenhouse, chatting amicably.

Thorvald kept looking at his companion, enthralled, and upon noticing it Sylverna doubled her coy glances and her cajoleries, telling him about her fears and openly asking for his help and protection.

"It's not just for me that I'm afraid, Thorvald! I think of my father as well, of his reckless disregard for all this, and..." She awkwardly lowered her eyes, brushing with her fingertips the laces on the young man's jacket, then she ended hurriedly, "... and of others, in the castle."

His gaze glued on that small hand, the squire reconsidered his decision not to speak anymore of Sylverna's nightmares, a decision he had come to also out of loyalty toward his benefactor. But if the Count was in danger as well—as Sylverna rightly supposed he was—then he was being disloyal in keeping silent, wasn't he?

"You're right, my lady."

"Sylverna," the girl immediately corrected him, offering him his tempting hand. Holding it in his own, Thorvald finally admitted to having heard frightening sounds, which had been heard by many others at the castle; he also admitted that Sylverna's nightmares had reawakened in his mind vague memories, buried so deep that he could not bring them back to the surface.

Upon hearing the steps of the gardener heading in their direction, they had to cut short their conversation and leave with a hurried goodbye, both thoughtful.

For many days they weren't able to meet alone again, and in the meanwhile the new moon was getting nearer, and Sylverna's fear was growing. She was now drinking her herb tea every night, but she had realized that the sleeping drug in wasn't having any effect on her anymore... or rather it just prevented her from getting up, lighting a lamp or calling her maidservant, thus locking her in a sort of stupor full of nightmares and terror. In the morning she would usually have no memory of it, remembering only her fear, until one morning she woke up with a single memory quite clear in her mind: an old woman's evil face looking through her window, white in the darkness, the toothless mouth grinning triumphantly.

Aghast, indifferent to the possible consequences, she immediately sent for Thorvald and desperately asked his help, telling him what she remembered and her awful feeling of a threat looming over her. She told him he was her only friend, the only one who could protect her, and she cried in his arms until the young man, both flattered and frightened by her words, because the girl's dreams mirrored more and more his lost memories, promised he would try to learn something more from the men-at-arms.

"Almost all of them once belonged to your father's mercenary company, and they have been here since the castle was rebuilt, so they should know all its secrets, if there are any," he told her. "They are hard men, not prone to fearful superstitions, so they won't either exaggerate things or indulge in gossips. Moreover, by now it seems clear to me that those sounds come from the underground... don't they?"

At Sylverna's uncertain nod, Thorvald thoughtfully went on: "There are some cells on the ground floor of the great central tower, but they are empty most of the time. However..." He stopped in midsentence, then he shook his head, a gesture whose discomfiture was belied by his sudden smile. "It's still too early to be sure, but we might discover that what's engendering so much fear is not so terrible, after all."

He then raised a hand and smiled, to forestall Sylverna's impatient queries, and added that he was going to make the men-at-arms talk, maybe with the help of a few bottles of good wine, if Sylverna would manage to steal some from her father's cellars.

While the young man carried on his investigation, however, the young chatelaine's situation deteriorated, suddenly and disastrously.

By now she had gotten used to the sleeping drug, which wasn't working anymore and, in the rare occasions when it did have some effect, locked her into awful nightmares, in which she wasn't able to distinguish what was real and what wasn't. Often her handmaid found her wandering half-asleep, shivering with cold, in the hall or on the stairs, and escorted her back to her bed; the next day, Sylverna had no memory of the night's events.

She never knew if it was a dream or if she really met that old, mysterious servant she had already seen once in the courtyard. All she could remember were her honeyed and enigmatic words.

"Young Countess, beautiful Countess! All alone here in the courtyard? Go to the tower, the great tower, my dear, go! And climb down, down, deeper and deeper in the earth, until what was obscure will be clear, and what had to happen will happen. There will be silence then, forever, my heart, and you will be able to sleep peacefully!"

The next day the maidservant found Sylverna curled up in the courtyard, a shawl thrown over her nightgown, her body so rigid that the woman feared she would not be able to take her back to her room. Then, once the girl was back in her bed and apparently asleep, the maidservant gave vent to her worry with the governess.

"We cannot go on like this! This is way too much responsibility! I can't wait for our lord Count to be back: he must be told..."

"Shut that mouth of yours! This certainly isn't the right moment to trouble our master, who already has his hands full with those damned brigands! The young Countess is in a difficult age, but she will soon get over it, you'll see."

"Let's hope so. If I think of what they told me about her mother, and her death, tough..."

"Gossip, that's all! Instead of wasting your time listening to all sorts of rumors, you should take better care of your young mistress!" fumed the governess, as she dismissed the maid, but then she lingered thoughtfully at the foot of the wide staircase, staring at the flagpole by which the Countess had been found sixteen years before, barefoot, half-naked and drenched with the rain that had been pouring down all night long.

In spite of her swearing to herself she wasn't going to be dragged into the young Countess' business again, Ghitta finally gave in to Thorvald's pleas, and to his gift of a couple of silver coins, and agreed to bring a message from him to Sylverna.

The girl had not yet recovered from her fright, and hadn't been leaving her room for two days, but when she read the message a little color flowed back to her pale face.

'I have news,' Thorvald wrote. 'I gained the confidence of a couple of old-timers and the Count's wine loosened their tongue to the point that I could bring them to talk about those night sounds, pretending that their unknown origin frightened me. They laughed and made fun of me, then they admitted they hear those noises as well, but know their source quite well: they are the moans and screams of about a hundred prisoners the Count has segregated into a deep well, with no light nor fresh air, dug into the very foundations of the castle, and the shouts of their guardians.'

'I let my perplexity show, because I couldn't believe our lord the Count could do such a thing, but the two men insisted. "Those are men who committed particularly heinous crimes," they explained, "and among them there are some of the brigands he captured."'

'When I appeared unconvinced, they laughed and added they knew quite well what they spoke of, because they were among the men charged with watching over those criminals, in the great tower dungeon.'

The young man then anxiously asked about her health, and suggested that they met as soon as possible.

The relief Sylverna had felt in reading the first words of the letter subsided substantially as she went on reading: on the one hand, she could not believe her father to be capable of being so cruel, and on the other hand she did not really believe to that tangible explanation.

The existence of that dungeon would certainly explain many things, but those still without an answer outnumbered them, first and foremost the old woman's upsetting apparition. That white, cadaverous face haunted her dreams more and more often, and it usually was the only, frightening memory she retained of them in the morning. By now, Sylverna felt certain she must have seen her not only in her nightmares but also with her own eyes, because she was persuaded that the old woman of her dreams and the mysterious servant nobody in the castle seemed to know—but who had already spoken twice to her—were one and the same person.

She hesitated for a moment, then she came to a decision: she wanted to see Thorvald. Regardless of what the young man had—or believed he had—discovered, she wanted to see him, talk with him, be comforted by him, who was the only person in the whole castle who would believe her. So, she ignored Ghitta's shocked complaints and protests, and had the maidservant bring him to her right away.

They met in Sylverna's small parlor, and once they got over the self-consciousness of being alone together in the same room for the first time they had a long talk. Even if she was still rather skeptic about the explanations Thorvald had discovered, Sylverna had finally realized that the threats connected to her visions, and the sinister warnings by the unknown servant all pointed to the dungeon under the great tower, so there might really be a connection, after all.

The two young people then speculated about mysterious enemies who might hate the Count and his lineage, and Sylverna remembered something she had heard from her aunt and uncle, about the Lorfeils' matriarch and how they had destroyed Stättenecke. At her mentioning those events, however, Thorvald suddenly looked distressed.

"The castle, the first castle... the one that was razed to the ground.. yes!" he exclaimed, as he jumped to his feet, thoroughly shaken. "The rubble, all around, and the drenched soil, and the stone, the black stone..." He broke off abruptly, a bewildered look in his eyes.

"What are you saying, Thorvald?" Sylverna was staring at him worriedly. "What's wrong with you?"

"I... I don't... I don't know, not anymore! For a moment, I thought I was remembering..."

His sentence was cut short by a sound of trumpets that came to break the relative silence of the castle. Thorvald and Sylverna looked at each other, uncertain and a little frightened by that new development, then Thorvald began, "But this is..."

Sylverna threw the window open and the well-known notes of the national anthem filled the small room, immediately followed by the door flinging open and the handmaid running in, excited and frantic.

"You must hurry, my lady! The prince-bishop is coming and you must get ready to greet him. Your father is with him. Hurry!" As she pushed Sylverna toward her dressing room, the maidservant added, now addressing Thorvald, who still stood rooted in the middle of the room, "And you must beat it, young man, unless you want the Count to find you here!"

281

"Sylverna?" the young man stammered, as he grabbed his hat and cloak. The girl reappeared for a moment on the dressing room door, her hair already loose on her shoulders, the dress half unfastened.

"Go, my dear, you really must hurry up!" She then blushed as she realized the endearment she had used; in the meantime, Thorvald ran out of her apartment, down the stairs and out into the courtyard, where now men-at-arms and servants were working frantically to get ready to welcome their lord. As he ran, he carried with him the memory of that cloud of dark hair framing the suddenly blushing face, and of those slim, naked shoulders, while that 'my dear' that had slipped out of Sylverna's lips kept ringing in his ears like some heavenly music.

He couldn't wait to see her again, but in the following days he had no way of approaching her, because they were both very busy with a succession of celebrations and banquets.

On her part, Sylverna not only had to suspend her investigation, but she also had to hide her growing disquiet from her father and his exalted guests, forcing herself to appear as the perfect lady of the house, which was what her father expected of her.

Thorvald, on the other hand, once the very first moment of confusion due to the guests' unexpected arrival was over, managed to take advantage of the general chaos to carry on his search, strengthening his friendship with the soldiers charged with watching the dungeon.

The relative laxity of those festive days, together with the abrupt change in the usual schedules and the wine Sylverna had given him, helped the young man to get from a couple of those men a description of the mysterious dungeon, which could be reached only through a trap door in the tower floor.

While the men laughed among themselves as they recalled some vicious prank played at the prisoners' expenses as they escorted them to their dungeon, Thorvald committed to memory the corridors and stairs leading to the wide underground hall and to the trapdoor leading to the well where those wretches were imprisoned. In the meanwhile, the two men told him that the underground hall was cut in two halves by an iron grating, beyond which the trapdoor was set. Only the Count himself and Tonio, their unyielding sergeant, held the key opening that grating, and it was only in Tonio's presence that they were allowed to lower a basket with food and water to the prisoners.

Ever since he had started worming his way into the two men's confidence, Thorvald had been determined to get into that mysterious underground hall, but now things were beginning to sound more difficult than he had expected. He pondered on the problem for a good long while, but in the end he had to give up: he clearly was going to need Sylverna's help again, while he would have liked to keep her out of that dangerous business, at least for the moment.

With the complicity of the handmaid, Thorvald managed to let her know he absolutely had to speak with her, and the next evening Sylverna came out on her room balcony. The conversation was perforce brief and furtive, but those few moments together made Thorvald realize that the girl was reaching her breaking point, worn out as she was by the need to feign a serenity she did not really feel in the presence of her father's important guests, coupled with her responsibilities as the lady of the castle and, most of all, her persistent nightmares. In spite of all this, however, the young man had to ask her yet another effort in order to carry out his plan.

"The dungeon is split in two parts by an iron grating," he explained, "and I need the keys to open its gate. The Count has them, on his key ring, and if you know where he keeps it and could manage to take them for just one night..."

"The key ring is on a hook, inside his dressing room," the girl stammered, but then she immediately added, "No, Thorvald, no! Don't ask me to do that, I cannot! I'm afraid, and... and it is a shameful thing to do! No!"

The squire had already worked out many justifications with which to counter her objections, but he did not even had the time to voice them because Sylverna, quite upset, bade him a good night and drew back, closing the shutters.

Now that his plan had gone miserably awry, and that he was also fearing of having lost the friendship and respect of the girl he loved, Thorvald sadly went back to his room, where he slept quite poorly because wild cries and the howling wind disturbed his rest. On the next morning, however, while going on duty he saw Ghitta hasten toward him furtively, one hand clenched on the pocket of her apron.

"Thank God I found you right away!" she whispered, as she reached him, and put in his hand a small package she took out of her pocket. "Otherwise my lady might have had a fit! You have no idea what kind of night we spent," she went on, grabbing Thorvald by his arm and dragging him to a secluded corner. "She kept trying to run away in her nightgown, screaming that a decomposed corpse was coming out of the moat to get her, and I had to try to restrain her and make her see reason, to persuade her it was just another nightmare! Of course, my poor lady has been having many such nightmares, and it is clear she's suffering from them: she's grown so pale and thin, just like her mother, God rest her soul, who..."

With good grace, the by now quite worried Thorvald managed to stem the maid's flood of words and to send her away after thanking her, then he closeted himself in his room and opened the package, staring at its contents with a satisfaction already tinged with a shade of fear: hidden inside a skein of wool were the keys he had asked for... the keys that would open the grating and allow him to look into Stättenecke's mysteries.

The sergeant stared at Thorvald with some perplexity. According to the young man, two of his men had been summoned by the Count as reinforcements for the prince-bishop Honor Guard, and he had been sent in their stead.

It was highly irregular, but on the other hand the boy was the Count's ward... maybe even his son, according to some rumors!

He cleared his throat, uncertain, shuffling his feet on the courtyard cobblestones.

"If there is any problem, sergeant, you can ask Captain Halmer, or the Count himself. To tell the truth, they are both in the great hall now, waiting for his Eminence the Prince-Bishop, but I'm sure that..."

That was just all they needed! Bothering the Count at such a time, and about what was, after all, a paltry problem! Of course, Thorvald's loyalty was unquestionable, and at worst he was covering up for his comrades.

Summoned, my foot! he thought. *They are drunk and the boy offered to replace them to get them out of trouble. It must have been easy for him to obtain permission from the Count, considering that right now, with all these noble visitors around, we certainly are understaffed.*

With a nod, the sergeant grunted his assent and motioned for Thorvald to line up with the others.

They opened the trapdoor, revealing a narrow spiral staircase. The young man climbed down in silence with the others, the grating keys hidden inside his doublet, thinking that taking the place of the two soldiers he had drugged with the wine and locked up in an empty closet had been far easier than he had expected.

Now he had to find a way to escape the sergeant's attention and hide in the underground hall, in order to open the grating and reach the well as soon as the patrol left; as he walked on, however, it was more and more difficult for him to put together a rational plan, as if those low, dark vaults confused him, flooding his mind with chaotic, fragmented memories and bits and pieces of disturbing, only vaguely remembered scenes.

His mind was making an effort to commit to memory every turn, every door, every step, heedless of the dampness and the darkness—broken only by the light of the torches held by the soldiers themselves—that wrapped itself around them as they climbed down those long corridors and narrow stairs framed by huge boulders that seemed to try and choke him.

While his brain was carefully recording every detail of their route, however, his heart was thundering in his chest. He tried to explain his anxiety away telling himself he was simply afraid that his subterfuge would be discovered , that he feared the Count's anger, even that he was suffering from lack of air and light, from his cramped surroundings... as soon as he reached the great underground hall, however, and saw beyond the dividing grating, right beside the well, a huge block of black granite, he suddenly felt confused and lost, while his incoherent memories slowly blended together, becoming a single, dreadful memory from his unknown past.

The stone, the black stone! Boulders and ruins all around, and a strong, hard hand forcing him down on the cold, wet stone, keeping him still...

Thorvald staggered as he fought against the awful images parading vividly in his memory, and he had to lean against the wall to stay on his feet.

The old sergeant, who had been keeping an eye on him, swore silently.

Spineless young people! he thought. *But he is the Count's protégé...*

So, instead of giving Thorvald a shake, together with a couple of kicks, while yelling at him, the sergeant forced himself to go to his aid, and felt quite relieved when the boy managed to ask—in a very weak voice—his permission to leave the dungeon and get back outside, in the open air.

"You can go," the sergeant readily answered, glad to get rid of him. "And then you are free to get back to your room, without waiting for us."

Thorvald thanked him and stumbled out of the hall, heedless of the ironic, compassionate stares of his companions. The more distance he put between himself and the underground chamber, however, the less confused and anxious he felt, so much so that by the time he reached the spiral staircase, he had almost managed to persuade himself that he had been very good at taking advantage of his brief spell of dizziness—probably due to the stale air in the dungeon—to be able to remain down there unnoticed.

He quickly went back over what he knew. The patrol, always under Tonio's command, would make its rounds every three hours, inspecting the dungeon and then leaving it unguarded. Taking advantage of the semi-darkness, and of the fact that everybody thought he had already left, he could hide under the staircase, wait there for the men-at-arms to leave, and then get back to the great chamber, open the gate and speak with the men in the well. As he nestled under the staircase, he reckoned he was going to have two hours at his disposal before the next patrol would climb down there.

That seemed like a very short time to him then, but once the soldiers had left and he came out of his hiding place to brave the darkness again, he wondered how he was going to last that long down there. He already had trouble breathing and the surrounding, slimy stones felt like they were closing on him, but he managed to get back to the wide chamber and to open the gate in the grating. He stopped for a moment, then he stepped forward. The air, already stale and heavy throughout the dungeon, there got even worse, made even heavier and sickening by a foul smell. Thorvald had to fight against bouts of nausea and at the same time against mixed feelings of fear and extraneousness; finally, a vague sound raising from the well shook him out of his confused state: it was a sound of voices, hoarse but human, and in that moment of dismay it heartened him. As Thorvald headed toward the sound, treading carefully in the uncertain light of his torch, he was struck by two words the prisoners kept repeating in a fearful, anguished way: *new moon*. His heart missed a beat as he remembered that the oncoming night would be the first of the new moon... the night when those mysterious, hostile forces haunting the castle manifested themselves more strongly.

That was not the only thing making his blood run cold, though. There was something else, which up to then he had been able to keep hidden in the deepest recesses of his memory, and that was now fighting to resurface.

What forced him to get near the well, in spite of his growing terror, of his feeling he was gradually becoming somebody else, was not just his curiosity, his wish to help the girl he loved... it was the unescapable need to do so, a sort of obsession: he had to reach the black stone, to touch it... to remember.

Darkness was almost absolute, broken only by the flickering light of his torch, but Thorvald slowly kept feeling his way forward, slipping repeatedly on the slimy, uneven stones of the floor. Every time, getting up required a greater effort on his part, as he stared, mesmerized, at the bulky black stone set between the thick wall of the chamber and the well. By now, however, Thorvald had almost forgotten the well, even if screams and moans kept coming up from its depths: his attention was now totally drawn by the black stone. He finally reached it and spent a long moment just staring at it, stock still, as if spellbound, while blurred feelings fought in his mind. Slowly, almost against his own will, he then reached with his hand to brush his fingers against it. A shudder ran through his whole body as his face lost any trace of color or expression, then he looked around, dumbfounded.

The walls surrounding him, even the vault arching over his head seemed to slowly change their shape, losing substance... he knew it was impossible, and yet the chamber had vanished under his eyes and now it—and the whole castle around it—existed only as the ghost of a possible future. The thick walls surrounding it were gone, and now the black stone rose menacingly under a black sky on whose background the shape of the hill of Pican and, further away, the dark Balest could barely be seen. By the stone stood a monstrous female figure, her clothes filthy with mud and blood, her gaunt face lifted toward the starless sky.

She held a curved sacrificial knife in her bony left hand and a naked boy was lying on the stone, paralyzed with fear, with barely enough strength left to cry softly.

Thorvald felt on his own body the cold night air, as if he were the one lying on that unholy altar, and he fell prey of a nameless terror, while all his life memories vanished from his mind, leaving only the nameless horror of his impending, hideous death, as the *bregostana* bent over him and held him still with her claw-like right hand, raising the knife in her left hand.

A thin wail, the cry of a defenseless child, escaped the squire's lips while his past surfaced from that vision; upon reliving the full horror of those dreadful moments, the young man crumpled to the ground by the sacrificial stone, while a voice that he would now been able to recognize rose in a bloodcurdling scream, followed by the prisoners' cries and curses.

Sylverna was in the depths of distress.

The previous night she had heard again that awful scream rise from the foundations of the castle. More frightened than ever, she had thought she could recognize a word... *castle*... in that dreadful howling.

As she always did in such situations, Ghitta had ignored her calls, and Sylverna had spent the night alone, beside herself with terror, shivering on a chair, with the thought of Thorvald as her only comfort.

The sun had already been up for some hours now, but the squire had not come yet, and he hadn't even let her know anything. Worse still, he hadn't sent the keys back to her, with the risk that the Count might discover they had disappeared.

She stood up, wringing her hands, and in that moment Ghitta appeared at her door.

"So, have you found him? Is he coming or did he give you something for me?" Sylverna pressed her, but the woman shook her head.

"No, my lady. Not only I did not find him, but nobody seems to know his whereabouts and Captain Halmer is quite annoyed. I think there will be trouble, a lot of trouble, and..." The maidservant pressed her lips knowledgeably, then she added abruptly, "And the lord Count wants to see you. Right now."

Sylverna collapsed back on her chair, her legs turning to water, as the fear that her father might have discovered the theft of the keys preyed on her mind, on top of her the night's terror and her worry for Thorvald.

She didn't say a word while her maidservant dressed her and combed her hair, then she headed for the study, where her father was waiting for her and entered, silent and trembling. Contrary to her fears, however, a smile softened Ruthgard's stern face as soon as he saw her. He greeted her kindly, had her sit down in front of him, and congratulated her on the way she had performed her duties as the lady of the castle in the presence of so many noble guests.

"You made me understand you are a woman now, my daughter, and that your tantrums and childish fears are but a memory. I'm proud of you, and I know I can leave the whole castle, and the fief itself, in your hands without any qualms."

Secretly relieved, Sylverna forced a smile and tried to find the words to thank her father, but the Count went on, still smiling, "I mean it, you know! His Eminence is leaving today with his retinue, and I'll go with him part of the way. In my absence, you will be the mistress of Stättenecke, the lady of the castle. Aren't you happy?"

Flabbergasted, Sylverna barely managed to stammer a few words, while she thought frantically that this turn of the events would at least give her time enough to look for the keys and to put them back where they belonged, provided that her father didn't realize they were gone before he left.

"Aren't you listening to me? Aren't you curious?" Ruthgard was asking her in the meanwhile. Not having the barest idea what he had been talking about, the girl managed another wan smile, stammering: "I... my lord Father, I'm just..." She didn't know how to end that lame sentence, but the Count burst out laughing and finished it for her.

"Shy and self-conscious, aren't you? Just as well, modesty and restraint are a marriageable girl's best dowry!

I'm sure somebody else I'm soon going to meet will share my view on this point... how about one of those handsome Wulfstaffen cousins of yours? No, I'm not going to add anything else, at least for now!"

Stunned by that new, unexpected blow, all Sylverna could do was to smile and curtsy, while she followed with her eyes her father's movements. When the man, who was already dressed for the journey, got near the cabinet where the keys should have been, the girl almost fainted with fear, but after hesitating for a moment, the Count simply closed its door.

"No," he said, his hand still on the latch. "You already have all the keys you might need, and in any case Captain Halmer has a copy of these particular keys, which open rooms that fall under his exclusive jurisdiction." And he left the door closed. This time, Sylverna's smile was far wider, and more sincere.

Brushing her cheek with his hand, the Count left the study with her.

A short while later, the prince-bishop and his retinue left the castle, escorted by a patrol of elite man-at-arms from Stättenecke, led by Ruthgard himself.

As soon as she was left in charge, Sylverna took immediate advantage of it to have the whole castle combed in search for Thorvald, but the search only confirmed that the previous evening the young man had climbed down to the dungeon with the patrol led by Sergeant Tonio.

"Our duty is to..." The old soldier, clearly ill at ease, swallowed with difficulty as he stared at his lord's daughter, uncertain about what he could say and what he'd better keep to himself. "Yes, it is to check on... the... I mean, to check that everything is in order."

He thought he had managed to answer quite well and sighed with relief, but the young lady looked at him quite sternly.

"Sergeant," Sylverna then said, making an effort to speak in a firm, hard tone, "as per the Count's orders, I'm the one in command in his absence. Do you think you master would have left me in charge if I didn't know everything about what happens in the castle? So, do not mince words with me, or I'll complain about that with the Count when he comes back."

Swearing inwardly against his commanding officer, Captain Halmer, who had left with the Count, leaving him to face trouble, the poor man tried to beat around the bush a little longer, but Sylverna pressed him with a shrewdness and strength she didn't know she possessed.

"I wouldn't be wasting my time with you if the Count hadn't left taking the keys with him, and telling me to turn to you, if necessary. And it is necessary, now: I have reason to believe that your master's squire might have been locked in the dungeon, and maybe even thrown in the well—as you can see, I know what is hidden down there!—in jest or even out of sheer malice. Yes, I know Thorvald has always been the object of envy and jealousy on his comrades' part, because of the affection shown to him by the Count!"

As she uttered those last words, which only confirmed to the poor sergeant that the young man they were talking about was in fact his master's protégé, his favorite, and that he would certainly avenge him, Sylverna leaned back on her seat, apparently quite self-assured, as she stared at the sergeant.

A long minute went by, then two...an eternity to the girl. Finally, the poor sergeant caved in. Sighing again, he unhooked the keys from his belt and handed them over to the girl.

"Here they are, my Lady. I will escort you personally, and we can go even now, if you want."

The big keys clenched in her hand, Sylverna followed the sergeant down the narrow spiral staircase and along the damp corridors, calling Thorvald and looking for him, until they reached the wide chamber, half lost in the semidarkness shrouding it.

One glance was enough for Sylverna to see that her friend wasn't there either, then she turned her gaze toward the grating: he had to be beyond those bars. As dread slithered in her mind, she realized she had known it from the start.

The sergeant looked at her and shook his head.

"No, my Lady. I realize Thorvald might be there, even if I cannot fathom how he got there, but it would be unwise to get too near to the well, just the two of us. The patrol should be here in a few minutes, though, and..."

"Call them, then, go get them on the run!" snapped the girl, who was still trying to penetrate with her eyes the almost absolute darkness surrounding the well.

"Won't you come with me?"

Sylverna hesitated. She was afraid to stay there by herself, but she also realized that it would take less time for the sergeant to go by himself. And time was crucial, if Thorvald was in danger or wounded.

Gritting her teeth, she forced herself to reply with a self-assuredness she was far from feeling.

"I'll wait for you here. I'm too tired to walk all the way twice, along the corridors and up the stairs. Go, then, and hasten to get back with the patrol. It is an order."

The sergeant hesitated, far from happy with the whole thing, but he finally shook his shoulders and hurried toward the door.

Alone in the wide chamber, by a torch that produced more smoke than light, Sylverna was already regretting her choice not to follow the sergeant when a faint noise made her start. Raising the torch aloft with trembling hands, she got nearer to the gate. Again, she heard that moan, a thin whimper as if of an exhausted child. Uncertain, she reached without thinking for the keys the sergeant had left by the torch. The faint moan echoed again, grew into a childish whimper then died with a sob.

Feeling she could not hesitate any longer, the girl strode toward the gate and with some difficulty unlocked it. She then entered the other half of the room, walking in small, cautious steps toward the well, from which she could hear moans and sounds drift up to her. She fought back her fear with the thought that the sergeant and his men were but a few steps away, but she was also heartened, in a strange way, by the disgusting smell wafting up from the well, because it clearly meant that its prisoners were men, and not ghost. In fact, the faint light of the torch she had taken along allowed her to see a very deep hole opening by one of the chamber walls, and down in its depths she could vaguely glimpse some shapes... men, dressed in rags, some of them chained, who were reacting to the light trying to move, to come forward, dragging themselves as they screamed, moaned and cursed.

Appalled, she was instinctively backing away the way she had come when a different, hoarse cry froze her in mid-step. Turning, she searched the darkness with her eyes, holding the torch aloft in an attempt to have a better view of the chamber, and she finally glimpsed a huge black stone, set between the well and the thick stone wall. Uncertain, she moved toward it, one step, then two, before she stopped with her heart hammering in her chest. A human figure could be seen at the foot of that huge boulder; curled up on the floor, it was almost invisible in the semidarkness, but for a moment Sylverna's terror lent it the evil face of the old woman she had seen in her nightmares.

She wanted to go back, to run beyond the grating, to call for help, but in that moment the figure looked up with a faint moan, and to her astonishment the girl recognized Thorvald.

Mustering up her courage, she got closer and shook him, but the squire looked at her as if he did not recognize her, as if he didn't even know who or where he was. Only when Sylverna repeatedly called his name, shaking him, he seemed to regain some measure of consciousness.

"You!" he stammered out. "No, go away! The *bregostana*... she's there, can't you see her? The knife! The knife!"

And he burst into tears, the desperate crying of a terrified child. Shocked, the girl held him in her arms, trying to understand what had happened.

"Stay calm, Thorvald, and don't worry: there's nobody here, just me, and the soldiers will soon be here to protect us from any danger. But there's nobody, as I said, nothing is threatening you!"

Since the young man was lying still in her arms, a heavy, almost dead, weight, she looked anxiously at him asking, "Are you wounded? One of the prisoners managed to strike you?"

"No, no... nobody touched me. I..."

For a moment, the squire seemed to come back to himself and he sat up, dragging his fingers through his ruffled hair, rubbing his face streaked with dirt and tears, and Sylverna sighed with relief. Immediately afterwards, however, Thorvald looked terrified again and as he extended one arm toward the surrounding darkness, he sobbed, "She's back! She wants me, I'm the one she's looking for! The knife... no!"

He struggled out of the girls arms and flattened himself against the floor, crawling back toward the wall and trying to creep between it and the back stone, as if he wanted to hide himself, while he kept raving about a monstrous ghost, a dreadful sacrifice and a knife threatening him. In his delirious state, he kept switching from the present to the past, now speaking in his normal, even if somewhat hoarse, voice, and now stammering in the thin voice of a very small child.

Distraught, Sylverna called out loud for help, and a few instants later she felt relieved as the room beyond the grating filled with men and torches. Staggering, she got to her feet and opened the gate.

"There!" she ordered to the sergeant. "Thorvald is wounded.... I mean, he is ill. Take him out of here and call for Nirika, but hurry! Hurry!"

Obeying without question, the men picked up the young man and headed for the door, supporting him.

Sylverna immediately moved to follow them. She would think later about what she could do for those wretches imprisoned in the well, about an excuse, a story to tell her father to explain her actions—a prospect that made her shudder— because right now the most important thing was to heal Thorvald and get out of that place. She clearly felt that grim place had not revealed all its horrors yet, and she was afraid, as if something even more dreadful was waiting for her in the shadows.

Resolutely, she turned her back to the black monolith and the well, but as the group of soldiers walked away, disappearing along the dark corridor, she suddenly froze, as if a will stronger than her own was forcing her to stay there, to walk toward the well, to look inside it.

Waves of dread and horror ran through her, but she could not resist and mechanically pulled a torch out of its holder, slowly advancing toward the well, step by step. She kneeled by the opening, the torch gripped into her trembling hand, and looked down.

An immediate cacophony of shouts made her realize that the prisoners had seen her, and that mixed assault of pleas and curses prevented her from hearing another sound, behind her, until it was too late: it was the tread of those heavy, shuffling steps she had already heard on the stairs and in the corridor outside her room. She froze for a moment where she was kneeling, while a fetid smell of putrid flesh assaulted her and stunned her. A moment later a gust of chilly air made her stagger on the edge of the well, and she lost her grip on the torch, that fell from her hand.

Sylverna turned to see who—or what—was behind her, and in the last flickering light of the half extinguished torch she vaguely glimpsed a bundle of dirty rags, a mass of grey, disheveled hair framing a decayed face, frightening talons reaching for her... beside herself with terror, she drew back, rising her arms to protect her face, and she fell in the well, landing on a heap of rotten straw.

She lost consciousness, and when she came back to her senses she found herself surrounded by the ugly faces of the prisoners, barely visible in the faint light filtering down there from the chamber above.

Their sneering faces, their gestures and mocking comments terrified her, and her fear grew when she realized she was impaired in her movements.

"I'm the Count's daughter," she managed to moan in a barely audible voice. "You can ask your freedom in exchange for my life and my safety, but if you hurt or kill me, the guards..."

She stopped in mid-sentence, because upon hearing the words 'I'm the Count's daughter' the men had drawn back from her, staring at her with a strange, frightened expression in their eyes; a moment later, they started shouting again, calling for the guards.

After a short time—that felt like an eternity to Sylverna—the patrolmen came back to the chamber to look for her, and the prisoners' shouts made them realize right away what had happened.

"Shut up, down there!" yelled the sergeant, nervously running his hands through his grey hair. "If what you're saying is true, let our young Lady speak."

Shouts and sneers slowly subsided until they died down, and in the silence Sylverna's trembling voice rose from the well.

"I fell, and now I cannot move! For God's sake, call my father! He's the only one..."

She broke off, bursting into tears, and her words became desperate sobs.

In the meanwhile, the prisoner had been whispering among themselves and one of them finally spoke for them all.

"The damsel is right. Let the Count come to bargain for his daughter's life! We won't touch her while we wait for him... provided that we don't have to wait too long. But should one of you try to get down here or to strike us from above, I'll break that delicate neck of hers with my own hands."

"You'd never dare..." the sergeant began, but the prisoner merely sneered.

"Why not? Because we would then all die? We don't have much to lose, as you can see, but you on the other hand..."

"What are you hinting at?"

"You know quite well, we all know. Month after month we have all listened to what the castle screams at each new moon."

"You're raving mad, you all are! The imprisonment made you all go mad!"

A chorus of guffaws followed those words.

"Look at yourself!" sneered the prisoner. "Your face is grey with fear and your hands are trembling! If you want to go on living, send for the Count, right away!"

The sergeant drew back, biting his lips, and turned to his men who were all crowding behind him, pale and worried. They'd been coming down into that dungeon for years, and they all had doubts and suspicions, which the brigand's words had now confirmed. They all avoided the sergeant eyes and—slowly at first, then more hurriedly and

301

with growing anxiety—huddled against the grating, asking, demanding that he opened the gate.

"Line up! Are you men or fearful women?" shouted Tonio. "We'll get back upstairs, of course, but in a disciplined way, like the soldiers we are!"

They walked away in a semblance of order, leaving two big lit torches behind, and the sergeant immediately informed his superior office, who in turn informed the lieutenant—since the captain was absent—but in the end all they could do was to send a messenger on the Count's trail with the order of trying to reach him as soon as possible, at any cost, to tell him what had happened.

In the meantime the sun set and the night fell—a dark and moonless night—and with the darkness came also those mysterious sounds that had always tormented and frightened the whole castle household. Down there in the well where Sylverna lay terrified and hurting, but still conscious, they sounded much nearer and more powerful and dreadful than ever.

She had already guessed from the fear and the words of the prisoners that some awful story was linked to the castle, and her terror grew to unbearable levels when the dreadful death scream, which so many times before had dragged her from her sleep, rose from a place even deeper than the well itself... from the very foundations of the walls.

Shaking with fear, helpless, she heard it grow louder, so terrible, full of terror and menace, while the prisoners screamed too, trying to cover it with the sound of their own voices, thus generating the cacophony she had heard so many times. Even so, that dreadful scream emanating from the bowels of the earth rose higher and higher, reaching the battlements, and the tower walls. Then some words seemed to hiss under her feet, clinging to the stones and echoing through the whole castle. She could hear them clearly, even if she could not understand them: '*I take away*'. Sylverna finally lost consciousness, overwhelmed by her terror and the pain from her wounds.

Since the Count was already heading back to the castle, the messenger reached him in a few hours and immediately handed him the message in which the lieutenant told him what had happened.

Ruthgard hastened to open and read it, then he slowly let it fall on his knees. His frozen face looked like that of a dead man, and it took him a few minutes before he found the strength to motion for the messenger to come closer to the coach window.

"Speak freely, soldier, and without any fear. My daughter... is she alive?"

"My lord Count, the damsel was hurt when she fell, but she was alive when I left."

"When you left..." Ruthgard echoed him, almost mechanically, as he looked toward the mountains as if he hoped to be already able to see from there the great castle of Stättenecke. Then he roused himself, and added, "She's still alive, yes. And she's wounded... how seriously?"

"I don't know, Your Excellence." The soldier peered into his lord's face and immediately tried to soften his answer. "She might just be stunned, and perhaps she'll recover as soon as we'll take her to safety and entrust her to Nirika's care."

He leaned forward again to peer at the Count, who was leaning against the backrest of the seat, and what he saw left him speechless.

He knew that Ruthgard had a deep love for his daughter, who was all the family he had left, but what he had just seen on his face was not grief... or at least not just grief: it was sheer, blind, hopeless terror.

They traveled in silence for a while, until the Count asked abruptly, "What about Thorvald?"

The messenger stared at him in surprise, because neither he nor the lieutenant in his message had mentioned the young man, then he hesitantly told his lord how they had found the squire semi-conscious and delirious, in the dungeon.

"Where? Where?" asked Ruthgard, his voice heavy with anguish.

"We carried him into his room and the healer is now looking after him" the soldier answered, misunderstanding his lord's question, but immediately a curse from the Count made him realize his mistake.

"Where did you find him, you idiot! I want to know where you found him, not where he is now! You know, don't you? You are in the patrol in charge of the dungeon."

"Yes, I am, my lord, but..." Dumbfounded, the man lowered his head, giving up any attempt to understand what was going on. "I was among those who came to his aid, yes. The boy was by the well, at the foot of that huge black stone... I don't know if you have any idea what I'm talking about, if you have ever seen it, but..."

"If I've ever seen it? If I've ever seen it?" The Count burst into a hard, dreadful laugh, then he made the coach stop and jumped down.

"Give me your horse, immediately!" he ordered to his captain, who was at the head of the group. "Follow me as you can."

Then he jumped into the saddle and spurred the horse toward Stättenecke.

In less than an hour he reached the already sleeping village and left it behind, swiftly riding up the slope to the castle; at this point, however, he was forced to slow down, because groups of men, carts and animals were coming down the road as swiftly as the darkness and the uneven ground would allow them. Ruthgard recognized one of them, two, ten... they were servants, peasants, artisans and shopkeepers who had been working at the castle for years and were mow leaving it together with their families, their furniture and trade tools loaded on the carts.

He stopped some of them, asking why they were running away in that hard and commanding voice that through the years had guaranteed his troops' blind, immediate obedience, but those men merely looked away and silently bowed their head. Here and there, however, from the wagons and the shadowy figures that could barely be glimpsed toward the end of the long column, a few voices spoke of a curse and of evil spirits, while some of the fugitives even signed themselves to ward off evil before setting off again. Slowly they all silently moved on around him and disappeared behind a curve of the road in a cloud of dust.

For a moment the Count looked after them, sitting still on his horse, then he rose on his stirrups, waving his fist at the dark heavens while shouting a curse before he spurred his horse again, riding faster and faster up the slope until, upon negotiating another bend of the road, he finally saw the five high towers of his castle. With an exultant shout, Ruthgard covered the last yards at breakneck speed, jumping over the moat and galloping into the courtyard.

"My lord Count!" the lieutenant greeted him, silently thanking God they had managed to open the gates before their lord crashed into them. "The situation..."

"A squad of men with me, now!" the Count brusquely cut him off, and he hurried toward the dungeon followed by the few soldiers the unlucky officer had been able to gather in a couple of minutes. The lieutenant tried to ask for instructions, to justify himself, to explain, but Ruthgard ignored him. Like a person possessed, he ran down the spiral staircase, along the dark corridors and into the underground chamber without answering or listening to anybody.

The gate had been left open, so he hurried toward the well opening, motioning for his men to wait for him on the other side of the grating as he shouted for the brigands' chief, calling him by his nickname.

"Fist, where is my daughter? If you killed her, you bastards, I swear..."

The brigand's guffaw cut him off.

"She lives, my noble lord, she lives, but then you already knew it! If she weren't alive..."

"Shut up, you rascal!"

"As you wish. In any case, it's almost midnight, a new moon midnight, and soon *somebody else* will speak!"

Scorn and hate filled the prisoner's words, but there was fear in them as well, and other voices rose from the almost absolute darkness of the well, echoing it.

"We know it only too well!"

"We've been hearing those words for years, and they grow more dreadful every time!"

"We scream, not to hear that voice, that prophecy..."

"But we know every word by now! Branded in our memory, they are!"

"Do you want us to repeat them for you, your most noble Excellency?"

To which, the others immediately chorused, "*With the…*"

"Shut up! That' enough! Sylverna is wounded, and you don't want her death, do you?"

Shouts and hoots answered his words, then Fist spoke again.

"Maybe we do, or maybe we don't, my fine lord. They say everybody holds his own life dear, but then it depends on what kind of life we speak of! The life we lead here, thanks to your generous hospitality, is such that we prefer death to it… death and vengeance. Therefore, you can get ready either to say goodbye to your daughter, or to let us go, in which case we won't touch one hair on her precious head."

The Count had a long moment of hesitation, his hands balled into fists, as he stared at the thick walls surrounding him, and at the soldiers huddling around the lieutenant, behind him. Finally, he called his daughter.

"Sylverna, Sylverna!"

His only answer was a faint moan, but that was enough.

He slowly rose to his feet, his face turned to stone, and ordered the soldiers to lower a rope ladder into the well, escort the prisoners out of the castle and let them go free.

They obeyed him in silence, nobody daring to say even one single word, and as soon as the last of the bandits had left, shouting insults and threats, Ruthgard had a stretcher—which his men had put together in them meanwhile—lowered in the well before turning to Halmer, who had finally reached him.

"As soon as the young Lady is in her room, get some twenty men and chase those wretches down," he ordered.

"As you wish! We'll catch them in no time and bring them back!" the captain zealously guaranteed, but the Count shook his head, a malevolent smile on his lips.

"No. You will kill all those you manage to catch," he curtly replied. Then, while the old officer still tried to come to terms with that order, he went on, his voice growing louder, more frantic: "And you must catch them all... all! There must be no survivors among those who know..." He broke off abruptly, biting his lip, then he seemed to calm down as he concluded, "Among those who dared to blackmail the Lord of Stättenecke."

In the meanwhile, with the utmost care the still unconscious Sylverna had been taken to her room, where Ghitta, tearful and trembling, was waiting for her together with the healer, who had just left Thorvald's room.

"Cut it out with those tears, girl, and don't just stand there!" she ordered brusquely. "Help me to put her in her bed. Uhm..."The healer quickly looked Sylverna over, then she shook her head, and added, "Go look for her father, now."

The Count had gone to check on Thorvald, who was sleeping uneasily under the effect of a sedative drug, but upon hearing Ghitta's confused words he rushed to his daughter's room.

Night had fallen by then, a moonless, starless night. Darkness hung heavy on the castle, like a shroud, and in her room, barely lit by a single lamp, Sylverna already looked dead, lying there on her bed.

Ghitta followed her master to the bedroom door, but then she stealthily ran away, crossing herself. She did not even stop to pick up her shawl, running down the stairs to join a group of servants who were leaving Stättenecke with the help of some of the guards.

"So, healer, what can you tell me?" the Count asked, after kneeling for a long while by his daughter, anxiously peering at her colorless face.

Nirika shook her shoulders.

"My lord Count, the damsel fell from a great height. She has a broken arm, and some ribs are broken too, but these are damages that could have been healed. Unfortunately, her fall also caused serious internal damage. She's been hemorrhaging, she spit blood and is barely breathing, and I think... I fear..."

The woman's voice died down in a whisper, while her eyes never left Sylverna, whose breathing was getting weaker by the minute, and more similar to a death rattle.

"Don't mince your words, woman!" snapped Ruthgard, clenching his fists as he glared at her. "You don't know what hangs upon this single life!"

Nirika held his burning gaze with her own, unflinchingly.

"Perhaps I do, my lord," she whispered. "This is why I dare to speak openly to you. Your daughter still has but a few hours of life."

The Count started, while the healer went on, "She won't open her eyes again, nor regain consciousness. She will slip from this sleep into death without even feeling it.

But while she still breathes, you must order everybody to leave the castle, and you should leave too."

"How dare you? Are you out of your mind?"

He lifted his hand, as if to strike her, and Nirika backed away toward the door, but after that first, angry reaction, Ruthgard calmed down and turned his back to her, dismissing her from his attention. Sighing, the woman cast a compassionate glance to Sylverna's still body, another to her lord, and she left, whispering, "May God have mercy on you!"

The Count didn't even register her leaving: he threw the window open and leaned out, staring at his castle, whose high towers were barely visible in the darkness. He stood like that for a long while, then he sighed and closed the window, almost reluctant to walk away from it, to kneel again by his dying daughter's bed.

The girl seemed to have grown smaller, thinner, so much so that the shape of her body was barely visible under the heavy layer of the covers; her face was deadly pale, with dark rings under her eyes. The only sign she was still alive was her slow, rattling breath, but it was becoming slower, weaker, more wheezing. The Count covered his face with his hands and knelt like that for a long time, while Sylverna's breath grew more labored. Realizing his daughter wasn't going to see the next dawn, finally Ruthgard rose to his feet, looked at her one last time, reaching with his hand to brush her cheek, then he went out on the balcony, calling out loudly to his servants and soldiers.

"Run away! Run away, all of you! Leave Stättenecke, now!" he shouted in a terrible voice.

Most civilians had already left, and many of the soldiers were away because busy chasing down the released prisoners. Those who were left gathered under the balcony in an uncertain, bewildered group.

"Don't waste any time collecting your possessions, leave now if you value your life, you idiots! Sergeant, have everybody leave the castle. It's an order!" the Count shouted, seeing Tonio among that small crowd, then he went back into the room and locked the balcony doors, ignoring the questions and the calls of his people crowded in the courtyard, where chaos was rapidly taking over. All the castle inhabitants were running here and there, bumping against one another, looking for each other, going back and forth from their rooms to look for a last object or memento. In a few minutes, however, Tonio managed to take charge of the situation, and soon the narrow road between the castle and the village was alive with torchlight, full of animals, men and women running away, until the last flicker of light vanished beyond the last bend of the road, leaving behind only silence and darkness.

In Sylverna's room, the Count slowly closed his dead daughter's eyes, then he went to the window and leaned his forehead against it, waiting.

He didn't have to wait long, because just a few minutes later a dreadful voice rose from the foundations:

"Through perjury you had it built
Through my blood its stones you knit...
But your blood the spell does destroy
And your castle thus I take away."

Ruthgard nodded his head, as if agreeing with those words and accepting his own end. He might still have saved himself by running away, instead he picked up his dead daughter's body and went to the armory, where he donned his full armor, just as he would have done going to war. He then picked Sylverna's body in his arms once more and climbed to the top of the great tower, where his flag waved in the night air. His back leaning against the flag pole, he proudly raised his head and waited there for his castle to crumble, swallowing him while the first, deep cracks opened in the huge walls, like black talons reaching out to grasp and destroy that castle built on blood and treachery.

"My Lord! My Lord! Sylverna is dead! It's my fault, it's because of me..."

A frantic voice sounded nearby and a human figure appeared on the battlements: Thorvald, whom the servants had totally forgotten about, leaving him in his room, and who had run outside as soon as the effect of the sleeping potion had vanished.

"Now I know, I finally remember!" the young man shouted, still half dazed. "I was the one who should have been sacrificed on that unholy altar, so that my blood would knit Stättenecke's foundations! Such was the price the *Bregostana* had asked for her infernal gods, the price you had promised her!"

"Thorvald..." Ruthgard wanted to reply, to deny it all, but in that moment the tower swayed under their feet; behind them, a cloud of dust rose from the stairs, while plaster rained on their steps.

The Count stared at Sylverna's body, than at Thorvald, the boy he had stolen from his parents so that the bregostana could make Stättenecke eternal through her evils spells. He then looked at the pitch-black sky as the floor trembled under his feet. There was no time left. The hour of his death had come, and with it a time for truth.

He looked at the squire again, and in his distraught face he found again the face of a little boy he—in his folly—had deemed expendable.

"Yes, Thorvald. You should have died on that black stone. Such was the nefarious pact that cursed hag offered me, and to which I agreed with the most binding oaths. But when I saw you on that altar, helpless, terrified and crying, I could not stand that appalling sight... and it was the *bregostana's* blood that flowed on that hellish stone."

"But then..."

"Human blood had been asked to cement Stättenecke's foundations and make it indestructible, and human blood was shed. The spell was done, and that cursed hag couldn't undo it, but as she died she used her last breath to cast a curse: those foundations cemented with her blood were going to hold firm until the blood of a Stättenecke was shed in the castle. Then they were going to crumble and dissolve like snow under the sun," the Count explained, tonelessly, then he knelt by his dead daughter, brushed her hair with his hand, and got up again holding her in his arms. "You can still save yourself, my boy! You are young and nimble... and innocent," he added, looking at the squire with affection. "You can still leave this tower, this castle, and live!"

Live.

Thorvald looked at Sylverna, his love, and at Ruthgard, who had always been all his family and who had defied for his sake those same evil forces that were now killing him.

"We'll go together, my lord!" he exclaimed. "I'll help you and we'll save ourselves! We can still live, both of us!"

313

A bitter smile curved the Count's lips. He looked down at Sylverna's pale face, then he stared at the walls of his castle, where the cracks were multiplying, widening by the moment.

"Live! Why, and for whom? No. I'm the last of the Stättenecke, and I won't run away, I won't leave my castle," he said quietly, with pride.

Thorvald hesitated, wringing his hands. He realized he had only scant minutes to try to get to safety, but he couldn't bring himself to leave the man he still considered his benefactor, and while he still hesitated a chasm opened under the cursed foundations of the castle. The powerful walls and the high towers all bent on themselves and fell down into that abyss, crumbling and breaking into pieces. From the chasm then rose a vortex of black dust that turned into a bundle of rags and of long, grey, disheveled hair... and into two skeletal hands that closed on the ruins of the castle in a supreme gesture of ownership.

Historical notes to "The Screaming Castle"

Even if set in the Gardena Valley, this legend originates from the Livinallongo area, and for many years the castle that mysteriously sprung up on Mount Balest and as mysteriously crashed down into the river below, the Rio di Pincan, has been thought to be just that... a legend.

In 2000, however, some archaeological excavations on the Pincan hill, in the d'Anna Valley, which lies at the foot of Mount Balest, unearthed various parts of a castle dating back to the fourteenth century, such as sections of its walls, most of the keep and a gate framed by a Romanesque arch. Those undoubtedly are the ruins of the castle belonging to the Counts of Stetteneck, who at the time were vassals and law officers of the Bishop of Bressanone, which is why I chose an imaginary member of this family as the main character of my story, which is quite different from the previous ones.

It goes without saying that everything in the story, besides the existence and the collapse of the castle, is just a product of my imagination, from the names of the characters down to the curse that destroys the castle.

Historically, the Counts of Stetteneck's lineage ended with Adelheid, the last to inherit the name and the castle, who married Reginbert de Jevun around the year 1350.

Iron Hands

"Tu cavalier, ciantor, poet de nomanza
Zenza speranza tu jiras
Ravacian per el mondo a chierir Gloria
Ciantan la rista storia
La storia de n amor"
(Da "L poet e la vivana" di Fabio Chiocchetti)
You knight, minstrel, renowned poet
Hopeless you wandered
Around the world seeking Glory
Singing the sad story
The story of a love
(From "The poet and the viviana", by Fabio
Chiocchetti)

Oswald threw down his staff and drew back, looking with clear satisfaction at his adversary who, disarmed, was splashing around in an attempt to get out of the water through, while all the squires, servants and grooms gathered around laughed and hooted.

The defeated squire, a young man of about sixteen or seventeen years of age, the son of the local blacksmith, looked in amazement at his vanquisher, a boy at least half a head shorter than he was and a few years younger, who had made up for his physical inferiority fighting with a courage and—most of all—a fury totally uncalled for by the offence he had received.

Offence? As he dragged himself out of the through, drenched with water and shivering, the young man shook his head. *There had been no offence, he had just said the sheer truth, inviting him to stand aside and keep quiet not to spoil the chorus they were starting to sing, and to refrain from touching the instruments, so that he would not damage them with his 'iron hands'.*

Anyhow, he now regretted his words, not so much because of the way the young boy had reacted, or of having made a fool of himself in front of his friends, but because he had remembered too late that the pestiferous little monkey was the son of his lord, the powerful Count of Wolkenstein.

Dripping with water, he climbed out of the through, uncertain if he should apologize, which would make him lose whatever face he had left with his friends, or simply walk away, at the risk of being punished later on.

He was spared making a decision by *anda* Bertha, the Countess' maidservant, who came running into the courtyard—as swiftly as her bulk would allow her— followed by two snickering valets.

"Young master! Your lady mother, the Countess..." the woman began, in her shrilly voice, bearing down on Oswald who, upon seeing her coming, had been trying to beat a retreat toward the stables, only to find his way blocked by the onlookers. "She saw it all, the poor woman! She almost fainted, and she wants to have a few words with you, right now! Come with me!"

The servant then took advantage of the boy's hesitation to grab him by the hand and pull him toward the castle doors with the silent but efficient help of the two valets; at the same time, the head groom came out of the stables, dispersing the onlookers with a couple of angry shouts and a few whiplashes, while the blacksmith grabbed his son by his ear and dragged him into his workshop, promising he was going to teach him a long lasting lesson.

In a few minutes the courtyard was empty and silent again, only proof to the previous confusion only a wide puddle of water that was already beginning to evaporate under the warm rays of the sun of May.

Oswald stood silent in the wide hall, on whose frescoed walls were portrayed the legendary deeds of the funder of his lineage. His back to the huge majolica *stube*, the boy faced his mother, who sat pale and dignified on a seat covered with cushions, and kept shuffling his feet as he looked longingly out of the wide mullioned window, through which he could see the far shapes of the mountains surrounding Castel Forte and the swallows darting through the clear sky... freedom, in other words.

In the meanwhile, his mother's sorrowful voice droned on.

"I really don't know what's the matter with you! You are the Count of Wolkenstein's son, with a future anybody else would envy you for, and you keep demeaning yourself, mixing up with all sorts of riff-raff, such as your servants, coming to blows with them, even running away from home! This way you keep risking..." The woman suddenly broke off in midsentence, staring through a veil of tears at the bandage covering her son's right eye.

The previous winter, during last Carnival days, Oswald had managed to give his tutor and servants the slip and, restless as usual, he had hurried to Pruca, where he ended up in a disreputable tavern, picking a fight with some drunkards. In the ensuing brawl, he had lost his right eye, but it had been impossible to get a word out of him about the how and why of that scuffle, or to get the name of his attacker from him. Oswald had met all their questions with silence, full of pent-up rage, just as he was now an always.

The Countess had always had a special fondness for that son of hers! For his sake she had even done something no good believer should ever have done... a tear rolled down the woman's round cheek. Before she could wipe it away, Oswald jumped forward and took her hand in his.

"Don't cry for me, mother! I'm fine, my eye doesn't bother me at all. It's just that..." He broke off, biting his lip, and it was only after much tender cajoling that the woman managed to drag a few more confused words out of his mouth.

"It's this thing inside me that wants out, but cannot find its way... I can't... and yet I hear them inside, the words, the music..."

Blanching, Katrina got to her feet.

319

"That's enough, my son!" she exclaimed, now as anxious to have the boy shut up as much as she had been to make him talk. "You are the son of Count Friederik von Wolkenstein, and what suits you are weapons, chivalric challenges and fighting the infidels, not brawling with street urchins or loiter about the taverns with wandering minstrels!"

"They don't want me there," muttered the boy, in a barely audible voice. "Not after I tried to handle their instruments." With his only eye he cast a burning glance to his big, strong hands and nimble, sturdy fingers.

Right then Don Antelmo—the undisciplined progeny of the Wolkensteins' unhappy tutor—came into the room, thus allowing the Countess to put an end to the discussion, which by now was worrying her far more than his son's usual recklessness.

"Ah, here you are, Reverend! There's no need for more punishment, because I have already scolded my son, who regrets his behavior..."

"Not at all," the ungrateful boy murmured, but Katrina pretended not to hear him and went on, "and promised me... yes, he did... that from now on he'll be obedient and respectful... Oswald! Where are you going?"

Turning his back to his mother, the boy had nimbly avoided the grasping hands of his tutor and run for the door, tripping the man-at-arm who tried to stop him and then disappearing along the corridors and down the stairs. Once out in the wide parade ground surrounding the keep, Oswald climbed on the walls surrounding it, vainly chased by the guards; once on the battlements, he bowed mockingly to his pursuers and with a series of jumps and bounds disappeared down the escarpment abutting the walls.

"Holy Virgin Mother, protect me!" moaned Katrina, who had seen it all from her window, shouting in vain to her undisciplined son to come back, then she collapsed on her chair, while Don Antelmo shook his grey head disapprovingly. "He needs a very strong hand, my lady," he commented, absently toying with the handle of his riding crop. "Mercifully, our lord the Count is soon coming back. You'll see, he will know how to instill some healthy fear of God in that child!"

"Yes, of course, of course," the Countess mechanically replied, fanning herself with an embroidered handkerchief. "But in the meanwhile my distress is going to kill me! I wonder what I did to deserve..."

She abruptly broke off. Perhaps she knew, after all.

Crouching between two strong boughs of a great elm that had been for years one of his favorite hiding places, Oswald finished eating some pie he had stolen at the tavern, wiped his mouth with the back of his hand, and his hand on his velvet doublet, then he looked around in satisfaction. He was free... free from his mother's stifling attentions, from Don Antelmo's boring lessons, from all the shackles always imposed to him as if he were a fragile maid. He was a man, instead, as he was going to tell his father very clearly as soon as he got back. And he was also going to ask his father to take him along on his next journey, even as his squire, and if there was going to be any fighting, well... even better, then!

His hands were as good as the others'—or even better—when it came to fistfights!

321

With that thought, he lowered his eyes to his strong, grazed knuckles, as his satisfied smile, which up to a moment ago had lit his wide, determined face, disappeared.

In that moment a bird's song came from above and the boy, suddenly grave and focused, tried to reproduce it, first with his voice, which came out as a hoarse, graceless whisper, and then whistling. Even his whistling turned into a hoarse puff of breath, and Oswald sulkily resigned himself to playing the role of a mute listener of the small singer.

As he listened, his expression changed, became gentler, enthralled, and his eyes grew softer, as if he were lost in a magic dream nobody else could see. When he tried again to accompany that sweet chirping with his voice, however, all he could obtain was a hoarse and tuneless sound. With a curse that would have elicited a couple of blows from Don Antelmo's cane, he slid down from the tree branches, ripping his clothes in a couple of places, and since the sun had finally set, he hang his head and headed for the castle.

The sweet notes he had listened to kept haunting him. He rehearsed them in his mind and—still just in his mind—added his own variations and words to them.

I want to try it on some instrument, he told himself, as he hurriedly crossed the castle doors. *I cannot sing, I'm tone-deaf… fine, but it isn't possible that I end up breaking into pieces any musical instrument I touch!*

It was quite possible, however, as in a few minutes his mother's lute and an old cithern once belonging to his grandmother Zwenna proved to his dissatisfaction. As he stood there, looking at their pieces with a lump in his throat, he heard the sound of many horses trotting into the courtyard, followed by joyful welcoming shouts. Leaving the broken instruments where they lay, he ran to the window and immediately a smile curved his lips: the courtyard looked suddenly smaller, full as it was with horses, weapons and knights, around which almost all the castle household had gathered: Friederik von Wolkenstein was back home.

Standing by the big majolica *stube*, the Count of Wolkenstein was pondering, his lips pressed in a tight line, his arms crossed on his strong chest. Sitting by him on her usual seat covered with cushions, a fur blanket on her knees, his wife was pressing a handkerchief against her lips, trying not to cry.

It was not enough that her husband was going to leave again, not even a month after coming back home... now her son was demanding that he could leave with him! He had shown his father a knowledge of the political situation worth of a diplomat, and in the previous days he had shown off his ability in handling horses and weapons. Katrina felt almost certain that his husband was going to allow him to go, that her second-born would be leaving, that... Friederick's voice drew her out of that whirlpool of misery.

"You're still too young to leave your home, but your mother and your tutor have filled my ears and my head with their accounts of your escapades." The Count fell silent, thinking, then he lightly cuffed his undisciplined son on the back of his head as he went on, "It might be that some months of military life will lead you to better appreciate the safe and calm life you have here. You will leave with me, and I'll entrust you to one of my companions, as his squire."

The boy's shout of joy, as he threw himself into his father's arms, before running away along the corridor, shouting for his servants to pack his things, blended with Katrina's distressed moan.

Friederik had felt certain that Oswald would stay away at most for a year before getting tired of his life as the squire of a wandering knight and deciding to get back home; instead, he never saw his second-born son again, because he wandered all over Europe for more than ten years, doing all sorts of jobs, and finally came back to his castle only when he got news that his father had died.

He had grown into a strong young man, but he was still unhappy and irritable, as his family immediately realized. He immediately quarreled with his older brother, Michael, and only their mother's timely intervention—with the support of her four daughters—prevented the quarrel from becoming an all-out fight.

"Sit here by me, my son, and tell us something about your adventures," Katrina invited him, after the two young men shook hands while still scowling at each other.

Sitting astride a chair, Oswald began to speak, but the words came out of his mouth graceless and abrupt, while his eyes kept lingering on his mother's great harp, and on his sisters' small lutes. He brusquely brought his tale to a close, then he suddenly burst out, "I cannot express what's in my mind, even if I can feel inside both the words and the music that should accompany them! But I'm not able to..." He broke off, walking resolutely toward one of the lutes, trying to tune it up. Immediately, one of the strings broke with a snapping sound, followed by another.

Barely choking a curse, Oswald threw the poor instrument to the ground and left without a word, going to the village tavern in search for some comfort.

"Iron Hands," Michael commented mockingly.

The young warrior had left in a fury, fully intedting to go to Pruca and make a round of all its taverns, but once he left the castle behind, and before the first houses of the village came into view, he fell prey to the enchantment pervading that spring morning, with the sun rays gilding the buds and the new leaves on the trees, drawing a thousand shining reflections from the dew beading the first flowers already dotting the new grass; a light breeze rustled among the brushes, which sported their first, shy shoots, and brushed grass, branches and flowers, making them sway to its breath. High above, in the blue sky, small white clouds seemed to chase each other, racing the swift swallows, before hiding behind the mountains, and the far, gurgling voice of the River Isarco blended with the birdsong, the chirping of the crickets and all the other, small sounds of the land as it woke up from its winter slumber.

Forgetting both his anger and his intent to get drunk, Oswald stopped, drawing a deep breath and letting his eyes wander all around. Inside him, that wonderful sight, its sounds, and even the scent of the flowers turned into a flood of music, verses, songs... a whole poem he knew he could not express, even if he felt it fight to be born, deep inside. His old frustration overwhelmed him, but before it could fester into pain and rage, another sound drew his attention.

It was a woman's voice, sweet and intense, whose singing was accompanied by the crystal clear notes of a cithern. That melody, more beautiful than any he had ever heard, seemed to blend with the surrounding natural sounds, becoming the flutter of a wing, the breath of the breeze among the leaves, the slow flowing of the river.

Spellbound, the young man froze, to avoid frightening whoever was singing, but then curiosity got the best of him and he slowly moved one step forward, then two, three... until he reached the clearing the music came from.

Sitting on a musk-covered stone, her back propped against a big willow half hiding her under its foliage, was a blond girl, with her shiny, fair hair loose down her back and a small cithern in her hands.

> *"White and golden in the sunlight*
> *The King of the Ràjes saw you, o Merijana,*
> *And searched for you so you'd be his bride."*

Thus she was singing, and it seemed to the young man, who was watching her unnoticed, that those words were almost a faithful description of the singer herself. In the last few years, Oswald had met and known both noble and peasant women, but none of them could compare to the beautiful stranger. He had never seen her before, and he could not infer her status from her clothing because she wasn't wearing a noblewoman's rich dress, but her clothes weren't those of a peasant, either: the tunic she wore, trimmed with silver along the waist and the arms, seemed to be made of silk, but its color was strange, shimmering, now as green as the grass the beautiful singer was sitting on, now more of the blue-green shade of the clear water of the River Isarco, lapping at her small, bare feet.

> *"Grateful I am, my fine Lord*
> *But first the nuptial gift I ask:*
> *Be full of joy that day for all,*

Be they men, plants, or beasts.
One day, just one, and I'll say yes."

Mesmerized, the knight moved forward again, inadvertently stepping on a small dry branch, which broke with a snap. At the faint crack, the girl started and stopped singing as she turned toward him and moved as if to run away.

"No! No, I beg you. I don't want to hurt you, but just to listen to your singing. If my face frightens you, I'll hide behind that tree over there, but please, keep singing! Your song is so beautiful, your voice so sweet!"

The girl shook her head, brushing her long hair back from her face, the most beautiful Oswald had ever seen, made even more beguiling by the faint blush her confusion had brought to her cheeks. She stared at him for a long moment, with eyes whose color was that of the meadows, but also of the water, and of the thick, dark foliage of the trees. Suddenly, she smiled.

"I'm not afraid at all, even if I can sense something strange and dark in you. I know you don't want to hurt me, though, and there's no need for you to hide. Come and sit here beside me and feel free to listen, if you like my singing. It's Merijana's story. Do you know it?"

"No, but I'll be glad to learn it from you. Sing, I beg you!"

The stranger nodded, and bent over her instrument to tune it up again.

"Merijana was a beautiful nymph," she explained, as she worked. "The powerful King of the Ràjes fell in love with her and asked her to marry him." The unknown girl's nimble hands brushed the strings, drawing from them sweet notes

327

that seemed to blend with her melodious voice, the gurgling of the river, the whisper of the wind. "Merijana was good and generous, and marrying the king made her happy, but she wanted everything and everybody around her to share her happiness. She would have loved to extend to the whole creation the joy she felt in her heart, forever, but since this was clearly impossible she asked her lover to ensure that at least for one day—the day of their wedding—everybody was happy, free from pain and worries. The wise men of the kingdom, however, declared that such a thing was impossible as well."

Slowly, the girl's sweet voice rose again in a tender, moving melody that gradually grew in a cheerful crescendo.

> "Precious little is one day! And even less one hour.
> Let it be so, though: when I give you my hand,
> A bride's hand, all the world will rejoice,
> Everybody on earth of my joy
> And yours will be glad, forgetting
> Of ennui and pain the bitter chains."

She broke off for a moment, looking at the young man sitting beside her, who was staring at her as if inebriated with her song, mesmerized by her beauty; then she went on singing, raising a little her crystal clear voice,

> "At noon, my bridegroom, at noon!
> High and warm the sun will be, and to us, happy newlywed,
> The world will smile, free from pain."

Nimbly, her fingers played on the strings, drawing from the instrument a merry rhapsody, and Oswald almost felt he was really living that magic moment when everything had been perfect and the whole creation had rejoiced in the nymph's wedding. He envisioned the green meadows, and the people dancing on them holding hands, without crushing even a single grass blade under they feet; the river running like a silver ribbon, and the fish darting in its current with nobody trying to catch them; small birds perching on the tree branches, side by side with birds of prey, in peace; the cattle resting under the trees, well fed, without breaking a single branch or grazing on one leaf, with wolves and other predators resting quietly nearby. And he saw the flowers—wide colorful, perfumed patches of flowers—blossom under the sun to greet the newlywed, he heard the trees rustle softly in the wind to wish them happiness, joining the light caress of the breeze.

He smiled, almost without realizing it, and tried to put his feelings into words, but as usual his lips refused to form them, and he finally had to settle for a simple, hoarse, "Nice." His smile vanished and he grew grim faced again.

The girl finished her song with a last warble, then she looked up at the scowling young man. A faint smile curved her mouth, and in staring at those pink lips Oswald unwillingly found his own smile again.

"What happened then?" he asked, in a softer voice.

The beautiful stranger stood up, threw back her long, blond tresses and shook her head.

"Merijana then sacrificed her bridal veil to give life to the larch, and went away with her husband, not to be seen again. I'll tell you about it at another time, because now I have to go, and you are sad. I'll come back."

"When? Where?"

The young man had jumped to his feet too, his hands reaching toward her, his wide, square face flushed with hope.

"Here, tomorrow, at the same time. Don't try to follow me, or you'll never see me again."

She then escaped his imploring hands and glided swiftly toward a grove of trees and bushes, disappearing in it, or at least so it seemed to Oswald, who didn't dare to run after her. After waiting hopefully for a few minutes, he went back home, totally oblivious by now of Pruca and its taverns.

They met again the next day, and the day after that, until their daily date became a cherished routine for them both. The knight told her his name and about his life and wanderings, but the mysterious girl—with whom he had fallen in love by then—told him nothing about herself, not even her name. Finally, when spring had already turned into summer, she confided, almost fearfully, "Don't look for my name and my bloodline among your people, because I'm not human. I'm a *vivana*..."

"A *vivana*?" Oswald cut in, astonished. "But they exist only in legends!"

"Look at me," the creature exhorted him, with a sad smile. "My people were already here when no man had yet set foot among these woods or looked at these mountains. We helped you, and you gave us many names, you loved and hated us, feared and hunted us. Now there's just a few of us left, a dwindling people, doomed to extinction."

330

Sabja de Fek

The young man shook his head, far from persuaded. "But you are a real woman, made of flesh and blood," he countered vehemently.

"I'm water and air; I'm the breath of this land, and for a short while I've been allowed to walk as a woman on these meadows, among these woods. It's only for a short while, though, until the cither will play the song of my fate. Then I'll go away, I'll have to."

"Where?" shouted Oswald, as he jumped to his feet and instinctively brought his hand to his sword, as if to protect his love from an unknown kidnapper. The *vivana*, however, shook her shoulders, refusing to say more.

A few days later, the knight finally confided his secret sorrow to her.

"You don't... you cannot... know what a torture it is for me not to be able to give life to the melodies, the verses I can feel singing inside me! But if I try my voice cracks, and my hands break into pieces any instrument I try to play. Iron Hands, that's what they call me! In is a yearning, an ongoing torture that gives me no peace."

"It's weird." The girl knit her brows thoughtfully. "Since the first moment I saw you, I could feel a dark shadow loom over you, through no fault of yours."

She bent over the young man's hands but did not touch them, as if they strangely repelled her.

"These hands have been cursed!" she exclaimed, rising her eyes to stare at his face. She then brushed his lips with her fingertips and jerked as if she had burned herself. "There's a curse on your voice as well! And yet music and poetry are powerful in your soul. It's the work of a *bregostana*."

331

"A *bregostana*," the knight repeated, thoughtfully. "That's some sort of witch, isn't it? But who may have wanted to... oh, well, it doesn't matter now. But... couldn't you free me from this curse?"

A shadow crossed the *vivana*'s delicate face, and she shuddered, as if a chilly wind had brushed her. It was however with a firm voice that she replied, "I don't have the power to do it, Oswald. I'm sorry, my love, so very sorry, but I cannot do it."

Sadly, the young man lowered his head, trying to resign himself to his fate, and the girl opened her arms, drawing him close to her.

The months swiftly went by, and Oswald kept meeting his *vivana* in secret, without saying anything about it to his mother and siblings who, on their part, were quite bewildered at his behavior.

"He's always been weird," Michael said, "but now he's overdoing it! He disappears somewhere almost all day long, and nobody knows where he goes, or what he does, or whom he is meeting with!"

"You should be the last to complain about it, though, since this has made him stop quarrelling with you over the inheritance," retorted Leonard, the younger brother.

"Enough!" Katrina ordered, cutting in the bud a new argument. "I'm quite concerned about him, for I cannot understand what..."

"He must be in love, mother!" her younger daughter interrupted her, raising her face from her embroidery, while her three sisters giggled.

"Shut up, you gossipers!" their mother ordered; but a moment later she threw them a piercing glance, asking, "What do you know? Did he tell you something?"

Giggling, the four girls gladly set aside needle, loom and spool to enumerate to their mother's benefit all those little things they had noticed and that, in their opinion, proved beyond any shade of doubt that their brother was in love, to begin with his unusual care for the way he looked and dressed.

"And then yesterday we found him searching among our music..."

"He was copying a witty poem on a piece of paper..."

"... and as soon as he saw us he thrust it inside his doublet..."

"... and then he hurried away without any explanation!"

The four girls were speaking all at the same time, interrupting each other, their words overlapping.

"Iron Hands?" snickered Michael, poking at his brother who immediately cut in, "A witty poem? But he is hoarse and tone-deaf like a cracked bell!"

They both burst out laughing; the four girls, instead, looked uncertainly at their mother, who was forcing a smile belied by her frown.

"If the reason for his weird behavior is his being in love, then it's not such a bad thing," the Countess finally decided, apparently calm and in a good mood, and she made it clear to them all that she considered the subject closed. Deep down, however, she felt an ancient woe reawaken.

That morning, when he arrived at the usual clearing, even if the sun had barely risen Oswald found the beautiful *vivana* already there, busy playing on her cyther a music he had never heard before. It caught his attention and fascinated him right away with its slow, enchanting melody that expressed both a deep mournfulness and a passionate plea.

He stood still for a while, just listening, then he stepped forward, deeply upset, and bent on the girl, who immediately stopped playing to reach for him with her hand.

"What ails you, my dear? Your music..."

"Didn't you like it?" the young woman interrupted him.

"That's not the matter. It was beautiful, but..." He broke off, unable to find the right words, as the *vivana* lowered her gaze, staring at the ground.

"I had an omen," she finally whispered. "A sinister omen, as if some tragedy were looming over us, as if we were to part forever..."

"No, this will never happen! I'm strong enough to defend you from any..." Oswald suddenly fell silent as the girl stood up.

A sweet, sorrowful melody—such as no human ear had ever heard—was rising from the air, the trees, the earth itself. Those notes were so intense, so full of pain and yet of strength and passion, that Oswald could not stand them for long and fell on his knees beside him, the *vivana* still stood straight, her eyes staring at something only she could see. Something changed on her face: love, pain and fear blended into a new awareness, which brought a shadow to veil her eyes, but also a smile on her lips. Slowly, she bent her head and spread her arms in a resigned gesture of acceptance.

In the still air, the mysterious notes faded away one by one. Silence fell again, and the knight then rose to his feet, still shaken. He tried to take the girl into his arms, but she drew back and lifted her gaze to his face, her eyes bright with unshed tears as she shook her head, whispering, "Now I can see my fate clearly. Now I know why we met and loved each other. Listen to me! It had been foretold that you would become a great minstrel, but that the price for that would be your happiness. Wanting to spare you this sad fate, your mother asked the *bregostane* to put a spell on your hands and your voice, to make it impossible for you to touch a musical instrument without breaking it, or to sing a single note, or to recite a single verse. But I can—and want to—free you from this curse."

Picking up her silver cither laying in the grass, she brushed its strings, drawing from it a bittersweet melody, full of strength and power. She then threw back her shining, long hair, and sang with resigned sweetness,

> *"Playing is for me my last song:*
> *Fulfilled is my fate,*
> *Broken is your spell.*
> *And so, my knight, fare thee well!*

"Hurry now, give me your hands!" she whispered then, as she reached for him.

Surprised, Oswald put his strong warrior's hands on the girl's small palms, and she held them for a moment, brushing those long fingers with hers.

The young man then felt a sort of light quiver—just like the fluttering of a small bird's wings as it tried them in flight for the first time—run through his body. He looked questioningly at his friend and what he saw frightened him. His unknown lover was beautiful, more than usual, but her beauty now had some quality that frightened him, and made him step forward resolutely to grab her by the shoulders. Bending on that diaphanous face, he whispered hoarsely, "What's wrong? What's happening to you?"

The girl had a soft, choked laugh that sounded like a sob and lifted her sorrowful eyes to his face, without trying to free herself from his grip.

"Your hands are free, now." Rising on tiptoe, she brushed Oswald's lips with her own. "So is your voice as well," she whispered, drawing back. She then stopped with a gesture her lover who, rapturous with that first kiss, wanted to hold her to himself again.

"No. Listen to me. Your mother's blind, fearful love deprived you of music and poetry, and my love gives them back to you. Here, the cither and the song that belonged to me are yours now: this is my gift for you, this is my destiny, and yours."

"The melodies I hear echoing in my heart but cannot play! And the verses that flow in my brain but that I could never say aloud! Is it really possible?"

Excited, Oswald had barely heard the last words the girl had whispered as she handed him her cithern. Instead, he grabbed the instrument and brushed its strings, which answered to his touch with a melodic sound.

His face shining with joy, the knight finally looked up, and what he saw left him dumbfounded.

The girl's beautiful face and slim body were losing substance; her long hair, barely fluttering in the breeze, looked like wisps of mist curling around a slender birch, or the foam crowning a wave, in a lake. And her voice, when the *vivana* spoke to him again, was just the whisper of the breeze among the leaves, or the soft murmuring of a stream.

"Farewell, my knight, my only love. I become wind and water again, but I leave you my song, and the memory of our love. Goodbye."

Then the faint sound vanished as well, and her image dissolved into smoke and fog in Oswald's arms, who had jumped forward to grab and hold her.

He left a few days later, deaf to his mother's protests and pleas, his face as hard as stone. His heart, however, brimmed with music and verses, and hanging from his saddle, beside his long lance and shield, was the small silver cithern the *vivana* had left him.

Sabja de Fek

Historical notes to "Iron Hands"

According to tradition, Iron Hands' figure is modeled after Oswald von Wolkenstein, the last of the minnesinger, and I've decided to stick to tradition, also because Oswald's figure—still enigmatic and under many respects contradictory—appears to be more than worthy of the love of a *vivana*.

Oswald was born in 1377, probably at Schoneck in the Puster Valley. Of high birth, he left his home and family as a boy to travel around the known world first as a squire and then as a knight, in the retinue of kings and emperors.

He was an adventurer, a counselor, a diplomat and an ambassador, and he traveled all over most of Europe, also visiting the Holy Land (1408-1410). He fought against Lithuanians, and belonged to the Order of the Dragon, founded by Emperor Sigismund II, Order to which also belonged Vlad II and Vlad III of Wallachia (the notorious 'Impaler'). He also took part to the Council of Constance (1415), at the orders of Frederick IV, Duke of Further Austria and Tyrol.

In the second part of his life, always characterized by contrasts with his family and by his unfortunate love for Sabine Jager, Oswald played a relevant role in the fight of the Tyrolese feudal lords against Duke Frederick II, ended up in prison more than once and was also tortured, but in the end he found refuge at the court of Sigismund II, whom he followed till his death. He took part to the Diet of Nuremberg and then probably joined the knights of the Order of the Dragon in their Crusade against the Hussites, before following his lord to Basel, Piacenza and Parma.

At Sigismund's death, Oswald became one of the members of the board protecting the Emperor's underage son's rights; in 1445 he took part to the Parliament of Merano, but he died a few months later, apparently in the contended Castle of Hauenstein.

He is buried in the Augustinian abbey of Novacella, in the municipality of Varna, not far from Bressanone.

With his restless and adventurous spirit, Oswald is considered the last minnesinger and the last chivalric romance poet, as well as the first modern poet, because in his verses he sings about all his life's experiences, alternating verses so realistic they are almost vulgar with others that are very lyrical and full of arcane symbolism, while always demonstrating an extraordinary fluency and mastery of the language and of the music.

Most of his poems and eighty-five lieders still survive him.

As far as the legend of the Merijana is concerned, all that's known about it is what I hinted at here, turning it into the *vivana*'s song, even if many of its elements hark back to ancient beliefs, far older than Iron Hands' story. Unfortunately, too little is known about it for me to try and make it into a full story in its own right.

The Hike

"Marmoleda ch'el soregie
De ses raies incoronà
De silenzes fond resona
Le to giazzes incantà"
Marmolada that rise
Crowned with sunrays
Of deep silences the echo
Suffuses your enchanted glaciers.
(From the folk song "Marmoleda" by Pomarici and
De Bernart)

Even while driving his new 1750 Alfa Romeo, Alfredo
of Castellalto could not help but admire the wonderful sight
swiftly flowing under his eyes. Certainly, it was not the first

time he went to Trentino, and to the Fassa Valley, but every time he came back there he still felt the same wonder at the sight of the wonderful mountains getting nearer and nearer, revealing their castles, the welcoming villages, the green fields and, higher up, the shining, immaculate snowfields.

Beside him, curled up on the comfortable seat, his daughter was napping, her thick, dark blond eyelashes shadowing her rose tinged cheeks. As he looked lovingly at her, Alfredo realized once more that his beautiful child was growing into a wonderful young woman, and that ten years had gone by since his wife had died. The war—the one now labeled as the 'Great War', even if there had been nothing 'great' about it, if not the tragedies and the grief it brought in its wake—had just ended, little Annina was three years old, and he had just come back from the frontline, anxious to be back by his beloved wife and to finally get to know his little daughter, who had been born while he was away, when Death—clearly not yet sated by the toll He had exacted during the war—had made his appearance again, this time as a ruthless illness, the 'Spanish flu'.

The death toll exacted by the war had been of ten million victims, where that terrible flu killed fifty million people, among them his beloved Angela, in spite of all the care and attentions he had for her.

So, he had been left alone with his child in the large white villa, which had never felt so big and empty, almost buried as it was in the heart of the surrounding estate, hidden by its ancient trees. The Adige River flowed not far away from the estate, and in the long summer nights its soft murmur and the chorusing crickets had been his only companions.

He still had Annina, who had to be enough; and she had been enough for him, until... until he met Eleonora.

Donna Eleonora, as dark haired and dynamic as his Angela had been fair and shy, of noble Sicilian descent, had fired his blood with her haughtiness and her aggressive beauty, so different from the Trentino women's charm. She was much younger than him, but Alfredo knew she would accept to become his wife: he could read that truth in the woman's midnight black eyes, which shone with a new light when she looked at him, and in the pleased smile that curved her beautiful cherry red lips every time he gave her his arm. Moreover, he knew quite well beautiful Eleonora's situation as the fifth daughter of a noble family that had lost most of its original wealth due to a series of wrong investments and to Don Sebastiano's—Eleonora's father—addiction to gambling.

He was rich, instead, and could give his bride the luxury and comfort she wanted. The only obstacle to a happy ending for their relationship was his daughter, Annina.

With that thought, Alberto lowered his gaze for a moment on the young girl who was still asleep, her blond head leaning against the seat backrest, her long braids a little tousled, and he smiled at her, almost to beg her forgiveness for having seen her, even if for a moment only, as an obstacle to his happiness.

They had already met a few times, the beautiful and haughty woman and the shy girl, and none of those meeting had been such a success as to make all the parties involved wish to repeat the experience, but Alfredo had insisted, and was still perseverating. Even that vacation in the Fassa Valley was part of his plan to make his beloved daughter and the woman he planned to marry grow closer to each other. That was not the only reason he was getting back to the mountains he loved, there was also the iron path to Punta Penia, a hike he had long planned to make together with an old comrade in arms of his, who was now a mountain guide.

As he thought of the new adventure waiting for him, he smiled again, almost unwillingly, and was still smiling when he reached Vigo, and the small square where the hotel he had chosen for their stay was located.

The owner immediately came forward to greet them, all smiles and bows.

"Did you have a good journey, Lord Marquis of Castellalto?" he asked, as a doorman took charge of the luggage and Annina—who had finally woken up—looked around and beamed in recognizing the mountain landscape. "The Lady Baroness has already asked twice about you." The hotel owner allowed himself a small, knowledgeable smile as he went on, "She was worried, because according to the forecasts the weather will change for the worse, and..."

"Fred!" Eleonora's beautiful, vibrant voce came from the balcony above; a couple of minutes later, the woman appeared on the landing, very elegant in a white silk dress, her hair gathered in a large chignon on the back of her head, her arms open wide and the red lips already parted in a welcoming smile.

A smile that froze as soon as she glimpsed Annina's slim figure, half hidden behind her father. The woman stopped at the head of the stairs, her face suddenly hard and haughty, while the girl grabbed his father's hand, holding tightly to it.

Alfredo sighed: perhaps the idea of spending a week of vacation with the two most important women in his life, hoping they would end up getting along well, had not been so bright, after all.

Four days later he was sure of it.

Eleonora's stinging comments, her rebukes barely veiled by formal courtesy made Annina silent and petulant, so much so that she ended up putting herself in the wrong.

"Fred, I know I'm not very patient, but even an angel wouldn't have patience enough to deal with your daughter! I gently pointed out to her that she cannot wear that ridiculous costume all the time, and also offered to help her choose something different, but she first burst into tears and then screamed that I should go away! To me!"

Taking advantage of Eleonora's falling silent for a moment, as she remembered the suffered wrong, Alfredo tried to intervene, but was not very successful.

"She's still a child... I mean, she's going through a difficult time..."

"Nonsense! She's jealous, that's all."

But it was Eleonora who was jealous of her future stepdaughter, instead. Alfredo had guessed that much from a thousand small details, but he was trying to justify her, telling himself that it was another proof of her love for him. In spite of himself, however, the glances the woman shot to Annina generated in his heart a painful feeling of diffidence and suspicion.

Lost as he was in those uncomfortable thoughts, he didn't realize the Baroness had asked him something and was now staring quizzically at him.

"Your hike, Fred!" she pressed, her small, elegantly shod foot tapping the floor. "You know I don't like the idea of you wandering around on those mountains!"

She shot a furious glance at the peaks surrounding the valley, her eyes lingering with particular hatred on the white peaks of the Marmolada, which Alfredo was going to tackle the next day.

"That's why I came here!" he countered, not hiding his annoyance. "I want to see how they rebuilt the Contrin mountain lodge, which I remember as a heap of rubble, and then…" He turned to stare at the Marmolada as well, but with a far different expression in his eyes. "The Penia Peak, 10,967 feet, my *Marmoleda*'s highest peak! Look: I'll leave from Alba to reach the mountain lodge, and from there, through the Rosalia Valley, I'll head for the pass, and then…"

Bending on the maps spread on the white painted iron coffee table that, together with four chairs of the same material, two deck-chairs covered with cushions and a large sunshade, furnished the terrace of their hotel. Alberto showed with his index finger the path he planned to follow, his smile barely hidden by his short, curly blond beard. Eleonora however shook her comely shoulders and turned her back to him to go and lie down on a comfortable deck-chair.

"I'm not enchanted by your words, or by your mountains!" she countered, with a little frown. "I have to acknowledge that it is pleasant to find some relief from the summer heat in a comfortable hotel, here in your beloved Fassa Valley, but I feel quite indifferent toward those mountains you love so much! Even worse, they remind me of sweat, fatigue, danger… in other words, all sorts of unpleasant things. The further I am from them, the better I feel."

She tempered her words with a laugh, her white teeth shining between her red lips, and threw Alfredo an alluring glance.

His hand still on the maps, Alfredo was at a loss for words. He had long known that beautiful Eleonora was not the kind of woman who would gladly follow him in his hikes, and had found a thousand ways to excuse her. Born under a different sky, by the sea, and grown up between the southern coast of Sicily and the Aeolian Islands, Eleonora could not understand the fascination, the lure those mountains had for him, but he had hoped that two summers spent together at the foot of the Marmolada had made her dislike subside, and that she was at least beginning to appreciate the wonderful sight offered by those white peaks, that to him were home and family.

"And I'd also like that you would learn to stay away from those climbs!" the Baroness went on in the meanwhile, leaning a little toward him. "Didn't you have enough of danger during the war?" She glanced at Alfredo again, and upon realizing his face had clouded over, she immediately switched to a sweeter tone of voice. "Oh, you men! If you just would think about us poor women, from time to time!" And with a jingle of bracelets she extended her shapely hand—on which two big rings shone—toward him.

The Marquis' face cleared right away and he bent on that hand to kiss it; in that moment, in a whirlwind of long, flowery skirts, embroidered apron and golden braids, Annina ran out on the terrace.

"I'm coming too, daddy!" she exclaimed. Then, while Eleonora ostentatiously brought her hands to her small ears, the girl went on, laughing, "To Contrin, I mean, tomorrow. Usèpp has been telling me about your hike, and he says I can certainly make it at least till there! And at Contrin I'll find Tita... I haven't seen him since last year!"

And she jumped up and down with joy both at the idea of an outing with her father and the old local man who for years had been their jack of all trades here in the Fassa Valley, and at the thought of seeing again Tita, the mountain guide who had been Alfredo's orderly during the war. His cheeks were as red as the apples of Trentino, his blue eyes shone, cheerful and confident, under his short shock of golden hair. Standing on the threshold, behind her, Usèpp smiled and nodded emphatically in answer to the questioning look Alfredo had shot him, above Annina's head since the girl had thrown her arms around his neck and was hugging him.

Momentarily forgotten, Eleonora let her hand fall back by her side and a frown creased her brow. Father and daughter shared that absurd passion, she thought, and the long hike together scheduled for the next day was going to strengthen even more the bond they shared, and which she saw as an obstacle to her wishes. Then Alfredo's voice broke into her broodings, and she immediately looked up at him, forcing herself to smile.

"I was saying, my dear, that you might consider coming with us just this once! It is an easy outing, reasonably short, and the mountain lodge is very well equipped." He smiled at her, hope in his eyes.

For a moment, Eleonora's expression showed plainly what she thought of Annina's intrusion and of the scheduled outing, then her shapely lips curved in a light laugh.

"Well, yes, I think it's a good idea," she forced herself to reply. "I'll be glad to come: I'm really curious to understand what makes you like so much all that hiking!"

Alfredo checked his watch for the umpteenth time. They had already left the hotel one hour later than scheduled to wait for the Baroness, and now—after negotiating the first one hundred thirty feet of switchbacks with a constant, steep gradient—the small group was trekking along a comfortable stretch of the path that ran through the beautiful Contrin Valley, enclosed between the Colac and the Marmolada. Behind them rose the Sella group.

Their pace had been slower than usual, and they also had had to stop twice to rest, so that Eleonora could catch her breath; Annina, however, kept running back and forth, her cheeks tinged red by the sun that was getting hotter by the minute, her braids partially disheveled, her clothing untidy and a shine in her wide, clear eyes. At times, she would run by them all, challenging them to catch up with her, then she would linger to study a flower or some small animal, and her voice—unusually loud and cheerful— echoed through the whole valley.

Alfredo looked at her with pleasure, recognizing in his daughter his same love for the mountains, but Eleonora shook her head, her black braids encircling her head like a dark crown.

"Fred, you should tell her to stop and behave properly! Look at that! She grabbed that Usèpp's hand, and so much familiarity with a mountain man..."

"We've been knowing him for years, since Annina was quite young" Alfredo interrupted her, but the Baroness shook her head.

"But she isn't a little girl anymore, now, and she must learn to behave as befits her age and social standing."

"Poor child! You know Angela died when our daughter was just three years old. I took care of her upbringing as well as I could, but..."

Eleonora had her usual haughty, pleased smile.

"Of course, it's not your fault, but now your daughter needs a strong, firm female hand, perhaps even a boarding school..."

"A boarding school? Sending my Annina to a boarding school?" Alfredo burst out, stopping to stare at the Baroness.

"Oh, come on, what's the fuss? I'm not talking about some dismal orphanage for abandoned children, you know! Nowadays there are first class boarding houses for young girls of high social standing, where a girl can learn all that a young noblewoman must now, and also make useful friends."

Far from persuaded, Alberto was going to reply heatedly when Annina came running back toward them and threw herself in his arms, while glaring challengingly at Eleonora.

"We're here, dad! And I'm not tired, not at all!" she announced cheerfully.

In fact, the Contrin mountain lodge was but a few steps away, and Tita—who was going to be Alberto's guide in the second, more dangerous, half of the hike—was standing by the door. With his usual, small pipe hanging from his mouth and disapproval written all over his tanned, lined face, he approached them with a familiarity born during the long, painful years of the war he had fought by the Marquis side, and addressed him using his old military title.

"It's late, colonel, sir! You should have been here two hours ago. We have a long, hard hike in front of us, and we must reach our goal before nightfall."

"What can I say, Tita... women! But we'll make it all the same, my old friend, I swear we will!"

As he spoke, the Marquis pointed at Eleonora and Annina, who stood behind him, a few feet from each other, looking at each other with very little fondness. Alberto caught that look and sighed, before he bent to kiss the Baroness' hand.

"My dear, we have to part ways here. The two of you will spend the night here and tomorrow morning Usèpp will take you back to the hotel, where I'll join you within two days, at the latest. I entrust Annina to you."

The Baroness shot an unreadable look at the girl, then she said goodbye to Alberto, telling him to be careful; the man however was not listening to her as he hugged his daughter.

"Take me with you, daddy!" the girl whispered.

"What are you saying, you silly girl? These aren't things for women!"

"Yes, they are!" Freeing herself from his arms, Annina stared firmly at him. "An English miss climbed the Marmolada, many years ago, you told me yourself! If she—a foreigner—did it, why cannot I do the same?"

Beatrice Tomasson, before the First World War, Alberto remembered, but then he shook his head.

"It's true, but you're still too young, and you have no training. Maybe, in a few years…"

"No, let it be now, I beg you!" Annina hugged him again and lowered her crystal clear voice as she whispered in his ear, "Don't leave me alone with her! She hates me, I know it! She would like to have me disappear, go away forever…"

"That's enough, Annina! Don't want to hear such things again!" In spite of his stern tone, the girl's words had left Alberto quite shaken, most of all because he was thinking back to what Eleonora had been telling him a short while before, so he added, in a milder voice, "In any case, you aren't alone, Usèpp is here with you, and you know he loves you!" He motioned for the old man—who was speaking with Tita—to come over, then he pointed at his daughter. "I'm leaving, Usèpp, and I'm entrusting my women to you. Have good care of them, Annina most of all!"

"Don't doubt none, Lord Marquis" the mountain man answered, brushing with his huge hand the girl's golden hair. Waving again at Eleonora, who was standing silently by the mountain lodge door, Alberto left with Tita, walking fast not so much to recover the lost time as because he was trying to fight the unpleasant feeling his daughter's last words had awakened in him.

He concentrated on the path in an attempt to push that disturbing thought away. In fact, he wanted to climb the steep, deep gully running through the Rosalia Valley and leading to the Marmolada Pass before the sun set; once at the pass they would camp for the night and start climbing toward the Penia Peak at daybreak. However, not even the sight of those wonderful peaks he loved so much could bring peace to his trouble heart, as it had always done in the past.

He answered in monosyllables to Tita's attempts at having a conversation, so much so that the guide, not a very talkative man to start with, soon shut up, and the two man climbed in silence up to the place where they had chosen to spend the night, in the shadow of the imposing side of the Marmolada that was crowned by Penia Peak.

"I don't like those clouds down there," muttered the mountain man, as they unrolled their sleeping bags. "If the weather turns, a coating of ice may form on the rocks, not to speak of the danger of lightning!"

Alfredo looked up toward the progressively cloudier peak of the mountain and pressed his lips."

"The west crest is already an iron path," he reminded his companion.

"Yes, Fersuoch did quite a good job," admitted the guide, "but it's better to be safe than sorry."

"We'll see how things stand tomorrow," concluded the Marquis, as he settled in his sleeping bag."

The next morning, however, offered clear skies, with the surrounding, bare rocks tinged with pink reflections by the dawning sun.

"We go," Alfredo decided. Tita nodded his assent, even if he commented, "The temperature got lower, during the night."

Picking up ropes and alpenstocks, they looked up at the climb in store for them: the iron way winded up along sleek and steep rock plates, and far above it was possible to see the West Crest of the Marmolada.

"It should take a couple of hours to get there," Alfredo said, but Tita didn't agree.

"You'd better say three or four, colonel, sir. The wind is picking up in a way I don't like at all."

"All the more reason for moving right away."

They climbed more slowly than Alberto had thought they would, because here and there the stirrups and steel ropes were still totally coated with ice, and in the meanwhile the wind grew stronger and colder, while large black clouds hid the sun.

"The weather is changing for the worst," the guide muttered worriedly, glancing quickly the way they had come. "We cannot stop here, however, we've almost reached the crest."

It was true, and the scenery was at the same time gorgeous and frightening: on their right there was a deep gorge of sheer rock extending down into the emptiness below, and some yards wide ledges made of white snow and bluish ice extended over the precipice.

"We'll stop at Penia Peak, if necessary, since we aren't far from it now," Alberto countered, worried as much as his companion by the violence of the wind, which forced them to hold to the ropes with all their strength and slowed them down.

As it the wind weren't enough, they heard a deep rumble of thunder in the distance.

"We really didn't need this!" Tita exclaimed, between a curse and a prayer to the Virgin Mary.

They had to work around a dreadful funnel made of ice and rough edged rocks, beyond which the shining glacier could already be seen in the livid light heralding the imminent storm. The air was freezing cold, and even if the wind had suddenly stopped, the progressively darker sky promised a storm.

Another thunder, much nearer than the previous one, echoed among the rocks.

The two men looked at the wide expanse of ice ahead, then at the stormy sky, and hesitated. By now, however, their only choice was go on in the hope of crossing the glacier before the storm broke. Putting on their crampons, the alpenstock ready in their hands, they started crossing the glacier, Tita opening the way and Alberto following him, with a rope securing them to each other. Even if he realized that the sudden bad turn in the weather was making the hike much more dangerous than he had foreseen, Alberto could not find his usual concentration because in a corner of his brain he kept brooding over the difficult relationship between his daughter and Eleonora; perhaps that was why—as they were nearing the far edge of the glacier—he realized only when it was too late that a layer of snow sticking to his crampons was preventing them from properly gripping the slippery ground. Before he could use his alpenstock handle to remove the snow, he slipped and lost his footing. He was still fighting to regain his balance when a sudden gust of wind threw him face down on the snow. He slid down on the ice for a couple of yards before the rope tensed, halting his fall, and Tita—realizing what had happened—came back gripping the rope in his hands.

"Colonel! Are you hurt, sir?"

"No, I don't think I am." With the guide's help, Alberto rose to his feet, but a cry of pain immediately escaped his lips. "I fear I banged my knee against that rock... it seems to be better now, though." He told the guide, as he tried to straighten his leg. However, a sudden wave of pain blurred his eyes and he had to desist.

The guide cursed a couple of times then, for the sake of consistency, he invoked the Virgin Mary before grasping firmly the colonel by his arm.

"Lean on me and on your alpenstock. Just a few steps and we'll be on solid rock. We'll then be able to see to your knee. Come on, let's go!"

Those few steps, however, turned into sheer torture, also because in the meanwhile the gusts of wind multiplied. Neither of them was a beginner, though, and besides his experience, Tita could count on a considerable physical strength. In about ten minutes spent slipping and getting up again, but always going forward, he managed to drag his companion to the rocky little expanse of Penia Peak, where they found shelter in a small iron plate shack.

"No," the guide sadly decided, after checking the Marquis' knee. "You cannot keep walking on this."

They had just settled inside the small building, using the equipment they had brought with them in their big backpacks, and Alfredo was opening the basket containing their supplies. Upon hearing those words, he looked up at the guide.

"Perhaps, if I rest for a while..."

"Don't even think about it! You cannot go anywhere on that leg," the other brusquely interrupted him. "The knee may not be broken, but it's sprained, at least, and it will take much more than three or four hours of rest to heal it!"

The Marquis tried to move his leg, but a sudden, throbbing pain immediately made him stop.

"Alright," he surrendered, then he suggested, "You must then go back to the Contrin mountain lodge to seek help."

"You want me to leave you here alone, at night?" Tita was dumbfounded at the proposal. "Even if the weather hadn't taken a turn for the worse, I'd get there after nightfall and we would then have to wait for dawn before coming to get you." Tita broke off, thinking. "We'll both stay here, and I'll leave tomorrow morning at daybreak."

"I don't want you to spend a night here because of me..." Alfredo began, but the guide interrupted him.

"It wouldn't be the first night I spent in the cold, and it won't be the last, I hope!" he laughed, then he turned a deaf ear to his companion's protests and concentrated on making that forced stop as comfortable as possible, and on getting some food ready.

The storm was raging outside, and the brightness of the bolts of lightning filtered through the cracks in the walls, filling the small room with a livid light while the wind blew with frightening violence through the gullies and crevasses, and thunder rumbled over their head.

"You see? Traveling now is really out of the question," Tita calmly commented, his pipe between his teeth, as he handed Alberto a canteen. "Have a sip of grappa, now, and you'll sleep like a baby! By this time tomorrow we'll both be home."

Whether because of the pain in the leg or because he was worried about managing to get back home, Alberto could not sleep. He moved cautiously inside his sleeping bag, careful not to wake up his companion, who was placidly snoring by his side, as comfortable as if he had been in his bed, and listened to the sounds of the mountain. The thunder was further away now, its rumble weaker, and the howling of the wind was losing its force, becoming just a whisper. The mountain, his beloved *Marmoleda*, seemed to be talking to him in many secret voices. He listened to them, finding again its usual appeal in those whispers and rustles, in the faint gurgling sounds the ice produced in settling after the storm.

His thoughts grew more and more pleasant.

Yes, in the morning the weather will be fine again, and Tita will therefore be able to get back to Contrin and find help to carry me away from this place. In a few hours I will hug Annina and see Eleonora again.

At that point he halted his reflections, newly upset at the thought that those two women—both so important to him—were always at odds with each other. Or rather, it was Eleonora who was always impatient with the girl, because of her behavior, her upbringing, and Annina reacted to her open dislike with an equally open rejection. Perhaps Eleonora was right, perhaps he should accept to part from his beloved daughter for a few years, for her own good, to allow her to get the kind of education befitting a young woman of good standing, and yet... he sighed, his heavy heart rebelling against such reasoning, and with an effort he moved slowly, until he got near to one of the cracks, so that he could look outside.

The sky was still dark, even if that darkness was getting lighter toward the east, as if with the promise of the oncoming dawn, and it was already possible to glimpse around Penia Peak the shapes of the other giants, the Rosengarten group, the Sella, the Langkofel... once more, the spell wrought by that scenery fascinated him, making him pay attention to each shadow, each rustle. Suddenly it seemed to him that he could hear, faint and far away, a sweet female voice. Surprised, he concentrated on it...

could that be Annina? No, it was not possible, and yet the voice kept sounding, weak but clear, intoning a monotonous, painful and resigned song. He felt certain he knew it, even if he could not remember its name, even if it was impossible that a woman was singing at night among those rocks.

I'm running a fever, he tried to tell himself. *It's just the wind whistling among the crags, the ice settling, a crumbling stone...*

He closed his eyes, and afterwards never knew whether he had fallen asleep or not, but suddenly both the melody and its words sounded quite clearly in his mind.

> *"Stone I am, I cannot move*
> *Rock I am of Marmoleda*
> *I'm a daughter who's been forsaken*
> *Nor I know the reason why."*

It was Conturina's eternal crying, she who had been the victim of her stepmother's hate.

Tita's hand shaking him gently brought him back to the real world: the sunlight was filtering through the crack and there was only silence all around them.

"Colonel, sir, are you okay?" asked the guide.

"I cannot move the knee. It's very swollen now, but it doesn't hurt anymore. Not much, at least. Besides that, I'm fine."

Yes, he *was* fine, and he suddenly realized that the doubts, the problems that had been upsetting him through the last few days had turned into absolute—even if resigned—certainty.

"I'm leaving, then, and in a few hours I'll be back, bringing help." The guide said, opening the door. "Cheer up, sir, soon you'll be back with your daughter and Donna E..."

"With my daughter," the Marquis interrupted him, in a tone that didn't brook no argument. "With my daughter, always." And he smiled, while the first rays of the dawning sun shone on the eternal, and yet always new, scenery of the Dolomites, painting their pale rocks pink as if to create a light wreath around the high peaks of Marmolada.

Historical notes to "The Hike"

Very little still exists about the original legend of Conturina, the beautiful girl turned to stone on the Marmolada: only four verses that, up to a few years ago, were still sung in the Fassa Valley, most of all by the *resteleris*, the women who raked the hay. Ugo Pomarici added more stanzas to those verses, and set the whole composition to music with the title "Marmoleda", later harmonized as choral music by De Bernart.

However, nobody can tell for sure what was Conturina's story and what was the meaning it carried in ancient Ladinia. Of course, there are some analogies with the myth of the Delibana, a virgin confined into a mine to guarantee that it would be productive. One of these analogies is the symbolic number seven recurring in both legends: seven were, in fact, the years the Delibana had to spend inside the mine, before a parent or a lover could free her, and Conturina could have been freed from the spell turning her to "rock of Marmoleda" within seven years, after which time she would have been beyond help. On this subject, it is also worth remembering that on the Marmolada existed lodes of geodes, which fact brings us back to the mines factor.

All this, however, doesn't help us to discover the real legend of Conturina, heavily influenced by the fairy tale about Cinderella, which is a very ancient story in its own right, since we can find versions of it in ancient Cina— country from which it probably originated—and also in Egypt, but that certainly is alien to the Ladin culture and tradition.

This is why I could—or would— not make up a story about this unhappy girl and her fate, and preferred to use only those few original verses, to which I entrusted the solution of the story, leaving Conturina mysterious and elusive legend shrouded in the mist of the past.

All the other references to the history of mountain lodges and local mountaineering are real.

The End

Sabja de Fek

BASIC BIBLIOGRAPHY

AA.VV. Mondo Ladino XXII-a. 1998 "L'entità ladino dolomitica – Atti" ed.

Bernardi Rut "La storia della letteratura ladina delle Dolomiti e la letteratura ladina di oggi" da Quaderni d'Italia n.7 2002 pag. 41-61.

Berardi Walter "Breve storia della lingua e della letteratura ladina" ed. Istitut Cultural Ladin Micurà de Run

Birkham Helmuockeck "Ad gredine forestum" atti del Convegno ed. Istitut Cultural Ladin Micurà du Ru

Bolognini Nepomuceno "Leggende del Trentino" ed. Nordpress

Cavaste Enrico "Quale presenza romana nelle valli ladine dolomitiche nell'età romana e nell'alto medioevo" su Mondo Ladino XV pag. 196 e seg.

Chiocchetti Fabio "Nota sulla comunità ladino dolomitica tra storia e sociolinguistica" su Mondo Ladino XV 1991 pag. 352-353

Idem " Appunti sulla storia della letteratura ladina" su Mondo Ladino XXIV 2000

Idem "Ladino nel canto popolare in Val di Fassa" estratto da "Mondo Ladino" a.XIX (1995)

Dal Lago Brunamaria "Il Regno dei Fanes" ed. Oscar Monadadori

Dal Polver Piere "La storia vera del Drach de Dona" postfazione, Istitut cultural ladin "Majon di fascengn" ed.

De Rossi di S. Giuliana Hugo "Fiabe e Leggende della Val di Fassa" Istitut cultural ladin "Majon di fascengn" ed.

Sabja de Fek

Forni Marco "La realtà e l'immaginario nelle valli ladinio dolomitiche" ed Micurà de Ru

Eco Umberto (a cura di) "Il Medioevo" – vol. 1- La Storia e vol. 2-Filosofia, letteratura, arte La biblioteca di Repubblica e dell'Espresso ed.

Kindl Ulrike "Le Dolomiti nella leggenda" ed. Frasnelli-Keitsch 1993.

Mazzel Massimiliano "Dizionario Ladino fassano-italiano", Istitut cultural ladin "Majon di fascengn" ed.

Palmeri Giuliano "Le antiche voci dei Monti Pallidi" ed. Canova

Palmeri Giuliano e Marco "I regni perduti dei Monti Pallidi"ed. Canova

Richebuono B. "Breve storia dei Ladini Dolomitici" ed. Istitut cultural ladin Micurà de Ru

Scroccaro M. "De Fascia ladina- La questione della Val di Fassa dal 1918 al 1948" ed. Istitut Cultural Ladin.

Wolff Karl F. "IL Regno dei Fanes", Cappelli ed. Bo.:"I Monti Pallidi" , Cappelli ed. Bo.; "I rododendri bianchi delle Dolomiti", Cappelli ed. Bo.

Zangrandi Giovanna "Leggende dell Dolomiti"ed. Nordpress

INTERNET SITES I CHECKED

Provincia autonoma di Bolzano dipartimento Cultura e Intendenza scolastica

Tuttofassa.stepdev.org

www Vejin.com

www ANSA. it – Dolomiti

www Il Regno dei Fanes.it (Adriano Vanin)

Sabja de Fek

www Istladin.net

AUTHOR'S NOTE

I already know I failed in listing all the texts and the sources I used in putting together this book, fruit of a research I began many years ago and later carried on, therefore I beg forgiveness from those I might have failed to mention.

If you enjoyed this book, please visit Inknbeans.com and discover our other fine authors.

www.ingramcontent.com/pod-product-compliance
Lightning Source LLC
Chambersburg PA
CBHW070908260626
47162CB00007B/2599